COURAGE
OF FALCONS

ALSO BY HOLLY LISLE

Diplomacy of Wolves

Vengeance of Dragons

Available from Warner Aspect

THE SECRET TEXTS
BOOK • 3

HOLLY LISLE
COURAGE OF FALCONS

ASPECT®

WARNER BOOKS

A Time Warner Company

This book is a work of fiction. Names, characters, places, and incidents are the product of the author's imagination or are used fictitiously. Any resemblance to actual events, locales, or persons, living or dead, is coincidental.

WARNER BOOKS EDITION

Cover design by Don Puckey
Cover illustration by Fred Gambino
Hand lettering by Carl Dellacroce

Aspect® name and logo are registered trademarks of Warner Books, Inc.

Warner Books, Inc.
1271 Avenue of the Americas
New York, NY 10020

Visit our Web site at
www.twbookmark.com

For information on Time Warner Trade Publishing's online program, visit www.ipublish.com

 A Time Warner Company

Printed in the United States of America

First Trade Paperback Printing: October 2000
First Mass Market Printing: August 2001

10 9 8 7 6 5 4 3 2 1

For Matt
With love and hope

Acknowledgments

Thanks go to Matt and Mark and Becky, who worked overtime and double-time and helped me in a thousand different ways to make sure I had the time to write.

To Russ Galen, for keeping the wolf from the door, and for pushing me and encouraging me until I created Matrin, and Kait.

To Peter James and Nick Thorpe, whose *Ancient Inventions* gave me goose bumps and inspired a whole lot of the primitive tech in all three books of the Secret Texts.

And to, in no particular order, those members of Lisle's Lunatic League who gave their all that the *Courage of Falcons* body count could be met: Robert and Keely Bush, Gretchen Woehr, Kathy Napolitano, Celia Hixon, Guy Beall, Ilari, Jacob Somner, and Scott Schuler.

COURAGE OF FALCONS

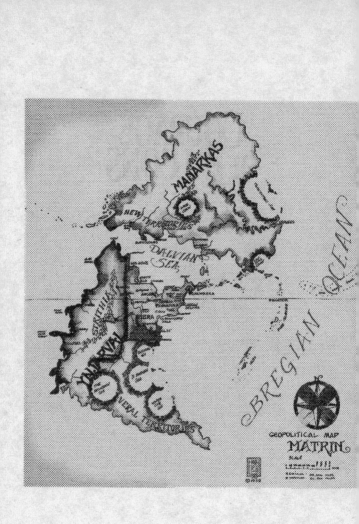

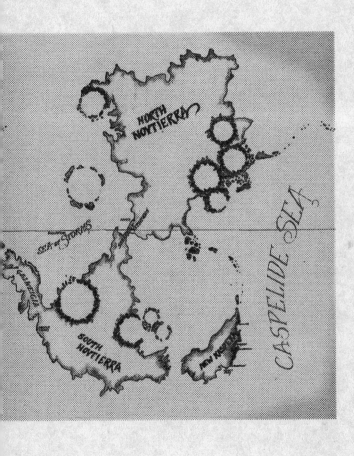

In Diplomacy of Wolves . . .

Magic, in the world of Matrin and especially in the Iberan lands where the last of the true humans live, has been a study both forbidden and reviled for a thousand years. But Kait Galweigh, daughter of the powerful Galweigh Family and promising junior diplomat, has survived to hide the secret scars of old and dangerous magic. While chaperoning her cousin prior to the girl's wedding to a second son of the Dokteerak Family, with whom the Galweighs desired an alliance, Kait's need to hide her Scarred nature—which causes her to skinshift, and which would lead to her immediate execution even by members of her own Family—puts her into position to overhear a plot involving the Dokteeraks and the Galweighs' longtime enemies, the Sabirs. These two Families are planning to destroy the Galweighs at the upcoming wedding.

Kait survives a harrowing escape from Dokteerak House with her information, aided by a stranger who, like her, is Scarred by the skinshifting curse, which is called Karnee. She is drawn to the stranger, but is dismayed to discover that he is a son of the Sabir Family. She returns to the embassy, where she informs the Galweighs of the Dokteerak-

Sabir treachery and tries to put her attraction to the Sabir Karnee out of her mind. Her Family takes both military and illicit magical steps to foil the conspiracy and crush the conspirators—steps that would have succeeded had the Sabirs not been planning all along to betray their allies the Dokteeraks, too. The Sabirs never intended to share power with the Dokteeraks; instead, they used them to get the Galweigh military away from Galweigh House and out into the open. Then, on two carefully managed fronts, they wipe out the Dokteerak and Galweigh armies as they meet in battle in the city of Halles, and use both treachery and magic to overthrow the unguarded Galweigh House back in the grand city of Calimekka.

However, magic used forcefully against another always rebounds. Both Families' wizards, who call themselves Wolves, expected to strike unprepared targets with their spells, and have readied sacrifices sufficient to buffer that amount of rebound, but their attacks hit each other at the same time, and the magic feeds back on them. It overwhelms their sacrifices, breaks out of the boundaries with which they controlled it, and wipes out the majority of both Families' Wolves.

It simultaneously does two other things as well, both seemingly irrelevant but both destined to change the face of the world of Matrin and the lives of everyone in it. First, the magical blast sends a shock wave across the face of the planet—a wave that wakes an artifact called the Mirror of Souls. The Mirror is a beautiful and complex creation designed by the Ancients before the end of the Wizards' War a thousand years earlier, and it has been waiting for just such a powerful *rewhah,* or rebound wave, for *rewhah* demonstrates that the world has returned to the use of magic . . . and more importantly, magic of the right sort. The Mirror awakens the souls it holds within its soulwell, and they reach out to people who might be able to help them.

Second, the *rewhah* horribly Scars a young girl named

Danya Galweigh, a cousin of Kait's, who has been held for ransom by the Sabirs and who is used as a sacrifice by the Sabir Wolves when the Galweighs fail to meet the ransom. Danya is changed beyond recognition, and the baby she unknowingly carries, a baby conceived through rape and torture during her capture, is changed, too, but in more subtle ways. The force of the *rewhah* throws Danya into the icy southern wastes of the Veral Territories, where, were it not for the help of a mysterious spirit who calls himself Luercas, she would die.

Kait, sensitive to magic, is knocked unconscious by the *rewhah* blast as she and her uncle Dùghall and her cousin Tippa are escaping from Halles via airible; Kait awakens alone to find that someone has hidden her in the airible's hold, and that the airible has landed in Galweigh House, but her Family's House is in Sabir hands and many of her Family have already been executed. She steals the airible and flies it to the nearby island of Goft, where the Galweigh Family has other holdings, hoping to get help. However, the head of this lesser branch of the Galweigh Family sees the demise of the main branch as his chance to advance, and he orders Kait killed. A spirit voice claiming to be her long-dead ancestor warns her of the treachery, and she escapes again, this time after stealing money from the House treasury.

The spirit tells her another way she can hope to aid her Family, even though it says they are now all dead. Following its advice, she hires a ship from the Goft harbor to take her across the ocean in search of the Mirror of Souls. The spirit tells her that this ancient artifact will allow her to reclaim her murdered Family from the dead. She enlists the aid of the captain by telling him she is going in search of the undiscovered ruins of one of the Ancients' lost cities. Such a place would make any man's fortune, so Captain Ian Draclas takes her on as a passenger and sails immediately.

Onboard the ship she runs into a man named Hasmal rann

Dorchan, whom she met briefly on the night of the party celebrating her cousin's upcoming marriage. Hasmal, a wizard of the sect known as the Falcons, had been trying to escape the doom that an oracle had warned would befall him if he associated with Kait. He is not pleased to see her.

Hasmal's oracle mocks him and warns that he must teach Kait magic to protect himself. He does, but grudgingly; she learns, but denies the relevance of the shared destiny he claims will send both of them to their doom if she fails to learn his lessons well.

Kait is plagued by dreams of the Sabir Karnee she met while escaping the Dokteerak House; she becomes certain that he is following her across the sea. To break her obsession with him, she accepts the advances of the ship's captain, Ian Draclas, and they become lovers. But her obsession only worsens.

As the ship nears its destination, it sails into the heart of a Wizards' Circle, a place where magical residue from the Wizards' War a thousand years before is still so strong that it can affect and control anyone moving within its reach. Hasmal works magic to free the ship, and Kait, in her skin-shifted form, saves the life of the captain. In saving the ship and the captain, though, Kait is revealed as a monster and Hasmal as a wizard, and the crew turns against them. They reach the shore and discover the city, but while Kait, Hasmal, Ian, and two of his men set out to retrieve the Mirror of Souls from its distant hiding place, the crew mutinies against the captain and his loyal supporters and maroons them in the unexplored wilds of North Novtierra.

In Vengeance of Dragons . . .

Kait, Ian, and Hasmal escape the brutal dangers of the Novtierran wilderness when Ry Sabir, a Karnee son of her Family's Sabir enemies, rescues them; Kait discovers that the gods have done more meddling in her life when Ry and Ian reveal that they are half-brothers . . . and bitter enemies. They transport the Mirror of Souls across the Bregian Ocean and get close to their goal, but the Goft Galweighs and Sabir House have formed an alliance to acquire the Mirror. They use airibles and magic to attack the *Wind Treasure;* they kill or capture most of the crew. Kait, Ry, Ian, Hasmal, and Ry's surviving lieutenants escape in one of the longboats, hidden by Falcon magic, and would have succeeded in getting the Mirror of Souls to safety, except that the Mirror, acting on its own, breaks through their shields with a beacon, drawing the enemy allies to it. Kait is forced to abandon the Mirror to the sea. She and the rest of the longboat's occupants find refuge on one of the islands of the Thousand Dancers, where she discovers her uncle Dùghall waiting, as he was instructed to do by his magic.

Meanwhile, Crispin Sabir, Ry's cousin and a powerful Sabir Wolf, successfully retrieves the Mirror of Souls from the sea, then kills his Galweigh allies. With his ownership of the Mirror undisputed, he returns to Calimekka, where he follows the instructions of the spirit of a long dead Dragon that has been guiding him, and activates the Mirror before a crowd of prayerful Iberans. He does not become immortal as he was led to expect; instead, his soul is ripped from his body and replaced by the soul of the ancient Dragon Dafril. Throughout the city, the freed Dragons choose other young, strong bodies to steal, and the Mirror rips those bodies' rightful souls away and inserts the souls of the Dragons.

Kait, Ry, Dùghall, Ian, and Ry's men sneak into Calimekka in disguise and attempt to locate and reclaim the Mirror. Even though the Dragons have been freed, they hope that by acquiring the Mirror they can reverse the damage it has done. So, pretending to be traders of ancient artifacts, they manage to discover the identities of several Dragons and acquire an idea of where they might find the Mirror of Souls. But Kait, following up on a lead, falls into the hands of both Dragons and Sabirs. They prepare to torture her to find out who she's working with and what she knows about the Dragon conspiracy to achieve immortality.

Dùghall and Ian, meanwhile, have located the Mirror of Souls, and Dùghall has discovered the general principle by which it works. Now, watching what is happening to Kait via magic, he creates a miniature version of the Mirror and draws the soul of the Dragon preparing to torture her out of the body it has stolen and traps it in a ring he'd been wearing. However, the man whose body was previously inhabited by the Dragon's soul isn't able to save Kait before she throws herself off of the tower.

Meanwhile, Kait's cousin Danya, hiding in a Scarred village in the uncharted wastelands of the Veral Territories, gives birth to a son. The baby bears no physical signs of the Scarring that changed Danya from a beautiful young woman to a hideous monster; he does, however, bear the markings of enormous magical power. Further, his mother, once a Galweigh Wolf, has the training to see and feel the newborn's magical connections to Falcons across the known world. The Falcons' magical interference, which has enraged Danya since it began, grows more intense once the baby has drawn his first breaths. Luercas tells Danya that the baby is the Reborn, the long-awaited Falcon hero, and that his mission in life is to create a world of enforced peace . . . a world in which Danya will forever be denied her revenge against the Sabirs who destroyed her and the Galweighs who failed to rescue her.

After terrible internal struggle, she chooses to sacrifice her son to prevent him from carrying out his mission. She decides that she must have her revenge. In his dying, her son first attempts through magic to save his own life; then, when it becomes clear that he cannot, he uses what remaining power he has to revert Danya to human form, excluding only the two talons that she drove into his heart. Even at the moment of his death, he loves her and she can feel his love.

Once he is dead, Luercas—one of the most powerful of the Dragons—claims the infant body for himself. He revives it and uses its inherent magical talents to force Danya to care for him until his new body is physically mature enough to allow him to care for himself.

Back in Calimekka, Kait, falling from the top of the tower, Shifts frantically, and for the first time in her life she develops wings. Expecting to die, she instead soars to safety; when she returns to the inn where she and the rest of her comrades are hiding, her brush with death has made her realize that she cannot spend whatever time she has hiding from her life. She and Ry become lovers. When Ian discovers this, he leaves the group in secret and offers to sell his knowledge to the Dragons in exchange for power.

At the same time that Ian is making his deal with the Dragons, the Falcons are shattered by the death of Solander, whose rebirth has been prophesied for a thousand years, and who was supposed to lead the world to a new age of peace and enlightenment. A thousand years of prophecy and an entire magic-based religion have just been destroyed, and many of the faithful take the paths of despair and even suicide. Dùghall gets Ry, Kait, Hasmal, and the surviving lieutenants out of Calimekka when he discovers proof of Ian's betrayal, but he is certain that the Dragons have won the world—he sinks into despondency. Hasmal and Alarista, the Gyru-nalle Falcon who once saved Hasmal's life and later became his lover, debate the merits of fleeing east to the unexplored lands of Novtierra, since they, too, are certain that everything is lost. Even Ry, who converted to Falconry after contact with Solander's love, withdraws.

Kait Shifts to the Karnee; in beast form she avoids thought and loss. But when she reverts to human form, she is forced to face the fact that Solander's death has made one thousand years of hope and prophecy a lie. After long thought, she finds hope from this truth instead of despair, for nowhere in the prophecies was Solander's death ever mentioned as a possibility. Therefore, all prophecies in the Secret Texts become invalid—any guarantees of either Falcon defeat or Dragon ascension to immortality and godhood are equally false. The Falcons have no guarantee that they will win, but neither are they guaranteed defeat because Solander is no longer with them.

Kait rallies the surviving Falcons and develops a plan—she and Ry will go back to Calimekka and magically mark any Dragons they can find. The Falcons, from the relative safety of their camp in the mountains of southern Ibera, will draw out the Dragons' souls and trap them in rings, the way Dùghall trapped the first soul when trying to rescue Kait. They will find a way to recapture the Mirror of Souls, too, and as soon as they do, they will reverse the spell the Dragons had cast. They hope doing so will recapture all the Dragons' souls within the Mirror.

The first part of their plan goes well: Both Ry and Kait find work within the Dragons' city-within-a-city in Calimekka, and both mark a number of Dragons. They have no luck finding the new hiding place of the Mirror of Souls, but are patient, trusting that sooner or later they will succeed. However, the Dragons become aware of their presence and take them prisoner.

Dùghall and Hasmal attempt to rescue Kait and Ry via magic, but the magic backfires—Dùghall is left weak and nearly helpless, while Dafril, the Dragon who wears Crispin Sabir's body, has the luck to connect with Hasmal. Dafril rips Hasmal's body and soul from the Falcon camp and deposits him in an interrogation room in the center of the Dragon compound. There Dafril tortures Hasmal; Hasmal manages to mark Dafril with the magic that will allow a Falcon to capture his soul in a ring, but there are no Falcons capable of controlling a soul as powerful as Dafril's left in the camp.

While this is going on, Ian replaces the guards watching Kait and Ry, and they are certain that he plans to kill them. Instead, he tells them how he joined the Dragons in order to find the Mirror; he still loves Kait and though he knows he cannot have her, he decided when she chose Ry to do what he could to assist her. He releases both Kait and Ry and the three of them retrieve the Mirror from its hiding place. They haul it to a carriage that Ian has waiting, and the three of them take off for Galweigh House, which had been abandoned once the Dragons created their new city.

Book One

✤

Nothing tears at the thoughts like a house abandoned. Its empty rooms whisper of tender memories forgotten, of the ghosts of joy and pain left to wander unheeded, of dreams dead of neglect. Here, where once people lived and loved, brought forth life and faced death, I run my fingers along crumbling masonry and shiver at the unimaginable loss of the unknowable dead, and I flee in dread lest the soul of this forgotten place waken and cling to me and claim me . . . and refuse to let me leave.

VINCALIS THE AGITATOR,
FROM *THE LAND BEYOND LOSS*

Chapter 1

A late-season blast of cold wind set the walls of the tent snapping and blew icy mountain air through tied-down flaps. Alarista crouched inside, looking from viewing glass to viewing glass, fighting down panic.

In two glasses, she had twin views of the inside of a carriage cruising through Calimekka's narrow back streets—Kait and Ry escaping from the Dragons with the Mirror of Souls. Over the steady clatter of the horses' hooves she could hear Kait, Ry, and Ian recounting what had happened to each of them since last they'd seen one another.

In another glass, she could see the remains of some delicate contrivance of crystal spires and silver gears lying in ruins on a worktable. The two voices whispering from that viewing glass were shrill with fear.

". . . I just found it this way. Shamenar was in here working on it, and now he's gone, too. It will be a month's work at least to restore it, if we can even find Shamenar—"

"You think *they* got him?"

"I don't want to think. . . ."

Another glass, another view. Through the eyes of someone running, a long, dark corridor illuminated by the runner's coldlamp—shadows dancing back, then leaping forward, fantastic shapes crawling up the walls and resolving into mundane objects. The only sound at the moment was the runner's harsh breathing. Whoever he was, he'd been down four branches of the corridor already, asking the first guard he came to if anyone carrying anything had passed that way.

A dozen more glasses showed groups of people standing or sitting and talking, or revealed fountains, or gardens, or books or papers being slowly perused. Several glasses were temporarily dark—their sources asleep, or possibly dead. A hundred more glasses were lined to one side, these never activated. With Kait and Ry gone, they probably never would be, but Alarista kept them nearby because doing so was the procedure that Dùghall and Hasmal had worked out. More than once in the past several days a glass had come suddenly to life, and Dùghall or Hasmal had learned something valuable. Until all hope was gone, she would cling to that procedure.

Hasmal had been gone, she estimated, half a station—snatched bodily from the tent by some unimagined Dragon magic and taken . . . somewhere. So far, not one of the viewing glasses had revealed the view she sought—a glimpse of Hasmal. She whispered an unending prayer to Vodor Imrish, asking that if he still listened and he still loved her he would give Hasmal back. If she could see him, just for an instant, just to know that he was still alive, she would be able to breathe again.

Hands pulled apart the tent flaps and Yanth slipped between them. He dropped to the tent floor beside Jaim, who had been sitting quietly behind Alarista, offering support simply with his presence. "The healer is on the way," Yanth told Jaim. "Any sign of Hasmal?"

Jaim's voice was soft. "She hasn't moved, so I don't think so."

Alarista summoned the energy to answer them, just to let

them know she could hear them and that she was still aware of the world around her, if only marginally. "No sign yet."

"I'm sorry. Is there something I can do to help?"

"Stay close," she said. "If anything changes, I might need both of you."

The healer came through the flaps a moment later, dragging her kit. She knelt beside Dùghall and unrolled it. The woman was one of Dùghall's people—part of the army he'd built months earlier. She was a Falcon, older and well trained in the healing magics, and calm enough, considering the circumstances. If he had any chance of getting better, the healer would make the most of it.

Guards knelt quietly along the tent walls, swords in hand; they hadn't laughed or joked since Hasmal vanished in a scream and a flash of light. They watched, tense and scared. It had been their responsibility to kill Dùghall or Hasmal if a Dragon soul, drawn through but not successfully locked into one of the miniature soul-mirrors, possessed either of them. Now Dùghall lay unresponsive on one of the mats, and Hasmal was gone, and Alarista had already told them she didn't have either the strength or the magical skills that had let Dùghall and Hasmal successfully capture so many Dragon souls. They knew that if she took on a Dragon, they were likely to have to kill her.

A hand gripped her shoulder, and she jumped. "Look!" Yanth whispered, and pointed at one of the viewing glasses that had until that instant been dark.

She turned to the sudden light, to the quickly resolving image, and she gasped. Hasmal's face was suddenly very close to her own; it had been cut across both cheeks and over both eyelids, and blood caked the wounds. Always pale, his skin had taken on the color of bleached bone. She could count the beads of sweat that rolled across his forehead and marked his upper lip. "We found a way to make our own Mirror of Souls," he whispered.

The image danced down to a long, bloody knife, and to a thumb that tested the edge of it. "Really? Tell me more."

"I'll . . . I'll tell you anything you want to know. Anything."

She heard a soft chuckle that raised the hair on the back of her neck and made her stomach churn. "I know you will. First tell me *how* you made it. We'll get to how you used it soon enough."

Alarista gripped Yanth's hand and squeezed. "He's torturing him."

"I know."

"Oh, gods! Oh, Hasmal! We have to help him."

"I know. But how?"

Alarista couldn't turn her eyes away from the nightmare in front of her. "I'll have to draw the Dragon's soul to me. I'll have to capture it."

"You couldn't do it before," Jaim said quietly.

"I'll just have to do it this time."

"And if you fail, we lose Hasmal *and* you. We're going to need you."

She turned to Jaim, snarling. "I can't sit here and watch him die!"

Jaim jumped back. "I wasn't suggesting that you watch him die."

"Then what?"

Jaim looked over at the healer working on the unconscious Dùghall. "Dùghall could beat the Dragon if he had his strength."

"As could I, if I had his skills."

"Dùghall said you had as much control of magic as he did, only in other areas. Could you use your magic to help the healer heal him?"

Alarista stared at Jaim. She wasn't a healer, and just healing Dùghall wouldn't do her any good. Even healed, he would be drained of energy and incapable of besting the soul of a rested, powerful Dragon. But where the healer could make him well, *she* could give him strength. Her strength. The price she would pay . . .

She chose not to think about the price she would pay.

She asked the healer, "Namele, are you nearly finished?"

"I've done all I can—he hasn't woken up yet, but now he's merely sleeping. A few days' rest and he should be able to sit up again. He's very frail—whatever happened nearly killed him."

"But he's healed."

Namele looked over at her, eyes wary. "As much as magic can heal him, yes. He's old, he's worn out, and simple healing can't fix that. He won't be able to do any more Dragon fighting."

Alarista turned to Yanth and Jaim. In a low voice, she said, "Drag him over here. Then sit by me—when I finish what I have to do, I'll need you to catch me. Finally—and this is the most important thing—when Dùghall wakes, the *very instant* he wakes, show him Hasmal. Don't let him waste time on me. Tell him he has to stop the Dragon before he kills Hasmal."

Yanth said, "What do you plan on doing?"

"The only thing I can. He needs youth and strength to fight the Dragons. I'm going to give him youth. And strength."

She heard the healer gasp. "You can't—"

"Shut up. I can." She glared at Yanth. "You'll take care of this?"

He nodded. "I will."

They dragged Dùghall to her, assisted by two guards and impeded by the protesting healer, and propped him across from her in a sitting position. Then, while the guards held him upright, Yanth moved to Alarista's left shoulder, and Jaim to her right. She heard Hasmal scream once, and she shuddered.

Hold on, Has, she thought. Hold on. Help is coming.

She summoned all her courage, and rested her hands on

Dùghall's shoulders. Then she lifted her chin, and stared toward the heavens where Vodor Imrish held his court, and in a loud, clear voice, she commanded:

"From my strength,
From my blood,
From my flesh,
From my life,
I offer all that I am,
All that I have,
All that Dùghall Draclas needs
To make him whole.

Take from me to give to him,
Strength and blood,
Flesh and life,
Even unto my own death.
I freely offer my gift,
And in his name accept my offer.

Vodor Imrish, hear me."

She did not draw her own blood, nor scrape her skin. She had no need of that. Their bodies touched—hers strong and whole, Dùghall's weak and worn. She would not limit her offering or mark off with a circle that which she would give and that which she would hold back. Whatever Vodor Imrish chose to take from her to give to Dùghall, he could take.

She knew in offering that she might die—that Dùghall, so near death, might take from her more than she could give and survive. He might absorb her. But Dùghall knew what she did not, and he could win for them where she could not. If she died, she would do so fighting to destroy the Dragons and to save Hasmal, and that would be enough. If she died, her soul would go on, and she would someday find Hasmal again. And meanwhile, her Hasmal would live.

She felt the fire flow into her veins, Matrin's magic stirred by the godtouch, and she knew that Vodor Imrish had heard her. She rejoiced for just an instant, for until that moment he had been deaf to all prayers and all entreaties. Then, as the fire filled her, it burned through her and emptied her. Her world grew dark and she heard a rushing in her ears. Her mouth grew dry, her body heavy, and a giant weight pressed down on her, making each breath a fight.

She knew she was falling, but could not stop herself. Her soul tugged at the moorings of her flesh, called by the wind of approaching death. She did not fight that wind, but at the last instant, when she was sure she would leave her body behind, she felt a surge of energy flow into her, binding her soul tightly to her cage of skin and bones. She was too weak to move—too weak even to open her eyes—but she lived, and knew she would live yet a little longer. Her last coherent thought was a prayer: that Dùghall had received from her enough to do what he needed; that Hasmal could hold on until he did it.

Chapter 2

Dùghall Draclas came roaring out of unconsciousness like a man trapped underwater who at the last possible instant breaks free from his trap and bursts to the surface. He lunged to his feet, gasping, his eyes open but for an instant unfocused.

His body burst with uncontainable energy. He felt as if he could fly, as if he could run from one edge of the known world to the other without his feet ever touching the ground, as if he could rebuild the Glass Towers single-handed. He had a hunger that he hadn't felt so overwhelmingly in years; he desired sex with the obsessive full-body yearning of a young man.

He stared around him at blurred bright colors and at shapes that he could not force to resolve into anything meaningful. The voices in his ears were clear and sharp, startlingly loud, full of nuances and depths but lacking meaning. Smells filled his nostrils, pungent and heady and rich. It was all new, all wondrous, all incomprehensible but glorious.

I've been reborn, he thought. Have died, have come into the world in a new body. I am once again a squalling infant,

and in a few moments or a few days I'll forget that I am
Dùghall Draclas. . . .

Sound was the first thing to resolve into comprehensible
patterns, the first thing to shatter his illusion. ". . . don't
know whether she's going to survive the shock."

"What about him? He looks healthy as peasant hell."

"Dùghall? Can you hear us? Can you see us?"

"Nothing. She's paid a terrible price for nothing."

Sight resolved next. He was in a tent . . . no. He was in
the tent, where he and Hasmal had been pulling the souls
out of Dragons. He was standing up, weaving back and
forth, with a soldier at either side keeping him from falling
on his face. He was looking down—Jaim stared up at him,
Yanth and the healer Namele were crouched over a white-
haired woman that he did not recognize.

He licked his lips, and they felt . . . different. Thicker,
firmer, moister. He still felt that wondrous energy, that illusion of incredible strength, that inescapable sexual fire.
"What . . . happened?" he asked, and wondered at the new
depth of his voice, at the richness and the range. At the clarity of the sound when he spoke, at the presence of soft sounds
he hadn't heard in years. Decades.

A relieved smile flashed across Jaim's face. "Dùghall?
You with us?"

Dùghall nodded. "Yes."

"No time for explanations, then. A Dragon pulled Hasmal physically through the connection between them. He's
torturing him now. If you can't pull the Dragon's soul from
his body, he's going to kill Hasmal. You don't have much
time; Hasmal looks bad."

Yanth and the healer dragged the old woman out of the
way, and Dùghall dropped to his knees beside Jaim. He
stared into the viewing glass Jaim indicated and saw quick
flashes of Hasmal, of a knife, of blood and horror. He heard
a scream—whisper-soft through the viewing-glass connection but no less chilling for its lack of volume—and heard

a gentle, soothing voice say, "More. Or I'll cut out a lung, dear fellow, and pull it out through your back. You really only *need* one, you know."

Jaim said, "Hasmal managed to plant a talisman on the bastard only a few moments ago. It's been going on like this ever since. He's been lying—making up all sorts of wild stories and talking as fast as he can. But the snake-futtering whoreson keeps cutting him anyway." Jaim's voice sounded tight and dry in his throat.

"I'll get him," Dùghall said. "I'll stop this."

For the moment he didn't question his strength. He accepted it, and with it the miracle that had brought him back from sharply remembered pain and utter exhaustion. Jaim handed him a featureless gold ring attached to a tripod of twisted silver wire; this would become a tiny Mirror of Souls—a house and a prison for the soul of the Dragon who tortured Hasmal. He set it on the rug directly in front of him and with a quick swipe of his index finger scraped a bit of skin from the inside of his cheek.

He'd refined his technique since the first time he'd snatched a Dragon soul from its captive body, but the process was still fraught with danger. He glanced at the guards. "Have them watch me," he said to Yanth. "If you have any reason to think the Dragon has won and has pushed *my* soul into the ring, give them a signal. They're to kill this body without question."

Jaim paled. "How can I know?"

Dùghall shrugged. "You might not. You might make a mistake. But, Jaim, you listen to me. Better that you make a mistake and kill me by accident than that you accidentally let a Dragon live. You understand?"

The young man looked at him with frightened eyes and nodded slowly.

Hasmal screamed again.

"I have to do this," Dùghall said. "What's the Dragon's name?"

Jaim said, "Hasmal has called him Dafril."

Dùghall nodded. "Dafril." He crouched over the tiny tripod. He rested his hands on the viewing glass that connected to Dafril's soul, and willed his soul to link through that ethereal connection to the monster at the other end. When, after a moment, he felt the hot darkness of that evil other, he concentrated all his will on the band of gold and said:

"Follow my soul, Vodor Imrish,
To the Dragon soul of Dafril,
To the usurper of a body not his own,
And from this body expel the intruder.
Bring no harm to the intruder,
The Dragon Dafril.
Instead, give his soul safe house and shelter
Within the unbroken circle before me—
Unbroken that it may guard
Dafril's immortality, and
Protect the essence of his life and mind,
While safely reuniting the body and soul
Of him whom Dafril has wronged.
I offer my flesh—all that I have given
And all that you will take—
Freely and with clear conscience,
As I do no wrong,
But reverse a wrong done."

White-hot magical fire burned through him once more, searing the anchor that held his soul to his own body, searing the tenuous connection between him and the Dragon; and within the blink of an eye it enveloped the Dragon's soul.

The fire pulsed and drew, and he felt first astonishment and then rage from Dafril. Because Dafril's soul could have no permanent anchor in the body he had stolen, the fire ripped him loose and pulled him toward Dùghall as fast as light raced through a keyhole. Dùghall braced and the enemy soul was upon him in the same instant; and this enemy held power he had never experienced before.

Dafril's soul dug into his mind and burrowed into his flesh seeking purchase; the Dragon fought with a thousand years of experience and cleverness to pry Dùghall from his body and force Dùghall's soul into the eternal prison of the ring. Dùghall strengthened his connections with his own flesh. He felt he was fighting an octopus—no sooner had he shored up one weak spot than Dafril had wedged a tentacle into another and dug in. Every self-doubt, every half-remembered shame, every wrong he'd ever done anyone became a weak point that the Dragon exploited.

He caught brief thoughts and images from his enemy's mind; he discovered he was fighting the head of the Dragons. Dafril was the monster who had conceived the immortality engine a thousand years before, and had planned out and designed the Mirror of Souls. This was the very monster who, when the Wizards' War turned in favor of the Falcons, had gathered his faithful followers and locked all of them into the Mirror of Souls, priming it to bring them back when the world was ripe for their return. This was the master.

Dafril reached into his mind with a will forged of iron, and drove commands like knives into his soul. *Give in. Give up. Surrender.*

Dùghall gathered his strength and channeled his purpose and determination. He visualized himself as the core of a sun, burning everything that was not him, expanding with unstoppable power, filling all the cracks and crevices, all the weaknesses and shames and uncertainties of his existence with the pure fire of his life. He accepted his self-doubt and admitted his imperfections, and when he did, he no longer questioned his worthiness to exist.

At the moment that Dùghall accepted himself as he was,

Dafril lost his hold. His soul erupted from the center of Dùghall's chest in a fiery river that poured into the center of the ring. The light began to spiral around the rim, and the room filled for an instant with a deafening wall of sound—a wail of terror and rage so loud Dùghall felt it more than he heard it. Fog poured out from the center of the fire, white and dense and ice-cold. And for just an instant, Dùghall choked on the stink of rot and honeysuckle.

Then the air cleared and quiet returned.

Before him, pure golden light rose upward through the center of the tiny tripod and swirled into the ring, spiraling slowly. It had become the Mirror of Dafril—a thing of beauty with a heart of evil.

Dùghall shuddered and looked up at Jaim. "I beat him," he said quietly. "I beat that monster. Hasmal should be safe now."

Jaim stared into his eyes, and Dùghall became aware of the point of a sword pressed lightly against his back, high on the left rib cage. A downward thrust would shove it through his heart and kill him in an instant. He recalled his peril and realized its extent as he saw the doubt and the distrust in the eyes of the man who held his life in a word.

Jaim's hands trembled. He nibbled at the corner of his lower lip. He stared at Dùghall as if staring could strip away the skin and bone and reveal the shape of the soul beneath. "Tell me something that only you and I would know," he said.

Dùghall took a deep breath and let it out slowly. He shook his head. "That wouldn't work. Dafril's soul would have had immediate access to my memories. He could tell you anything I could."

Jaim frowned. A spot of blood appeared on that lower lip, quickly licked away. Abruptly he laughed and looked up at the guard. "He's Dùghall," he said, and the pressure of the sword at Dùghall's back vanished.

Dùghall nodded. "I am. But how could you be sure?"

Jaim said, "Dafril would have told me something to convince me he was you, in order to save his life as quickly as possible. Only *you* would say something that wouldn't give me any reassurance at all."

In the viewing glass, Hasmal was smiling through blood and pain. "You're the rightful owner of the body, aren't you?" he was saying.

Dùghall felt he could relax. Hasmal would be taken care of by the grateful man who had gotten his life back. Meanwhile, he, Dùghall, could take the time to find out what had happened to him. He stretched and pulled his hands away from the viewing glass that still showed images of Hasmal. "Tell me how I got my strength back."

Jaim glanced at the old woman still lying where Yanth and the healer had dragged her. "Alarista knew she couldn't take on the Dragon who was torturing Hasmal and win. So she fed her youth and her strength to you. You look like you're in your late thirties or early forties now."

Dùghall looked at his hands—really looked at them—for the first time since he woke up. The skin was smooth; the arthritis that had bent his knuckles sideways and swelled them into knots was gone. He made a fist and saw the muscle below the webbing between his thumb and index finger bulge, big as a mouse. The air flowing into and out of his lungs moved slowly and easily. His spine felt straight and strong, and no dull throb of pain grabbed at him when he arched his back or turned his head. And lust coursed through his veins and filled his groin with urgent hunger.

He was young again.

And Alarista was old.

He twisted around and stared at the wasted body and wrinkled face of the woman across the tent. *That* was Alarista? She had sacrificed herself to save Hasmal; had torn most of the years of her life away and gifted them to him. He tried to conceive of a love that would do that—in all his years, he had known and desired and enjoyed many women, but he had never found the one woman for whom he would move the world.

He envied her the power of her passion, and realized in the same instant that he could not keep the gift that she had given him. He had to return her life to her, though he didn't know how.

He turned back to the viewing glass as he heard Hasmal say, "Will you cut me loose? I need a healer."

"You don't know who I am, do you?"

Through the eyes of the man Dùghall had just restored to his life, Dùghall saw Hasmal shake his head. "Someone who appreciates having his body back, I hope."

The man watching Hasmal laughed, and Dùghall's attention snapped fully back to the viewing glass. He shuddered at the sound of that laugh. It was wrong. Cruel. It would have sounded right coming from Dafril—but Dùghall knew he'd banished Dafril to the ring in front of him. Which suggested that the man whose body Dafril had claimed had been evil, too.

"You have no idea how grateful I am," the man told Hasmal. "There I was, ready to do wondrous things, and suddenly that lying Dragon ripped me from my body and threw my soul into the Veil. I wasn't dead, but I wasn't alive, either. *Things* hunt between the worlds—did you know that? Vast cold monstrous hungers that seek out the bright lights of souls trapped in their lightless void so that they can devour them. Annihilate them. Other souls were trapped there with me—I watched darkness swallow some of them. They're gone forever. I barely evaded that same fate twice. Twice. Being trapped in the infinite blackness of void, hunted by roving nightmares-made-real, facing eternal extinction at any moment—I still don't know if there's a true hell, but the horrors of that place will do for me. You, or rather the one you summoned, pulled me out of that."

He'd been watching Hasmal's face while he talked,

moving closer step by slow step. Twice he'd glanced at the knife in his hand.

His words created an image of gratitude, but some edge to his voice spoke of darker emotions. "You and your unseen friend have powerful magic at your disposal. You're Falcons, aren't you?"

Hasmal's face showed that he had heard that edge, too. He nodded, but warily.

"Working with Ry Sabir."

Another slow nod.

"I thought as much. Ry's my cousin."

Hasmal tried a cautious smile, but it died on his face.

"Good guess," the man said. "We weren't friends, Ry and I. My name is Crispin Sabir. Perhaps you've heard Ry speak of me?" A soft chuckle. "I see from your expression that you have, and that Ry was careful to tell you all my best points."

Dùghall's fists clenched into tight balls. *Crispin Sabir.* Of all the Sabirs Dùghall had encountered in his years of service to the Galweigh Family, Crispin was the closest thing to incarnate evil he had ever encountered. Hasmal couldn't have fallen into worse hands.

"I helped you," Hasmal said.

"Well, yes. Undeniably. But I don't give that fact much weight. I'm grateful to have my body back—please don't think I'm not. But you were only trying to save your own life when you summoned your friend."

"Are you going to let me go?" Hasmal asked.

Crispin Sabir was quiet for a long time. A very long time. Dùghall felt his muscles ache with the tension of waiting. Beside him, he heard Jaim's shallow breathing, and movement as Yanth crouched at his left shoulder.

"You're a Falcon. My magic can't touch you. You're shielded somehow—I can't even see the shield, but I can feel its effects. I can't control you. I can't make you work for me. If I set you free, nothing I could do would guarantee that you won't turn on me."

"My word—"

"I have no love for the trappings of honor, you. I've given my own word countless times, and have broken it in the next breath. Expediency rules honor—you know this and I know it, and I would have it no other way. But because that is true, your word is no currency I'd care to spend."

"I've done nothing to harm you."

"Not that I know of. I grant you that. But you can't guarantee that you won't do something to harm me in the future."

Hasmal grimaced. "I swear on Vodor Imrish, my word—" he started to say again, and again Crispin cut him off.

"No. Don't waste your breath or my time. I must do something with you. You might make a good prisoner or fetch a decent ransom. But I doubt that any ransom I could get from you would be worth the trouble you would cause me."

Jaim asked, "Can't you do something? Travel back through the viewing-glass link—force that Sabir bastard to let him go?"

Dùghall gritted his teeth. "Falcon magic cannot coerce. It is purely defensive. Most times, that's enough. But Crispin Sabir is the rightful soul in his own body—I cannot do anything that will force him from the choices he makes of his own free will."

Dùghall felt fingers tighten around his arm, and he turned from the viewing glass to find Yanth a mere hand's breadth from his face. "Dragon magic could force him. *Wolf* magic could force him."

Dùghall rested a hand atop Yanth's and willed himself to calm. "Agreed. But I am neither Dragon nor Wolf. I am Falcon, and sworn to follow the path of Falconry. As is Hasmal."

"You have to *save* him," Jaim said. "Alarista gave you her life so that you could save him."

Dùghall turned to face Jaim. "Perhaps I could save his body, but it would be at the price of my soul, and his. Jaim, if he chose to turn away from the Falcon path, he could, perhaps, save his own life. Instead, he holds his shields in place and so protects his soul."

"*Save him,*" Yanth snarled.

"There are things worse than death," Dùghall said softly. "Things more terrifying, more painful. And far more lasting."

"You quaking coward," Yanth said. He started to draw his sword. In a flash, three guards' blades pointed at the young swordsman's throat. Yanth glared at them and turned to Dùghall. He said, "If I could, I'd cut you a spine, you jellyfish."

In the viewing glass, Dùghall saw Crispin rest his blade against the rope that held Hasmal's left wrist. He had moved closer to the trapped Falcon. He said, "Perhaps I *ought* to let you go. I wonder if you would be as grateful for your freedom as I am for mine."

Hasmal suddenly smiled and said, "Dùghall, hear me. I want more time. I am not done here."

"You're done here," Crispin said, and in a stroke almost too fast to follow, buried his knife to the hilt in Hasmal's heart.

Yanth roared, "*No!*" and Jaim made an inarticulate cry. From her place on the floor near the healer, Alarista awakened from her motionless sleep, keening.

Hasmal gasped. His eyes went wide, and then closed. Dùghall held his breath. Hasmal's words rang in his head— *I want more time. I am not done here.* Hasmal's message had been a code; it spoke of a plan that Crispin Sabir could not suspect, and would not believe.

"More time," Dùghall whispered, praying that Hasmal would succeed. "More time."

Within an instant, a faint white light formed around Hasmal's face, so that his features seemed to be hidden by a thin fog. The expression of pain that had twisted his mouth slowly seeped away; he looked peaceful, and somehow triumphant. The faint white cloud of light grew brighter and spread down his body, setting his torso glowing first, then illuminating his arms and legs. Dùghall could see the changes clearly—Crispin was unmoving, staring at the body. The only sound to come from the viewing glass was the sound of his breathing, which grew harsher and faster as the light surrounding Hasmal's body grew brighter. When Hasmal's entire body was bathed in the light, the nimbus surrounding him grew brighter, then brighter yet, until it was too brilliant to look at directly. Crispin averted his eyes, then glanced back as shadows in the room where he stood changed.

The light had lifted away from Hasmal's body. It maintained its man shape for a moment, then coalesced into a tight, brilliant ball of white fire.

"Get away from me," Crispin whispered.

The sphere of light began to float toward him, soundless, slow, inexorable.

In the viewing glass, Dùghall saw one of Crispin's hands raise to form a Wolf power-hold. Light streamed from Crispin's fingertips, pouring through the radiant sphere. But the sphere was undamaged. Indeed, it grew brighter, then larger. It kept floating toward Crispin, still silent, unhurried, utterly implacable.

Crispin turned away at last and began to run.

In the next instant, the view in the glass became whiteness—brilliant blinding light.

Then blackness.

In the tent in the mountains far to the south of Calimekka, wind set the flaps shuddering and snapping, and cold air blew through the gaps in the waxed cloth. Yanth and Jaim stared at each other, and then at Alarista, who still lay unmoving, her head thrown back, her eyes open and focused on nothing. She did not cease her keening; her thin, frail voice shredded the silence.

Yanth spoke first. "What happened? What was that?"

Jaim said, "Hasmal took over Crispin's body—like the Dragons did."

Dùghall shook his head. He said, "Hasmal's last words were quoted lines from the Secret Texts, from the Book of Agonies. The whole passage goes:

> 'Then, at the moment of his death, Solander spoke into the Veil. "More time," he cried. "I am not done here."
>
> 'From within and beyond the Veil the gods listened, and though his body was broken beyond saving, they had pity on Solander, and did not call his soul away from the world. Instead, in sight of Dragons and Falcons, Solander took form as a sun, as a light unto the world, rising from his shattered shell.
>
> 'And he spoke to all who watched, saying to them, "I am with you still."
>
> 'And at his words the Dragons feared, and the Falcons rejoiced.' "

Jaim said, "His body is dead, but his soul is . . . that light?"

"I believe so."

"Then what will happen to him now?"

Dùghall touched the darkened viewing glass. "We can only wait to see."

Chapter 3

The carriage rattled over the cobblestone paving of Shippers Lane, in the Vagata District of Calimekka—one of the few streets open to wheeled traffic during daylight hours. It made poor time; the driver jockeyed for place with wagons filled with ships' stores bound for the harbor, with donkeys, mules, and oxen pulling farm carts laden with produce just arrived from the country, with public coaches carrying merchants to and from their warehouses and private coaches bringing the rich to and from their ships.

Kait held Ry's hand; it was the first time she had been able to touch him since they came to Calimekka to infiltrate the Dragons' city. Now the two of them were alone except for Ian, and Ian kept his eyes pressed to the peephole at the rear of the carriage. Kait knew he was looking for trouble that might be coming after them, but she suspected he didn't want to have to watch her sitting so close to Ry, either. Both his desire for her and his pain in knowing she loved Ry had been clear in his eyes when he'd rescued the two of them from the cages. And every time he looked in her direction, she could see it still.

Ry leaned over and brushed the side of Kait's neck with

his lips. "I love you," he whispered, too low for any but another Karnee to hear.

She squeezed his hand and murmured, "I love you, too."

"I have rooms waiting for us in one of the harbor inns," Ian said. He was still on his knees on the rear bench of the carriage with his back to them, clinging to the handholds and staring out the peephole. "You'll find forged papers in the packet beside you. You're to be Parat and Parata Bosoppffer, from the village of Three Parrots Mountain, first names Rian and Kaevi. Those were as close to your actual names as I could come using backcountry names. You're minor affiliates of the Masschanka Family taking passage for Birstislavas in the New Territories, where you're to homestead. You attended the funeral of Tirkan Bosoppffer, who was buried today—his legacy to you was the lands in the Territories that you now go to claim. Your papers are very good," he noted in an aside. "They would hold up if you used them to take passage, and would probably get you your homestead deed when you arrived if you chose to leave Calimekka."

"We won't be leaving the city," Kait said. "The Dragons are still here, and as long as they are, no one and no place is safe. As much as I would like to never see this city again, there's nowhere else we can go."

Ian turned and nodded at her. A wry smile twisted one corner of his mouth. "I expected you'd say that. I still wanted to give you the option of escape." He turned back to his peephole. "We'll have to be in the inn for two or three days. Traffic along the Palmetto Cliff Road is watched now—for us to get to Galweigh House, we're going to have to get a donkey to carry the Mirror of Souls and pack in over one of the mountain paths."

"You have forged papers that will explain what we're doing heading there, too?" Kait asked.

"No. No one goes to Galweigh House by any path. If we're caught on our way there, we'll most likely die."

Ry sighed. He told Ian, "Since Kait and I jumped off a cliff to get here, I've been operating on the theory that I'm already dead. It's given me a whole new appreciation for every moment of my life, and has allowed me to keep from panicking."

Kait looked at him, interested. "Does that work?"

He looked over at her and grinned. "You'd be amazed. The guards came running at me with swords drawn when they caught on to us; I thought, I'm already dead—what can they do to me? So I shouted to warn you, and stood to fight, hoping to create a distraction and give you time to escape. Didn't work . . . but I still think it was the right thing to do."

Kait thought about it for a long moment, and decided to give it a try. She visualized herself still, gray-skinned, eyes dulled and open and staring at nothing, breath stopped. I'm already dead, she told herself, and forced her protesting mind to believe it. Already dead. Already dead. In a strange way, it was comforting. The instant she conceded her death, she had already lost everything she had to lose. She became indestructible. She could suddenly focus on what she had to do instead of on her fear of dying. Her goals and the logical steps she would have to take to reach them rose smoothly out of the background chatter of her mind, and the ceaseless shrill monkey voice that howled warning of her imminent destruction stilled. "That works," she said. "That actually helps."

Ry nodded.

Ian was less impressed. He said, "As I was saying, you have new identities to use before we get to Galweigh House. But you'll need to change into the clothes I brought for you now. We'll have a checkpoint coming up soon— you need to look like poor relations just come from a funeral." He had stripped off his soldier's uniform as soon as they'd jumped into the carriage, and already wore his disguise. Dressed in a silk tunic embroidered with copper thread, deep blue pleated balloon breeches, and calf-high embroidered black cloth boots, and with his cropped hair covered by a long blond wig, he looked like the sort of man who could afford to rent a four-horse funeral carriage for himself and his poorer relations.

"Where are the clothes?" Kait asked.

"Compartment above your heads. You have a few moments, but do hurry."

Ry stood, swaying with the movement of the carriage, and handed down a bundle of green cloth to Kait. He pulled out another bundle, this one brown.

Kait pulled on the outfit Ian had obtained for her. It had once been intended to ape the fashionable funeral wear of the upper classes, though its dyes were muddy and its fabrics cheap. With the cut of it several seasons past its prime, it had descended from merely ugly to truly hideous. As she tightened the laces on the bodice and adjusted the ankle ties of the leg wraps, she decided she definitely looked like somebody's poor third cousin.

In the time she had taken to get dressed, Ry had scrambled into his new clothes. His were equally ugly—but she thought he looked good in them nonetheless.

He looked at himself, grimaced, then looked at her. "Yodee hoder," he said in a broad backcountry accent. "Let's send Uncle Tirkan off with banana beer and an all-night stomp. And when we're done, you can tuck up your skirts and we can go plow the fields."

Ian turned away from the peephole for a moment and studied the two of them. He shrugged. "You look like every other poor parat or parata leaving Calimekka for a fresh start. If you could afford silks and jewels here, why would you be traveling to the New Territories to make your fortunes?" He turned around and sat down on the bench facing the two of them. "Get your papers out," he said. "The checkpoint is just ahead. By the way, should you be asked, I'm Ian Bosoppffer, your first cousin, just arrived from the Territories to take you back with me."

Kait nodded, memorizing his story and Ry's as well as her own. Her heartbeat picked up. The Mirror of Souls lay nestled in the compartment beneath Ian, easily found by even the most cursory search.

"Get ready," Ry said, and gave her hand a final squeeze.

"I'm ready," Kait said. "At least as ready as I can be."

He told her, "They may know by now that we're gone. If they question us, or if they want to search the carriage, we're going to have to kill them."

"I know."

Ry said, "We can't let them get the Mirror back."

"I know that, too."

The carriage rattled to a stop. A guard pulled the door open and leaned inside. "Apologies for interrupting you at your time of loss," he said, "but I'll have to see your papers." He gave each of their faces a cursory look, but Kait knew from experience with Family guards that in that quick glance he'd catalogued myriad details about them that he would be able to recall again if questioned.

Ry handed the man his and Kait's forged documents, and Ian handed over his own papers.

The guard studied her papers and Ry's first. He read the notations and snorted. "Three Parrots Mountain? Zagtasht preserve you!" He handed Ry the papers and said, "Here's some free advice, country boy. People in the city aren't like the ones you know. When you get to your rooms, stay there and hold your vigil in private. Don't play dice with the sailors, don't buy drinks for the whores, and don't go walking down backstreets with men who have a wondrous device to show you that is guaranteed to make your fortune."

Ry nodded solemnly. "I won't." His accent was pure hillslogger.

The guard said, "You think you won't. But you'll do something equally stupid, I'll bet you, and lose your ship fare—and then you'll be stranded here like the thousand other yokels who thought they knew what cities were about."

He studied Ian's papers next. After an equally quick glance, he shrugged. "You've made it to the Territories and back already, eh?"

"Yes."

"Then maybe you know a bit about the city. Keep them smart, would you?" He returned his attention to Ry. This time the glance was intent, not cursory.

Kait felt a chill crawl down her spine.

Ry shrugged.

The guard finally said, "You remind me of the last hill-slogger I warned to stay out of trouble. He ended up back at the guardstation the same gods'-damned night, weeping about his lost life savings and wondering how he was ever going to reach his claim in the Territories." The guard gave a disgusted snort and stepped down from the carriage. "As if—in this city—we could find the trickster who gulled him out of his gold and get the whoreson to give it back." He slammed the carriage door and waved up to the driver. "Move it. Next!"

When they were through, Ry sagged against Kait's side.

"What's the matter?"

"I knew him," Ry said. "He was one of the gate guards at Sabir House before I came after you. His name is . . . damnall. What is it. Lerri? Herri? No, but that's close. Guerri? That's it. Guerri. What's worse, he knows me, too. He hasn't connected my face with who I am yet, but he will."

Ian grimaced. "We should have killed him, then."

Ry shook his head. "No. We wouldn't have made it past the checkpoint. We may have time to lose ourselves at the harbor. We'd better get new papers, though."

Kait looked from Ry to Ian. "He knew who you were, Ry," she said. "He knew. I saw an instant of surprise in his eyes when first he looked at you. I didn't know what to make of it, and when he didn't say anything, I thought perhaps I'd imagined it."

"Nonsense," Ian said. "If he'd recognized Ry, he would have sounded the alarm. He could have been a wealthy man for turning him in—a fact I *know* he knows. The decree of Ry's *barzanne* is posted in all the guardhouses, in the dorms, and on the public posts."

Kait looked at Ry. "I'm sure he knew you," she insisted.

Ry leaned his head against the wooden headrest and closed his eyes. "I was good to him when he worked at the gate," he said thoughtfully. "Nothing spectacular . . . but I remembered his name, and I gave him small gifts for Haledan's Festival and the Feast of the Thousand Holies."

Ian raised an eyebrow. "Considering what the rest of our Family is like, you must have seemed a veritable saint to him."

"The Sabirs earned their bad reputation for their dealings with other Families," Ry said stiffly. "They weren't cruel to those who served them."

Ian said, "It was my Family, too, brother. Remember? I spent my first years in that House, and saw plenty of cruelty aimed at those who served. My *mother* was one of those who served."

Ry shrugged. "Perhaps you're right. In any case, he didn't turn us in, and if Kait's right and he did recognize me, I don't think he *will* turn us in."

"I hope she's right. He knows the names we're traveling under, our faces, our cover story, and our general destination. If he sends the Sabir guards after us in the next few days, they won't have any trouble tracking us down."

Chapter 4

asmal's last words still rang in his own mind like the pure tones of a meditation bell. *Dùghall, hear me. I want more time. I am not done here.*

He was dead, he knew—and he could feel the pull of the Veil still tugging at him like the waves of an outgoing tide pulling at a piece of driftwood. But the light that infused his soul gave him strength to resist the pull, and his mind remained his own—not confused, not lost and uncomprehending as he had heard minds became when people died suddenly by violence. He knew exactly what had happened to him. Crispin Sabir had finished killing him. And Vodor Imrish had heard his summons and answered his prayer. Even dead, Hasmal now had at least a little time to finish the things he had left undone, and though he was not sure of how everything worked in this new state of being, he knew that he had within his grasp the means to effect change.

He rose slowly, feeling an unnerving pull as his spirit separated from his body. As his flesh fell away, he felt both lighter and cleaner. But he also felt the first wave of terrible loss. His heart cried out for Alarista; he knew he would never hold her again; never touch her; never kiss her; never make love to her. The last words they had spoken were the last words they would ever speak; the last kiss they had shared would be the final one. His dreams of having children with her, of growing old together—those were gone.

He hoped their souls would reunite beyond the Veil—that they would share their afterlife, or that they would be reborn into other bodies where they could share other lives. It was something to hope for. But the happiness of *this* moment, *this* love, *this* life, was now behind him.

He hung in the air for a moment, staring down at his dead self lying on the table, and he grieved. He had wanted so much more.

Then he drew himself together. Vodor Imrish had not given him this second chance so that he could mourn his own death. He was a Falcon—he had sworn himself to the service of good, and while he existed in any form as Hasmal rann Dorchan, son of Hasmal rann Halles, he had work to do.

He felt certain that Dùghall had heard his last words. He'd felt the old master's presence just before the Dragon soul of Dafril was ripped from Crispin's body. He felt equally certain that Dùghall would realize that he intended to bind his soul to the plane of the living as Solander the Reborn was rumored to have done, so that he could carry out the destiny that had been stolen from him by the Dragons. Now he had to hope that Dùghall would find a way to provide an open channel for him, as the Secret Texts said Vincalis had provided an open channel for Solander after his death.

Hasmal would not try to become another Reborn. Not for an instant did he believe Vodor Imrish had intended any such destiny for him. But his god had put him in the hands of Dafril, a powerful Dragon who had bragged to him that he and he alone had been the creator of the original Mirror of Souls. And his god had allowed him to see Dafril captured and rendered helpless, while the body Dafril had inhabited had remained close at hand. If the rightful occupant of that body, Crispin Sabir, had killed him, Hasmal believed Vodor Imrish had allowed it for a reason. He believed he had died so that he could achieve the one form which would allow him to obtain the information the Falcons needed to conquer the Dragons once and for all.

Vodor Imrish was not a god of war; he didn't destroy perfectly good worshipers to take pleasure in the spectacle of their deaths as did the gods of war. He had no love of blood for the sake of blood, nor of pain for the pleasure of pain. He would make good use of the dead as he made good use of the living.

Crispin Sabir still stood in the spot from which he had killed Hasmal. Hasmal could tell that Crispin could see him, too; the Wolf's eyes were fixed on the place where he floated, and his breathing was faster than normal, and shallower. Hasmal could feel Crispin's fear vibrating in the air.

He found that he could will himself to move in any direction with a thought. He began to float slowly toward Crispin, not certain of what he would do when he reached him, but certain that Crispin needed to be his first destination.

The Wolf hummed with magic—power, Hasmal realized, that he had drawn from the energy of Hasmal's death. As Hasmal moved toward him, Crispin attacked with that magic.

The magic that Crispin had intended to be a weapon, however, did not act like a weapon when it encountered Hasmal's insubstantial form. It flowed through Hasmal, but didn't harm him. Instead, it fed him back the life-force that Crispin had stolen, making him stronger and further clearing his mind. The spell attached to the energy, though, rebounded on Crispin, and the *rewhah* energy that came from the death-powered spell hit the Wolf at the same instant. The combined forces of spell and *rewhah* stunned the Wolf, pinning his feet to the ground. Hasmal felt the vibration of Crispin's fear rise in intensity.

He continued floating slowly toward Crispin. At the last instant before they touched, Crispin regained control of his body. He turned and tried to run. Hasmal enveloped him, and their souls connected.

An immediate wash of sensations assaulted his heightened senses and sickened him. His first impression of Crispin's soul was of foulness layered upon foulness; of perversion and delight in perversion; of hatred piled upon rage stacked upon lust twisted up with greed and hunger for power. Each part of Crispin's soul yammered its desires in an unending stream; each separate memory and each separate perversion added to the babble. Hasmal tried to shield himself from the disgusting cacophony, but in this new form he could no longer summon a shield. Frustrated and overwhelmed by the noise of Crispin's mind, he pushed against the din, intending only to give himself a peaceful space in which to study his surroundings, unbothered by them. The blanket he created, however, did something to Crispin; the Wolf toppled to the floor, rendered senseless and still. He breathed and his heart beat, but his chaotic mind grew quiet, the many conflicting voices in it hushed completely or forced to whisper.

Which was an improvement, Hasmal decided.

He spent a few moments learning to read the shapes of the tumultuous thoughts, and sorting those which belonged to Crispin from those deep imprints which remained from Dafril's presence. Hasmal felt he was digging for diamonds in a river of filth, but he persisted. And he began uncovering his diamonds.

His first gem of information was that Crispin lived in paranoid terror of the discovery of the single secret he kept hidden not just from the rest of the world, but also from his brother Anwyn and his cousin Andrew. He had fathered a child, a daughter, a baby born to him by a woman about whom he had actually cared. The mother had been involved in an intra-Family intrigue; when Crispin discovered her treachery against him, he'd killed her himself. But the child the two of them created he had spared. Fearing that a member of his own Family or one of the other Five Families would use the babe as a lever to move him, he'd bought a wet nurse for her and sent wet nurse and infant to Novtierra. For years, he'd kept the child hidden in the city of Stosta in the Sabirene Isthmus. She had been there, in fact, until he discovered the existence of the Mirror of Souls and first decided to make himself a god. On the day that the *Wind Treasure* had sailed into the Thousand Dancers and into his reach, he marked three albatrosses with the compulsion to fly across the sea to her, and banded each with the message that she was to come home, and was to wait for him in a secret apartment that he had prepared for her. She was not to try to contact him—he would come to her.

Of course Dafril had taken over Crispin's body at the moment when he had thought he would ascend to godhood. He'd never experienced his moment of triumph. His vision of being the god-king welcoming his beloved child into the realm that would become her own personal possession had not materialized. She had arrived in Calimekka, and was in the apartment at that moment. Dafril had noted her arrival, and had kept a spy checking to see that the girl had the necessities and that she didn't stray, but he had not come up with any compelling use for her yet. So he had left her alone.

And because Dafril had controlled Crispin's body until the moment Dùghall exorcised him, father and daughter had not yet met.

Hasmal knew her name; he knew where she was hiding; he knew the words Crispin had given her that would identify him to her and let her know he was the one person in all of Calimekka she could trust.

Within the dark, strong traces of Dafril's presence, he

found memories far stranger than Crispin's, memories that shook him to his core. Dafril and a colleague named Luercas had been the wizards who took the life of Solander more than a thousand years earlier. He and Luercas had worked out many of the details of the immortality engine. Dafril had been the sole leader of the Dragons in Calimekka, too—for in returning from their long hiatus inside the Mirror of Souls, something had happened to Luercas. Hasmal could find Dafril's concern on that score. Dafril had believed Luercas might be working against him, or working on his own. Hasmal felt an uneasy chill at that thought, but kept digging.

His greatest find waited amid the foulest of Dafril's thoughts. The Dragon Dafril had been the primary designer of the Mirror of Souls. He and Luercas and a few other Dragons had created it when they began to suspect that they might not win the Wizards' War. Dafril knew the meaning of every sigil inscribed on the Mirror, the use of every inlaid gem, the nuances of every spell the Mirror could build and channel.

And as he knew those things, so did Hasmal.

Hasmal recalled suddenly and with crystal clarity the words of the Speaker he had summoned long ago—the Speaker who had launched him on his flight away from the safety of his home in Halles and into the path of Kait Galweigh and the fates. She'd said, "You are a vessel chosen by the Reborn, Hasmal. Your destiny is pain and glory. Your sacrifice will bring the return of greatness to the Falcons, and your name will be revered through all time."

Perhaps in the nest of clever obfuscations and intentional cloudiness she had spoken, she had told him that one clear truth without ornament or trickery. If Hasmal could be quick enough, and if he could hold his incorporeal self together long enough, he could hand the Falcons the keys that would rid Matrin of the Dragons for good, and in the same stroke could give them a way to control Crispin, who now led Ibera's remaining Wolves. Before he fell into the Darkland, before he heard the *karae* sing their welcoming dirges into his dead ears, he would seek out Dùghall. If he could transmit his message to the Falcons, he would not have died for nothing.

He focused his energy, located the talismanic connection that bound Crispin to Dùghall's viewing glass, and launched himself along it.

Chapter 5

Luercas said, "A little faster, Danya. It would not be seemly for you to trail behind me when we make our triumphant return to the village. You are, after all, my mother . . . and we know how the Kargans revere mothers."

They rode giant lorrags—bigger versions of the deadly predators who hunted the Kargans across the tundra of the Veral Territories. Luercas had lured two of the beasts to Inkanmerea, the citadel of the Ancients buried beneath the tundra near the Kargan village. When the two predators skulked down the steps and into the huge, vaulted entry chamber, they had been of normal size. Luercas had used one of the Ancients' magical engines to steal energy from the lives and souls of the Kargans, and had twisted that energy into a spell to increase the monsters' size and suppress their will. They were still vicious brutes, and still deadly, but now they could do nothing to harm either Luercas or Danya.

Luercas added, "This is the moment you've been waiting for, girl. You needn't sulk."

Danya nodded, but did not speak. She rarely said anything to Luercas anymore; he took delight in turning her words back on her, in humiliating her, in making her feel like a fool. He never did anything of the sort when anyone else could see them; his plans for the Kargans demanded that both he and she become not just beloved but actually worshiped by the furry Scarred tribe. But when they were alone, he goaded her mercilessly for her weakness, her cowardice, her lack of foresight, her poor magical abilities, and anything else he could think of to remind her that no matter what their outward appearance might be, he owned her.

She glanced over at him. Luercas looked about twelve years old, though he'd been born only half a year earlier. His golden hair hung down his back in a short braid, his blue eyes studied her guilelessly. He was as beautiful as any human child she had ever seen, and she hated him with a depth and a ferocity she did not even have words for. When she slept, she dreamed of hurting him; when she woke, she sometimes wept to discover that he had not died at her hands.

She comforted herself with the fact that she had sworn revenge against him at the same time that she had renewed her vows of revenge against the Sabirs and her own Family, the Galweighs. She had sacrificed her son to seal that oath—and if Luercas's soul now inhabited her dead son's body, her dead son's blood would see that the Dragon wizard would suffer and die for doing so.

They rode through a stand of fireweed, the flowers in full and glorious bloom. Had she been on the ground, they would have towered over her head. Astride the lorrag's gaunt back, she could just see above the waving sea of fuchsia blooms.

"So, Danya Two-Claws, are you ready to become a goddess?" Luercas asked.

She said nothing.

He turned and stared at her. As he did, she felt his gaze take on weight and form. Her throat tightened, and continued to tighten. She gasped, and her airway closed completely. Invisible fingers squeezed it shut, and though she grabbed her neck with both hands and opened her mouth and tried to suck in air, nothing happened.

"I'm tired of riding in silence," Luercas said. "I want someone to talk to . . . and since the lorrags can't talk, that leaves you. Are you going to talk to me?"

A faint film of red glazed the world, and darkness moved toward the center of her field of vision. She nodded.

He laughed. "You'll learn that you can't fight me, Danya. You might as well become my friend."

He still held her airway closed. She nodded.

"You'll be my friend?"

She nodded again, frantic. The world reeled around her and her skull felt like it would explode.

"Well, good. I'm so glad."

Suddenly air rushed into her starved lungs. She sagged forward, relieved and terrified at the same time.

He was staring at her, that same fixed, humorless smile stretched across his face. "Don't you feel better now that we're friends?"

She nodded again.

He smiled. "We're ready, then. Friend. I'll take Kargan form before we reach the village. Keep the red cloak on when you ride in, but after I change to human shape in front of them, throw it to the ground at my feet so that I can dismount on it. Their prophecy of their savior's arrival states that he 'walks on red.' The cloak should meet the requirement well enough. And as long as we ride the lorrags and I'm Kargan in form some of the time, they'll be ready enough to accept that their prophecy has come true."

Danya nodded. "You said you wanted me to say something."

He said, "Raise your right hand so that they get a good look at those two claws of yours. Say, 'You welcomed me and made me one of you. You accepted me in forms both strange and stranger, fed me from your tables, gifted me with home and hearth and friendship. Now, my good and faithful children, I reveal myself to you as Ki Ika, and I give you my son Iksahsha as I promised long ago.'"

"Ki Ika and Iksahsha—the Summer Goddess and her son Bountiful Fishing. You truly believe they'll look at us and see their heroes? I'm not even Kargan."

"Their legends speak of the day when they were human—they fully believe that they'll be human again someday. If Ki Ika reveals herself to them in human form, what of it? You're what they hope to be. Besides, we're riding lorrags, I can become Kargan at will, and we control magic. We're as close to their gods as they'll ever see walking."

"If you say so. Then what?"

"Then I'll tell them that the days of the prophecy have come, when the Scarred shall be returned to their rightful places in the lands and the homes of Man, and shall once again, if they so desire, take back their forms as Men." He shrugged. "I'll tell them to follow us—that we'll lead them to the Rich Lands, them and all the rest of the Scarred."

"And we use them to raise our army and attack Ibera."

"Yes. Why do you sound so doubtful now?"

"Because now I'm sitting on the back of the lorrag and not merely imagining it. And I'm looking at you on the back of your beast, and you look neither immortal nor particularly impressive. We have no cloth-of-gold robes, no jewels, no servants. I was raised in a House, gods know. I've *seen* what power is supposed to look like. We're not it."

"Dear foolish child, *I* was the leader of the most powerful guild of wizards in the known world a thousand years ago, when aircars flew through the skies powered by wizard thoughts and gardens grew in the air and people wandered through them walking on clouds. *I* have seen power in forms so beautiful and wondrous you would fall to your knees, believing yourself in the presence of your own puny

gods if you had ever seen them. I tell you they'll believe—
what is power to you would be an alien thing to the Kargans. What they will see when they see us will be power in
a form they can understand. We'll be what they have prayed
for and dreamed about for generations uncounted."

Chapter 6

Dùghall saw Crispin Sabir's viewing glass go dark. He waited, holding his breath, looking for a sign from Hasmal. He didn't know what his young colleague might do, but he hoped Hasmal might find a way to control Crispin's body. That he might even discover a way to oust Crispin's soul and claim the body for himself.

Then the darkness in the glass changed to radiant light, and Hasmal's voice filled the tent.

"We have to hurry," Hasmal said. "I have so much to tell you, and so little time. Crispin will wake soon, and before he does, much of what we need to accomplish must be completed."

Dùghall suppressed his desire to ask questions about where Hasmal was and what was happening to him, or to offer him comfort or encouragement. He said, "Tell me."

Hasmal's voice spoke from the light. "Take me into your body and your mind, that you can know what I know."

Dùghall hesitated only for an instant. Then he picked up the viewing glass and stared into its depths. Immediately Hasmal made the connection with him. Dùghall felt reassuring warmth and Hasmal's familiar personality flow into him—and half a heartbeat later, he felt the sharp memories of Hasmal's torture and death, his grief over his loss of Alarista, and his discoveries of Crispin's daughter and the operation of the Mirror of Souls. While he was learning what Hasmal knew, Hasmal was discovering that Kait and Ry had already escaped, that Ian had not betrayed them, and that the Mirror of Souls was already back in the hands of the Falcons.

He felt Hasmal's imprint on his soul—and Crispin Sabir's, and the Dragon Dafril's, too. And he felt Hasmal discovering the price that Alarista had paid to send rescue, and Hasmal's anguish at the discovery.

She loves you still, Dùghall told him.

I know. As I love her. Right now, it only makes what has happened hurt worse. Please just tell me you can use what I've found, Hasmal said. *That this has not been for nothing.*

We can use it. We'll get the girl before Crispin can wake and find her. We'll activate the Mirror and call back the rest of the Dragon souls, then send them through the Veil. And when they're gone, we'll destroy the Mirror. You've saved us, Hasmal. You've given us the chance to win everything. You will be written into the Falcon annals, your name remembered until the end of time.

And I would trade all the Falcons' memory and honor for a single day with Alarista. . . . Touch her for me, please. Let me be with her this one last time.

Dùghall moved to Alarista's side and rested a hand on her forehead. Light poured down his arm, and only in that instant did he realize that while Hasmal had been inside of him, he had glowed like a small sun. As Hasmal left him, he once again felt the cold of the tent. The light poured into Alarista's frail body and illuminated her, erasing her anguished expression and replacing it with a beatific smile.

Dùghall looked for just a moment. Then, feeling that he intruded on something private, he turned away.

"Get me Kait's and Ry's viewing glasses," he said to Yanth. He spoke around the lump in his throat, and his voice sounded rough in his own ears. He blinked back the blurring in his eyes and growled at Jaim, "Don't stare at them. For decency's sake, man, turn away. Better yet, bring me pen and paper and ink. I've spells to cast that have never been set before, and I'll only have one chance to set them properly. I'll do it the child's way, with the words before me."

When the tasks he had to accomplish were clear in his mind and on paper, Dùghall knelt again in the center of the tent. "Ry first," he said.

They had reached their inn. Ry and Kait were eating, Ian was pacing the room, stopping from time to time to stare out the window.

Dùghall felt the familiar darkness take him as he connected with Ry's viewing glass, and an instant later he looked out of eyes not his own.

Ry, it's Dùghall, he said.

Ry grew still. *I know your touch.*

We've almost won. Hasmal found out that Crispin has a daughter. Her name is Ulwe. He's hidden her in an apartment on Silk Street, in the outlanders' ghetto of the Merchants' Quarter, just beyond the Black Well and above the dyeing shop of Nathis Farhills.

Dùghall could feel Ry absorbing the information. The revelation of his cousin's daughter stunned him, but he moved quickly beyond that.

How will I get her? Why would she come with me?

She has not yet met her father. When Crispin wakes, he will no doubt go to her first—Hasmal's thoughts will be in his mind as clearly as his were in Hasmal's. He now knows everything Hasmal knew, and that's a deadly danger for us. But if you hurry, you can reach her before he does and take his place. With Crispin's daughter in our care—

You don't need to tell me. I'll hurry. What am I to say to her?

Tell her, "A daughter is her father's greatest blessing, his greatest weakness, and his greatest fear." She's young, Ry, and has been raised entirely out of her father's influence. She's an innocent.

I won't hurt her.

Protect her.

I'm on my way.

Dùghall broke off the connection with Ry. He waited a moment—Ry would tell Kait and Ian something, surely, before he raced out the door, and Dùghall wanted to make sure Ry was well on his way before he contacted Kait. What would happen next would be dangerous—perhaps deadly—and he didn't want Ry to hesitate when he discovered that Kait would be facing danger he would no doubt prefer to take on himself.

Either Kait or Ry could have activated the Mirror and done what needed to be done with it—but the girl, Ulwe, was expecting a man to come after her, and if she had ever seen an image of him, she would be more likely taken in by Ry's appearance than by Ian's.

Finally enough time had passed that he felt sure Kait and Ian would be alone. He grasped Kait's viewing glass and reached out for her.

Chapter 7

Kait leaned against the slatted shutters, staring through one gap at the place where Ry had been only an instant before. He had run out the door after only the thinnest of explanations, leaving her and Ian dumbfounded.

Behind her, Ian paced and fretted. "Where are we going to hide a little girl? We won't be able to use her papers—her father will have the city in an uproar finding her. And the first checkpoint we pass, she'll scream for help, and the weight of the city will descend on our heads."

"I don't know what we're going to do." Kait sighed and watched the unending stream of strangers that hurried along the harbor boardwalk. She wished one of those strangers would suddenly become Ry—that she could know he would return safely to her. "We'll figure it all out when the child gets here."

"Maybe I should buy a sleeping draught from an apothecary," Ian said. "If we fed her a healthy dose of nightbell or Phadin's elixir, we could get her to Galweigh House with only a bit more trouble than we'll have getting ourselves there."

Kait turned and stared at him. "You would truly pour Phadin's elixir into a child?"

She watched with some satisfaction as his face flushed. "No. I suppose I wouldn't. But we're going to have to do something."

"We will. But we don't have to do it now. Wait. We'll meet the girl and when she arrives her actions will dictate ours."

"She's Crispin Sabir's daughter. If we're going by actions, we'll probably have to kill her."

Kait gave him a hard look. "Don't even say that in jest."

Ian sighed.

Kait turned back to the window.

Kait.

"What?"

Ian said, "I didn't say anything."

Kait. It's Dùghall.

Kait grew still and inhaled slowly. She felt the faintest of touches through the talisman embedded in her skin.

I hear you, Uncle.

It's time to use the Mirror, he said. *It's time to send the Dragons through the Veil.*

Kait turned to Ian. "Help me get the Mirror out," she said.

He frowned at her. "You think you should be tinkering with it here—" he started to argue, but he faltered as he looked at her. "You're listening to him, aren't you?"

"To Dùghall," she said.

"He's telling you what to do."

"He says Hasmal found out how the Mirror works. We're going to get all of the Dragons out of Calimekka now."

"We?"

Kait nodded.

"Oh, *shang!*" Ian went to the wardrobe and, with Kait's help, dragged out the Mirror of Souls. "I suppose I never saw myself as an old man, anyway." When the three of them had arrived, they'd taken the spare blankets from the wardrobe and wrapped them around it; neither the blankets nor the wardrobe would do much to hide the Mirror if it decided to betray them as it had in the Thousand Dancers, but wrapping and hiding it had seemed more sensible than leaving it sitting in the center of the room. "Let me look out the window," he muttered as he shoved it in front of her. "I want to get a last look at life."

Kait managed to give him a small smile as she pulled the blankets off of the Mirror. She stood before the artifact, hands trembling. Its creators had made it beautiful; the beauty went far in hiding its evil. Her skin crawled as she looked at it; it could rip her soul from her body and fling it into the Veil and give her flesh to a stranger. She knew what it could do, and she was flatly and totally terrified of it, and now she alone would have to touch it and manipulate its jeweled glyphs and put herself at its mercy to send the Dragons away.

She became aware that Ian was standing across from her, watching her, and she realized she had been poised motionless in front of the Mirror for quite a while. "What are you waiting for?" Ian asked.

"Courage." She clenched her hands into tight fists. Altruism was a fine and noble sentiment, but when it came down to stepping into fire for strangers, or even for friends and colleagues and love, Kait discovered that the desire to survive rose kicking and screaming from the dark recesses of the mind, demanding second thoughts.

You don't have to do it, Dùghall told her.

I know.

She stared at the cool, sensuous curves of the Mirror. It represented evil and the foul path that the future would take without her intervention, as Solander had represented the path of hope and joy. She steadied herself with thoughts of Solander—she remembered what it had been like to touch his soul. For the first time in her life, someone had known her totally and still completely accepted her for what she was. She had not been a monster to Solander. She had been Kait, woman and Karnee, and he had loved her without reservation.

Until she'd met him, she'd thought of Solander as a god; she had been stunned to discover that he was a man—purely human. Yet in spite of his human limitations, he had found within himself a beauty that allowed him to love without reservation, and he had insisted the potential for that same beauty existed within her, and within all people, human or Scarred.

I have that potential in me. I can love like that.

From Dùghall, she felt a brief sharp stab of shame. *That is where I fail Solander's teaching. Where I have always failed,* he confessed. *Even now, what I do I do for myself more than for anyone else.*

Kait would have argued with him, but he stopped her.

I know what I am, he told her. *I know I must be more someday. Somehow. But right now, I don't matter. You do. And the Mirror does. And what you can do to save us all.*

Kait inhaled slowly, and took the single necessary step forward that permitted her to rest her hands on the smooth metal of the Mirror. The Mirror of Souls still made her think of a giant flower: a bowl formed of platinum petals resting on a tripod of delicately curved, swordlike leaves. What had been the stem when first she had seen the artifact—a slender pillar of golden light that rose upward from the base through the center of the tripod and swirled into a radiant pool at the heart of the bowl—was missing at the moment. It would return when she activated the Mirror . . . and once that light again flowed, Kait knew she would be in danger.

If you're ready, we'll begin. I'll look through your eyes, Dùghall said. *But I won't try to take over your hands. You are the one who will be in danger when we start this; you must be the one to decide at each step whether or not to continue.*

You could guide me—
I could. But I won't.
I understand.

She felt Dùghall's excitement, and also his fear. *Then let us begin.*

Through his eyes, she saw the rows of carved gemstones inside the bowl differently. No longer merely pretty decorations, each gem with its incised hash marks and curlicues suddenly meant something: "first power" or "drain" or "connect" or "increase" or "draw" or "modulate." She realized that she was not looking at the Mirror only through Dùghall's eyes—she had connected to the memories of a Dragon, too. She could feel the Dragon's connection to Dùghall—could feel a link, as well, to Hasmal, though she could not understand how that could be.

She took a few steadying breaths and let herself relax. She strengthened her connection with Dùghall. For an instant, she felt resistance as he pulled away, but she felt she needed a deeper link with the Dragon memories he held in his mind. When he let her reach past the buffer he'd created, she felt a sudden flood of recognition as countless other memories connected with hers. She discovered that the Dragon had been the one who had claimed to be her ancestor Amalee—the one who had led her across the sea in search of the Mirror. She discovered that he'd intended to take over her body, but had been denied access by the shield Hasmal had taught her how to cast. She discovered that the body he'd occupied—that of Crispin Sabir—had been one of the men who had tortured her cousin Danya, and had been the very one who had fathered Danya's child, who would have been the Reborn. She felt the full weight of Crispin's evil life, of Dafril's thousand years of plotting and manipulating, of Hasmal's many fears and great love and agonizing death, roll over her like a freight wagon pulled by a hundred galloping horses. The connections were dizzying, the memories—Hasmal's, Crispin's, Dafril's, and

Dùghall's—were overwhelming. Brutal, conflicting, incomprehensible images flooded into her mind, and her knees went weak. She sagged against the Mirror, queasy and sick.

Strong arms wrapped around her waist and pulled her back.

"Kait. Are you all right?"

The voice she heard from so far away was a real voice, and she rose out of the darkness that threatened to consume her and clung to that.

"I will be." She closed her eyes and hoped that was true. "Give me a moment."

"Let me use the Mirror," he offered. "Tell me what I have to do, and let me take the risks."

She took a steadying breath, then got her knees under her and locked them. Standing under her own power again, she turned her back on the Mirror of Souls. "I can't. I know you'd do this if you could, but to use the Mirror, you have to be able to reach and channel magic." She rested a hand on his forearm and said, "Just keep me from falling over if this gets to be too much for me again."

He stared into her eyes, and took her hand in his own. "I'll do that if that's all you'll let me do," he said. "But if you find that I can do more . . . please . . . let me."

She turned and looked at him. The love in his eyes was too clear and too painful. She hurt for him. She wished she could be the woman he wanted her to be. She nodded and felt a lump forming in her throat and tears beginning to burn in her eyes. Unable to find words, she gave him a quick hug, then turned to face the Mirror again.

Chapter 8

Crispin woke to blackness and ringing in his ears. For a long, painful moment he thought that he was still in the Veil, and that his memories of reprieve had been nothing but a dream. But the scent of his body was musky in his nostrils, and the sweetness of night-blooming jasmine reached him from somewhere in the distance, and from nearer he caught the stink of drying blood and piss. Then the ringing ceased, and he realized that in each of the city's hundreds of temples and parnisseries, the bellringers had been clanging out the Invocation to Paldin to mark the end of day. Twilight had come.

He sat and ran his fingers over his face. *His* face. He touched his hair, his neck, his chest, pressed his palms hard against each other and felt the blood pulse in his fingertips. He sucked in air until his lungs began to ache from holding so much, then let it out with a joyful whoosh.

He wiggled his feet and felt them move, stretched his arms high over his head, flexed his spine and felt the satisfying crack as joints popped all along it.

"Back," he whispered, and grinned. "Damn the Dragons to darkness, I'm back."

His eyes adjusted to the nearly lightless room, and he realized that he was in the torture chamber in the Citadel of the Gods, the Dragons' city-within-a-city in Calimekka. A body lay on the table, still strapped down; it was from that body that the various stinks emanated.

That body. . . .

Memories deluged him—not just his own memories, but those that had belonged to the corpse on the table, and those of the Dragon who had stolen his body and ridden him like a cheap nag, and those of a terrifying wizard hiding in the distant hills—a wizard, he realized, who could still see everything he did and who could, without warning, invade his body and listen to his most secret thoughts.

He snarled. Because of those memories, he knew much of what the old wizard knew—he saw how he could travel in trance to the place where the Falcon Dùghall hid with his followers, simply by following the energy strand from the talisman that the dead man had embedded in his skin. He could watch them; perhaps he could find a way to destroy them.

But even as he entertained that pleasant thought, he knew that he didn't have the time to persecute his persecutors. They'd found out about Ulwe. And they intended to kidnap her and use her against him.

He snarled again. The cold white fury that he felt toward the spying Falcons and the manipulative Dragons metamorphosed into something else—something hotter and redder and more primitive. His blood began to simmer and his muscles burned and grew liquid beneath his skin. He had spent his life mastering the beast that dwelt inside of him, but now he wanted no such mastery. He embraced the animal that bayed for blood inside his Shifting skull; he offered himself up to its hungry, wordless passions.

Quickly he stripped off his clothes. He bundled them neatly, took a bit of cord, and slung the bundle around his neck. His clothes were light silk—they made an unobtrusive burden.

He lusted for the taste of blood in his mouth, for the feel of bones crunching between his jaws. He yearned to maim, to rend, to destroy whoever sought to kidnap his daughter. He slipped into four-legged Karnee form, and the world became hard-edged and clear, scents sharper and suddenly full of meaning, sounds broader and richer and louder. He panted, tasting the air, and turned his muzzle to the door.

He had to hurry. The kidnapper would certainly already be on his way to get Ulwe, and she would not know her danger. She was only a child, ignorant of the dangers of the city and those who dwelt in it. She would go trustingly with the first man who uttered the right phrase—and Hasmal had learned the phrase from Crispin's own mind. He had no hope that Hasmal's agent would get it wrong. His only hope was to be fast enough to get to Ulwe first.

Or that the scent trail remain unsullied long enough that he could track the kidnapper back to his lair.

Crispin loped through the long white corridors of the Citadel of the Gods, avoiding the hurrying Dragons, ignoring their obvious agitation and dismay. He would deal with them later.

First, he had a kidnapper to kill and a child to save.

Chapter 9

Silk Street after twilight seethed with life.

The silk shops for which the street had been named were closed, and *om-bindili* bands were set up in front of them on the high sidewalks above the cobbled road. The inhabitants of the apartments above the shops moved out to their balconies to enjoy the cool evening air. They drank and danced to the music or sang with the bands' singers, or made their way down to the street itself, where they bet on rolls of the dice or strolled hand in hand in the nightly promenade, wearing their finest to see and be seen.

The songs of Wilhene and Glaswherry Hala and distant Varhees, sung in the original tongues of those places and those people, blended into a rich and oddly comforting stew. The outlanders' ghetto would make a surprisingly good place to hide a little girl, Ry realized. These people accepted each other and looked out for each other because they knew that they were all they had. Not citizens of Calimekka, they wouldn't have access to the many protections such citizenship offered. They had become neighbors and friends out of self-defense.

The promenaders were watching him. He was a stranger to Silk Street's nightlife; they were remembering his face, his clothing, the way he walked. He couldn't help being memorable. He couldn't make himself someone they knew. Inwardly he cringed, but outwardly he nodded politely, and made his way as quickly as he could through the gamblers and the chatters and the strollers.

His main landmark, the Black Well, sat in the midst of a square of greenery. Carefully shaped shrubs and sweet-scented flowers grew in boxes at the four corners of the square; the boxes themselves bore mosaics reminiscent of the bold, stylized street paintings that decorated the thoroughfares of the city-state of Wilhene. Benches surrounded the well itself, and on those benches old women sat talking to each other and watching the spectacle of the promenade, and old men told their old jokes and slapped their knees with laughter at tall tales they'd heard a hundred times already. As he walked past the square, their voices dropped to whispers, though, and he felt their eyes, too, fixed on his back.

When Crispin came looking for his daughter, a thousand people would be able to give a clear description of Ry.

He would have to find a way to render that description worthless.

Beyond the well and on the other side of the road, Ry saw the sign for the dyer's shop, and read the name Nathis Farhills scrawled out in Iberish and half a dozen other common scripts. On the balcony above the shop, a pretty girl stood, staring down at him. Small-boned, slender, and with hair that looked white in the twilight but that was likely pale gold, she leaned forward with her hands resting on the rail. Her eyes, light as his own, didn't seem to blink when he looked into them. He had intended only to glance in her direction, but her steady stare didn't waver, and he found that he couldn't look away. He would have thought her too old to be Crispin's daughter, but she had her father's features. She had to be Ulwe.

He came to a stop and stared up at her, feeling like a

fool. He couldn't hope that she would believe he was her father. In his early twenties, he was too young to have a daughter already approaching womanhood, and he knew nothing of the past that she shared with her true father. What could he hope to say to her that would not betray him as the imposter he was?

He almost turned away. But Crispin was . . . Crispin. And the Falcons would have to deal with him. And this girl, this watchful, still creature, was the key to controlling Crispin.

Ry's heart raced. He looked away from that steady gaze, hurried across the street, and climbed the steps at the side of the building. The girl was waiting for him with the door already open when he reached the top.

Her father should have warned her about the danger of this place, Ry thought. Surely he must have let her know that she should never open the door for strangers.

"I felt you would come tonight," she said before he could say anything to her. "All day the air has whispered trouble. The ground trembles with changes brewing." Her voice was high and sweet. A very young voice. Up close she was younger than she'd looked standing on the balcony. Her actions, her movements, her startling grace and amazing beauty, all gave her a maturity that belied her true age. He guessed she was no more than twelve, and perhaps as young as ten. She had an odd accent. After a moment he placed it—she had the drawling speech of the settlers of the Sabirene Isthmus. She'd spent the better part of her life in Stosta, he guessed, being raised by her mother, or strangers hired by Crispin. Things he didn't know and dared not ask.

"I'm . . ." He wanted to say, *I'm not who you think I am*, but he stopped himself. He said, "A daughter is her father's greatest blessing, his greatest weakness, and his greatest fear."

She looked at him, and one eyebrow slowly rose, and the tiniest of smiles twitched at the corner of her mouth.

"So the birds told me," she said.

"We can't stay here."

She nodded. "I know that. I feel danger following in your footsteps. Even now we have little time." Abruptly she threw her arms around him and hugged him. "Thank you for coming for me. I've been . . . afraid."

He nodded, not daring to speak. She was a sweet child, and trusting. Damn the fact that she was so trusting. He would rather she had snarled at him and been hateful—he wouldn't have felt so horrible about snatching her away from her father and taking her off to serve as hostage in the trouble that was to come. She had every right to be met by her father; she had every right to have the world meet a few of her expectations. The world wouldn't, and in many ways it wouldn't because of him, and he felt guilty just standing next to her.

She smiled up at him, then turned away and stepped into the room and spoke to someone—he hadn't realized until that instant that she wasn't alone. He should have heard the other person breathing, should have noted her scent in the air, but he had been too distracted by Ulwe and his own doubts. He needed to regain his focus, and quickly.

He heard the clink of gold and Ulwe's soft voice saying, "You've been very good to me, Parata Tershe. I hope we'll meet again someday," and an old woman answering, "I hope you're happy, child. You deserve happiness."

Then she was back, a bag in each hand. "Would you carry one of these for me?" she asked. "They aren't heavy; my nante told me be certain not to pack too much before I left Stosta. She said I'd have plenty of new dresses and toys when I got here and I needn't bring any but my dearest things."

"That's fine," Ry said. "I'll carry both of them."

"Then you won't be able to hold my hand."

He looked down at her. The solemn face looked up at him. "You want to hold my hand?"

"Yes. Please."

"I'll carry one if you wish."

"We should go now," she said.

He nodded. "You're right." He took the bag she offered him. It was light. He wondered what she'd brought across half a world with her—what "dearest things" might have comforted her during a sea passage alone, on her way to meet a man whom she had never seen before who had claimed her and pulled her away from the only people she had ever known.

They hurried down the steps, and he was surprised that she set the pace, and set it so fast. She was walking so briskly that he had to lengthen his stride to keep up; he could as easily have jogged beside her. She waved to some of the promenaders, and they called to her, "Is that him?"

"It is," she shouted gaily. "Isn't he as lovely as I said?"

Now the faces that looked at him wore smiles. A few of the people waved. An older woman said, as the two of them hurried past, "You have a lovely daughter. I'm glad you returned safely from your voyage at last."

"So am I," he said. He was no longer a stranger in their midst—by virtue of her presence and her words, he was Ulwe's father, and they knew Ulwe, liked Ulwe, accepted Ulwe. He could understand why. She squeezed the hand he held and looked up at him, and her smile was radiant. He wished at that instant that she *was* his daughter.

Then they were outside the outlander's ghetto, and the character of Silk Street changed. The people who hurried through the gathering darkness avoided each other's eyes, and stared straight ahead. The *om-bindili* bands were gone, the merry promenaders replaced by hollow-eyed women and gaunt-faced men who offered their bodies for pleasure, or who shilled for custom for the caberra-houses, or who waited for some unwary target to pass by. Ulwe moved closer to him. She didn't complain when he walked faster. He thought perhaps he should swing her onto his back and let her hook her knees over his elbows. He could carry both her bags that way and still run. He turned to her, ready to suggest it.

But she said, "We're going to have to get a carriage."

He said, "Are you getting tired?"

She shook her head. "Not me. I could run for days. But we're leaving a trail, and he's coming right now. And he's really angry."

Ry frowned. "Who is?"

"My father," she said simply.

Chapter 10

Grief cannot touch us here.

Alarista spread out her arms and spun in weightless circles, feeling warmth that surrounded her and penetrated her, feeling light that flowed around her and through her. She danced, lost in beauty and happiness, and Hasmal danced with her. This was life beyond death, joy beyond pain; she and Hasmal were united in a place where Dragons could not touch them and where evil could not come.

She could not name the forms that moved around her and shone in the shadowless brilliance, but the forms needed no names. They were a part of this eternal world, the keepers of this place, guardians against those beings that moved in coldness and darkness and hunted through the Veil beyond. They were part of the light, welcome and welcoming.

Grief cannot touch us here.

She knew that Hasmal's body had died—knew that hers was dying. She recalled her sacrifice with crystal clarity;

she could still feel the weight of unaccustomed age her dying flesh bore, the harsh pains and labored breathing. A thin strand still connected her to that constrictive, sense-dulled form, passing to her whispers of movement, hints of frantic activity aimed at saving her life. She knew only re-lief—her flesh-pains would soon end, her dance with Has-mal would continue through eternity, and she and he, soulmates reunited, would move beyond this greeting place to the infinite mysteries beyond.

This was her destiny.

They rejoiced and embraced.

One of the nameless guardians of the realm of light brushed against Alarista. Through her. She felt calm pres-sure building around her, an air of certainty, a sense of fore-boding.

The guardian said, *Wait.*

She moved closer to Hasmal, blending with him along her edges, flowing into him. She tried to silence the guardian, tried to push it back to the gate through which she had been admitted.

She said, *We are together at last. We are meant to be to-gether. Grief cannot touch us here.*

Grief cannot touch you here, the guardian agreed, *but the world behind you awaits completion of the task you chose. You have not yet finished.*

Hasmal pulled away from her, and their dancing ceased.

The time in which you can return grows short. Will you return, or will you move forward?

She felt within that question the weight of knowledge she had hidden from herself in life. She had chosen her life, had given herself a path, and had planned her path to inter-sect with that of her soul-twin, her beloved Hasmal. But other intersections that she had also chosen had not yet taken place. She had slipped away too soon, and if she left, her work left undone would remain undone. No one else had chosen her path. No one else would complete the task she had chosen.

The pull of the fragile strand that connected her to her body lessened.

She looked behind her, back into the slow, heavy world of flesh, and saw the healer crouched over her, spinning a final desperate spell. Her body breathed in ragged, irregular gasps, its mouth hanging open, its eyes open, too, and dully staring up at nothing. How could she don that weight again? How could she return to slow thoughts, to ignorance, to pain and weariness?

How could she leave Hasmal?

But her task remained undone, and none but she would complete it.

She reached out to Hasmal, palm upward and forward. He pressed his hand to hers, and she felt his yearning for her, his need that the two of them be together and complete. His hunger for her was as great as hers for him. After lifetimes of separation, they were finally together again. If she returned to her flesh-self, she knew she might face yet more lifetimes before the two of them could find each other again. They might *never* find each other again if he lost his way or she lost hers. Souls could fall into the maws of the dark hunters of the Veil; souls could die. This wondrous moment, which should have been hers for eternity, might instead end, never to be repeated.

No one else could do what she had gone into her life as Alarista to do.

The task she had chosen for herself mattered.

Is there any way that Hasmal can come back with me? she asked the guardian.

You know there is.

She did. But she considered the ways that he might, and shivered. He could be lost so easily.

She said, *Dear one, I cannot stay here.*

I know. He caressed her with a thought, and she discovered that grief, indeed, could touch her even in that place of joy and light.

Be careful. Wait for me.

Forever if I must.

She broke away quickly, racing backward along the fragile tendril that connected her to flesh and life: She had no more time. The tendril was already beginning to disintegrate as she poured herself back into her flesh, and the darkness and the cold and the dullness of her senses and the acuteness of her pain enveloped her. She felt fire in her lungs, and pulled in a hard, harsh breath, and let it out and pulled in another. She fought her way back into her flesh, a butterfly fighting its way back into the prison of its cocoon. The beauty of the place she left behind faded, and the memories she'd brought back with her shimmered into nothingness as if they were no more substantial than beams of light cast upon smoke.

She knew that she had something terribly important to do. She knew that Hasmal was dead. And she knew that she could have been with him, but had returned instead.

She woke, weeping.

Kait swallowed nervously and licked her lips. The gemstone glyphs lay beneath her fingers, their inscriptions now meaningful to her, their combinations something she knew with the assurance of a thousand years of certainty. *Caffell* was first. *Initiation.* She pressed the carved ruby, and it depressed with a soft click. A light sparkled through the gemstone she'd pressed from inside. The Mirror made a soft, whispering sound, and a swirl of mist formed at the base of the column and began to spiral upward slowly through the soulwell.

You're doing fine, Kait, Dùghall assured her. *I'm with you.*

I know, Uncle. But this is . . . She faltered.

Terrifying.

Terrifying, she agreed.

She located *benate*—marked in bloodstone—and *tirrs*—
of inlaid jade. She depressed the first, then the second.
Again the soft clicks, again the tiny lights that shone
through the pressed gemstones. A faint scent of honeysuckle appeared and soft golden light rippled through the
column of mist and flowed upward.

Her mouth was dry, her palms itched. She shifted from
left foot to right, then back. Dùghall's comforting presence
filled her, but could not take away the terror she felt at the
stirring of the ancient Dragon magics beneath her fingertips. She felt as if she were waking a monster, one that
could, when fully awake, turn and devour her without even
pausing to consider what it did.

She did not understand how she could have ever believed the Mirror of Souls was anything but evil. The slimy
touch of its magic licked across her skin, and she shuddered. She had wanted a miracle—had wanted her family
restored to her from the dead—and she'd been so desperate
to believe anything that might make that miracle happen
that she'd made herself blind. She wondered if evil so often
succeeded for just that reason—that it made itself seem
necessary, that it held out hope to desperate people like a
sweet-ice on a stick.

She breathed shallowly and closed her eyes. The memories of strangers played behind her closed eyelids, and
she watched them carefully. From Crispin's mind, she saw
tens of thousands of innocent people gathered in the parnissery squares across the city when he activated the Mirror. She saw it connecting through magic to the towers of
the Ancients scattered across the city, and saw the blinding blue light of immense power pouring out of the Mirror and tearing across the skies. Through Dafril's
memories she made sense of that picture—she discovered
that the Mirror drew its power from the life-forces of
those who had crowded into the squares, and used that

enormous power to force the souls of the Dragons' chosen victims out of their bodies and to insert the Dragons' souls and hold them in place. The Mirror had been working since then to hold those huge energies steady, as if it were a dam holding back floodwaters.

She was about to open the floodgates, and though she had Dafril's knowledge of what ought to happen then, she also had his awareness that the Mirror had only been used once—neither he nor anyone else knew for certain that their theories were right.

She opened her eyes. "I think you need to step out of the room," she told Ian.

He stirred from the place he had taken against the wall directly behind her. "I'm not going to leave you in here alone with that thing," he said.

She could smell his fear as clearly as she could smell her own. She cared about him—he was her friend, even if she couldn't love him the way he wanted. She said, "I don't want you to die unnecessarily if this doesn't work."

"That goes without saying."

"Please . . . I'll be able to focus on this better if I'm not worried that something might happen to you."

"Kait. . . ." He stepped into her line of sight. He was frowning. "I understand what you're saying, but I can't leave you alone. I can't. You don't know what will happen, so you can't know whether or not you might need me. So I have to stay."

She couldn't tell him that he was wrong. He was correct when he said she didn't know. So she nodded and said, "Thank you, Ian."

He pressed his lips together and retreated to his place behind her against the wall; he'd said nothing, but she could guess at his thoughts.

She rested her palms on the rim of the Mirror. The next three buttons she pushed would reopen the connection between the Mirror of Souls and the souls of the Dragons.

They lay in a neat cluster to her right, marked with the glyphs *pethyose* and *neril* and *inshus*. Modulate, gather, and set-hold. She pressed golden cat's-eye, glittering jacinth, and pale aquamarine—and then she held her breath.

Again the soft clicks, again the light shining through the depressed hieroglyphs. The soft whispering sound that emanated from the Mirror rose in volume and pitch, and a faint breeze stirred the air in the room. The light from the soul-well intensified, and began to take on a greenish cast. She began to think she could almost catch individual words in that soft, steady whispering. Gooseflesh rose on her arms and a bead of icy sweat rolled down her neck, slid along her spine, and left her shivering in its wake. The room felt both hot as a furnace and cold as death.

She could hear Ian breathing rapidly. She felt her own blood bounding through her veins as if racing for a way out. The energy that swirled in the pool of light in the center of the Mirror of Souls felt heavy, hungry, and watchful.

And she was going to have to embrace it. She had to let it use her body as a lightning rod—she had to ground that swirling green fire.

She sought the glyph *peldone*—draw—and let one index finger hover over it. She found *galoin*—reverse—and placed her other index finger over that. Pressing both together would reverse the direction that the souls had flowed before, and would draw them back to the Mirror. With them would come all the energy that had been stolen from the lives of the Iberan people. That energy would, if Dafril's theory was correct, leap from the Mirror of Souls to the nearest available living body, and from that body would stream back to the places from which it had come. It might be a violent process. It might destroy her. It had never been attempted before, so not even the memories of the Dragon Dafril could offer her reassurance.

Dùghall said, *I'm still with you, Kait. I'll be with you no matter what happens.*

She sent him her love, and jabbed her fingers against the two jeweled hieroglyphs simultaneously.

The green light changed to hypnotic, brilliant blue. She felt the slight breeze in the room become a rush of wind, and felt the wind pulling against her, tugging her nearer to the twisting column of light that burst upward through the ceiling and down through the floor. The whispering became shouts inside her skull. She felt the building around her begin to tremble, and saw ghostly forms erupt from the walls. The room filled with fog, cold and damp and thick as baled cotton. It swirled around the Mirror of Souls and fed itself into the column of light, and the scent of honeysuckle became a gagging, thick miasma overlaid by the sweet rottenness of decay—the scent which she'd learned was the smell of Dragon magic. The fog in the room kept her from seeing anything but the blue light that rose like a sword from the Mirror. But she heard crackling and rumbling in the distance—thunder and lightning, coming closer with the speed of a cyclone's wind.

The walls shook, the floor shook, and to the invisible accompaniment of ten thousand tortured screams, a cascade of blue light poured into the Mirror and burst from it, slamming into Kait like a man-sized fist. Her arms flew out to her sides, her legs pushed away from each other so hard that both her hips made cracking sounds, her lower jaw snapped open and stretched wider and wider, her fingers pushed away from each other, her hair stood on end, her eyeballs pushed outward as if they would crawl from their sockets and flee. Every joint in her body stretched and pulled, as if her bones could no longer stand each other's company.

She couldn't breathe, she couldn't move, she couldn't scream. Thousands of arrow-thin bolts of blue light erupted from her body and shot outward in all directions. Fire burned beneath her skin; screaming deafened her, thunder shook her, dust fell from the ceiling. Pain racked her; her sight dimmed from lack of oxygen; she began to die.

Then the blue fires pouring out of her weakened; first a few wavered and disappeared, and many in a rush, and finally the last dozen straggling bolts.

She sucked air into her tortured lungs and collapsed to the floor, pain consuming her. She rolled into a ball and stared at nothing, and her vision began to clear.

The fog around her thinned. The blue light dimmed. She held her breath. The screaming faded back to soft, steady whispering. And the last of the fog gathered itself by wisps and tatters into the column of light—Kait could only think of a giant sucking in smoke as she watched it swirling into the center of the room and vanishing.

The last of the light flowing into the Mirror seemed to crawl down itself, pressing and shrinking and squeezing to fit as it slipped inward. It filled the soulwell and spiraled around the basin of the Mirror of Souls again. It wasn't the same as it had been before she pressed the hieroglyphs, however. It felt at that moment the way it had when she found the Mirror back in the ruins in North Novtierra. It felt *full*, and she hadn't been aware of the difference until right then.

Now the whispers were clear—dozens of them, maybe even a hundred, all scrabbling at the same time, all fighting to reach her mind. When she felt for the energy that she needed to shield herself from those evil whispers, it was there, and she drew a shield around herself, and then around Ian. She knew what those voices had to say. She knew, and she wouldn't listen again.

It worked, Dùghall told her. *By all the gods, it worked. We're saved and the Dragons are defeated.*

Then she felt Dùghall react with surprise—the connection that bound him to her changed in shape and form, and a spirit that was not her and was not Dùghall moved through her and shimmered out of her fingertips, making the leap to the Mirror of Souls. Behind her, Ian hissed and drew his sword; she backed away from the Mirror. The smooth surface of the pool of light began to curve inward on itself, rising into a round bubble that stretched after a moment into an oblong, and then developed indentations that became eyes and a mouth, and protrusions that shaped themselves into a nose and ears. Kait's heart began to race.

"Kait," the face in the center of the Mirror said, "it's me. Hasmal."

"Hasmal?"

Dùghall said, *That was Hasmal. I left him with Alarista, but that was him.*

Hasmal said, "You aren't done yet. You're only where you would have been if we could have gotten the Mirror to Glaswherry Hala without the Sabirs getting it."

She nodded. "I know. I'm going to release the souls into the Veil."

"And then what?"

"Then Ian and Ry and I are going to hide the Mirror in Galweigh House."

"Not good enough. How many people would willingly ignore the promise of immortality—of godhood? If you permit the Mirror of Souls to exist, someday someone else will use it."

"The Dragons are captured. Soon they'll be gone forever. No one else knows how to build an immortality engine, or how to use the Mirror."

"I do," Hasmal said. "Dùghall does. You do."

She started to protest that of course she didn't know that. But she discovered that in fact she did. She knew everything the leader of the Dragons had known; she could make herself a god. She could make Ry and Dùghall and Hasmal and Alarista gods. They could live forever.

They could live forever.

She stared at the Mirror of Souls, feeling her skin prickle, tasting the scent of honeysuckle and rot growing stronger all around her. She knew the magic to stave off death. She knew, as well, its horrible price. She could feel the stain of the Dragon's soul within her, could feel the marks branded into it by the annihilation of uncounted other souls.

In her mind, Dùghall said, *It could be used for evil, Kait, but it could be used for good, too. Consider Hasmal. We need him to rebuild, Kait. And Alarista needs him. After you purge the Mirror of the Dragons' souls, you could use it one final time to put Hasmal into Crispin Sabir's body. You could give him his life back.*

The Mirror drew its magic from the lives of others. She considered that. She knew how it worked. She could draw energy for the spell only from those who had hurt others. The Sabir Wolves, murderers, thieves, rapists and torturers and pedophiles. Maybe slavers. Maybe . . .

She felt herself standing at the edge of an abyss. She didn't let herself look too closely at the gaping void beneath her feet. She said, "Hasmal, I could give you Crispin's body. You could be with Alarista again."

His image stilled. For a time that seemed like an eternity, he hung suspended above the Mirror, silent, unmoving, unblinking.

"Oh, Vodor Imrish," he whispered, "I would give almost anything to be with her. You cannot know. . . ."

Dùghall spoke into her mind. *Tell him I need him. I'm but one, and so many of the other Falcons are dead—I need someone to help me.*

Kait relayed the message, her voice quavering.

Again he was silent for a long time. "I can't lie, Kait. I want to come back. You don't know what it's like to know that this thing could put me into a strong young body and give me another chance with Alarista. You don't know what it's like to move beyond the Veil and know that another flesh-life waits for me, with its forgetfulness and struggle and pain and the truth that no matter when or where I find

Alarista again, she won't be Alarista anymore. And I won't be Hasmal." He paused, then said, "I love her. I want so much to be with her now. Not later, not different. Right now."

Kait felt a lump growing in her throat. She swallowed hard.

"I found the love I hungered for my whole life." A wry smile crossed his face. "I found a measure of courage, too, there at the end." He paused, and she saw remembered pain move across his face like clouds across the sun. "But it did end. My body died, and I can't get that back. Any other body I had . . . would be stolen. Right now, a little of that courage I found is still with me. While I can remember what is right and what is wrong, and while I still care, you have to listen to me. Shut down the Mirror. Shut it down, and when the Dragon souls are gone, destroy it. Don't give Dragon magic another chance to get free."

"What about you?" she asked. Her voice came out as a croak. "Isn't there some way I can save you?"

"There is," he said softly. "You can let me go. And I can be man enough to leave."

He started to dissolve. Kait was having a hard time breathing. "Wait! I have so much I want to say to you."

He was shaking his head. "We're friends, Kait. Friends don't need words. But you need to hurry. This may be the most important thing you'll ever do, for me or for Matrin."

She clenched her hands to her sides and dug her nails into her palms and did not allow herself to weep. She stood straight, and she said, "We'll always be friends. Good-bye, Hasmal."

He vanished without a ripple into the light.

She stared at the Mirror of Souls, at the gleaming metal petals that arched up to form the basin for the pool of light, at the graceful stems that surrounded the soulwell beneath, at the array of jeweled hieroglyphs before her.

Shut it down.

Other heads began to rise from the pool of light, panic-ridden faces that screamed, "You can't shut it down," and light-formed hands that reached for her and through her, trying to fend her off.

She was shielded, safe from them.

They'd planned for their own protection—shutting down the Mirror had been designed to be difficult. But a way existed, in case something went wrong. And one person could shut it down, because in an emergency, perhaps only one person would be able to do what had to be done.

There were three buttons that had to be pushed in unison—three that required the awkward stretching of one hand, the careful jab of the other. She pressed the three, and the Dragons in the Mirror of Souls erupted from the pool of light, clawing for her eyes and heart with ghostly hands, lunging for her throat with insubstantial jaws agape and teeth bared. Some screamed, some pled, some offered her anything if she would just return them to their bodies, to their new lives. They promised to change their ways, to do good things, to make Calimekka a better place.

The three buttons clicked.

She lifted both hands, and they stayed depressed. She knew that they would only hold for an instant. She steeled herself and reached through the mass of frantic ghosts to the other side of the bowl, and there found the button that meant *nothing*. Almost hidden beneath the edge of the most distant petal, unadorned, plain, it was a small onyx circle that anyone who didn't know better would have overlooked entirely.

She pressed it, and the ghosts only had time to scream, "No!"

Then the light that danced its stately dance through the heart of the Mirror of Souls flickered out. And was gone.

The smell of honeysuckle and rot vanished as if it had never been. The pressure of evil vanished, too. The weight of the presence of Dragons who had dared to name a world their prey and dared to stalk it across a thousand years fell into nothingness, without sound, without light, without spectacle.

"They're gone," she said, and realized that tears were pouring down her cheeks. "It's over. And we've won."

Chapter 11

Crispin, again in human form, dressed in his bloody silks, stalked through the crowd on Silk Street. Men and women scattered before him—he wore his Family status like a battering ram that none could ignore or overlook. When he reached the stairs that led to the apartment he'd rented for Ulwe, he took them three at a time.

He knew before he opened the door that she would not be inside; at the door itself, he smelled the presence of his cousin Ry. He snarled, but slammed the door open anyway; he might find something that would tell him where she was headed.

She'd been there, safe. Had he woken earlier, had he run faster, he could have reached her before his accursed cousin. She would have been with him, where she belonged. Now . . . now she was a captive, a hostage. And Ry hated Crispin as deeply and passionately as Crispin hated Ry. He might hurt the child, torture her, even kill her, just because knowing that he could hurt Crispin would give him power the bitchson had never had in his life.

Except, Crispin thought, that Ry had never had much stomach for the *real* exercise of power. He'd avoided Family politics—he'd kept himself to the sidelines while others jockeyed for position in the hierarchy of Wolves. He'd tried to give the impression that he was above all that . . . but Crispin thought Ry simply didn't have the balls to spill a little blood for his own advancement.

Ulwe might be safe for a while.

Crispin paced through the apartment. No signs of violence, no smell of fear. The woman he'd hired to care for the girl—through intermediaries, damnall, since that had seemed wisest at the time—was gone, the place left neat and orderly. No note from Ry, no note from Ulwe. Ulwe might believe Ry was her father, and he might be willing to pretend to be Crispin in order to keep her compliant.

Crispin hurried back outside, following Ry's scent and the smell of his daughter. He sniffed the air, retraced his steps down the stairs, and turned after them, moving through the crowd. They were staring at him, he realized— men and women with cold eyes and hostile faces.

If he didn't catch up with her, he would come back and question them. They might be able to tell him something useful.

The trail led well down Silk Street in the opposite direction from the one he'd come, heading south and east. It took him out of the Merchants' Quarter and into the Pelhemme District, through neighborhoods where no sensible person would take a child. Then, at a heavily trafficked intersection, the scent trail vanished completely. He fought his way across traffic to each of the four street corners, but the ground did not carry any further marks from either Ulwe or Ry.

So they'd taken a carriage. They could have gone in any direction, they could already be almost anywhere. And the longer he took getting back on their trail, the more difficult it would be to hunt them down.

He stared around him, clenching and unclenching his hands, feeling the tips that dug into his palms Shifting from neatly manicured human nails to hard, sharp points. He wanted to kill Ry, but Ry was temporarily beyond his reach. He noted shapes lurking in the shadows, and felt eyes watching him. Yes. Yes. One of the bits of human scum who inhabited the neighborhood would have seen them. A young man of Family, a lovely young girl—in this neighborhood after twilight—yes. One of the doxies or the pimps or the street jackals could tell him which way his daughter and her kidnapper had gone.

He turned toward a shadow, smelling hunger and rage and anticipation in the waiting darkness, hearing the quickening of breath and the soft snick of a blade leaving a scabbard, and he smiled.

"Ah, good sir," he murmured, pacing into the deeper blackness, letting a tiny trickle of his rage escape from his control, letting his hands—and nothing but his hands—embrace the Karnee tide. "I almost hope that you don't want to help me."

The man moved toward Crispin, long dagger in hand, feral grin on his face. "I'll help y' to yer grave, y' pretty bastard. None here'll cry Family when y' fall."

Crispin laughed and flexed his claws.

And then the sky lit with blue fire, and a wave of wild magic tore over and through him, and darkness denser than blackest night rolled over him, blinding him, deafening him, and dropping him to the ground like a bolt-felled steer.

He felt a quick, hard pain in his side as he fell, and another, and another. His last thought was, He's stabbing me! The whoreson is stabbing me!

Chapter 12

Danya felt the wave of magic wash across her as she tossed the red cloak to the ground. The Kargans were oblivious to it, of course; they had no sense for magic—they were blind and deaf to its manifestations. But from the way that Luercas paled, she could tell that he'd felt it.

He landed on the red cloak, but his dismount from the back of the lorrag was more tumble than leap. He said his lines, and the Kargans embraced him as the embodiment of their savior, and then hugged her—something they had not done since she had regained her human form. They began racing around the village to prepare a feast. Only then did Luercas get the chance to speak with her alone again.

"You felt it?"

"Of course."

He nodded. "You know what it was?"

"No."

"That was the destruction of my old colleagues." He chuckled and tipped his head back. Eyes tightly closed and grin spread across his face, he looked as satisfied as a cat in a sunbeam.

Danya had never liked cats.

She said, "You're certain."

"Absolutely certain. That surge of magic you felt was the Mirror of Souls—it discharged the life-force it stole, back to the people it came from. And the only reason it would do that was if my fellow Dragons had been ousted from the bodies they took and dumped through the Veil. A lot of drained people are going to be suddenly bursting with energy tonight, and I'll wager you Calimekka's birth rate nine months from now will nearly double." He shifted excitedly from foot to foot, looking very much the excited boy at that moment and not the monster he was. "I told them a thousand years ago that if they didn't find a way to lay sole claim to the bodies they took, this would happen." He smiled at her and spread his arms wide. "You don't see the Mirror flinging *my* soul into the Veil, do you?"

"No. More's the pity."

His expression became solicitous, and he patted her shoulder. "Ah, Danya—you really must lose that bitter streak of yours. We're well on our way now, girl. A handful of our enemies have eliminated the deadliest of our Iberan obstacles for us. We're gods to the Kargans already; word of our presence is traveling toward the other Kargan camps even as we speak. We'll be gods to the Hattra and the Ikvanikan and the Myryr peoples, too, before long. We'll have our army of fanatics, we'll have a clear path, and we'll have our city, our slaves, and our immortality before a year has passed."

"I'm sure you're pleased."

He opened his eyes and looked at her, surprised. "As you should be. My lovely child, we have only one more great obstacle standing in the way of our conquest of Ibera."

"And that would be?"

"The destruction of the Mirror of Souls."

"I thought you said the Mirror couldn't harm you because you were sole owner of . . . the body." She'd almost said *my son's body,* but caught herself in time.

"The Mirror didn't put my soul into this body, so it

wouldn't rip it out to replace it with the body's rightful soul. I *am* this body's rightful soul. Now, anyway . . . thanks to you." He never let the opportunity to goad her pass by. She glared at him. He smiled sweetly and continued. "However, the Mirror of Souls was designed to remove *any* soul from *any* body, and to hold that soul in storage indefinitely. That's how the rest of the Dragons and I weathered the centuries."

"So someone could use it to pull you out of your body—if they knew about you."

"If the operator knew *how* to perform a removal."

Danya studied him thoughtfully. "Is it difficult?"

"No."

"Pity *I* don't have the Mirror of Souls."

"Isn't it?" His eyebrow arched, and he said, "Perhaps you can entertain yourself with fantasies of reaching the Mirror before the people who have it destroy it. You can imagine getting hold of it and turning it on me and tearing my soul free from the moorings of this flesh—that picture ought to sustain you through the long journey ahead of us."

Danya turned and walked away from him, and this time he let her go. He laughed at her, but she thought, Well, yes, I can hope to get to the Mirror, you hellbeast. I'd take great pleasure in seeing you die, and greater pleasure if your death was at my hands.

In the meantime, she had an army to raise and an enemy to conquer. And vengeance to mete out. She could cherish the thought of Luercas's death while working alongside him. In fact, she thought that doing so would make their whole forced relationship much more tolerable.

Chapter 13

Kait looked up at the creak of the door. Ry staggered into the room, gray-faced and sweating, half-leaning on a lovely young girl. The girl said, "He passed out in the carriage, and it was all I could do to get him up the stairs."

Kait managed to get to her feet and helped the girl to get Ry to the bed. "How do you feel now?"

He sprawled and closed his eyes. "I'll survive. You beat them, didn't you?"

Kait nodded. "Dùghall found out how to use the Mirror. He told me."

"And waited until I was gone, sneaky bastard."

"You couldn't have helped. And you had something to do that only you could do."

"I'll still break his skull the next time I see him. You shouldn't have had to face that alone. I should have been here with you."

Kait didn't point out that Ian had been with her. That, she thought, would be terribly undiplomatic. Instead she said, "The Dragons are defeated. Gone. And you are here with . . ."

"Ulwe," Ry said. He managed to sit up. "Ulwe, I present to you Kait Galweigh, who is my love and who will someday be my parata. Kait, I present to you Ulwe Sabir, daughter of Crispin Sabir, who gave me news you don't want to hear."

Kait arched an eyebrow and glanced quickly from Ulwe back to Ry.

Ry read her look. "Ulwe knows I'm not her father. She knew it even before I got to her. She . . ." He shrugged. "She uses some magic I've never seen before."

"It isn't magic," Ulwe said. "I have no magic about me."

"You knew I was coming before I arrived," Ry said. "You knew that I wasn't your father. You told me that Crispin was after us. How else could you have known any of those things but by magic?"

Ulwe said, "I'm a *be'ehan khan jhekil*. A roadwalker. And I know you named me with my birth father's name, but that is not *my* name. I'm Ulwe Foxdaughter Walks-the-Road, of the Seven Monkey People." Her smile as she said this was a very adult, knowing smile. "Names matter to the Seven Monkey People. I had to work hard for mine."

Ry nodded to the girl and said, "My apologies. I would not willingly have named you wrongly." He smiled at Ulwe and asked, "But what is a roadwalker?"

The girl pulled off her shoes, climbed onto the bed, and tucked her feet beneath her. With her hands folded in her lap, she said, "If you stand in the center of a still path, the path seems empty to you. You think of that path as going to different places that you might wish to be. But the path doesn't go to those places. It is there already—the path that is still where you are standing is a busy road thirteen leagues away, and twenty-three leagues beyond that, it is the very heart of a busy city. The same road that feels your slow footsteps is at that same instant feeling the footsteps of uncounted others on its body. The road lives. It listens. It hears voices and thoughts and feelings. And if you know how to ask it, it will tell you what it hears." She gave them an apologetic smile. "I'm not a very good roadwalker, though. My nante can hear the road's voice from anywhere that it goes. I can only hear the near voices. And I can't hear old stories—only new ones. The road can tell me what it heard yesterday, or sometimes what it heard the day before . . . but I can't hear what it says of those who walked it a month ago, or a year ago." She sighed. "But I'm human, so it's harder for me."

Kait and Ry exchanged startled glances.

"Who *isn't* human?"

"My nante. I *told* you—I was adopted by the Seven Monkey People."

Kait shrugged and spread her hands palm up. "I don't know of them."

"My father sent me to Stosta when I was an infant. I don't know what happened to my mother, but considering what I've found out about my father, I imagine she's been dead a long time. A wet nurse accompanied me, but she died shortly after she and I reached the city of Stosta, and there were no wet nurses available among the Stostans—we arrived in a plague time, and the same sickness that killed my wet nurse had left many others dead as well. Orphaned infants would have been nothing but a drain on the survivors. So I was taken to the parnissery, where my papers were given to the parnissa. I was to be exposed, and news of my death sent back to Calimekka.

"But my nante—her name is Kooshe, which means *fox*—came through the gates of the city and walked straight to the parnissery. When she arrived, she demanded to see the parnissa. She told him that she had come for the baby. A number of orphaned babies were there, lying naked on the stones of the inner courtyard. A few of them were already dead, others were still quite healthy. I was in between—I had been outdoors overnight by that time, had not been fed in two days, and was weak and sick.

"The parnissa directed her to the healthy babies and said

she could have her pick, but she said she had come for the baby that had crossed the Western Water.

"She walked straight to me, picked me up, and told the parnissa she wanted my things. She said that she would care for me until it was time for me to go home."

Kait said, "She knew you were there?"

"The road told her. The road brought her to me."

Ry said, "So this stranger came out of nowhere and saved your life. Why?"

"The road told her my story, and when she listened, she decided that it was time for the Seven Monkey People to meet a human. She took me to the Seven Monkey People's *kezmoot,* their hidden clan city, and the People healed me and fed me. When I was old enough, Kooshe taught me to walk the road with her, telling me always that when I returned to the city of my father, the road would tell me how to survive. And when at last the message came from my father that I was to come home, Kooshe put me on the ship that brought me here, and stood on the dock waving until the ship sailed out of sight." Kait saw tears form in the corners of Ulwe's eyes.

Ry looked startled. "You sailed all the way from the Sabirene Isthmus to Calimekka by yourself?"

"Yes."

"Why didn't she come with you?" Ian asked. "That's a terrible voyage for a child alone."

Ulwe's smile became sad. "*This* place would be death for her. In this city, she would be called Scarred, and the road has told me what happens to the Scarred."

Ry and Kait exchanged glances. Ry said, "But if she was clearly Scarred, how could she enter Stosta? How could she enter a parnissery and demand that she be given a human baby—and why would the parnissa *give* it to her?"

Kait added, "No Scarred can enter the gate of a parnissery and live—that's the law."

Ulwe looked from Kait to Ry and back to Kait. She said, "The two of you still live, and both of *you* are Scarred."

Kait's skin crawled. Ulwe had looked at the two of them—looked through shields and careful disguise and lifetimes of passing as pure human, and had divined their secret. She had blurted out the secret that meant their death if it was discovered. She might only be a child, but she was a dangerous child. Kait said, "We look human, and the parnissas don't know about us." Her mouth tasted bitter with the sudden rush of her fear.

Ulwe said, "The Stostans don't know the Seven Monkey People exist. They think they are alone in the Red Hills. The Seven Monkey People can make themselves hard to see—when they don't want to be seen, they can . . . bend a picture of the world around them." She gave an apologetic shrug. "I have never been able to find words for this. And I can't do it, so I can't show you."

Kait thought it sounded a bit like shielding. She nodded, but said, "She spoke to the parnissa in order to get you, though."

"When they *must* be seen, they can make people believe that they are what the people would like them to be. For a short time, anyway. And if there aren't very many people. One person alone is easy for them. Two or three is still not too bad. More than that and the . . . trick . . . doesn't work very well. My nante doesn't look human. But the road told her when one parnissa would be there alone—the one who hated to hear the babies crying as they lay on the cold stones. She went to him when he was tired, when he felt guiltiest that he wasn't feeding them or caring for them. He *wanted* someone to save the babies, and was willing to believe what Kooshe wanted him to believe—that she was a human who wanted a baby of her own."

Ry was staring thoughtfully into space. Kait looked at him, curious about his sudden stillness. He seemed very distant. "The settlement in Stosta is ours," he said after a while. "It's been there for nearly a hundred years. My Family has been pulling caberra spice out of those hills, and logging in them, and gathering rubber and kaetzle and a multitude of other riches from the surrounding land, for the whole of that hundred years. I've read the reports from Stosta's paraglese when they arrived with the tax ships. No one has ever seen anyone except for settlers there. No one has ever found any sign of other habitation."

Ulwe grinned. "The Seven Monkey People have five cities as big as Stosta within the Red Hills. Two of them you could walk to in less than a day."

"That can't be."

Ulwe said, "It can, though. The Seven Monkey People have made the roads their friends. And friends keep their friends' secrets."

Ry was shaking his head doggedly. "In a hundred years, we should have found *something*. A campfire . . . a footprint . . . some trash." He seemed shaken.

"The Seven Monkey People watch the Stostans carefully. They don't want to be found. Humans wouldn't want to accept them."

"Some of the Stostans are *Karnee*," Ry said. "I can see how the Seven Monkey People could hide from humans, but how can they hide from the Karnee?"

Ulwe's smile held secrets. "If the road is your friend, it isn't so hard."

Kait could see uncomfortable realization in Ry's eyes. "You could have been anywhere—you *let* me find you. You didn't need me to protect you from your father—if you didn't want him to, he'd never find you."

She nodded.

"Then why were you there when I came for you?"

"Eventually I'll have to meet my father—I came here to save him. But the two of you are the point to which all roads lead right now. You're bringing trouble to you like the smell of blood draws hunters. Soon enough, my father will come to you, and when he does, I'll have the chance to reach him. Before he comes, I'll give you reasons to want to help me save him." She closed her eyes and clenched her fists, and for that moment, she looked so young and fragile and helpless that Kait's heart went out to her. "I know he killed your friend," Ulwe whispered. "I know he has done much that is evil. But long ago he risked everything to save me. I have to believe that there is something good inside of him." A tear slid down her cheek; she brushed it away roughly.

Kait reached out and touched the girl's shoulder. Ulwe couldn't help the fact that Crispin was a monster; all she could see was that he was her father, and that he had loved her enough to get her away from the city to a place that was safe. She wanted him to be someone she could love because he was all she had.

Kait could understand that.

Ry was staring at the two of them. "Which friend did Crispin kill?" he asked softly.

Kait winced. She'd forgotten that Ry didn't know. "He . . ."

She tried to find words that would soften the blow, but there were none. "Hasmal," she said.

"Hasmal is dead?"

Kait nodded. "Dragon magic does things we didn't even imagine were possible. The Dragon Dafril reached through the link Hasmal was using and snatched him, body and soul." She closed her eyes. Hasmal's memories of his torture still echoed in her mind. If she allowed herself to think about it, she could feel what he'd felt in the last terrible moments of his life. The memories made her sick. "When Dùghall captured Dafril, Crispin reclaimed his body. He didn't see any reason to save Hasmal's life, so he killed him."

"When Dùghall told me to get Ulwe, was Hasmal still alive?"

"No."

Ry's face darkened. "A second secret the old man kept from me. He has much to answer for the next time we meet."

"Let's hope it's soon," Kait said quietly. "We've beaten the Dragons, but we still have to destroy the Mirror of Souls. And I don't think we'll be able to do that without Dùghall."

Chapter 14

The Gyru-nalles had a dozen fires going around the perimeter of the clearing, and several tents set up for food and drink. They'd set nine wagons into a circle, and from that circle joyous music emanated, and laughter from dancers, and loud banter. Dùghall kept to the edges of the party and sipped at whatever the celebrating Gyru-nalles and soldiers pressed into his hands and accepted their slaps on the back and jovial congratulations with good grace, but his heart wasn't in the celebration.

"The Dragons are dead, long live the world," he muttered when the party momentarily swirled away from him, leaving him in relative silence. He raised the glass one singing Gyru girl had just handed to him and took a sip. It burned and tasted like hell. Lumpy hell. Fermented goats' milk—the drink the Gyrus swore by . . . and over. He realized he should have looked at his glass before swallowing.

But fermented goats' milk was the drink he had in hand, and he had words still to say. "To colleagues lost and friends fallen but not forgotten," he added, and lifted the glass and took a hard swig of the vile drink.

"And to the future—may it be better than the past." He

took a final drink, then dropped the pottery mug on the packed dirt and stepped on it to smash it, sealing the toast.

"You dropped your glass," one of his younger sons said, grinning at him. "Wait, if you will, and I'll get you another."

But Dùghall had smiled all he could for one night. He studied the young man—a product, like all of Dùghall's hundreds of sons and daughters, of Dùghall's Imumbarran status as a fertility god—and wondered how the lad had felt about being so far from home, waiting for a chance to die on foreign soil for foreign purposes. How he felt about Dùghall's sudden youth he had made clear the first time he'd seen his father after the change. He'd shrugged and smiled—gods did funny things, and Dùghall had, by growing younger, simply proved again his status as a god. The rest of Dùghall's sons had seemed equally unfazed. Dùghall shook his head and told the young man, "No more for me. I'm going to see how Alarista is doing. You . . . you keep the party warm for me."

A piper and three drummers had just joined the fiddlers who'd been playing for the last station. The whole motley band started into a rollicking staggerjig. His son grinned and grabbed the hand of the Gyru woman he'd been seeing, and the two of them lurched onto a bit of packed earth free of other dancers. They began stamping and leaping and clapping, their attention on each other.

Dùghall turned away and slipped into the darkness beyond the ring of fires. The main camp hadn't been abandoned—soldiers still kept watch around the perimeter, the healer tending Alarista still stayed at her post, and a slow trickle of folk who had already overindulged or had simply reached their limits for noise and motion meandered back to tents or wagons.

Dùghall stared up at the bright stars, wondering how victory could feel so hollow. We won, he thought. But we lost so much to get here. The Reborn is dead and lost to the world; most of the Falcons are gone; Hasmal is murdered and Alarista ancient and fragile and near death; the gods alone know how many people died and lost their souls to oblivion in the city of Calimekka to make way for the Dragons' great white citadel. I am young, but the coin of my youth was paid with the life of a friend—and I am young only in body. My spirit feels older and more tired than ever. What we suffered could have been much worse, I know . . . but it was bad enough. And one of us needs to spend this night of celebration by remembering the price we've paid, and looking to the future to make sure we use our victory wisely.

He stopped by Alarista's wagon long enough to confer with the healer; he'd said, after all, that he was leaving the party to visit her. The healer said she was sleeping well, and that the draught she'd received should keep her slumber nightmare-free for the rest of the night. Dùghall, satisfied that he'd done his duty and served his honor, moved on to his tent.

Inside, he tied the flaps shut and lit his lantern. He shielded it so that it cast its small circle of radiance downward, but left the rest of the tent in darkness. Light showing through the walls of his tent might invite well-wishers, and he didn't want company.

He unrolled his embroidered black silk *zanda,* and for a moment studied the embroidered circle—the silver thread outlining the twelve triangular sections that represented each face of the Falcon Double-Cube of Existence: House, Life, Spirit, Pleasure, Duty, Wealth, Health, Dreams, Goals, Past, Present, and Future. Each silver-broidered glyph gleamed at him in the dim light; he felt the presence of the gods in their pale shapes and in the blackness of the silk that represented the Veil—the medium through which men and gods communicated.

He removed the silver *zanda* coins from their silk bag. The silver was cool in his palm and heavy. In prayer, he thought, men ask the gods for help; in meditation, the gods answer. I'm listening. Speak to me.

Sitting cross-legged on the floor, he closed his eyes for a moment and stilled his thoughts. When the world disappeared and his mind was a deep lake over which not the slightest breeze blew, he tossed the coins onto the *zanda*.

He opened his eyes.

He wished he could close them again.

He had been hoping to find simple directives leading him and his people back to Calimekka; he'd desperately wanted to receive reassurance that the world had settled back into its appointed track, and that the only dangers were those that conniving people and corrupt governments created for themselves. But the shining coins lying on the black silk gleamed up at him in mocking defiance.

In the quadrant of House, the obverse of the *Good fortune* coin lay centered and alone. Not just bad fortune, then, but coming disaster. In the quadrant of Life, the *Family* coin overlapped the reversed *The gods intervene* to create an enigmatic warning. Dark gods and Family conspired against the world?

The quadrant of Spirit held the message he read as *Scattered forces gather*, but he wasn't sure if this was a good thing or a bad one, and the *zanda* gave him no clue. The quadrant of Pleasure offered the good news–bad news message *Trusted friends await* and *Suffering to one who is loved*. The damnable Duty quadrant said *You have not yet paid*—more bad news.

Wealth indicated coming massive expenses; Health noted only an affirmation of his own sudden return to youth with no comment on what he should do about it; Goals told him to plan for travel; Dreams suggested a nightmare; Past indicated a partial triumph that was not quite as it seemed; Present said nothing, and Future . . .

He looked at the Future quadrant and closed his eyes. Five coins had fallen into that quadrant, fitting themselves between the embroidered lines in such a way that none overlapped a border—which would have allowed him to discount them—and that all overlapped each other, so that each subtly changed the meaning of those it overlapped while being changed by those that overlapped it. He wasn't sure he could have *stacked* the coins in such a convoluted pattern.

He began puzzling his way through the reading, pushing away the temptation to sum up by saying *The future will be a mess* and letting it go at that. A man asked the gods' advice and then only at his own peril ignored it when it was given. Dùghall had asked. Now he had to listen.

First coin. *A known friend,* but obverse and reverse. *An unknown enemy* then, but overlapped with *Messages already received,* so that it became an unknown enemy that he had heard from before, or one that he knew but didn't know he knew. *Messages already received* overlapped a reversed *Hope* coin as well, serving as a warning that his hopes were either misplaced, or they would be dashed. *Travel* was in there, but lay partly beneath *Hope,* so that he had to assume he would be traveling but that the travel would not be of a sort he might desire, and partly above the fifth coin, which was *Triumph,* angled slightly to the right, so that it became *Possibilities of triumph.* He would have to travel if he hoped to win.

And *Possibilities of triumph* just slightly overlapped *An unknown enemy.*

Which seemed to be a message of hope, except that he'd already been warned in the same quadrant not to trust his hopes.

He'd planned to give everyone a day or two to recover from their celebrations before suggesting to them that they pack up and begin the trek back to Calimekka. He'd considered paying off the army he'd gathered, thanking the soldiers, and sending them back to their families and homes. He'd considered sending his sons back to the islands—perhaps inviting one or two of the younger and less traveled to make the journey to Calimekka with him just to see the city. He'd considered looking up surviving Falcons as he headed toward Calimekka, to find out if they had any idea of what the Falcons' future should be with the Dragons defeated and the Reborn gone.

But the strongest message in the *zanda* was that he dared not make plans without seeking further advice. He needed guidance that was clear and compelling and given in simple Iberish.

And that meant an oracle more dangerous than the *zanda,* but considerably more direct.

He got out his mirror and his pack of bloodletting thorns, and drew a circle of salt across the mirror's surface. Then he dropped three drops of blood into the center of the circle, and murmured a summons to the Speakers, asking for one of their number to assist him.

He quoted the final lines of the Directive for Safely Bounding an Oracle:

Speaker step within the walls
Of earth and blood and air;
Bound by will and spirit,
You must bide your presence there.
Answer questions with clear truth,
Do only good and then
Return to the realm from whence you came
And don't come back again.

In an instant, the image of a tiny, human-looking woman stood in the center of the mirror, penned in by the ring of salt. The wind of another plane whipped her long hair around her and blew her thin dress tight against her body. She stared up at him, eyes gleaming hungrily and lips curled in a dangerous little half-smile.

"What do *you* want?"

"I am to face an enemy that I don't know but have some-how met. I am to travel, but not in a way that I had hoped. My world and my people face danger when we thought we had eliminated this danger. I seek clarification of these mysteries, and practical advice."

"Don't we all?" She smirked at him, then shrugged. "Well enough. When you travel, travel with friends, but leave your army behind to guard your back. Go without stopping to that one member of your Family whom you know without doubt will fight with you, for a fight comes to you unlike anything you have yet experienced. Your enemy will reach you in due time—he will be stronger than you think, and cleverer, and if you falter for a moment he will devour you and your world. The time you have been given for preparation before his arrival is short and the work you must do immense. And even if you make no mis-takes you will probably lose."

Dùghall gave an exasperated sigh. "Who is this enemy? What can he do? What must I do to prepare?"

"When you confront life that is not true life, you will know him. When you remember death is not true death, you may, perhaps, defeat him."

"Speak plainly," he snarled.

"You want plain advice? Fine. Don't go breaking things you can't fix."

She laughed then, and tilted her chin so that, tiny as she was, she could stare down her nose at him. Arms crossed over her chest, she radiated defiance.

The flames within which her image danced flickered out, and she was gone. Weariness drove down on Dùghall like high seas in a hurricane—summoning the Speaker from her own plane required enormous energy, and he had already been tired. Now he could barely keep himself up-right. He didn't dare summon another Speaker right then, hoping to find one who might choose to be more helpful than the one who had just departed; he didn't have the energy to keep another Speaker bounded within the walls of his will. And he wouldn't chance being devoured.

Why couldn't she have plainly told him what he needed to know? He glared down at the mirror in his hand, wishing he could vent his frustration by breaking it. She'd given him some practical advice, though. "Don't go breaking things you can't fix." He might as well start following that admonition.

He drew out his journal and wrote down the *zanda* reading and the message the Speaker had given him. He didn't trust his memory to keep all the details straight, and he would need to puzzle over some parts of it for days, or even weeks.

He didn't need to puzzle over it right then, though. He put his things away and blew out the flame of his lantern and tucked himself into his bedroll with his blankets pulled over his head. Dawn would be coming soon, and he didn't want to greet it.

Chapter 15

Wolves howled along the ridge, their haunting song echoing through the darkness. Kait stood with her back to the gate of Galweigh House, staring down at the city spread before her feet. The peaks of the Patmas Range rose out of Calimekka like boulders out of a flooded stream bed, and from her vantage point on the highest of those peaks, the city flowed around them like a river of fire surging around dark and dangerous islands. Kait Galweigh stared down at that glowing river, yearning for its warmth. Then she turned back to the lightless hulk that waited behind her.

She rested one hand on the smooth, translucent white gate. Galweigh House had been her home for most of her life. It had held all the people she loved in the world; when she closed her eyes, she could still see them moving through the House, talking and laughing, arguing with each other, sitting in cozy little nooks or great halls debating and discussing and planning. As long as she stayed outside those gates, her mind could fill the corridors with her memories, and she could fool herself into believing they still held some truth.

Once she reentered the House and confronted the emptiness of the rooms and heard the echoing of her footsteps in the halls, her memories would grow fainter, overlaid by hollow new reality. Her longed-for family would then be dead for her not just in some distantly acknowledged way, but with the starkness of visible truth. Standing at the gate, she experienced a brief, painful desire to flee back down the way she had come, to never look at Galweigh House again.

The wolves howled once more, their mournful cries closer and louder than before. Kait sniffed the wind and tipped her head, listening to the voices.

She turned to Ry and Ian and Ulwe. "Go ahead without me. I'm going to wait here for just a moment. I'll be in . . . when I've finished."

Ry sniffed the wind, too. "They're coming this way," he said.

She nodded. Behind her, the donkey was starting to get nervous. It pranced from foot to foot, tugging at its lead and rolling its eyes. In another moment it was going to pin its ears flat against its skull and start bucking and lunging.

Ry said, "Ian and Ulwe can take it in. I'll stay with you."

She shook her head. "I'd rather be alone." A wistful smile touched the corners of her mouth. "A friend is on his way to see me."

Another howl, this time a single voice crying a deep and lingering solo. Both voice and smell were poignantly familiar. *Gashta.*

"A friend. A wolf?"

Kait nodded, not offering explanation. She closed her eyes, reading his scent in the air.

"Kait?" Ry rested a hand on her shoulder.

She shrugged his hand off and moved forward. She could hear movement now—light steps padding through the underbrush, rustling leaves, and the crackling on the leaf mold underfoot. Behind her, she heard Ian and Ulwe and the donkey hurrying into the walled safety of Galweigh House's grounds.

The underbrush parted and a huge, shaggy beast stepped

into the clearing. Kait took a few steps forward. "Gashta," she whispered.

The enormous wolf bounded to her side, mouth stretched back in a canine grin, ears perked forward, tail lifted and wagging. He stood on his hind legs and licked her face; she wrapped her arms around his neck and buried her nose in his ruff and breathed in the comforting, familiar scent.

Behind her, she could hear the gates closing, and from inside, the frantic braying of a donkey.

"I sense no magic about him," Ry said.

"He's just a wolf," Kait said, keeping her tone light and even. Gashta was sensitive to tones of voice. "I saved his life a long time ago. He returned the favor the night the Sabirs killed most of my Family."

"He's . . . wild?"

Kait heard the surprise in his voice. "Yes. He and I used to hunt these hills together when I Shifted."

Kait rubbed the big animal's ears and pressed her face into his fur again. She hadn't seen him in nearly two years; she was delighted that he still remembered her, and equally delighted that he'd found her. She'd lost so much that was dear to her—the survival of any friend seemed a miracle at that moment.

"We should get inside," Ry said. "We have a lot to do."

"I know." Kait didn't look at him. Instead, she ran her fingers through the wolf's fur, feeling the hard ridges of scar tissue that ran across the left shoulder. Marks of the past, a tangible reminder of his debt to her—now paid. She bore her scars on the inside.

She rose, and the wolf sat on his haunches and leaned against her side. He was big enough that, sitting, his head came to her rib cage. He panted happily, his tongue lolling out one side of his mouth as if he were a big dog, his eyes half-closed as her hand scratched the base of his ears. "I know," she said again, softer. Now she looked at Ry. He was as beautiful as the wolf and as wild, and a thousand times more compelling than anyone she had ever known. He was magic to her, the personification of things so wonderful she had never dared to let herself dream them. When he looked into her eyes, a light flickered in the darkness inside of her.

"I'm afraid to go inside, Ry. Out here, I can touch Gashta and pretend that everything will be as I remember inside the walls. Once I go inside . . ." She shrugged and fell silent.

"You fear the ghosts."

"No." She went to stand by his side. The wolf strode beside her, and when she stopped, he stopped, too. Ry held out a hand and Kait rested her own hand in it. "I don't fear the ghosts. I fear that the ghosts will be gone . . . that the emptiness will have killed even them, and that once I am inside the halls, I will have nothing. Even ghosts are better than emptiness."

Ry stroked her hair, and kissed the angle of her jaw. "I'll be with you. Whatever you face in there, you won't face it alone."

They stood outside the gate for a long time, the woman, the wolf, and the man. Then the wolf rose and trotted into the jungle, and in the hollow heart of the night, as the Red Hunter chased the White Lady across the skies, the man and the woman, hand in hand, stepped through the maw of the gate into the silence that waited beyond.

Chapter 16

Dùghall gave his son Ranan a hug. "All I know is that trouble is coming, and you're to be the guard at our backs. Keep the soldiers paid—if you run into trouble, send word to Galweigh House. Kait and Ry and Ian reached it safely and got both the little girl and the Mirror of Souls inside. So I will be going straight there."

Ranan looked down into the valley, where the camp had not yet begun to wake. He was a good man—sturdy and patient and reliable. He had little of Dùghall's impetuousness to him—he was much more like his mother. Watchful, determined, stolid. He'd taken many of his veterans through battles between the islanders; he'd walked fire; he'd borne his wounds and lived to tell of them. When times were good, he knew how to laugh and drink and wench, and more importantly, he knew how to listen to everything and how to tell nothing. He kept his own counsel—if he had ever been afraid, no one knew it but him. His men admired him. Dùghall was proud of him. He said, "I'll watch. Whatever comes will have to go through us to get to you."

Dùghall stared down at the campfires below. They had burned down to embers—now those embers glowed like the half-opened eyes of demons, heavy-lidded but watchful.

A shudder rode up Dùghall's spine and reached into him and grabbed his heart. He wondered if he would ever see this son again, and a hollowness in his belly suggested an answer he didn't want to know.

"Trust only yourself," he said, gripping Ranan's shoulder and turning him around. "Believe only what you know to be true, not what you hope *might* be."

Ranan's lips pressed into a thin line. He met his father's eyes and clasped the hand on his shoulder. "We'll be fine. There's plenty of silver still in the treasury, and the men are loyal. They saw what you were fighting against. They won't desert."

The premonition left him as quickly as it had come. He smiled carefully. Ranan did not need to be burdened by the shapeless wraiths of dread that hounded his father. Dùghall said, "If the money runs low, I'll do what I can to send more. I'll be looking in on you as often as I can. Put the men to work—morale will go to hell if you don't."

"The villages in the area are poor. The villagers need better roads, better houses, deeper wells. . . . I'll find plenty of things to keep them busy. And we'll build ourselves some goodwill in the process."

"Then I'll leave you to your business." Dùghall looked at his companions, waiting on the road just beyond. Yanth and Jaim sat astride horses given to them by the Gyrunalles. Alarista, white-haired and pale and bent, rode one of her own beasts. Dùghall's horse, and the string of horses that would carry their supplies and alternate as riding horses, cropped the grass by the side of the road.

His son hugged him quickly and whispered, "With you so young, you seem more a brother to me now. I cannot quite find it in me to dread your displeasure as I did when I was a boy and you came visiting."

"If all goes well, I'll be an old man again when next I see you."

Ranan said, "Love a woman well before you take back

your years. Fight once, drink once, dance once ... and once, watch the waves on the shore with young eyes, and see the flash of green as the sun rises over the water's edge."

Dùghall managed a rueful smile. "I will."

"Then go with the blessings of the gods."

"And may they bless you as you stay." He turned away and walked quickly to his mount. When he had his seat and turned to wave, Ranan was already gone.

The road unrolled down into grayness. Tatters of fog thickened into an impenetrable wall; as they rode, the sun made its way over the mountains but vanished almost as quickly as it had appeared behind the dark bellies of low-hanging clouds. The fog-thick air deadened the sound of their voices and the clopping of the horses' hooves; it blinded them to each other so that only when their horses brushed against each other did they see proof that they were not alone. No one felt much like talking, and the bleakness of the day brought an end to every awkward attempt. For people supposedly riding home in triumph, they were a sorry, dejected little band.

They would have nearly two weeks' ride to Brelst. From there, gods willing, they would get a ship to take them to Calimekka. And in Calimekka, Dùghall would find out what trouble awaited him, and would, perhaps, come to understand why he felt the earth itself had turned against him, why the sky above watched him with a mocking eye ... and why, though he was now young and strong, and though the Dragons were defeated and the Falcons were triumphant, he had never felt his death moving nearer than it was at that moment.

Chapter 17

The delicate light of dawn through translucent walls woke Kait, and for a moment she thought she was a girl again, and all the horrors of the past two years had been an ugly dream. She lay in her own bed, in her own room, surrounded by her belongings—silk dresses in red and black, skirts and shawls and wraps of Galweigh Rose-and-Thorn lace, tiny portraits of her father and her mother painted by a clever artist with a steady hand and a true eye. A thousand alto bells rang in the city below, their steady clear voices rising up from the distant valleys in waves—the song of a musical sea.

Almost, she could imagine stepping out the door and finding her mother in the hallway chastising her younger sister for playing pranks on the servants. Almost, she could place her father in one of the House's many studies with the paraglese, going over a trade map and discussing the latest diplomatic news from Galweigia or Varhees or Strithia. Almost, she could put her hand to the speaking tube and call down to Cook to bring her meat, rare and unspiced, and a bowl of bitter greens.

But when she sat up, she saw Ry curled up in his bedroll in front of her door, still sleeping, his tangled golden hair catching the sunlight. She didn't remember him coming into the room—he'd insisted on checking through the lower floors alone before retiring—and she couldn't imagine why he hadn't taken the other half of her bed when he had come in. But perversely, she was glad he hadn't. She didn't know how she would explain to the ghosts who watched from her memory that she was sharing her bed in Galweigh House with a Sabir.

She slipped silently from beneath her covers and walked to the east window. Leaning against the casement, her hands tight on the sill, she could see down into the hidden garden that lay beneath her window. Once it had been beautiful—full of wisteria and night-blooming jasmine and frangipani. The Sabirs had burned it when they took the House; now weeds choked the ground and the paths, and algae and burned branches and more weeds silenced the fountain. She closed her eyes tightly. The morning sun kissed her face as it had done so often when she stood there, and the last echoes of the bells made the memories sharper.

She should have been able to hear her sister Loriann in the room next to hers, complaining that her twin, Marciann, had borrowed her clothes again without asking. Down the hall, her brothers should have been chasing each other and complaining about getting to the parnissery for morning devotions. Her mother's voice should have been clear, talking to her sister-in-law about tutors or the women of lesser Families. Nieces and nephews and cousins and uncles and aunts should have been laughing and bickering and commenting on everything from food to clothes to politics; servants should have rustled through the corridors, knocking on doors and bringing food and fresh clothing and cut flowers and clean cottons for the beds. The ebb and flow of people through the House had made it live.

Now it was a dead thing. Silent, tomblike, cold, and unbreathing, its hollow shell held empty rooms that overflowed with pain.

Tears burned in the back of her throat and welled in the corners of her still-closed eyes. I'm here now, Kait thought. I have the Mirror of Souls with me—I crossed half a world and walked through hell to get it, and it's here now, and I can't change a single thing. I can't get even one of them back. I can't do anything more than I could have done if I'd stayed here.

But that wasn't true. If she had stayed behind, she could have died with them. Then she wouldn't be lost in the dead House, missing her family.

Warm arms slipped around her waist, and lips gently brushed the back of her neck.

She opened her eyes and stared out at the hazy blue of distant peaks and the warm gold of the sun and the illuminated whiteness of the House. "I miss them so much," she whispered.

"I know."

"I want them back."

His arms tightened around her and he pulled her closer. "I know."

"They're dead. Gone. I'll never see them again, and I can't do anything, *anything,* to change that."

His cheek brushed hers, and she felt the dampness of his tears on her skin. "I'm sorry. I'm sorry for what my Family did. I'm sorry that you're so alone. If I could do anything to change what happened, I would. I love you, Kait. I would never have had you hurt like this."

Her tears escaped her, sliding down her face. "I know," she said. She turned and pressed her face against Ry's chest. Her parents and brothers and sisters were gone for good. She would never find the magic that would bring them back to her—that magic didn't exist. Death was a final form of moving on, and they had moved on without her. The realization sank in at last, and she finally let herself cry. While she cried, Ry held her, stroking her hair as if she were a child. He said nothing, and she said nothing.

At last she took a deep, shaky breath and pulled away. She wiped her face on her sleeve and looked up at him. "We have a lot to do today. I suppose we should get started."

He nodded.

She rested her hands against his chest and stretched up on her toes and kissed him lightly. "I love you."

He hugged her close again. The sunlight streaming in the window warmed the back of her neck like a mother's kiss, and Ry's skin touching hers poured strength into her. She felt ready to face the empty spaces.

Ulwe and Ian were already waiting when the two of them stepped into the hallway.

"I thought we were going to start early," Ian said.

Ry arched an eyebrow. "This *is* early."

Ulwe said, "I'm hungry. Ian and I already ate some of the supplies, but Kait said there would be better things in the siege storage."

Kait nodded. "We won't have to live on trail food, or go back into the city to get the things we need. The siege stores were planned to keep a thousand people fed for a year. The four of us could live off of that much food for the rest of our lives . . . if it didn't go bad first." She smiled at Ulwe. "You won't go hungry. We'll do a quick inventory of what we have and where it is, and while we're about it, we'll bring up enough food for a week or two—that way we won't have to go all the way to the siege stores every day. Once that's done, we'll figure out what we're going to do next."

"The Dragons took enormous amounts of food out of here," Ian said. "I'm afraid you're going to be disappointed by what you find."

Kait shrugged. "I'm sure they cleaned out the main storage rooms. But the siege stores were hidden. The whole point of them was to give us food in case of emergency, and to have it in a place that wouldn't help our enemies if we were overrun."

"The Sabirs and then the Dragons . . . got information out of the survivors," Ian said quietly.

He'd worded that carefully—he hadn't said torture. But Kait had heard the word *torture* in the tone of his voice, and she saw it in the way he looked away from her. She stiffened and felt her blood chill; the pictures her mind threw at her made her want to scream. She kept her voice steady and said, "We won't know what they found until we check."

She led them downward via one of the multitude of servants' stairs. She had seen no sign of blood or bone, no smallest trace of the horrors that the House had witnessed, but she braced herself. She feared coming across skeletons that wore familiar clothing; she dreaded encountering the bones that had borne the people she loved.

Memories of better times assailed her. Grimly, she walked faster. Behind her, she heard Ulwe suddenly whisper, "Ry, I can't walk that fast."

She dug her nails into the palms of her hands and forced herself to slow down. They reached the first subfloor, which held the main kitchens and most of the common stores. Kait turned into a dark corridor, then looked over her shoulder at Ian. "Did you come this way?"

"I didn't personally, but someone else might have."

She looked at the floor. There was no dust on it. She frowned, realizing then that she had seen no dust anywhere in the House, though it had been shut up since the Dragons abandoned it for their Citadel of the Gods. She considered that odd fact and couldn't decide on its import. "Stay close to me, then," she said. "This becomes tricky. People have gotten lost in these sublevels and never been found again."

She walked into a passageway, turned left at the first intersection, right at the second, then right again into what looked like a little cul-de-sac with a semicircular stone bench in it. The lanterns weren't lit, but Kait lit them, and the dancing shadows showed familiar sights. The air smelled stale, but here the House still felt civilized. Comprehensible. As though it were merely a building. Deeper within the subterranean labyrinth, beyond the reach of the sun and air, scents rolled past the nose that hinted of terror, and sounds skittered and scritched and chittered just at the edge of hearing, and the darkness held within it the feel of eyes that watched, of claws that waited. Galweigh House's surface friendliness covered a core of patient, watchful mystery. Through those deeper, darker places, not even Kait had chosen to wander alone.

She knelt, reached under the bench, and slipped her finger against the back of the bench's trestle leg. She found the pressure point hidden there and pushed. The mechanism silently moved away from her finger, and with the faintest of whispers, the bench and the wall behind it moved backward.

"This is a fairly obvious one," Kait said. "If it's empty, there are others that are better hidden. We'll check them next."

She stepped into the gap that had opened in the wall to her left. The shelves were bare.

She stepped back out, shrugging, knelt again, and pressed the mechanism that closed the hidden passageway. She didn't feel much disappointment. "Downward, then. Deeper in the House, the stores are better hidden."

The Sabirs or the Dragons or both had found most of what the Galweighs had put by, though. After half the day and six more hidden rooms stripped to the walls, she finally led them to a storeroom that had not been touched. It lay well away from the main areas, in a corridor so utterly light-less that the lanterns seemed only to move the darkness around, not dissipate it. The hidden mechanism used two pressure points and a rhythmic pattern—Kait had to try five times before the door would finally open for her. But when it did, she was rewarded by the dark forms of lidded jars and wax-sealed amphorae, huge barrels and smaller casks, crates and bags and boxes and trunks. The air was thick with the scents of pepper and sage and cinnamon and a dozen other spices. Hooks hung empty from the ceiling, and a rack to the right held nothing but shelves of crumpled cloth, but even without whatever was missing, that one storeroom would feed the four of them for a year if necessary.

"I'd begun to fear you were wrong," Ry said. He moved up behind her and slid his arm around her waist.

"So had I. I never thought anyone could have uncovered the room just before this one."

"The Dragons created these places."

"I thought of that. But I also thought that only the Dragon who had created the place would have been able to find them all—and if that Dragon had come back, surely he would have reclaimed his house and stayed."

"It looks as if you were right."

Kait studied the stores. "We have enough of what we need to survive on. Still, I'd like to check on the other rooms I know of. It may be that we four will not be the only ones who have to live off the stores. We can eat first, and then you can carry up stores while I go through the rest of the House on my own. Or we can put off the rest of the inventory until tomorrow."

Ian had been looking through the contents of the room. "We'd best keep looking," he said. "This storeroom has no meat in it—I'm sure you'll want to find some before we quit for the day."

Kait was startled. She sniffed the air—she could catch the scents of smoked pig and jerked venison and beef and dried python. But she certainly didn't see any wrapped hams hanging from hooks, and the jerky bags on the shelves looked awfully flat.

"We made sure every storeroom had everything needed for survival. There's even a fresh water source in the back of the room, and plumbing, and a way to lock the door from the inside, in case survivors needed to hide for a while.

Some of those smaller trunks will even have gold in them." She started checking the shelves. But Ian was right. Nothing else had been touched, but every single piece of meat was gone.

"There will be salted fish in some of those barrels," she said. "Ry and I will be able to eat that."

Ry was frowning. He pointed to the empty hooks, and then to waxed cloth and binding twine that lay in crumpled piles on the floor beneath them. "Why would anyone unwrap all the meat before taking it?" he asked. "It wouldn't store well without the wrappings, and no one could eat so much at once."

Kait didn't know the answer to that. "Perhaps I ought to check on the fish," she said.

She pried the lid off of one fish barrel and looked in. Fish should have been packed clear to the surface of the brine, but the barrel was empty down to the last third. And that third—dark brine—held no sign that it had ever held fish. She couldn't find a single scale in the water or the tiniest piece of fin stuck on the side. She took one of the gaffing rods from the wall and stabbed it into the liquid. "Nothing," she said. "Not a single fish. If I didn't know better, I'd say that there had never been fish in here."

"Maybe someone intended to fill it later," Ry said.

Kait gave him a long look.

He shrugged. "I suppose not. We wouldn't have put anything into our storage rooms that wasn't ready to use, either. I can't imagine what happened."

"Neither can I. But you and I are going to *have* to have meat. These other two will do fine without it if they must—"

"I don't eat meat," Ulwe interrupted.

Kait nodded, but continued, "—but if you and I don't have meat to fuel us during and just after Shifts, we won't last long."

"To the next storage room, then," Ian said.

The next hidden room had been cleaned out. The one following it had supplies intact. Except, again, for the meat. Once again, all the herb-stuffed waxed wrappings were crumpled into piles, and the barrels were sealed. Kait lifted one of the empty wrappings and realized that it was still intact. The wax seal was untouched, the wax-dipped cloth uncut. No one could have removed the meat without cutting the cloth or breaking the seal. Nevertheless, impossible though it seemed, the meat was gone.

"It isn't even as if the hams turned to dust," Kait said, frustrated. "If the meat had spoiled and rotted away, we'd at least have bones in these wrappings. But there's *nothing*."

Ry dug through the stores, clearly mystified. "What *happened* to everything?"

"It doesn't make sense." Kait dropped wearily onto a trunk that still contained gold and silver in a wide variety of denominations and mintings. "Who would take only the meat, leaving wines and herbs and spices and fruits and vegetables? For that matter, who would take dried meat and leave the gold that could buy fresh meat a thousand times over?"

"And how in the hells did they take it?" Ian grumbled.

Ulwe crouched in the center of the room, her eyes squeezed tightly closed, her fingertips splayed to the floor. Kait became aware of the child's odd posture and the air of tense concentration that surrounded her.

Ry and Ian noticed Kait's stillness and followed her gaze. Both of them fell silent, too. The three of them watched the child, curious.

Ulwe began to speak, her eyes still tightly closed and her body rigid. "You're the first people in this room since before the . . . the evil day. The day of bad magics and bad deaths," she said softly. "Nothing alive . . . has moved across this floor since that day. No . . . human . . . has taken anything from this room."

Kait leaned forward, elbows on knees. "Then what did?"

"The dead fed here. The dead were given flesh. . . ." A shudder ran through Ulwe's body, and she squeezed her eyes closed tighter. "They were given dead flesh as an offering."

Her trembling grew more fierce, and her voice changed, dropping and slowing. "The promise made them still echoes in the walls. They still listen to it, and hold it as their due." In cadenced singsong, she began to recite:

"By the blood of the living
And the flesh of the dead,
I summon the spirits of Family
Who have gone before.
Without the walls of this room
But within the walls of this House
Enemies have come
And killed,
Have plundered
And pillaged,
Have conquered
And claimed.
Come, spirits of the dead.
All dead flesh within the walls of Galweigh House
I offer as your payment
If you will chase beyond the walls of this House
All alive beyond the walls of this room.
Harm none; draw no living blood;
Inflict no pain.
I ask not vengeance;
I ask only relief.

By my own spirit and my own blood
I offer myself as price to ensure
The safety of every living creature,
Friend and foe,
Now within the House's walls

Until this spell is done.
So be it."

"A spell," Kait whispered.

"Yes. Offered by a man both powerful and clever. I feel the echoes of his steps strongly through this place. He is tied here by his own blood and spirit, though he did not stay here long."

"So he summoned the dead."

Ulwe opened her eyes and looked up at Kait. "And they came. They watch still. They watch us now. The enemies that were here before came, but they could not live here. The dead are not as strong now as they were when first the spell was cast, but they are strong enough to . . . to do . . . things." She wrapped her thin arms around herself and Kait saw gooseflesh prickle on her arms. "No one can live in this place who is not your friend, or the friend of your Family. The dead claim all dead flesh within the walls as their payment, and when anything dies within the walls, or anyone brings inside the flesh of any dead creature, the spirits consume it and for a while grow stronger. And when they are strong, they work the will of the one who summoned them."

Ian began to laugh.

Kait looked at him. "What?"

"No wonder the Sabirs and the Dragons gave this place up. Meat-eating ghosts."

"That's going to make things difficult for us," Ry noted. "We *must* have meat to survive."

"We can hunt," Kait said. "And we can eat our meat outside the walls."

"I suppose. Yet doing so exposes us to anyone who might be watching."

Kait nodded. "There will be some risk. Still, I hunted here for years. I know where to go to keep out of sight of even watchful eyes."

Ulwe held up a hand, palm forward. "Kait. There's something else I found that might be important. Let me walk the road a little wider for you."

Kait nodded and waited. The girl closed her eyes again. For long moments she crouched to the floor, so still she barely breathed, eyes closed and lips slightly parted. She brought to Kait's mind the image of a fawn hiding in the tall grass, hoping to escape detection. The image jarred Kait—the child was in no apparent danger, but Kait's predator senses would not let her banish the picture or replace it with something more suitable. She wondered what she had learned from watching the girl that she did not yet know she knew.

At last, Ulwe said, "A mother and her two children took refuge near this room. There is another room . . . like this one. They locked it from the inside. They are eating the stores. They have been hiding since the House fell the second time. . . . But, no. Two of them have been hiding since that day. The third . . . came later."

Kait froze. "There are survivors still here?"

The child nodded. "So the paths tell me. So the road says."

The House could hide them. The House could hide an army, if the army could get to the right places and sequester itself within the cunning walls. So many had been unprepared. But someone, somehow, had survived.

Kait said, "Can you take me to them?"

Ulwe nodded, wide-eyed. "They're so afraid, Kait. They've expected every day to be caught. I can feel the terror. They don't know the House is empty."

They might live out a full span of years within their hiding place, away from sunlight and fresh air, growing weak and pale and feeble. She had to find them. A mother. Two children.

She tried not to let herself hope that they were her Family. Dùghall had told her that, as far as he knew, all of her immediate family was dead. But perhaps one of the cousins had survived. She reminded herself that the House had held more people who weren't Family than who were—the survivors were most likely a terrified serving girl and her two babes.

She stood. Even if they were, they might still be people she knew. She would take any link to her past that she could get.

"Shall we go after them, then?" Ry asked.

"Perhaps I should go alone." Kait rested a hand on the wall.

"I have to take you," Ulwe said. "I can follow the road to them. Their footsteps sing to me."

Ry shrugged. "I'm certainly not going to abandon the two of you down here alone."

Kait took a slow breath, and let it out even more slowly. "Perhaps we should wait until tomorrow, and come down here when the day is young." Either great joy or great disappointment waited for her in the hidden room she had not yet reached. The events of her recent past made her wary of pursuing hope; she had become cautious.

"Perhaps we ought to get it over with," Ian said. "Before you lose your nerve."

Kait winced and nodded. "Perhaps you're right."

Ulwe led them out of the storage room and toward the balconies. As they moved progressively through lighter corridors, past chambers with opened doors and fine furnishings, her mood lifted a little. The near-perpetual darkness of the deep heart of the House bothered her more than she could ever explain. She was as much at home in dark as in light—but she wondered still why the original builders of Galweigh House had created so many dark, airless, windowless rooms. Who had lived in them, what had they done in them? And why had anyone needed so much space?

Ulwe's path twisted like a serpent; they followed her down a level, then forward again, then down another level.

They were very near the balcony rooms; Kait hadn't known of any storage rooms that were so close to the balconies. And when Ulwe took her finally down a corridor that she recognized—one that dead-ended with two balcony rooms and two little storage rooms—she said as much.

"You've made a wrong turn. I know this part of the House."

"This is the right way," the child said. She kept going. Kait didn't argue. It would be simple enough to show her that she'd made an error, and if they wasted a little time, well, she would not complain about any delay that held off disappointment.

To Kait's left, the two doors that would open into the lovely balcony rooms. To her right, the two storage doors. All four were closed. The child opened the second storage room door and walked between the shelves. She rested a palm on the back wall. "They're in there."

Kait looked at the smooth face of the wall, then at the child. "In there."

"Yes."

Kait moved close to the wall and sniffed along its edges. She did catch human scents there. They were faint—far too faint for her to identify—but people had been here. She ran her fingers along the corners of the wall, then along the back edges of each shelf. To her amazement, she found the slight seams of a pressure pad on the far corner of the bottom right shelf. She pressed, but the pressure pad didn't give. Locked, then . . . from the inside.

Her pulse picked up, and she looked at the child. "You were right. There is a room in there."

"I can feel them in it," Ulwe said. "They're alive."

"Then they can hear me."

"Yes."

Kait stood and pressed both hands against the back wall, and shouted, "Heya! In the room! It's me! Kait Galweigh!"

She pressed an ear against the smooth surface of the

stone-of-Ancients, and listened. She heard no movement, no voices, nothing. She waited, then shouted again. "The Sabirs have gone. The three of you can come out. It's me! It's Kait! You're safe now."

Again she pressed her ear to the wall and listened. She heard nothing for a long time, then the faintest whisper. "It *might* be Kait." A child's whisper.

"Kait's dead. It's the bad people. Be still and they'll go away."

Then stillness again.

"It is me!" Kait called. "I can prove it."

No sound. No movement. The whispers could have belonged to anyone—but the child had spoken the name Kait with tones of hope. There were other Kaits in the world—there had been other Kaits within the House—but perhaps the people in there had known her. Had, perhaps, cared about her.

What should she tell them to convince them? Should she start with things the servants might have known, or things Family would have known? Which children had cared about her? Nieces and nephews? Very young cousins? The children of the upstairs servants?

"I had seven sisters," she said. "Two living brothers. My older sisters were Alcie and Drusa and Echo. My younger sisters were the twins, Loriann and Marciann, and then Luciann and Helena. Kestrell and Ewan were the brothers who died. Willim and Simman are the other brothers—both were younger."

No sound. No response.

Kait continued. "My chambermaid was Danfaith—she came from the village of Hopsett on the north coast, near Radan. My mother's name was Grace Draclas—she was from the lines of Imus Draclas and Wintermarch Corwyn. My father was Strahan Galweigh. His paternal line came from Ewan Galweigh. We lost track of his maternal line before Brassias Karnee and his mistresses."

Nothing. Please, she thought. Please answer me. Please come out. Please let me think of the right thing to say, so that I can convince you I am who I say I am.

"I had the corner room in the Willow Hall," she continued. "I kept a seashell in a carved puzzle-box beneath my pillow—I found it while walking by the shore at our country house. The shell was plain—brown on one side and white on the other—but when I held it up to the light, it glowed like pink fire. I had a jay feather in there, too, and a crystal my sister Echo gave me. I used to borrow Alcie's horse because it was the fastest and was a steady jumper, but it didn't like me, and she used to get angry with me for riding it."

She heard footsteps moving slowly near the wall. Coming closer and closer. Stopping just at the other side. She held her breath, waiting for the wall to move. But it didn't, and there were no more sounds.

"Please come out," she said.

"Tell me . . . tell me why your brothers died." Still the whisper. She did not know who stood on the other side of the door. She couldn't smell the people in there, she couldn't hear them.

"They were both killed by Sabir spies. They were infants when they died."

"Yes. But *why* were they killed?"

Kait's heartbeat picked up. Only her own family—her parents and sisters and her surviving brothers—had ever known the answer to that question. In truth, only they had known to ask it—and they had kept the truth secret to save their lives. It could still cost her hers.

She closed her eyes tightly and pressed her cheek to the wall. If she whispered the words, she invited death—but some leaps had to be taken on faith.

"They were Karnee," she said at last. "Like me."

She heard a small sob. Then the wall began to slide back, away from her. Scents rolled out of the sealed storage room, sweetly familiar, and a slender form stepped from the opening.

Kait's nose knew her sister before her eyes recognized her. In fact, her eyes might never have recognized the fragile woman that was her oldest sister.

"Alcie," she whispered.

They threw their arms around each other and wept. When they pulled apart, Kait asked, "Who's with you?" Alcie had had five children.

"Lonar. And the new baby. I named her Rethen."

She led Kait into the room where she'd been hiding. Kait's nephew Lonar hid in a corner, tucked behind a stack of crates, a baby girl clutched in his arms. When he saw Kait, his hunted expression vanished, replaced by a broad smile. "You aren't dead," he shrieked.

"And neither are you." Kait dropped to her knees and held out her arms, and he, clutching the baby, ran into them. "I'm so glad to see you, Lonar. And your new sister. You can't believe how glad."

The baby, startled, began to wail.

Chapter 18

Then you hadn't planned to be down there." Kait and Alcie sprawled in deep chairs in the salon of her family's apartment, facing each other. Alcie nursed her baby and nibbled fresh greens pulled from one of the untouched herb beds on the grounds. Kait sipped warm amber Varhees brandywine straight from the bottle.

Ry and Ian were dragging stores up from the closest of the intact storerooms; Ulwe and Lonar had already been tucked into bed. So Kait had been able to hear Alcie's story uninterrupted, and had been able to tell her own. Both sisters had done a fair job of horrifying each other.

"It was just luck. Lonar was lonely, and I knew with the baby coming soon I'd have less time for him. He wanted to go down to the balcony rooms, and I thought I'd show him the secret room I'd found when I was little."

"I never knew about that one."

"I never told the Family I found it. It was my hiding place. When I married Omil, I showed it to him, and we decided to stock it. Just in case. We kept it full and rotated stock out of it regularly. That was the main reason we claimed the balcony suite so far from the upper House. It gave us a plausible excuse to go down there as often as we did."

Alcie grew still. She stared down at her baby, and Kait could see the sudden gleam of unshed tears in her eyes. Memory was hell.

"I'm so glad you made it," she whispered.

"So am I . . . sometimes," Alcie said. She stroked Rethen's cheek and shifted her from one breast to the other. "When I look at her, or at Lonar, I'm grateful that I was away from everyone else when the screaming started. But I have to admit I've wished I'd died with Omil and my others more than once."

Kait took a long drink of the brandywine. "I've wished the same thing for myself."

"But you've done so much. And you and Ry . . ." She smiled. "I'm glad you found someone."

"You may be less glad when I tell you who he is."

"I already know who he is. He and Ian are brothers, right? And Ian is a Draclas. He told me so." She took a sip from a glass of springwater. "Don't worry. They aren't any of the Draclases who are closely related to us."

"That wasn't what I was worried about." Kait looked into the little fire that flickered in the fireplace. The flames danced comfortingly. "Ian and Ry are half-brothers. Ry . . . is a Sabir."

She heard no sound from Alcie. Not even breathing. She glanced over at her sister. Alcie was staring at her, face etched with disbelief.

"Sabir?" she managed at last.

Kait nodded.

"How closely related to *the* Sabirs?"

"He's a son of the main branch. He was to have taken over one segment of the Sabir Family upon his father's death." She didn't mention *which* segment. She thought she had enough trouble on her hands without linking Ry to covert wizards.

Alcie looked stunned. When at last she spoke again, it was only to ask, "How *could* you?"

Which was the question she had asked herself endlessly. In spite of her love for him, and in spite of the overwhelming feeling that the two of them belonged together, she still had no satisfactory answer. Her duty as a Galweigh had demanded that she forsake him, no matter how much she might desire him; she had, instead, forsaken duty for desire and love. She stared into the fire, trying to find words that could make Alcie see why she had chosen as she had. But she already knew the words. She just didn't want to say them about herself.

She was a traitor. A coward. A weak and foolish child.

"Dùghall must have known," Alcie said.

"He knew. He . . . came to like Ry. Ry stood with us against his own Family's interests. He helped us . . . helped Dùghall. In the fights we had." And how could she explain Dùghall to Alcie? Alcie thought her uncle was a diplomat— an elder statesman—a respectable man. She knew nothing of his secret affiliation with wizards, or his religion that had waited for the return of the Reborn. She knew nothing of the wonders their world had almost gained, nor that those wonders had been ripped away again forever by the hand of their own cousin, Danya. Alcie knew of Kait's escape, and the betrayal of the Goft Galweighs, and her long and dangerous voyage. Kait, though, had couched the whole ordeal in language that hid its magical nature.

"Dùghall accepted this . . . treachery of yours?"

Without knowing about the magic—about the battle between the Families' Wolves, about the Falcons and the Dragons, about the Reborn and the prophecies and Danya, Kait realized that Alcie would never understand what had happened. Kait thought perhaps that would be best; if Alcie didn't know about the return of magic to their world, it wouldn't taint her or endanger her children. She would be safe, even if she hated Kait for the rest of her life. Kait thought she could live with that hatred, as long as she knew Alcie and her two remaining children survived.

But what right did she have to keep the truth from Alcie? The bitterest truth was sweeter than the sweetest lie. Why did she assume that Alcie needed to be protected? Her sister had lost more to the Wolves and the Dragons than even Kait had. Along with brothers and sisters and parents, she had lost her husband and her children. If the situations were reversed, Kait would have wanted to know what had really happened.

In the end, that fact decided her.

"There's more you don't know," she said.

This time, she told her sister the whole truth.

Book Two

When men gather for battle,
Ravens fill the skies,
And wait to sup on war-spilled blood
And feast upon men's eyes.

FROM A FOLK SONG OF THE GYRU-NALLES
AUTHOR UNKNOWN

The outriders approached the Kargan fishcamp with green pennants flying. They came to a stop well outside the perimeter of the camp and waited.

Danya dressed in the beautifully embroidered split suede caspah and breeches the Kargan women had made for her. She mounted her lorrag and rode out to meet the outriders alone. She had to maintain appearances, after all. She was Ki Ika to the Kargans—the Summer Goddess, the mother of their long-foretold savior, Iksahsha. Luercas, in his role as Iksahsha, had done the necessary miracles, and the stories had spread. Were spreading. The Scarred—born of wizard magic and wizard madness a thousand years before—came, in all their twisted and perverted forms, seeking proof that their time of exile in the cold, harsh wasteland of the Veral Territories was coming to an end. When each new mob arrived, she greeted the leaders and Luercas convinced them, and they stayed—or if they left, it was only to bring the rest of their kin back to the camp. Already the summer camp of less than a hundred had grown to a city of nearly ten thousand. All of them would have to move northward soon, toward warmer lands and richer fields, for the hungry legions were stripping this place. It would be decades recovering.

"Hail, strangers," she said in Trade Tongue. "I am Ki Ika—Summer Mother and bearer of the Son of the Thousand Peoples." She held up her right hand—the hand still Scarred with two fierce, scaled talons where once her first and second fingers had been. Those fingers were her brand, her mark, the sign that she was not a true human, but was, indeed, as much one of these rejects as the most hideous of them.

The leader stepped forward and raised his own three-clawed paw in greeting. "We Stormeaters," he said. "We come see truth for ourselves. We hear Hammer of Man here now. We want fight for Green Lands." These latest Scarred were of a sort she had never seen before. Squat, heavy-furred, broad-bodied, they wore only leather harnesses hung with tools and weapons.

Hammer of Man. Another version of the Scarred savior, no doubt. Like Kempi to the bearish Wishtaka, or He Who Leaves No Footprints to the terrifying Flame People, or Arrow-heart to the cadaverous, eyeless Oauk, Hammer of Man would be another name for the myth she and Luercas were bringing to life—the myth that the wrongs done to past, lost generations could be somehow made right.

All of these poor, twisted freaks shared some version of the tale of the day when the true humans had stolen their birthright—their own humanity—from them and banished them to the world's wastelands. And all of them shared some form of the same prophecy—the story of the day they would bring down vengeance on the heads of unScarred humans. The prophecy seemed always to tell of another freak who would lead them, and promised that on the day when he came, they would no longer have to live on a bitter snowfield and wear skins and eat what they could scrounge from the hostile, ungiving earth. They would ride to the north, to the Green Lands, or the Fair Lands, or the Rich Lands, or the Fields of Heaven, and there they would conquer the true humans. And then they would reclaim warmth and softness, civilization and wealth, and all the comforts of a world they had never known but that they had made miraculous in their imaginations.

And she and Luercas were telling them what they wanted to hear.

It was so easy, really. Luercas took the form of whatever nightmare creature they expected to see—then metamorphosed into the form of a human. He told them that they would gain their rightful human form after the usurpers of the Green Lands were defeated.

They accepted the lies because they wanted to believe. All of them were going to end up throwing their bodies against the brutal wall of human civilization—adult males and females, the old, the children, mothers with babes in arms. Many of them—perhaps most of them—were going to die. And she and Luercas would ride into Calimekka atop their broken bodies and claim the city for themselves. And after the great city-state, all of Ibera.

It was an ugly future, but there was a price to be paid for revenge. She had paid. Paid with the life of her son, and, she suspected, with her soul. Having paid, she now accepted the offerings that came her way as her just due, and did not let herself think too much about the lives of those who made up the offerings. She smiled and welcomed the freaks because they were the coin with which she would buy vengeance.

This time she welcomed the Stormeaters, and Luercas did the necessary miracles to convince them that he was both one of them and something greater. They watched, they worshiped, and they stayed. And the army of the Scarred, the damned, the unwanted, grew by another thousand.

Chapter 20

Dùghall gave Kait a weary hug. "The trip was hell. And the worst of it was once we reached Calimekka. The city boils with insurrection—Dragons gone, Galweighs gone, Sabirs weakened and discredited, the parnissery in a riot over traitors among its number, and both the Masschankas and the Kairns trying to make inroads into the territory once held by their betters. . . ." He shook his head. "And stirring among the landsmen the idea that maybe they should be governed by their kind and not by our kind." He glanced back at Ry and Jaim and Yanth, who were exchanging their own greetings. He interrupted them. "Jaim, Yanth—see that you get Alarista to a comfortable bed, will you? And feed her. The trip up the mountain took most of her strength."

Kait stared at the old woman being lifted down from the back of her horse, then turned back to her uncle. "You're not much older than me, and she is now the age of Grandmother Corwyn. What *happened*?"

"A long and ugly story—one better discussed later." He lowered his voice. "Where is it?"

Kait didn't have to ask what he meant. "The night we got

here, I had it put in one of the treasuries, behind fingerlock doors. I locked the door myself. It's shut down."

"But you know that doesn't matter."

Kait had not even let herself think about the Mirror of Souls from the time she'd arrived at Galweigh House until the moment that Dùghall arrived. Dark fears within the memories she'd received from the Dragon Dafril had kept her away from the Mirror, from thoughts of the Mirror, from speaking of it to anyone else. She had not even dared examine those fears to find out what lay behind them. She'd simply kept her thoughts focused on other things, and waited for Dùghall's arrival. "I've suspected as much."

Dùghall closed his eyes and rubbed his temples. "I suggest you and I stroll about outside the wall while we discuss . . . our journey."

Kait nodded. She turned to Ulwe. "Follow Ry. Help him with Alarista. She'll need someone to get things for her."

Ulwe nodded. "I think I know her somehow. I'll be glad to help her."

Kait didn't want to take that moment to unravel the mysteries surrounding Ulwe. There was no way the child could know Alarista, but in the last two years, all sorts of impossible things had suddenly become not just possible, but true. So she said, "Good. Treat her gently."

Ulwe ran off, and Dùghall raised an eyebrow and said, "Crispin's daughter?"

"The same. Certainly not what he—or we—expected." Kait pulled the gate almost closed, propping it just enough that she and Dùghall would be able to get back inside quickly without help, should trouble come. Considering what they were about to discuss, that seemed more than a distant possibility. "How far would you like to walk?"

"How would you feel about the other side of the world?"

Kait's laugh sounded hollow in her own ears. They said nothing else for a while; instead, they strolled together down one of the back paths, along the ridge of the mountain, through a barrier of dense understory plants that quickly gave way to old rainforest. They walked with magical shields wrapped tightly around themselves, keeping everything in, hidden from any magical eyes that might watch and any magical ears that might listen. When they were well away from Galweigh House, Dùghall turned to Kait.

"This is far enough. If it can follow what we're doing here, I doubt there's anyplace we could go that it wouldn't be able to monitor."

She nodded. She found a seat for herself on the rotting stump of a fallen blackwood, and waited until her uncle had made himself comfortable in a loop of giant cut-by-night vine. When he was seated, she said, "You think . . . it . . . is alive." She did not speak the words *Mirror of Souls*. She would not.

"My memories tell me as much."

"As do mine. If it lives, what does it want now that the Dragons have been banished?"

"That I don't know. But a characteristic of living things is that they have a strong sense of self-preservation. And a strong urge to fulfill their purpose, whatever that purpose might be."

"It's a *thing*. It shouldn't have a sense of purpose."

Dùghall shrugged, and rocked himself back and forth in his vine swing. "It shouldn't have been created in the first place. It was born for evil, it lives for evil, and it will fight for its freedom so that it can do as it desires. I can feel it drowsing, now, napping. But it won't nap forever. It is waiting to do . . . something, and you and I are going to have to deal with it."

"We're agreed that it must be destroyed?"

"I see no other choice. Thanks to Dafril's memories, you and I know how to use it, and I'm uncomfortable enough with that. The temptation will grow greater as we grow older—impending death stirs instincts I would rather not face while gripping a gate to immortality in one hand. But Crispin, too, holds the old Dragon memories inside his skull—and while you and I value the souls of others, and so might face our own deaths without faltering, I hold out no such hope for him. If the Mirror exists and he can find it, he will use it and damn the price."

"Then the question remains—how do we destroy it? It was designed to prevent its own destruction, and it can pull power and life from every soul in Calimekka to fight us."

"I thought of little but the answer to that question on the way here." Dùghall sighed and leaned his head against the vine that held him. He pushed with one foot—back and forth, back and forth—and the vine creaked softly, and high above, the leaves of the branch that supported the vine rustled in rhythm to his movements. He might have been a child sitting there, dreaming of a faraway future in which he would be a hero.

"And . . . ?"

Dùghall focused his attention on her. His gaze, direct and thoughtful, sent a chill through her veins. "First, there's the question of you. I need you to become a Falcon, Kait."

She met his gaze, trying to see the threat in that, and after a moment, shrugged. "Hasmal was going to initiate me into the Falcons," she said. "He wanted to make me a Warden. It doesn't sound so ominous."

"It doesn't. But when you swear yourself to Falconry, you become oathbound to the Falcons."

She had assumed she would have to swear an oath. That still didn't sound like such an ordeal. "So?"

"Oathbound," Dùghall said, his voice slightly impatient.

She supposed she was failing to see what he was trying to get at. "I've sworn oaths before."

"You have never been oathbound. Oath . . . *bound*. Constrained by the power of your word—locked into certain forms of action by the ties that connect you to every other Falcon, alive or dead. The Falcon oath is not empty sounds whispered into the wind, Kait. It has a thousand years of lives bound into it. A thousand years of magic, poured layer upon layer, life upon life. You swear your oath and it's like . . . like . . ." He closed his eyes and for a moment seemed to go very far away. When he looked at her again, she saw the old man that he truly was looking out at her from inside that young body. "It's like throwing yourself from a dock into an angry sea. The waves pick you up and fling you where they will, and you're a long time finding your breath and your stroke and hauling yourself against the current and back to shore. And even when you reach dry ground again, for the rest of your life, you carry that angry sea inside of you. It's a weight, and you can feel it with every step you take and every breath you breathe. I won't deny that there are times when it's a comfort. In moments of trouble, you can feel the path that the Falcons would take—you can feel the current of that huge sea pulling you toward right actions and away from wrong ones. It can be a second conscience—one that won't ever weaken and tell you what you'd like to hear."

"That still doesn't sound so terrible."

He sighed. "It can also blind you to new paths, new ideas, new possibilities. When the Reborn . . . died . . . the tide pulled toward despair. There was a reason why so many Falcons killed themselves then, Kait. A thousand years of hopes and dreams and striving, a thousand years of having a specific reason to exist, died in the moment of his death, and the shock of that realization ripped through us like a tsunami. Falconry had no answers, no reason to go on, and no way to see clear to a new future. Bound together, we would have drowned together. You provided a bit of solid ground, Kait—hope and a new direction. You could see it because you were outside. Once you're inside . . ."

At last, Kait could see the danger for what it was. "Then it seems to me, Uncle, that I would serve better as a friend to the Falcons, without becoming a Falcon."

"And if enough Falcons survived to do what needed to be done, and if they were here where I needed them and when I needed them, I would agree with you wholeheartedly." He braced both feet on the ground and leaned forward. "But the . . . the *artifact* you have in there . . . it poses a danger that grows with every day and every moment that it watches us. A slip from us—a false word, a false move—and it will call other keepers to it. If it does, it can destroy us. It *will* destroy us."

Kait clearly remembered her own experience with the Mirror calling other keepers—the bloodred beacon cleaving the night sky, the Mirror of Souls tumbling into the sea, their frantic journey through the inlets and byways of the Thousand Dancers with Ry and Ry's men and Hasmal, with Ian at the rudder urging them to row faster . . . and faster. . . . She closed her eyes tightly and drew a steadying breath. "We don't want to give it the opportunity to do that again."

He knew the story of their narrow escape. He said, "No, we don't." He rose, and began to pace. "We need great power to destroy it—and we need that power quickly, before one of us makes a mistake. You and I and Ry can control an enormous amount of magic between the three of us. Alarista, too, might join us, though I fear that, frail as she is, she would become the weak link in the chain with which we seek to rip apart the Mirror. But three should be enough, if the three of us also share the oathbond of Falconry. Then, you see, we can create a *thathbund*—a ring of power. All surviving Falcons can offer their strength into the *thathbund,* and the Falcon dead whose souls still watch us can give us their strength, too. We become more than three. We become . . . legion."

"And with this added strength, you think we could destroy the M—the artifact."

"Yes."

"I wish Hasmal were here."

"So do I. If he were, I would ask only Ry to join me. I would leave you free from Falconry."

"Why Ry? Why not me?"

Dùghall pursed his lips, blew out a short, sharp breath. "Reasons that you will not care to hear," he said. "But you might as well."

Kait crossed her arms over her chest and waited.

"He's Sabir, Kait." Dùghall met her defiant gaze with a sad smile. "Born Sabir, raised Sabir, trained Sabir. For all his love for you, for all his newfound willingness to leave behind Wolf magic and Wolf training for the magic of the Falcons, and even for all his hatred of things his Family did to your Family, at core, he is a Sabir and will always be. If the Reborn had lived, things might have been different. The Reborn's love touched him. Changed the way he saw the world. If the Reborn had lived, he would have served, and he would have stayed strong, I think. But the Reborn died, and that love died, and now Ry runs on memories that grow fainter, and on his love for you, which, in the final accounting, has little to do with how he lives his life. Pressed, cornered, I cannot help but believe that he will use every weapon at his disposal to save himself . . . and if that weapon is Wolf magic, you and I could well pay with our lives. Or worse."

"He won't do anything to hurt me."

"You believe. And I hope. And if I had a gold preid for every woman who ever said, 'He won't do anything to hurt me,' of a man who later beat the life out of her, I'd be the richest man in all the world."

Kait felt the edges of anger twisting in her gut. "You think he'll beat me? Me?"

"No. I don't think he'll do anything of the sort. But I *know* that you don't know what he will do. You *cannot* know. He's a man, with free will and self-determination, and as such, he's as unpredictable as any other man." Dùghall leaned back. "Taking the oath of Falconry would . . . limit his options somewhat. In a *good* way. So that's why, if we had to choose only one of you, I would choose him. Bound to our side by oath and magic, he would cease to worry me so much."

Kait managed a small smile. "I understand. I can't say I like your thinking very much, but I do understand it." She picked at a soft spot on the rotting log beneath her. The rich wood smell filled her nostrils, comforting and familiar. "So how long will it take to prepare us to take the oath?"

Dùghall snorted. "You could take it today. It isn't like taking the Oath of Iberism before the parnissa—you don't have to memorize a catechism or a litany or learn the Obeisances or the Signs of Humankind. You swear to use only that power which is yours or freely given to you; to hold life—both mortal and eternal—sacred; to do no harm with your magic, either through your action or your inaction, or, if harm is inevitable, to work for the least harm and the most good; and to remain steadfast to the coming of Paranne and the return of the Reborn. Once you take the oath, it is perfectly capable of enforcing itself." He frowned thoughtfully and stared at the ground beneath his feet. "I don't know about that last clause anymore. The Reborn will not come a third time, and without him, there will be no city of Paranne, and no world of perfect love. I wonder if that ought to come out of the oath for new Falcons. . . ."

Kait got him back on track. "If you took our oaths today, we could destroy . . . it . . . today?"

"Eh?" Dùghall returned his attention to her. "Oh. No, I don't think so. We have to work out a plan of attack. The artifact will certainly defend itself—we need to be certain when it does that we react effectively together. I think we'll only be ready to take it on after several days of practicing together. Even so, I suspect our chances of success are about the same as our chances of failure."

"You're more optimistic than I am." Kait remembered only too clearly the way the Mirror of Souls shattered her shield as if it weren't there and called Crispin to it when she started to take it in a direction it didn't want to go. She feared the Mirror, and wondered how the three of them, even strengthened by Dùghall's Falconry, could hope to fend off its attack.

"Perhaps you're less optimistic with reason," Dùghall said quietly. "You've been around the thing. I haven't. Your sense of it is certainly more clear than mine."

They sat without speaking for a few moments, lost in their own thoughts. Finally Kait stood and brushed wood chips and wood dust off her clothes. "I suppose we should be getting back."

"I suppose we should." Dùghall rose, too, and looked toward the House. "Talk to Ry, will you? I'll tell him about the oath if you'd like, but I think it would be best if he understood both the positive and the negative aspects of becoming a Falcon from your perspective before he talked to me. I will not . . . and cannot . . . coerce him into something he doesn't want."

"He might refuse." Kait considered that possibility. She was tempted to refuse herself. Without the promise of communion with the Reborn and the eventual building of the city of Paranne, Falconry seemed to her to have little to offer. And while it had lost the Reborn, which would have made any sacrifice worthwhile, it had kept its drawbacks intact.

"I realize that. If he refuses, we have little chance of success. But he must come to Falconry freely." Dùghall glanced at her. "As must you. If you do not take the oath with a willing heart, your oath won't be accepted."

She realized she must have looked surprised by the smile on Dùghall's face.

He chuckled. "You thought if you said the words, you would be bound to the oath whether you wished to become a Falcon or not?"

She nodded.

"I told you, the oath isn't just the words. If you truly have no wish to become a Falcon, *nothing* can make you. The words you will say must match the desire in your heart and the willingness of your soul to be bound beyond life itself to the precepts of Falconry. Nothing less will make you one of us."

She thought about that for a moment. "I'll tell him," she said at last. "And when we've talked, we'll let you know what we decide."

"That's all I can ask."

Chapter 21

Dùghall completed his session with the *zanda* and rose, his face troubled. He did not understand the directions he'd received; he did not like the direction in which the gods were pointing him. Always, he had used magic to bring harmony, to create peace, to guide in positive directions. Now he was being directed to do something that ran counter to his every instinct—and yet three times the *zanda* had insisted this was the direction he must take if he and the Falcons were to triumph against the last Dragon and the army he raised.

He gathered the accoutrements of spellcasting and settled cross-legged onto the floor. He thought for a long time, composing the spell in such a way that it would do no harm, even though it would certainly seem to. Then he clipped a bit of hair from his head and scraped a bit of skin from the inside of his cheek and offered those into the blood-bowl. On a scrap of black silk that he had spread onto the stone floor, he dropped two tiny white spheres. When he dropped them, he dipped his fingertips in a little vial of clear gel and let the coating dry.

When he finished his physical preparations, he recited:

"Vodor Imrish, hear me now—
This path which leads through seeming night

Must come at last to light of day
And all my actions be revealed
To mark me for this seeming crime.
I give my flesh to pay my price
And ward my deed in pure intent.
Upon the utterings of gods
And spirits do I cast this lot.
Send honesty among us, place
The fire of anger and the seed
Of discontent on those I mark.
Let thoughts that prudent men would keep
In chains be spoken, and let ears
That would incline to understanding
Hear instead each syllable that's
Said and take each word to heart.
I ask for nothing save the truth,
Knowing that truth can be unkind.
No pain or hurt would I then cause
Save only that which can't be spared
To do the work that this must do."

He held a hand over the silver-lined bowl and waited—
and it began to fill with white light, as Vodor Imrish took his
offering, and then the light took on a cold and shimmering
quality, and formed itself into the shape of a flame. Dùghall
channeled that lovely flame into the two little spheres,
which absorbed it as quickly as water would douse a candle.

When the last sparkle of the godlight was gone, Dùghall
pressed his left index finger to one sphere and his right to
the second. They stuck, unobtrusive so long as he didn't
wave his hands around.

Then, hurrying, for he sensed that he had only a little
time to do what he must do if he hoped to succeed, he went
through the halls, searching.

"Kait," he said when he passed his niece, "bring Ry to
my quarters later and we'll go over the details of the Falcon

ceremony." He patted her bare arm in a gesture that looked like absentminded affection and moved on, lighter by one sphere, aware that behind him, Kait stood in the hallway, watching him with suddenly uncertain eyes.

And in an upper passageway, he met Ry. "Oh, son," he said, tapping Ry on the wrist with a single finger, and feeling the slight pop as the second sphere came free, "Kait was looking for you mere moments ago. I just saw her in the hallway by the west salon, but I believe she might have been headed elsewhere."

And he moved on to his quarters, and took a seat in one of the fine brocaded chairs, and shook. He thought he might throw up, and he hung his head between his knees until the feeling finally passed.

There. It was done. He did not know what his spell might accomplish, and he did not know why this was the path he'd been directed to take. He wished he could uncover a clear picture of the future—a map that would let him see clearly the consequences of his actions and the prices that others would have to pay for the things he did.

And at last he prayed that he had not been misguided.

"I don't like it," Ry said. "With the death of the Reborn, the Falcons have no reason to continue. They existed to clear a path for him . . . and now he's gone, and there isn't going to be a Paranne, or a world of perfect love." He turned from stalking back and forth through the ruined garden and faced her. "I would have given my life for him, Kait. For the Reborn. But not for a stuffy, secretive association of pacifist wizards. They have no head. No direction. No objectives once—" He caught himself just before he mentioned the Mirror, and shuddered. So close. "Once they've accomplished this one last thing."

Kait sat on the edge of the fountain, still as any of the statues around her. Sunlight played across her hair and the lean planes of her face, and shadowed her dark eyes and the full curve of her lower lip. She watched him, thoughtful and wary and worried. "I know. And yet, without us, they aren't going to accomplish this one last thing."

"You can't be sure of that."

"I can't."

"You know we could wait to see if any of them respond to Dùghall's call."

"I know that."

He gave her a hard look. "Stop trying to sound so reasonable. Show a little emotion about this. A little *feeling,* for the gods' sakes."

She almost smiled at that. He saw the corners of her lips twitch. Then she shook her head. "Passion can't decide this. Logic is going to have to—and I'm being reasonable because if I don't, no one will."

"So you think it's reasonable to bind yourself for life, unbreakably, to a group of people who stand for nothing, who have no fixed goal or aspiration, who have become nothing but a remnant of a lost civilization?"

Now she did smile. "Put that way, it sounds insane."

"It *is* insane."

"It would be if you were right. But with or without the Reborn, the Falcons don't stand for nothing. They stand for the responsible use of magic—for using only that power which is rightfully yours, for defending instead of attacking, for protecting the innocent from the voracious and the predatory. They stand for self-sacrifice, for the triumph of love over hatred, for leaving the world a better place than they found it." Now, now he could hear passion in her voice, and his heart sank. Her conviction flushed her cheeks a darker red and made her lift her chin and glare at him like the parata she was but rarely acted—and he knew he would not like what came next. She said, "The Falcons cannot stand on the promise of Paranne any longer, but the things they've been fighting for these last thousand years are as true and as important now as they were the day Vincalis started writing the prophecies for the Secret Texts." She rose, a statue no longer, and walked over and rested a hand on his arm. "Ry, the Falcons are much of what was best about the Ancients' world. They can be much of what is best about our world."

They stood staring into each other's eyes for a long, uncomfortable moment. "You're going to take the oath," he said at last. "You've already decided."

She looked a little surprised. "I hadn't decided, until you tried to convince me that it was the wrong thing to do. Then suddenly I could see the truth. Yes. I'll become a Falcon." He could see, then, the pain in her eyes. "And you will not take the oath."

He said, "I'll take it if you do."

She shook her head. "I already told you, if you don't truly wish to become a Falcon, the words will not bind you."

He turned away from her. "How can I wish to become a slave to someone else's philosophy?"

"If you had stayed in Sabir House, in the fullness of time you would have become a full Wolf for the Sabir Family," Kait said quietly. "You would have embraced *that* philosophy."

Her words were a little knife, digging at him, probing for weakness. He said, "Don't try to manipulate me, Kait. Perhaps I would have done what my Family required, but perhaps not. I've shown considerably more spine in standing against *my* Family's wishes than you have shown in standing against yours. You are the one who has put a wall between us for the sake of Family . . . of *appearances*. I received my own apartment in the House the day you found your sister—not one with a door that connects to yours, either. *She* has that apartment. She has your time in the mornings, your first smiles of the day, the first sound of your voice each dawn. *I* have an apartment I don't want, and distance I don't want, and the feeling that you're ashamed of me—that I'm not good enough now that your big sister is around to pass judgment."

"I *don't* feel that way and you know it. I love you. I want to spend the rest of my life with you. I just want to be able to share my life—including you—with the little that remains of my family. Alcie is slowly coming around," Kait said. "She will accept you."

"And I think she would accept me faster if we declared ourselves *incanda* and took our own apartments and shared our bed."

"That's too . . . abrupt. My way is taking longer, but it's better. Alcie understands that you're not truly Sabir—"

Ry's skin crawled. He spun and stared at her, and she faltered and fell silent. He said, "What did you say?" and his voice was flat and hard.

She flushed. "I've been explaining to her that you left the Sabirs rather than take charge of them, and that your own mother declared you *barzanne* in consequence, and that you aren't really Sabir anymore. . . ."

"And that is all that will make me acceptable to her? That I'm some gelded, tamed, caged thing that lives with you because I have no place of my own?"

She was shaking her head. "No . . . no, of course not—"

"I should have seen this coming. I should have realized that we had no future together—should have seen it when you presented me with separate quarters and a stupid explanation about how it was just temporary and just for show." He took a step back from her. "I'm still Sabir," he whispered. "My mother took my birthright, but she could not claim my blood. I will live and die a Sabir, and you will live and die a Galweigh, and all the Reborn's love and tolerance and acceptance can't change that, and all your wishes that I be something other than what I am can't change that, either."

They stared at each other across the widening gulf of who they were and who they could not be.

Kait's fists clenched and Ry saw tears well at the corners of her eyes. "I love you," she said.

"And I love you. You are the only woman I've ever wanted. The only woman I've ever loved." He took a deep breath and continued. "But if you can't accept who I am, we can't be together. I won't be your embarrassment, Kait. I won't be your shame or your mistake, the thing you did to yourself that you wish you could hide from the world. I won't pretend that I'm not Sabir so that your sister will accept me."

"Why not? You pretend all sorts of things. You pretend not to be Karnee every day to save your life."

"And so do you."

"Yes. I do. We *both* pretend, Ry. Neither of us has ever let the world see who we are. Neither of us has ever been who we really are, except with each other. We share secrets no one else will ever know. We know each other—we're the only ones who know each other. Why can't you give up being Sabir so that we can have that?"

He stared at her, seeing a stranger in familiar flesh. "That you could even ask me that tells me that everything I thought I shared with you doesn't exist. I never asked you to give up being yourself for me. I never would, because who you are is much of what I love about you. If you weren't Galweigh, you wouldn't be you." He paused, then said, "And if I weren't Sabir, I wouldn't be me."

He wanted her to take back what she'd said. He wanted her to say she was wrong, to say she was sorry for asking him to become someone else, to run to him and throw her arms around him. But she didn't. She stood there staring at him and crying, and at last he turned away. He had his answer.

"Where are you going?"

He didn't look back. "To pack. Once that's done . . . I don't know. It's a big world. There's bound to be a place in it for me somewhere."

She said, "Ry . . . please don't go. I . . . need you. There's no one else in the world for me." Her voice sounded very small when she said it.

He turned back then, just for a moment. "If you really needed me, Kait, I'd stay. But you need someone who isn't Sabir to fit all the pictures you have in your head of what a dutiful daughter is supposed to be. I can't be who you need me to be, and I won't try."

He left the garden, and packed his few belongings, and found Yanth and Jaim and told them what was going on. The whole time, he kept hoping that she'd come to him and say something—anything—that would let him know she could love him without regrets; that she could find a way to put their pasts behind her and accept him as he was. But she didn't come.

At last, he and his lieutenants left Galweigh House. He tried not to look back, but he couldn't help himself. She was standing atop the wall, silent, watching. When the wind shifted slightly, it brought her scent to him, and the yearning he felt for her was so great he almost couldn't breathe. But she didn't run after him. She didn't plead with him to stay. She didn't take back her words.

So he turned and trudged toward the jungle, toward the hidden paths that would take him down to the city. He didn't know where he would go from there. He didn't care. Who he was and what he did mattered to him only if he was with her. Without her, the world was bleak and empty, and so was he.

Chapter 22

Kait sat in the far corner of her sitting room, her back to the door, staring out the window into the ruined garden where she and Ry had fought their last fight. She should have told him that she didn't care if he was Sabir. She could have kept him if she'd said the words he wanted to hear—she knew it. But just saying it wouldn't make it true, and if she could only have him with a lie, she would live without him.

She heard the knock on her door and ignored it. This time, unlike the last few times, the door opened anyway.

"You can't sit in here forever," Alcie said. "You have to come out eventually."

"Why?"

"Don't be stupid. Dùghall's frantic. He's demanding that you come downstairs and eat something and talk to him. He says the two of you have unfinished business, and that the world won't wait for your broken heart to heal."

Kait said nothing. She kept staring out the window, shutting out her sister's voice.

"Oh, for the gods' sakes, Kait," Alcie snapped, "you're better off without him. You were infatuated with him, and I can see why. He was handsome, he was clever, he was passionate—but he was *Sabir*. Some night he would have remembered that, and he would have rolled over and strangled you while you slept. And then he would have crept through the House and finished off everyone else."

Kait felt rage beginning to build in her gut, but she didn't show it. She kept her voice calm and said, "You didn't know him."

"I didn't *need* to know him. I know what the Sabirs did to the rest of us. You and I are all that remain of our family, almost all that remain of the Calimekka Galweighs. Maybe his weren't the hands that wielded the sword that killed Maman and Papan and my Omil and my children and our brothers and sisters, but the killers' blood runs through his veins."

"It does," Kait said evenly. "And most of his Family is dead, too, destroyed by the same fight, on the same day, and by much the same means. We used magic, we broke the agreements and the covenants, and you can just as honestly say that killers' blood runs through your veins. The Galweighs' hands weren't clean."

"Maybe not, but we didn't start that fight. The treachery was theirs . . . and you admit he had a part in that treachery."

Kait turned away from the window and looked into her sister's eyes. "The treachery was theirs *that* time. You and I cannot know about other times or other betrayals. With four hundred years of hatred between us and them, I cannot believe that the Galweighs were always innocent victims, or the Sabirs always vile aggressors. Ry did what his Family told him to do; he served out of duty. As did you. As did I. We were all obedient to our Families—"

"And now he's gone and you can cease to shame yours," Alcie said. "It could never have worked, Kait. Passion dies after a time, and the newness fades, and all that lovers have left are those things they share in common. You could never have shared common ground with that . . . beast."

Kait turned back to the window. *I could never share common ground with anyone but that beast,* she thought. *We were both Karnee. Both kept outside the core of Family life because we were different. Tainted. We share a bond Alcie couldn't understand, and wouldn't believe—if I told her I know where he is right now, that when I sleep I can still feel his hands interlaced with mine, or that at this moment I can sense that he hasn't eaten in two days, she would tell me I was suffering from the taunts of spirits and visions, that I could not know such things. Or that I was simply mad. But I'm not mad. We share something that is for us alone—in all the world there will not be another like Ry for me.*

"I could have," she said. "I did. It's over, but I will hunger for him for the rest of my life."

"You'll get over him."

"As you've gotten over Omil?"

Kait turned in the chill silence that followed her question and regarded her sister. Alcie's lips were bloodless, her face pale, her body rigid with fury. "How dare you compare Omil with a Sabir, or your little infatuation with something you know nothing about?"

Kait nodded. "If it's yours, it's sacred; if it's mine, it's something of no value. Is that what you think?"

Alcie turned and stalked out of the room without another word. Kait stared after her thoughtfully, then returned to her place by the window. But Alcie's words and her attitude kept interrupting her reverie. And Alcie was like Ian, who had stayed, and like Dùghall. None of them would see what she had lost; none of them would understand the depth of her pain. Perhaps none of them could. They saw only her duty, and that she neglected duty out of grief.

At last she went to her armoire. From it, she pulled one of her presentation dresses—red silk in the Galweigh weave with a stiffened collar of black Galweigh Rose-and-

Thorn lace, the soft black underblouse chastely high, the sleeves cut and turned and heavily embroidered in black-on-black silk so that the roses stood out from the cloth almost like real flowers. She put it on slowly. She laced on formal shoes, watching their gems gleaming in the morning light as she caught the cord through the hooks in the back. She brushed and braided her hair, then pinned it up in a heavy loop at the base of her neck.

She rummaged through her room until she found a kit she'd acquired as part of her diplomatic training; she opened it, found that its contents—powders, brushes, glues, and gems—were intact, and smiled grimly. She took the case, sat before her mirror, and powdered her face with *iliam,* a concoction of ground gold and bone dust and gods alone knew what else that made her look like she'd been cast of precious metal. She brushed lampblack on her eyelids and eyelashes and pressed little rubies at the outer corners of her eyes with spirit gum. She painted a red line carefully from the center of her forehead down to the tip of her nose, her hands only shaking a little as she did—she had painted such lines before, but never on her own face.

Finally, she found the case that held her best head-dress—the one with the woven platinum band that rested across her brow and held in place a cascade of gemstones that hung halfway down her back—and settled it on her head. As its immense weight came to rest on her, four hundred years of Galweigh history settled on her shoulders; four hundred years of ghosts told her what she must think and what she must feel and what she must do to honor them.

She bowed to the mirror and to the ghosts, and then she went down to the solar to greet her uncle.

When Kait stepped into the solar dressed as if for her own funeral, Dùghall resisted the urge to beat his head against the cool stone wall only with difficulty. He had hoped to pretend cheerfulness with Kait, and to act as if Ry's absence were only a temporary misfortune, but obviously he could no longer consider that an option. He could not offer her a meal and chat about inconsequential nothings while she ate. She presented herself as one already dead, and he couldn't see any polite way to ignore that.

He could, however, resent the melodramatic gestures of youth, and that he did.

"Don't you look lovely," he said after an instant's hesitation, and Kait gave him a hard look.

"I've come to do my duty," she said.

"Oh, lucky, lucky us." He leaned against a wall and crossed his arms over his chest. "You're all enthusiastic about it too, I see. So few corpses rise from their pyres to attend the needs of the living."

"I'm doing my duty to my Family because it *is* my duty." Kait stood before him like a paraglesa, chin up, spine rigid, shoulders squared. She would have looked quite grand, he thought, if it weren't for the fact that parading around as an upright corpse was inherently ridiculous.

"Duty for the sake of duty. . . . I'll tell you something that may serve you well in the future. Families thus served are better left to rot into oblivion." He looked at her standing there in all her outraged glory, and he gave in to the impulse and laughed at her.

That, of course, was like throwing water on a cat. "I at least know my duty," she snarled.

"Right. Right. And you're going to shove this magnificent sacrifice you're making down our throats—you have loved and lost and you're dead inside but you'll bravely go on, giving your life up to serve your Family and the world, and all you want is for us to pity you and admire you for being the poor, brave creature you are."

He'd shocked her speechless. Her mouth dropped open and she stared at him, and he could see her fingers digging into the palms of her hands—he could see, too, a blurring at the fingertips, as if her hands couldn't decide whether to have fingernails or claws. He recalled, then, her Karnee heritage, and decided he might be wise to take a less antagonistic approach.

"I'm not saying the world doesn't need you, Kait," he said. "But it doesn't need you to be a martyr."

"Really? You're saying I don't have to die. I just can't have my Family *and* the man I love. Is that it?"

"You *had* the man you loved. You sent him away."

"He left."

"You had nothing to do with his leaving?"

"Family came between us."

"Family stood between you from the beginning, but you seemed to be managing well enough. Then all of a sudden he leaves and you go into mourning, and you declare the problem was Family. I don't see it." He didn't mention his own part in their breakup—he still wasn't certain exactly how significant that part had been, or why what he had done had been necessary.

Kait was quiet for a long time. Finally, she seemed to come to a decision. In a quieter, less angry voice than before, she said, "He couldn't leave being Sabir behind."

Dùghall shook his head. "You asked him to give up being Sabir?"

"Yes. I had to—for you and for Alcie, for all the Galweighs who died."

"I see. And did you ask him to give you his balls on a plate at the same time?"

"What?"

"You might as well have. You can't ask a man to be someone else for you."

"The longer I was here, the more I realized that I could not have him if he was still Sabir in his heart."

Dùghall sighed. "You're young, Kait-cha, and youth has its charms, but that bullheaded idealism of yours is not one of them. You still think the world is made up of sharp edges and clear divisions, of good that has never known evil and evil that has never known good—and in spite of everything you have seen and done, you think you can force the real world to fit your picture of what it should be if you just want it enough."

"That isn't so," Kait argued, but Dùghall held up a hand to stop her.

"It is so. You're a good girl and you loved your family and you served the greater Family with your whole heart. And then you discovered a piece of the puzzle of your life that didn't fit the rest of the picture . . . but that piece fit you. Ry fit you, girl, and you fit him. There was something more to the two of you than simple desire; magic coursed between the two of you through the Veil itself. You were shaped for each other by the forces of fate or the gods."

"You're saying I should go after him."

"No. I don't know that going after him would bring him back. You don't see yet why what you did was wrong. You might never see it, or truly understand it, and until you do, you can't hope to fix the rift you've created between the two of you. So, no. Don't go running after him. You'll likely only make things worse."

Kait pulled her heavy headdress off and dropped it onto a brocaded bench. It rattled and clanked, and Dùghall winced. She dropped into a deep chair, oblivious to the damage she was doing to her dress, which was not made to be sat in, and leaned forward, elbows on knees. "You really think our fight was all my fault, don't you?" He realized that she was crying; tears carved little runnels through the gold powder on her face.

He dragged another chair to a position across from hers and settled into it. "You look at Ry as a sacrifice you made for your Family," he said. "And there are sacrifices you will have to make in your life—some of them may be as painful as sending him away. But"—he held up a finger—"you don't sacrifice a gift the gods have given you."

"You say that so lightly—that he was a gift the gods gave me. How can you know that? Why would the gods give me a gift that would divide me from my Family?"

"Why would the gods . . . And you question the gift itself. . . ." He rested his head in his hands and closed his eyes for a long moment. His own weaknesses rose before him, unbearable specters of failure, of insufficiency, of inadequacy. "Ah, Vodor Imrish, give me the words." He sighed and looked up at her. "Love—true, abiding love—is the greatest gift the gods bestow. Solander felt it for every living creature—he was so moved by love that he transcended time and death to touch us with it. Vincalis felt it for his friend Solander, and for Janhri, who became his wife, and love so changed him that he marked the future with his words, and gave many of us a path to follow and a star to sight by.

"Love is no small thing, no weak power. It is the greatest force in the universe, stronger than hatred or death, more powerful than any magic." He shrugged and looked down at his hands. "Some say it is the true source of magic, or even of life itself, though I wonder at that. There is too much that is evil and cruel in the world for that to be true, I'm thinking. I am an old man, no matter this young body. I've known friendship and caring, passion and compassion, in my years. I've shared the beds of a multitude of women, and have even been named a minor deity in the service of their fertility. But when Solander touched me with his love, that was the first time I had ever felt such love. And the last. Whatever exists within you that lets you love with your whole heart and your whole soul . . . it doesn't exist in me. Or if it does, I have not yet found that one person or that one thing that I can love completely. Not the Falcons, not a lover, not anything." He looked into her eyes and wished he could force her to feel the things he felt inside himself at that moment. "I would give my life, my soul, my eternity, to feel that kind of love, that love that you have thrown away out of some misbegotten sense of duty, and out of guilt that you survived when your family did not."

He looked down at his hands again—the strong young hands whose youth belonged not to him, but to Alarista, who had loved so deeply that she had given him her years for the merest chance to save the life of her beloved Hasmal. "The dead are dead, Kait, and the living can be blind and stupid and heedless—and if you give up the best and most perfect thing in your life for either the dead or the living, you're mad . . . and undeserving of the blessing the gods gave you."

"And yet you say I should not go after him."

"I do."

"Because I'm likely to make things worse. To ruin everything."

"Yes."

"Then what do I do?"

He sat up straight and took a deep breath. "You go wash your face. You remove that ridiculous outfit. You come back here and eat a good meal, and when you've finished, we'll figure out what we must do next—for I'm guessing that Ry did not wish to become a Falcon, and that does change our plans." He stood and crossed to her and rested a hand on her shoulder. "And then you and I will sit down and figure out how you might apply the arts of diplomacy, which you know, to the art of love, which you obviously do not. And we'll find a way for you to win back your love."

Kait rose and wiped off her tears with the back of her hand, streaking her face further. She nodded. "I'll be back quickly."

He gave her a hug and said, "Don't waste any more of

your *iliam* on the living. Real corpses never cry and wash your artistry away."

She managed a small smile before she turned and hurried from the room.

Chapter 23

Ye'er the hardest whoreson t' kill I ever did see," the stranger said, and Crispin opened his eyes. His skull screamed with pain—white lights sparkled in front of his eyes, the only images in a sea of darkness. His bones, his skin, his muscles, his gut . . . his very hair felt like it was on fire.

"I know ye'er awake again. If y' don't start talkin' t' me soon, I'm gonna smash all those pretty teeth of yours in."

Where was he? The stink that surrounded him was unbearable: rotting fish and filth and decay, the sounds of lapping water and seabirds, the babble of a thousand shouting people off at a little distance, the rattle of cart wheels, the clop of hooves. . . .

And how had he come to be where he was?

"I'm getting m' stick now."

He managed to say, "What do you want to know?" He vaguely recalled images of a cudgel smashing into him again and again, and darkness falling, and Shifting, but it doing him no good. No good at all.

He heard a coarse laugh. "Thought you could talk. Tell me who you are, y' bastard. When I found you in the alley, you weren't talking. If you hadn't been such an interestin' catch, I'd a left you there for the bodywagon."

Alley, he thought. And he remembered a knife.

"Someone stabbed me."

"I know that well enough. And robbed you, too. Lying there naked as a babe, you were, but a damn sight uglier. Hands all twisted into claws, and a bit of a tail growing from yer backside, and yer face all stretched long like a wolf's. Or a lion's. Blood everywhere, and holes in yer hide would have killed a dozen men, and you still breathin'. Weirdest thing I ever saw ... so I brought you here t' tend you for a while. See what use you might be, so t' speak."

What use might he be?

He had his own purpose, didn't he?

He recalled pursuing someone. Being angry. Wanting to kill—and then his memories cascaded over him, and he recalled his cousin Ry kidnapping his daughter, and he realized that he was running out of time. Ry might be anywhere with Ulwe—if he hadn't killed her already, he might soon. Crispin had to get away. He had to save his daughter. He tried to leap at the man, to kill him to get him out of the way.

Something held him back. Cut into his throat, his wrists, his legs, his chest, his thighs. He fought against the unseen restraints, howling with pain and wordless rage, and heard his captor say, "Damnall, you do this every time. No sense my tryin' to get you back t' health—you'll never be of use t' me."

The words stopped him. He remembered again that cudgel falling, and bringing darkness with it, and he lay still, and this time the blows did not fall.

"Ye'er learnin', anyway. 'Bout damn time." He heard shuffling; the man had been very close to him, but now moved away.

"I need water," he said. "And food."

"And I need answers."

The man wanted to know who he was. Which would serve him better: a lie, or the truth? The truth had its own power, but was in its way more unbelievable than lies.

"My name is Crispin Sabir," he said after a moment.

The man was silent for so long that Crispin thought perhaps he had spoken too softly. In a louder voice, he said, "My name is Crispin Sabir."

"Yah . . . yah. I heard you the first time."

Crispin's vision was beginning to clear a bit. He could make out light, and fuzzy shapes. He could tell enough to figure out that he lay in a darkened room with two small windows high on the walls, filled with boxes and crates and oddly shaped equipment. A warehouse of some sort, surely. He couldn't see anything but the vaguest shape of his captor. From that, though, he could tell that the man was immense—broad of shoulder and thick of neck.

"I figured it was something like that," the man said softly. "Who but Family or someone with Family connections could get a monster-child past Gaerwanday, what with the parnissas poking and prodding and sticking their pins into squalling brats and killing the weird ones."

Crispin saw an opportunity and took it. "I could be of tremendous advantage to you," he said. "Can put my Family and my connections at your disposal—I can give you a secure position with the Sabirs. You saved my life—that's worth wealth, and power—"

The man's laughter cut him off. "It's worth shit in a sewer, laddie. Just proves you ain't been around lately. The Sabirs ain't what they was the day you was stabbed, y'hear? We've had done with Families in Calimekka—done with parnissas, too. The riots have sent your kind runnin' for cover—what Sabirs there is, is hidin' t' save their skins, or left fer friendlier cities. If you've got nothin' more t' offer me than your name, I'll kill you now and sell your meat t' the knacker."

"You said I was hard to kill."

"Hard ain't impossible. I'm thinking I take yer head off and you won't be coming back to hurt me."

And that was true enough. Crispin stayed silent. He wondered at the changes his captor described—Families overthrown, the parnissery gone, the survivors fleeing the city—and he wondered what he might offer the man that he would save his life and set him free.

"I can give you gold."

"Gold's worth about the same as any other rock these days. You can't plant it, you can't eat it, and you can't wear it—and with the troubles in the city, shipping's dried up like grass in a drought. If you know where I could get my hands on a large supply of food, now . . . ?"

Crispin did, actually. The Sabirs had siege stores put by in Sabir House, and hidden in other places within easy reach. Crispin had several such stores for himself—places he alone knew of. He figured with his hidden stores, he could live in Calimekka for years.

"I have siege stores," he said.

"Tell me how to get to one, and when I get the food, I'll come back and release you."

Crispin smiled. "Ah, no. I'm afraid once you have the food, you might forget how to find your way back here. I must insist that you release me before I tell you where it is."

"An' let you change into a beast and try to rip my throat out again. . . . No. That ain't going to work, either."

They stared at each other across the room. "We need to come to some accommodation. You want the food, I want my freedom."

"And I don't want t' get my throat torn out." The man watched Crispin thoughtfully, thumbs tucked into the rope belt that wound twice around his thick middle. He was silent a long time—Crispin doubted that concentrated thought was familiar to him, so he kept silent while the stranger struggled his way through the unaccustomed terrain. Finally the man smiled and said, "Yah. That'll work."

Crispin would have asked him what would work, but he didn't have the time. The man leaped at him and slammed him in the head with the cudgel, and all was darkness and pain.

"Sorry I couldn't warn you 'bout that. Figgered it'd be easier on you if you didn't know it was comin'."

Crispin's head was bouncing up and down on rough boards, and the rattling of wooden wheels over cobblestones jarred through his bones. He'd been tightly bound in an awkward position—everything hurt, and he couldn't move anything but his eyes. He could see nothing but filthy straw and the boards beneath him.

"How thoughtful of you," Crispin said.

The stranger laughed. "Oh, I'm a darlin', I am. Ask any of the whores in the Red Dish."

Crispin chuckled and said, "I'll be sure to do that," but he made a note of the name. Red Dish. A tavern with whores, or an inn with whores, or simply a whorehouse. Somewhere in the waterfront district, perhaps—that would help him narrow it down. He might not be able to kill the stranger immediately, but he would certainly keep that offhand remark in mind. Finding him later and killing him slowly might be even more pleasant than finishing the job right then.

"We're on our way t' the Sabir District," the man said. "You're goin' to tell me where your stores are. I'll go there, and load t' food in with you, and we'll go someplace else. When I've finished gettin' all the food, I'll drive this wagon out away from where I live, and tie the horses out o' sight o' the night traffic. Come day, someone will come along an' find you, and if you're lucky they'll cut you loose 'stead of cuttin' yer throat."

"Doesn't seem like such a good deal for me," Crispin observed.

"Y' ain't dead, are you? I ain't gonna kill you, am I? I

could have you take me to yer stores, then kill you anyway, but I'll honor my word if you honor yours. You'll have yer chance, even if it ain't a comfy one, and even if it ain't guaranteed. We don't none of us get guarantees."

Crispin said, "No. We don't. With that in mind, then, I'll thank you, and tell you that you need to go to Manutas Street near the Durgeon Tree, and just beyond that, take Firth's Lane back to the potters'. . . . You know the Sabir District?"

"I'll find the place," the man said calmly. "Never you worry about that."

Chapter 24

Ian worked in one of Galweigh House's ruined gardens, salvaging the plants that could be salvaged and clearing out those that were dead or ruined. It was pointless work—no crowds wandered through the gardens anymore seeking solace, and in fact he thought he might be the only one who had even rediscovered this out-of-the-way spot. Beyond carrying food from the siege storage rooms to the kitchen, he had nothing useful to contribute to those inside. But he found comfort in work, and with tensions between Dùghall and Kait and Alcie so high, he preferred to work alone and away from everyone else. The earth was warm and welcoming, and responded to his touch. It invited contemplation. It offered peace.

Ry was gone, Kait despaired in her room, and though Ian tried to find hope for his own cause with Kait in Ry's leaving, he could not. Kait did not love him and never would, though he believed she cared about him. Caring, though—that wouldn't be enough. Even if Ry never came back to her, even if she decided to accept Ian as a substitute, that wouldn't be enough. He could love her forever, but if she didn't return his love with the passion and the hunger he felt for her, he would always be a starving man at a banquet table—able to see the great feast he desired and needed, and perhaps even able to touch it, but never permitted to eat.

He'd done everything he could to help her, but he could no longer help. Here in the House, he was useless. He stayed out of loyalty, or out of some futile hope that circumstances or magic would suddenly transform him into the man she desired. Or because he got some masochistic pleasure from seeing her every day, even knowing that he could never have her.

He pulled at an entrenched weed, working it free down to the tip of the root, and tossed it into the pile with the other plants to be burned later. He needed to leave. He contributed nothing of value here, and he needed to get on with his life. Perhaps find another ship, hunt down the mutineers who'd stolen the *Peregrine* from him and left him to die on the other side of the world. He had no business among wizards and skinshifters and secret societies and pacts with old gods.

Ulwe came out into the garden and crouched down next to Ian. She didn't say anything—she simply began pulling out weeds with him.

He glanced over at her and saw that her skin was pale as bone, her lips compressed, and her eyes bright with unshed tears. He didn't say anything to her; he simply pointed out additional weeds that were within her reach. And he waited.

The child stayed quiet for a long time while they worked together. At last, though, she looked up at Ian and said, "He just killed someone. Someone who *helped* him, though the man did it for gain. He didn't kill him in self-defense, he didn't kill him out of fear—he killed him because he thought it was fun, and because he likes to kill, and because he could. He broke his own oath."

Ian nibbled his lower lip and looked at the girl out of the corner of his eye. "Your father."

"Yes."

He sighed, thinking of his own father, who had kept his

mother as a mistress but who had loved her deeply, who had cared about him at least a little, yet who had been, from everything he'd ever been able to find out, an evil man, hungry for power and willing to do anything to keep it. "You wanted him to be a good man," Ian said at last. "Because he's your father, you wanted him to be someone worthy of your love and your admiration."

"He loves me. I know he does. I thought that meant there was good inside him. That he could become good."

"You hoped if you loved him enough, he would change." She nodded.

Ian said, "He won't change, Ulwe. He likes himself as he is. I know him—I've known him since we were both children, though he's older than me."

"Everything I feel from him is terrible—except for what he feels when he thinks of me. I touch the road and I can feel his love. It's real. I can feel it." She rested a hand on his arm and looked directly into his eyes. "How can that one bit of goodness survive in the midst of so much evil?"

Ian brushed the dirt from his hands and turned to face Ulwe. He held both her hands and said, "I'm going to tell you something that will be hard for you to hear. But you have to understand. Will you listen and let me finish?"

She looked at him with wide eyes. "Yes."

"Very well. The daughter that Crispin loves is a tiny, helpless, perfect baby he sent away a long time ago. He holds that picture in a place in his mind that is never touched by the rest of his life. It's like . . . like a beautiful place that you only saw once, for just a moment, and never forgot. Do you know a place like that?"

She nodded.

"Good. You keep that place safe in your memory and cherish it, and for you it is always perfect. The day is always clear and lovely, the temperature always just right— and when you look at that memory, it never disappoints you. So you can love it." Ian sighed. "If you were to go back to that place right now, it would be different. And the longer you stayed, the more different it would become. Sooner or later the weather would grow cold. Flowers would die, rain would fall, storms would blow down the branches of the trees. A fire might rush through and change everything. The place would be the same, but it wouldn't mean the same thing to you anymore. Your cherished memory would be erased. What you had in its place would depend on you. You are a good person, so you would probably find a way to love the real place as much as you loved the memory."

Ulwe was watching his face with the intensity of a hawk watching a mouse. "But my father is not a good person."

"No. He isn't."

"And I'm not a tiny baby anymore."

"No. You aren't."

"I've already done things that will disappoint him."

"Have you?"

She arched an eyebrow and smiled a half-smile, and for just an instant, she looked very old. "I chose to let Ry bring me to all of you, when I could have easily hidden and waited for my father to arrive and claim me. I wasn't ready to meet him. And I'm still not. Somehow, I don't think knowing that will make him very happy."

"You're probably right."

She stood up, a determination on her face that he found almost frightening in its intensity. "Life is full of difficult choices, isn't it?" she said.

He almost laughed, thinking about the quandary he'd been pondering before she joined him. "Life is full of hellish choices."

"He'll be coming after me soon, Ian. He's gone home, but not because he's defeated. I can feel his . . . fury. He's gone home because he thinks he can get help there. He thinks of a brother and a cousin . . . of people who owe him favors . . . of magic. He will use everything in his reach to come after me. He intends to destroy everyone and everything that stands in his way."

Ian's blood chilled at that thought.

Ulwe said, "I have things to do here. But so do you. They need you here, more than they know."

She left without another word, and he looked after her, unsettled. She was a frightening child—she couldn't read minds, but she could read paths. She'd found him in his hiding place, something he hadn't even thought about until that moment. She'd known he was thinking about moving on—she'd sought him out not just for her own comfort but because she had something to tell him that would change his plans.

She was as alone in the world as any child could be—her mother dead, her father someone she needed to fear—and still she managed to be brave and fierce. And kind.

And she was his blood. His kin. Perhaps he could be a father to her, to replace the monster she dared not love too much.

He returned to the weeds, but his thoughts wandered down the mazy paths of the future, looking for signs that would point him in the right direction.

Chapter 25

Did he listen?" Alarista turned from the window and carefully let herself down into a well-padded chair.

Ulwe nodded. "I feel that he'll stay."

"Good. The *zanda* says we must not let him leave." She closed her eyes and rubbed her hands over her frail arms, hating the papery feel of her skin, the stiffness of her joints, the sluggishness of her blood that left her cold even while she sat in the sun, out of the wind.

Ulwe brought her a blanket and helped her wrap it around her shoulders.

"Can you feel your father now?"

"Not really. He is off the road and so am I—the stream no longer connects us."

"We need to go back to the road, then. I need to know if any Falcons come yet—and I need to know what your father is doing, and . . ." Alarista's voice trailed off to nothing. She hated her body—that it could be so frail and useless that a simple walk to the road that began just outside the compound could defeat her.

"If you want to sleep for a while, I'll wait," Ulwe said. "Or I can go now, and check, and come back to tell you. I know what Falcon magic feels like now. If any Falcons are coming to us who are not hidden by their shields, I'll be able to find them for you."

"Please. I fear we have so little time. I'll . . . just rest here while you're gone."

Ulwe nodded. "I'll bring you something to eat when I come back."

"I'm not very hungry."

"I know. But Dùghall says you have to eat anyway."

"Bring me some fruit. It doesn't hurt my stomach the way other things do."

"I'll find you some lovely fruit." Ulwe gave her a bright smile and ran out the door.

Alarista looked after her, wistful. Being with Ulwe, she missed her own youth—the boundless energy, the unquenchable hope, the certainty that somehow she would find solutions to every problem. Adulthood shined an ugly light on such childish optimism—at that moment she faced a problem that would probably be her death. If other Falcons did not answer the call that she had put out, and quickly, she would have to be the third in Dùghall's and Kait's *thathbund*, and the strain of that would kill her.

She didn't fear death—Hasmal waited for her beyond the prison of her flesh, and she yearned for her return to him with an impatience she shared with no one. But she feared that if she died too soon, the task she had to complete—the task that no one else could accomplish—would remain undone. Then her life would be a failure.

She wished she could remember what that task was. That imperative had been so clear when she floated beyond the Veil. She'd known it—and though it had been daunting, she'd been sure she could return and carry it out. Back in the newly ancient and decaying flesh of her body, though, the crystal clarity of the realm beyond death vanished in a haze of muddled thoughts, bodily needs, pains, and hungers. What did she still have to do? The *zanda* would not tell her. Summoned Speakers would not tell her, and the strain of summoning them had weakened her to the point where she dared not try again. Dùghall did not know and his magic could not find it out for her, either.

She closed her eyes to think, with the warmth of the sun pouring onto her skin and the soft blanket wrapped around her shoulders. She fought to connect with the answers she had once known. And once again her flesh defeated her.

She slept.

anth turned to Ry and said, "You think she holds the patent on stubbornness and stupidity, but she isn't the one who left."

Jaim said, "Eat the damned food before it spoils. It's no pleasure watching you stalking across the floor like a caged beast, wasting away to nothing."

Ry paced the floor, gray-faced and dead-eyed. "I gave up everything I had to be with her. My home, my position, my family, my future. But she wasn't satisfied with that—she wanted me to give up myself, too, and I won't do that."

Yanth said, "She was wrong. We've been over that more times than I want to think about. She was wrong, you were right . . . but *you left*. You're the one who said, 'You aren't worth spending any more time on. I decree that our problems can't be fixed. Good-bye.' So you can't complain about the fact that she didn't run after you. If you cared, you would have stayed."

"I did care," Ry growled.

"*Excellent* way to show it," Yanth said.

"Both of you shut up. Ry—sit down and eat. Yanth—don't antagonize him. I'm sick of this subject. I'm sick of your fighting. I'm sick of both of you, if truth be told."

Ry and Yanth both turned on Jaim. "Then you can leave, if truth be told," Ry said. "No one barred the door."

And Yanth said, "I'll show you the way out if you'd like."

Jaim said, "I *can* leave. Unlike you, Ry. I'm not Family or *barzanne*. No mob is hunting me for the one—no zealot will want my skin for being the other. No one is going to take me out for a day or three of public torture before ripping me into pieces and nailing the pieces to the city wall just for being in this damnable city. Look out there." He pointed to the window, half-shuttered, that opened onto the bay. "There are ships out there. Ships. We could be on one of them, bound anywhere, and not shut in here hiding because you don't dare show your face in the street."

"I won't leave the city."

"Why? Because she might come to you and tell you how wrong she was and how sorry she is?" Jaim stood up and stared at his friend. "She isn't going to do that. She was wrong until you left—but when you walked through the gates and didn't go back, you ended things. You closed the door on her apologies. You told her nothing else she could say mattered to you. So if you want to hear what she has to say, you're going to have to go to her to hear it."

Ry was quiet for a long time. "I can't go back," he said at last.

Yanth snorted. "You *can*. Your legs work. We can climb the damned mountain and knock on the damned gate. You just don't want to, because if we go back up there, then it's her turn to decide whether she wants to open the gate or not—and you don't want to find out she won't open it."

And Ry thought, Yes, that's probably true. He'd left her with a hellish chore waiting for her—destroying the Mirror of Souls—and he'd made it clear that he wouldn't do the thing he had to do to help her destroy it. He'd refused to become a Falcon with her. He didn't understand what had gotten into him—he'd been upset with her, but he'd *never* intended to say the things that he'd ended up saying.

Which wasn't to say he hadn't meant them. He had. But if she was wrong for wanting him to give up being a Sabir, perhaps he was wrong for not caring if his presence offended the last surviving members of her Family. Being suddenly without Family of his own, he found it hard to care about her relationships with her relatives.

Which was simple jealousy, and petty of him.

In the end, though, the thing that decided him was the same thing that had let him walk through the gate—she hadn't tried to stop him. He could see where he had been wrong to leave. But if she had truly loved him—if she had felt about him the way he felt about her—she would not have let him walk through the gates and out of her life without making some attempt to make him change his mind.

His head hurt, and his body ached as if he'd spent two days Shifted and hadn't eaten after. He turned to Yanth and Jaim, wishing that she would come through the door right then, knowing that she was still back in Galweigh House, not coming after him. Not going to fight for *them*. He said, "We're leaving Calimekka. Get us transportation."

Jaim and Yanth exchanged wary glances, and Yanth said, "Where do you want to go?"

Ry turned his back to them. "Do you think I care? Do you think I'll *ever* care? Just make the arrangements to get us out of here."

He heard only the faint clinks of coin-filled purses being tied into belts, and the soft click of the door as it opened, then shut. When he turned around, they were gone.

Chapter 27

The Army of the Thousand Peoples rolled northward, into warmer terrain, into the embrace of land not always hunkered against the onslaught of ice and snow and darkness. It passed the Wizards' Circles that had once been the lustrous cities of a great civilization, and that had become glassy sheets of water that cried out with the voices of the dead. The army walked first west, then north, gathering soldiers and believers, clearing villages of their young and strong and hopeful, growing huge. And hungry.

The Army of the Thousand Peoples became a plague on the land, swarming like the poisonleapers that hatched every thirty-one years and flew through the air in clouds so thick they blotted out the sun. Where the army passed, the land lay bare, stripped of everything edible, both animal and vegetable. It grew—from ten thousand to fifteen thousand to twenty thousand—and it crawled inexorably forward.

And then, on the rough and rocky banks of the Glasburg Sea, where once, in the city named Glasburg, a million people had danced in perfumed streets and strolled down grassy lanes between gleaming white arches and delicate spires, it came to rest. It foraged from the sobbing sea, and from the cruel and twisted land. And it waited. Patiently. Hungrily. In sight of the southernmost borders of Ibera, in sight of the promised land.

For the final miracle on which it waited had not yet come to pass.

Chapter 28

Kait knelt in the darkened chapel with Dùghall by her side. She wore a simple gray tunic with fitted sleeves and fitted gray suede breeches, and at Dùghall's insistence, no shoes. Dùghall had told her that she must wear no jewelry, nor any other metal, and that her hair should be bound back in a braided bun that could not move around—and that she must accomplish that without the use of the silver pins and clips she preferred. She'd wrapped the ends with linen thongs and twisted the long braid around two long wooden sticks, and tried to imagine why it could matter.

Dùghall, similarly attired, but wearing shoes, dropped easily into cross-legged repose across from her. "You're certain you want to do this?"

She nodded.

He began pulling implements and powders and long, hair-thin silver needles from a rolled kit. He unwrapped a roll of black silk and spread it between the two of them. It had a large divided circle embroidered in silver thread in the center, with a single glyph centered in each section. "The *zanda*," he said, and passed a handful of heavy silver coins to her. "When I tell you to, drop these into the center, from about here." He held his arms straight out in front of him, pantomiming the motion he wanted.

She nodded again.

He gave her a searching look and said, "If you aren't sure about this, it will just waste your time and mine. You will not become a Falcon unless it is something you truly desire."

"It is something I desire," she said softly.

"But . . . ?"

She clinked the coins from one hand to the other, eyes closed. "He left Calimekka," she said. "He's on a ship headed to the New Territories right now. He's gone, and I've lost him." The coins clinked faster.

Dùghall put a hand on her arm. "Don't damage those," he said. "I've had them a long time."

She opened her eyes and stared at him. "Did you hear me?"

"Of course I heard you. You didn't expect him to stay in Calimekka, did you? Think what would have happened to him if he'd been found here."

"But he's gone."

"For now. Things change, Kait. He's alive and you're alive, and life and hope ever embrace."

She straightened her shoulders. "Yes. And meanwhile, I'm ready."

"I hope so," he said. Then he smiled at her. "I'm sure you are. I simply wish it didn't come as such a shock, that first moment."

"I don't see why. You've warned me about it."

He chuckled. "Words are not the thing itself. If they were, life would be so much simpler. Well, we might as well begin. Close your eyes and breathe deeply. And hold those damned coins still. That racket you're making will drive me mad."

She stilled her nervous hands, and the warm coins settled against her skin.

"With your eyes closed, look upward, as if you were looking at the top of your forehead from the inside."

She did as he asked and felt suddenly dizzy, as if she were falling backward. Her pulse thudded in her ears, and the world began to feel far away.

"You are at a crossroads," he told her. "At this branching of the road, you choose to live either for yourself or for others. Down the road of self, there are many other paths that can bring you back to this point if you so desire, and there are many other ways to serve—but once your feet are set upon the Falcon road, there is no turning back. Listen to the voice of your heart and the voice of your soul, asking if this is the road you should follow."

Her knees hurt from kneeling on the hard tiles. The small of her back ached, and her shoulders felt cramped, and she wanted to move around, but Dùghall had impressed in her the importance of maintaining her kneeling position throughout the whole of the ceremony. "It will keep you from getting hurt," he'd said—she'd thought that cryptic, and still wondered what he'd meant. Still uncomfortable with the god Vodor Imrish, she prayed to the gods of Ibera for a sign that the path she sought would be the right one. She listened, but her thoughts refused to still, and any answer she received from the gods was buried in her mind's noisy chatter.

After what seemed to her a very long, uncomfortable, and unprofitable time, Dùghall said, "With your eyes still closed, hold your arms out and drop the coins on the *zanda*, asking for guidance from Vodor Imrish as you do."

She raised her arms and let the coins fall—they hit the silk with a musical clatter. Then she waited.

Dùghall said nothing for a long time.

Then he said, "The Fates would have plans for you no matter which road you choose. You are marked to change your world—marked to touch the lives of those around you—marked to carry a burden from the old era into the new one, but always in secret. You will never be acclaimed a hero by the masses, you will never rule in name, you will never receive praise or thanks for your many sacrifices, though you will be a hero, and you will rule in fact, and you will make great sacrifices throughout your lifetime that will be deserving of great praise. Your life, no matter which road you take, will bear the scars of hardship and want, of pain and loss, and of great regret. You will lose a great friend, and regain a great love." He sighed. "And from all I see before me, the Falcons need you more than you will ever need them. Vodor Imrish watches you with interest and some admiration, because you have chosen never to lean on the comfort or promises of the gods, and have proven time and again that you can make your way without them. Not all lives are bound to the gods—yours is not and never will be, and though you may ally yourself with Vodor Imrish, you will always be a comrade, not a worshiper."

She maintained her posture, eyes closed and focused upward, trying to puzzle out from Dùghall's words whether he was telling her that she should join the Falcons or shouldn't. They needed her more than she needed them. She was destined to rule, but in secret. She was destined to heroism, but in secret. She was to be the comrade of the gods, not a worshiper. She would lose a friend and regain a love.

Oracles annoyed her. She wished that they could offer advice not couched in confusion. She would have liked Dùghall to read the *zanda* and tell her, *The gods decree you are to be a Falcon,* or conversely, *The gods decree that you are not.* Simple, direct, clear.

"I choose the Falcon path," she said at last. No oracle had convinced her, no god had whispered in her ear, and even her soul had failed to offer her compelling reasons for saying yea or nay—in the end, she decided simply because she believed that the Falcons had much to offer the world even without the promise of Paranne, and she wished to add her strength to their numbers.

"Open your eyes, then, and tell me again, for no path should be chosen with eyes closed."

"I choose the Falcon path."

"Then repeat after me," Dùghall said.

"I offer all that is mine to give:
ka-erea—my will;
ka-ashura—my blood;
ka-amia—my flesh;
ka-enadda—my breath;
ka-obbea—my soul . . ."

He paused, and Kait repeated the words after him, feeling weight building in the silence around them. As she enunciated the final *ka*, she felt a presence in the room with them, eyes that watched out of the edges of shadows, ears that listened from a place outside of time.

Dùghall continued.

"And that which is mine I will offer only,
Now and ever.
I will not partake of the *ka* of others,
Nor benefit from *ka* so taken.
I will do no harm by magic,
Either through my action or my inaction,
But if harm is inevitable,
I will choose the path of least harm
And the most good,
Knowing that I am fallible
And that if the path is not clear,
I may err."

Each time he paused and she repeated, the sense of presence grew stronger. She smelled the cold clean scent of fresh-falling snow and felt behind her eyes a vast plain unfolding. Unfamiliar terrain in her mind. Places she had never seen, never imagined, with paths—well trodden—leading off in all directions toward unmarked, unknowable destinations . . . destinations fraught with danger.

> "I will carry the weight of my errors
> On my own soul,
> And bear such punishments
> As magic and the gods mete out
> On my own flesh."

And there the bite of the oath. That mistakes, even mistakes innocently made and with the best of intentions, would stay with her. She could not confer blame or punishment; neither could she escape them. Her mistakes would be hers alone, always. Always.

She could accept that. She had borne the consequences of her own actions all of her life—perhaps not happily, but the oath did not demand of her that she rejoice in punishment. Only that she take it on herself, not pass it off to innocent others. She breathed in and out slowly and repeated the words, feeling the metallic taste of them on her tongue. And as she finished the last word, a light sprang up between her and Dùghall, a soft, cold white flame that flickered on every metal object in the room, casting slender, dancing shadows all around.

Dùghall's eyebrows rose, but he kept going.

> "I will not oppress by magic,
> Nor be party to such oppression,
> Nor view such oppression and fail
> To act in the benefit of the oppressed,
> Though it cost me all that I have
> And all that I am;
> For I will hold life sacred,
> Both flesh life and soul life."

She repeated her promise, and the fire grew into a blaze, and somehow, though its color did not change and though it shed no physical heat, it seemed warmer. The scent of snow still hung in the room, and her skin still felt like ice, but somewhere in the back of her mind, a word whispered of spring, and the dancing of buds in an early morning breeze, and the fall of apple blossoms like snow across green meadows, and the rolling of the sea, and salt air sharp and biting against her face . . . and somewhere, somewhere, green and growing and lush and rich with decay and rebirth, her own beloved jungles, riotous with life, steadily green, fecund, powerful. Her own power, her own memories, to add to those odd and frightening memories of strangers, her own essence to add to the stream, for every bit of water that flows changes the shape of the river, and her life, her presence, would carve out a bit of bank, wear away the corner of a pebble, feed the roots of a tree, and she would pass on, changed, too.

She felt all of that within breathe in and breathe out, and felt, too, a sense of belonging that was alien to her very soul.

You are us, we are you.

And Dùghall, clearing his throat, starting, stopping, starting again, pain in his face, but also wonder—and certainly he felt what she felt, the touch of the river that welcomed her into its flow. Changes came already—she felt them against her skin, inside her blood, in the chirring of the tiny bones within her ears.

"And . . . I will hold fast
To the vision of Solander,
That all people are bound together by love
Now and forever.
I will hold Paranne
Within my heart.
For if it must be a dream withheld,

Still it is a star by which
I may steer my life."

New words, a new promise, a new branching of the
stream, and she said the words and the blaze filled the room,
blotting out all vision, and the river embraced her and the
water flowed in that new way, to that new place that still
went to the sea. Life, the sea . . . and blinded by the flame
that was a thousand years of lives and deaths, her mind
showed her bloodshed and childbirth and parade and battle-
ground and hearthfire; her skin felt gentle kiss and thrust of
passion and stab of blade and lash of whip; her ears rang
with song and whisper and lie and scream; her tongue tasted
poison and feast and thin gruel; her heart knew fury and
vengeance and comfort and love.

And acceptance. She was not alone. Never again alone.
She was part of life, and had always been, but now she was
the river and not the riverbank. Now she was shaper and not
shaped. Now she was found, who had never known before
how deeply lost she had been in the corridors of her own
mind.

You are us, we are you.

Fire was her blood, her breath was richest purple and
truest green, her heart beat roses, and every faintest whisper in the world humped and skittered and slithered and
strolled before her in shape and color and scent and taste reborn a living thing.

And in that pageant, that maelstrom, that wonder, a soli-
tary cry of pain.

No! Don't leave me.

Over that, louder—as the crashing of the sea is louder
than the falling of a single drop of water onto a leaf in a
rain-soaked forest—the great susurration of the body that
enfolded her. *You are us, we are you.* Wordless, soundless,
and nonetheless immense, bone-melting, skin-searing,
sense-drowning . . . and wonderful. So wonderful.

You are us.

We are you.

And the desire, the hunger, the blind, seeking, nuzzling, pleading, raw-edged *want* to be part of that, part of that, part of that, when that was the thing she had never had, never been, knew she could never be. Part of a group, part of a herd, part of the masses. One of many, not one alone. Never one alone again. To heal the hurt of her losses—her family, her greater Family, her childhood, her pain at being Scarred, and finally her abandonment by Ry.

And that single drop of water fell on that single wet leaf in that distant stand of trees that whispered again, and again she felt its movement, heard its soft plink, saw it shimmering in her mind: *You were not alone with me.*

She rose from the depths, slowly, as if from a deep and bewitching dream. She rose, shaking layers of warmth from her skin and her soul. She rose, leaving behind the alien vistas of a thousand years, the sweet touches of welcoming brothers and sisters, the gentle lulling rocking embrace of that timeless, waterless sea. She rose because that single tiny voice called her—against time, against the tides of eternity, against even her own desires—and let her see herself as she was. She could hear the calling of that voice, and that set her apart, made her unlike others, gave her both individual identity and distance.

She was Karnee, born strong, raised to be alone, destined to be a hunter. A protector . . . or a predator.

But never, never, never part of the herd.

The soft and muffling comfort of Falcon souls fell away completely; she was above them then, as if she stood on the churning surface of the water. She could still dip into that storm of memories and thoughts and hopes and fears, but she would not be a part of it again. She was no longer the riverbank, but neither was she the river; she had become the sailor—on the water, but never truly part of it.

Her vision cleared, and she was once again in the close,

dark room with her uncle, kneeling on the hard tile floor, her knees sore and her back aching. The instep of her right foot burned, and she had to fight the urge to change position, to twist around to see what had caused that pain.

Dùghall shook his head and smiled at her. "I should have realized," he said.

She waited for clarification, but none came.

Annoyance pricked her, and she gave vent to it. "What should you have realized?"

"That the Falcons would never swallow you. You could no more lose yourself in the comfort of others than I could fly."

"Ry called to me when I was in there," she said.

Dùghall shook his head. "He couldn't have. Nothing can break through the sound of those voices when they have hold of you. . . ." He looked at his hands. "But you aren't me. They don't compel you as they do me."

Kait said, "That was the place you came back from, wasn't it? When the Reborn died and you sank into trance, that was the place where you were hiding."

"Yes . . . but it was not the warm and comforting place you felt. It was full of despair then. It was . . ." He shook his head, lost for words. "It was a sea trying to swallow itself. It was hell, and I was lost in it."

She considered that for a moment, and said, "You were strong to come back from there."

"I was. The only thing more seductive than your own self-pity is self-pity you share with your entire group. You did well to get my attention."

She thought a moment longer. "So . . . am I a Falcon, then, or am I not?"

He said, "You are. You've been marked." He pointed to the silver needles that had lain beside the *zanda* when the two of them began. They were twisted into knots and lumps, unrecognizable. "The Falcons marked your skin with silver—somewhere. The place will be unique to you, but the mark will be the same."

And she thought of the pain in her right foot, and said, "Dare I move?"

"Now you can."

Gratefully she shifted position and, cross-legged, studied her right instep. The mark on the skin was blue, deep, but clear. A circle no bigger than the pad of her thumb, with a stylized falcon within it. The falcon plummeted from the sky, beak open, wings cupping the air to slow his descent, talons spread to catch his prey.

She angled her foot and showed him her mark, and he stared at it for a moment, and swore softly, and then he began to laugh. He peeled his shirt off, and twisted his left arm around until she could see the pale skin of his underarm. The small blue circle marked him, too—but the falcon silhouetted in his circle sat in profile, talons clutching a branch.

"This is the mark of every Falcon I have ever seen. Yours is different; they acknowledge that you're different. A new kind of Falcon."

"And what sort of Falcon am I?"

"That I don't know."

"Why a mark?" she asked him. "It seems to me only a good way to be found out and executed, especially since you can feel each other's presence within that . . ." She couldn't find a word to describe the sea of souls that had flowed over her.

"Falcons call it *sha-obbea*."

Our soul. "Yes, then . . . why the mark, since you can touch each other within *sha-obbea*?"

"Several reasons. First, because most Falcons cannot sort out an individual soul within the mass of *sha-obbea*. Second, because almost always, even for those Falcons who can, we have been forced by danger to stay shielded. Even when we met—sometimes especially when we met—

we dared not enjoin *sha-obbea* because of the danger of sudden magical attacks if we lowered our shields. The marks—well, you feel a burning in your foot."

"Yes."

"That burning tells you another Falcon is nearby. The mark isn't terribly sensitive—the burning doesn't get stronger as you near a Falcon, or weaker as you move away. It is either there or it isn't, and the range has always seemed excessive to me. There have been times in my life when I've occupied a city for months, and have felt the presence of another Falcon, and have sought him or her without success. We might have been on the same street, or only in the same district, with our paths never crossing."

"You have no safe way of reaching each other?"

"We have ways. They are awkward, but in times of extreme danger, when no shield can be lowered, they work well enough. A bit of graffiti scrawled on the corner of a public building, a crier hired to call for a lost lover, with the code phrase 'I burn for you' inserted in his message. In any case, when we meet, mostly we exchange the Falcon words of greeting. That is usually enough. If we doubt, we show our marks."

"It's a simple enough design," Kait said. "I should think it would be easy to forge."

"Hold your foot close to my arm."

"What?"

"Hold your foot close to my arm."

Kait raised her foot, moving the instep toward Dùghall's mark. Suddenly, when the two marks were less than a hand span apart, a brilliant blast of light erupted between them. She yelped and pulled her foot back, and Dùghall laughed.

"Not so simple to forge after all, eh?"

"Well, *that* must be awkward on the streets."

"Never happen. Clothes, shoes . . . they block the spark." He began gathering up his supplies and storing them. She noticed that he cleaned the coins before he put them in the bag, that all of them had been horribly tarnished, though they had gleamed before her trance. And that he didn't just drop them in when he'd finished, but placed them carefully. He glanced up at her, noticed her watching, and smiled. "Good tools are precious things." He scooped up the ruins of the silver needles and handed them to her. "You'll make your own. These will become the silver coins for your *zanda*. You'll have to create that, too. I'll give you such guidance as I can, but no two are alike. That way, no one else can ever use what they've learned from another Falcon to tamper with your tools, or twist what the *zanda* tells you. But that is for later. For now—Alarista awaits us."

Kait realized then what he had not told her before. The three of them were going after the Mirror of Souls immediately.

Chapter 29

I don't like the look of this place," Yanth said.

Jaim rested a hand on the pommel of his sword and glowered, which would have made him look more imposing had he not then sneezed. "Hellish pighole."

They'd put ashore in the New Territories, in Heymar, a rough coastal trading city run by the Heymar Galweighs, who from all accounts were little better than pirates and thugs. Riches came through Heymar, but it didn't look to Ry like they stopped there. The houses were almost all built of poorly made mud brick with roofs thatched instead of shingled; the streets ran to mud and deeper mud, with a few planks strewn over the worst bogs to keep unsuspecting strollers from falling in at night and drowning; the air—redolent of night soil—told of a place where the locals' preferred treatment of raw sewage was to throw it out into the street on unwary passersby. The women ran from merely bedraggled to downright ugly, and the men started at ugly and got progressively worse from there. Everyone wore a sword, or a sword and daggers, and Ry thought that if the weapons looked to be of poor quality, they would probably still kill a man well enough. And there were Scarred in the streets, too, with misshapen bodies and unreadable faces and eyes that watched everything.

"I think we ought to find a place to stay for the night," Ry said, "and by tomorrow morning be sure we are on our way away from here." He'd wrapped the pommel of his sword so the Sabir crest wouldn't show—he thought it alone would be enough to give mortal affront in such a rough place as Heymar. He wore commoners' clothing—coarse homespun breeches and a thick wool shirt that itched abominably. He could walk with a slouch to hide his fighter's body and his fighter's gait. He'd darkened his hair to a muddy brown with dye. But nothing would hide his pale eyes or the angle of his jaw or the shape of his face. He looked Sabir still, and he knew it.

Yanth smiled coldly, the scars on his cheeks blanching white when he did. "We could find some sport here, I think, without looking too hard for it. My blade hasn't fed on any blood but mine in far too long."

Ry glanced over at him and said mildly, "And if you think they'd fight you for sport here, you're madder than poor Valard."

The mention of their absent friend who, possessed by some demonic spirit, had fallen into the employ of Ry's mother and betrayed him to her, erased the smile from Yanth's face. "I've not gone that mad," he said after a moment. "I simply tire of all this running and hiding and hiding and running. I want an enemy I can fight."

Ry nodded. "I know. I do, too. I'd love to see a familiar face in these streets. Donnauk, maybe, or Kithmejer." He referred to rivals he and his men had crossed blades with back in Calimekka, in the days when the world still seemed sane.

"Donnauk!" Yanth turned to Ry, eyes unfocused, voice soft and dreamy, and quoted:

"You say I would do nothing for you? Lies!
For I would set a thousand babes-in-arms afire

To light your footsteps into hell.
Thus do you mark me—and if that is not caring,
I know not care and never shall."

Ry stared down at his boots sinking into the mire and thought for a moment. His lips pursed in frustration, and at last he shrugged. "Seems vaguely familiar."

Yanth's eyebrows rose. "Oseppe to his arch-enemy You-rul in *The Dancing Blades of Wiwar.* We saw it twice while the players were in town—don't you remember? The swordplay was particularly good, especially the part where the captain of the guards swings across the stage on a curtain and . . . ah, never mind. Your thoughts are still in Calimekka. I simply recalled those lines because I always wanted to say that to Donnauk when we met again . . . but of course we never did. I used to practice that speech before the mirror."

Ry was startled. "You did?"

"So that I could sound right when I said it. Get the words all out coldly, you know, and with the proper degree of fierceness. And so I wouldn't stumble over them. That would have ruined the effect. I thought I'd say them just as we crossed blades, but before we began to fight in earnest."

Jaim snorted. "I can just see you in front of your mirror, trying to decide which shirt would best complement the color of Donnauk's blood, and striking poses with your blade. 'Ah, Donnauk . . . a bit of poetry before I skewer you.'" He struck a foppish pose, then laughed.

"And if you weren't my friend, I'd skewer you for that," Yanth said, face flushed.

"Then thank the gods my luck still holds and I remain unskewered." Jaim sighed. "I don't hunger for blood. But I would love to have a plan."

Ry laughed. "Here's your plan. We'll find an inn for the night, and food for our bellies, and on the morrow we'll walk back to the harbor—"

"Swim, on these roads," Yanth muttered.

"—and take passage elsewhere on the first ship that will accept us." So he told them, but his true plan was different. He was too far from Kait—across a sea, with his feet on the wrong continent. The pull between them wore at him like an unreachable itch, disturbing his sleep, invading his waking hours. For a terrible few moments they had pulled her from his grasp and he had known that he lost her—he'd fought back to her, but only through great pain and nightmarish fear.

He'd nearly lost her. No more. If being together those last weeks had been painful, being apart was agony. He intended to be sure that the first ship that would take them would be a ship heading back to Ibera, if not directly to Calimekka.

They trudged up the street under gray skies and a miserable cold drizzle that made the station of the day unguessable, keeping to the center of the street to avoid the rain of anything more noxious than water from the balconies and casement windows overhead. They did not speak, and were not spoken to, but they could feel people watching them, sizing them up, weighing the wealth they might offer against the length of their swords and the breadth of their shoulders. Heymar would have been a bad place to be a stranger alone.

Horses, goats, cattle, and other beasts had preceded them down that central path in the muddy road, leaving it fragrant with their droppings. Wagon wheels had churned it to tenacious soup. By the time they reached the first clearly marked inn, they were gray to midthigh and stank like a barnyard.

A cowbell rattled against the heavy door as they entered the room. The interior of the Long Comfort was bright enough, if smoky. A cheerful fire burned in the hearth and fine brass lamps with glass chimneys made up for the lack of windows. Deep sawdust covered the floor, fragrant of cedar and pine, and the red-painted tables and booths gleamed from recent polishing.

"Take a seat and state your preference," someone called from out of sight. "I'll be with you in a breath."

"Food first, then?" Yanth asked.

Ry noted the many empty booths. "Suits me. And then a place to wash off the dirt."

They took the booth farthest from the door, arranging themselves in it so that they could watch both the entrance and the stairway that led up to the next floor. They kept their swords loose in their scabbards and avoided looking directly at any of the other customers—a sure way to provoke fights among those already in their cups—but some of the customers were exotic enough that it was hard not to stare. The Long Comfort apparently had no qualms about serving the Scarred, for one trestle table nearest the hearth held three of them, along with three humans.

Two of the three Scarred had heavy overlapping scales like those of rattlesnakes, and thick squat bodies; they moved not at all, then so suddenly and quickly that the eye blurred their motions. Ry recognized them by name and reputation—they were called Keshi Scarred, and were said to be brilliant sailors and formidable adversaries, as hard to kill as any snake. The third Scarred he could not place at all.

She—at least he guessed by the delicacy of its features that the creature was female—had skin dark as a starless night, but iridescent as mother-of-pearl. He caught gemstone flashes of amethyst, sapphire, emerald, and ruby every time she turned her face. Her hair was white, almost feathery—stray hairs floated around her head in a nimbus turned golden by the reflected light of the fire—and was incredibly long. She wore a single braid that she looped through her belt like a length of rope; her hair unbound would without question reach the floor and probably could double back again to touch her head, but Ry wondered if, loose, gravity would actually pull it to the floor, or if it would float around her like a cloud. Her eyes were huge, bottomless wells of purest black, and over them arched two snowy eyebrows of the same feathery floating stuff. The eyebrows grew long at the outer corners, and she had braided them, too, and decorated the braids with beads and bits of shell and feathers that hung to the sharp angle of her jaw. Her ears, huge and doelike, swiveled independently. One stayed focused on the people with whom she talked, the other was in constant motion. When she laughed, he caught a glimpse of pointed white teeth. For all the whiteness of her hair, she looked quite young. He'd never seen anyone even remotely like her, yet something in the back of his mind insisted there was something about her that was familiar.

Her eyes flicked over him and away, instant assessment and dismissal. He turned his attention to Yanth and Jaim before staring got him into trouble.

The hostler came out of his back rooms then, arms laden with trays of food. He caught sight of the three of them and said, "With you in a moment." He set the food down in front of the six at the trestle table, and Ry glanced over to see how it looked—it smelled good enough, and he was pleased to see that the servings were large and were presented with a bit of care. He was not pleased to discover that the Scarred woman was staring at him, her expression unreadable but unnerving.

"Now, then," the hostler said, wiping his hands on his white apron as he hurried to their table, "I'm Boscott Shrubber, the owner of this place. My wife Kelje cooks. You'd like a meal? Rooms?"

Ry gave his voice the flat inflection of the Wilhene commoner and said, "Both, I think. The meal first. Then a single room with several cots—we haven't much money; we'll have to save what we have. Perhaps a bath if the cost is not too high." He studied Shrubber while he spoke. The man was of average height, but, for all the corded muscles in his hands and forearms, bore a slightness of bone and frame that spoke of years of hard times and missed meals. He wore a beard and bright tattoos on both cheeks, and within the right tattoo, Ry noticed the scars of an old brand. Though much of the brand had been removed and the rest had been tattooed over, he recognized what remained. The brand would have once been two stylized trees—and Boscott Shrubber would have once been a Sabir slave. Ry made a note of the mark but was careful not to stare—time and circumstances changed for many men. If Shrubber had once been property, he was no longer. And if Ry had once owned property, he did no longer.

Shrubber nodded. "We have a good room in the attic— two beds and a sturdy door with a solid lock—I can put a third cot in there if you don't object to being cramped. I give better rates by the week than by the day, and better rates by the month than by the week, and if you help out with the heavy work around the place, I'll make your price even better." He sighed. "If you're looking for short work, the Galweighs are hiring up at the big house right now— tree-felling in the forests, and some packing of cargo to go south. Runners just came in to say the next traders' caravan will arrive in two days—we'll have work and plenty then for a week or so."

"We're sailors," Ry said. "We're looking for places aboard a good ship."

Shrubber sighed and turned away. "They always are. The ones with good backs move on, and the ones too broken down to be of worth stay." He glanced back at them. "*Sailors*. Listen, you—I'll have no whoring in my house, and no gambling, and no loud noises or late nights. If you've come ashore for that, there are places nearer the water's edge that will give you satisfaction."

When he'd vanished back into the kitchen, Jaim laughed. "You disappointed him," he said. "I believe he fancied us as permanent boarders."

"Didn't fancy us so much when you told him we were sailors," Yanth said. "And why did you—"

Ry tapped him on the wrist and shook his head in warning not to continue. He had been about to ask why Ry had called them sailors when they were nothing of the kind. The Scarred woman had her ears cocked in their direction, though, and Ry could feel her interest in them.

Yanth, quick to pick up the signals, changed the direction of his question. "—not get us separate rooms? Surely we could have afforded them for a single night."

"We don't know if we'll only be here a night. We might not find a ship that will hire us on for a week, or maybe a month. I thought it best that we not spend what we have too quickly." He inclined his head slightly toward the table where the woman sat, and saw first Yanth, then Jaim, find excuses to look in that direction.

When Shrubber brought the beer, Jaim spilled a bit of his on the table, and with his finger wrote, "They're all watching us now. Why?"

Ry shrugged. He listened to them talk, his Karnee hearing picking up much more than they could suspect, but they were discussing matters aboard their ship, and had said nothing that might explain their interest in Ry or Yanth or Jaim. Finally, though, while they waited for the sack-puddings they'd ordered, the woman said, "He looks familiar."

"He has Ian's look about him. The same bones, the same height."

The Scarred woman said, "I believe you're right. That is who he reminds me of."

"But he isn't Draclas. He's nothing but a ruffian."

A knot twisted in Ry's stomach, and suddenly his appetite was gone.

"Of course not." The woman was picking at a flake of red paint on the table with the point of her dagger. "He has the look of my Ian, but not his bearing."

"*Your* Ian? If it hadn't been for—"

The conversation ended abruptly with the sound of a boot kicking hard into a shin and the Scarred woman giving a long, thoughtful look at the man who'd almost dared to question her; the next instant, the six at the trestle table rose as one and called out the hostler. They settled their account quickly, refusing their puddings, claiming they had forgotten they were due back at their ship, and raced out the door at a pace that tried to look like a walk, but gave the impression of being a run.

When they were gone, Ry asked Jaim and Yanth, "Did you catch any of that?"

"Those six hurrying off? I thought it looked odd, but I have no idea what sent them out the door in such a hurry."

"I did," Ry said. He pursed his lips. They might not be who he thought they were, but Kait had described the cabin girl on the *Peregrine* to him more than once, in bitter tones. The woman fit that description. The Scarred woman in turn had spoken of an Ian Draclas, and in the past tense, and had remarked on his resemblance to that captain. Ry was willing to consider the possibility of coincidence, but if she was the bitch responsible for abandoning Kait in Novtierra, he'd kill her. "I think they were part of the crew that mutinied against Ian and marooned him and Kait in Novtierra."

"You jest," Jaim said.

"It should be easy enough to find out. If the *Peregrine* is docked here, I'm betting they'll be on it."

Yanth sat still as a stone for one long moment. Then his eyes met Ry's and he smiled. "I'm thinking my blade will have the meal it hungers for after all."

"I'm thinking if those are the bastards who left Kait to die, your blade may have more of a meal than it can finish. If that *is* her, she's mine. I'll rip her throat out with my teeth."

"Considering we are only three, and may stand against a whole shipload of them, I'm thinking we're likely to die before your teeth get anywhere near her throat," Jaim said. "I mention this not because I think you'll listen, but because I'd like to think the gods heard me pointing out a sensible course of action to you when I have to explain to them how I came to die in such a fool's mission."

Ry laughed softly. "I'm sure the gods are shaking their heads in agreement."

Chapter 30

Kait went into Alarista's room; she'd been in her
chair, where she sat almost all the time, a blanket wrapped
around her shoulders, her head tipped back in sleep. Her
skin was so thin it was almost transparent, her white hair
wispy and thin—a far cry from the thick red mane she'd
had before she gave her youth to Dùghall.

Kait rested her hand on the old woman's shoulder and
felt the fragile bones so clearly she almost pulled her hand
back. "Alarista? Alarista? Wake up. It's time."

The eyes opened—cloudy eyes now, no longer clear
and alert—and Alarista coughed and wheezed and sat up.

"Time?"

Kait nodded. "I am Falcon now."

The old woman managed a smile that, for a moment,
erased the years from her face. "*Katarre kaithe gombrey;
hai allu neesh?*" It was the Falcon greeting, part of a rit-
ual and a language that had survived in secret for a thousand years. It meant, *The Falcon offers its wings; will you
fly?*

"*Alla menches, na gombrey ambi kaitha chamm,*" Kait
said, struggling a bit to remember the response. *I accept,
and for the falcon's wings I offer my heart.*

"Those were almost the first words Hasmal and I said to each other," Alarista said. "They marked us. They changed us. The Falcon offers its wings, but there is a price to be paid for flight." She coughed again, leaning forward as she did—her lips turned blue and her face turned a dusky tinge that frightened Kait. When she finally straightened herself in her chair, she said, "I hate being old. It's hell. Nothing works, my body won't listen to me anymore, I have to think even to breathe."

Kait wished she could let Alarista go back to sleep. But she couldn't. Dùghall had pushed her to get Alarista right then, certain that they were almost out of time, that the Mirror of Souls tired of its captive state and grew restless and hungry for change, that he could feel it beginning to stir in the locked room deep in the heart of Galweigh House.

So Kait offered her arm, and Alarista, after only an instant's hesitation, took it. They moved slowly through the House, Alarista having to stop often to catch her breath, Kait waiting with well-concealed impatience and a growing sense of dread. The old woman was too frail to serve as third for their *thathbund*. Dùghall had been working hard—he had the spell prepared that he thought would restore Alarista's youth to her and return him to his old self, but he dared not try it until after the Mirror of Souls was safely destroyed. Alarista's magical skills were different from his—if a soul of some sort remained in the Mirror that had to be channeled through a living body and out into the Veil, which Dùghall and Kait had come to believe was the case, he could do what needed to be done. Alarista could not.

"After we've . . . finished," Kait said, dreading even then to mention the Mirror out loud, "Dùghall is going to try to give you back your youth."

Alarista, stooped and stiff, looked up at Kait slowly. "I gave freely. He doesn't have to give it back."

"He knows. But I don't think he's comfortable being young anymore. He says the guilt is a heavier burden than the years."

Alarista chuckled. "He's an idiot—or he's already forgotten what this feels like. I'd keep the youth and take the guilt—but if he feels differently, I won't complain." She wheezed, caught her breath, and added, "Maybe youth will clear my memory—I know I have tasks yet to accomplish, but on my life I swear I cannot recall what they are."

They went down and yet farther down, deep into the House's secret recesses, to find Dùghall waiting before the locked door. "Hurry," he said. "It's waiting in there for us. It's awake."

He slid his fingers into the fingerlocks warily; one mistake in placement and the door mechanism would cut all of them off. He made no error, though, and the heavy lock clicked, and the door slid open.

Hellish red light illuminated the treasure room; it poured up through the central soulwell of the Mirror of Souls in a tight, blindingly bright beam that seemed to cut into the ceiling.

"Oh, gods," Kait whispered.

Dùghall said, "This is the light you saw before?"

"Yes. When it summoned the Sabirs who hunted us, when we were escaping through the Thousand Dancers. It shattered the shield I'd cast around us and it."

"I would guess the structure of the House is of little consequence to it," Dùghall said. "No doubt a beacon burns from the top of the mountain now, letting all of Calimekka know someone is here."

"It isn't calling everyone," Kait said. She felt certain of this—dark memories that had never belonged to her still lurked in the quiet corners of her mind. "It's calling Crispin Sabir. He has enough of the Dragon Dafril still inside of him to know how to use it—and he is enough like Dafril to want what it has to offer."

"It's found us out," Alarista agreed.

Dùghall stood with his head bowed, adding to the shield he'd created around himself. "I'd hoped to take it by surprise."

"Well, we didn't. So now we fight it strength to strength," Alarista said. Kait looked at her, surprised. Suddenly she didn't look so old, or so weak. Her eyes burned with determination, her spine straightened, and in the garish red light, her color looked almost healthy.

Dùghall said, "The *thathbund,* then."

The three of them moved close together, and Dùghall extended his shield to embrace both Alarista and Kait. The shield would come down when they finished the binding spell that would call the power of all willing Falcons to them, and they would be vulnerable then to whatever evils the Mirror could throw at them, but while they cast the spell, they had some protection.

Dùghall, Kait, and Alarista, holding hands to form a ring, closed their eyes and sought to connect their souls within the space of the Veil. Bound by touch of flesh and soul, they then cried out the words of the spell enjoining *thathbund*—words both ancient and fraught with need, testament to the great terrors and dangers that Falcons had faced from the first.

> *"Gombreyan enenches!*
> *Inyan ha neith elleyari . . ."*

The old tongue, lost except to Falcons, with power embedded in the words, from the thousands of souls that had spoken them, had heard them, had heeded them, in the thousand years of Falconry.

"Falcons, heed us!
Now in the station of our need,
Now as we stand in mortal danger,
Now as our enemies threaten
And death beckons,
We call *thathbund*.
We summon all willing souls,
We entreat all who would
Pit themselves against the
Reign of evil,
We call all who would hear and fight.
Come now!
Come now!
Come now!"

The entreaty was short, the response swift. Kait felt the river of souls that ran beneath her feet swell up to embrace her again. The shield that had protected her shattered, blown away like thinnest spun glass by the mighty upwelling. Her body felt hot and cold all at once; it seemed to vibrate; it seemed to float in a place with neither walls nor doors, floors nor ceilings. It was a place unmarked except for the red light that blazed like a flaming sword just ahead of her. She could see Dùghall, but though she knew him to be Dùghall, he looked nothing like the lean, dark-haired man who held her hand in the world of flesh. Dùghall stood like a fire-haired god to her left, a dark giant whose every step scattered sparks as he moved toward the Mirror's ghastly beacon. To her right Alarista stood, and she, too, was a giant, a glowing goddess formed of cold white light, youthful once more, taut-fleshed and unstoppable. Between them, Kait was a small creature, fragile, slow, and uncertain. Thus she discovered that in the realm of magic, she, who had feared Alarista would become the weak link in the chain, had herself become that weak link.

The souls of the other Falcons fed into them, and all of them grew bigger, stronger, brighter—but Kait could not shape the magic that she received with the skill that her partners could. She could not accept everything that was offered to her. She remained smaller, weaker—and she felt the mind of the Mirror drawn to her.

She would be the point of attack. If she failed, they would all fail.

In the world of flesh, the three of them had moved to surround the Mirror, their hands linked around it. They did not touch it, but its energy pressed against them, seeking weakness. Within the Veil, the Mirror's beacon changed form. It gathered itself into the shape of a winged man with eyes of fire and claws like knives. It grinned at them, and blue lightning struck it from a hundred different directions, and it began to expand. It fed itself from the lives of the Calimekkans, using their strength as its own. It stretched out a hand, and the knives of its claws glittered like diamonds, and it spoke directly to Kait. "Come, we have nothing to fight about, you and I. You have lost your love, your family, your past—but you need not lose your life, and you need no longer be a monster. I can give you that which you most desire. I can give you humanity."

Dùghall said, "You can give nothing. You can only steal."

Alarista said nothing, but she shoved against the monstrous soul of the Mirror, trying to break the lines through which it sucked out the lives of the people in the city below.

Kait said, "I want nothing you have to offer."

But the pictures were in her head, brighter than the voices of the Falcons who held her up—pictures of her soul inside the smooth curves and seductive lines of a perfect human body. A body that would never Shift to beast, would never dip a long muzzle into the raw gore of some still-twitching carcass and lap up its blood, a body that

would never shame her with its crude desires, its crude
wants, its crude form. She would not fly as a human, but
neither would she crawl. She would not taste the heights
of Karnee ecstasy, but neither would she bear the ugly
dullness that weighted her down after Shift. Her Scars
would be gone. Her pain, forgotten.

The threat of death that hung over her head . . . lifted.

Human.

She could be human.

The souls of the Falcons cried out, telling her that she
was one of them, but though she was Falcon, she had set
herself apart. No Falcon before her had ever been Scarred.
No Falcon before her had ever borne the mark she bore,
the mark that told her she was different even in the one
place where she could have hoped to find complete acceptance.

Dafril's memories were in her head—the simple task of
switching bodies with the use of the Mirror came to her as
clear as if she had done it herself. No one would die, no
one would truly bear hurt—she would give her body to a
stranger, and the stranger would give her body to Kait. No
loss—simply . . . change. The press of a few glyphs and
her pain would be a thing of the past.

"Stand with me," the Mirror's soul said. "No need for
destruction. No need for suffering. I offer good things,
good gifts, good magic. They are yours to take."

No voice could reach her through the powerful wall the
Mirror's soul created. Dùghall was silenced. Alarista was
silenced. The uncounted souls of Falcons living and dead
could not touch her in the place where she stood, faced
with the one dream she had never dared speak. She realized that what the Mirror offered her, she could truly have.
She realized that the gift would be real—not trickery. And
she realized that no one could stop her from taking it if she
chose to do so. She was free—truly free—free in a way

that no other Falcon could ever have been, for no other Falcon had ever stood beyond the bonds of Falconry.

My difference is my strength, she thought. Strength to do what I want, to find new paths, to go where I choose free from the imposed guilt of uncountable ghosts.

She looked at what was offered, tempted beyond words. To be human, to be acceptable, to have a place in the world that was hers by birthright—she would give anything to have that. Anything that truly belonged to her.

But she would not take what was not hers.

I am Falcon, she thought. Even if I stand apart from all other Falcons, I am Falcon still, sworn by oath to give only what is mine to give, to take only that which is freely offered.

"Somewhere, dear girl," the soul of the Mirror said, "there is a woman who would give up her body willingly to have yours. Somewhere, there is a girl who does not appreciate what she has, who would relish the hunt, the gore, the rut, who would not care if she ate her meat raw and choked down the fur and dirt to get to the tender, stinking offal. I will help you find her, and then you will not have violated your Falcon oath."

But the pictures the Mirror's soul cast at her had lost their luster. The enchantment broke, and she saw how close she had come to falling, and she drew back.

Dùghall was calling to her. "Kait? Kait? Can you hear me?"

"I can."

"We have to force the Mirror's soul from the Mirror into the Veil, and we have to do it now. It's getting stronger—we don't have much time."

They'd already prepared the spell—the same spell that had drawn the souls of the Dragons from the bodies they had stolen and forced them to take residence in the tiny homemade soul-mirrors. They did not have a little mirror for the Mirror's soul, though—they feared that if it were given any sort of physical form, it would draw people to it and use their lives to feed itself. It could grow strong again, even trapped within a simple gold ring. But if it were cast into the Veil, it would have to face the gods and the cycles of birth and death. It might become human. It might have a chance to leave behind the evil that it did—the evil that it had been created to do.

They quickly chanted:

"Follow our souls, Vodor Imrish,
To the soul of the Mirror of Souls,
To the usurper of the lives of the Calimekkans,
Faithful children of Iberan gods,
And from its false metal body expel it.
Bring no harm to this made-soul,
The Mirror's soul,
But give it safe house and shelter
Within the cycle of birth and death—
To teach it love and compassion
To guard its immortality, and to
Protect the essence of life and mind.
We offer our flesh—all that we have given
And all that you will take,
Freely and with clear conscience,
As we do no wrong,
But reverse a wrong done."

Now, now, the magic of the Falcons poured into Kait faster and harder, and she grew stronger and brighter, keeping pace with Dùghall and Alarista—but not with the soul of the Mirror. Its explosive growth outstripped the three of them—it raced outward in all directions like a Ganjaday fireflower exploding silently in the sky.

Their spell hooked into the Mirror's soul, and Kait felt furious lines of power clawing into her, trying to drag soul from body, trying to eject her and claim her place within her flesh—but though a line of blue fire arced between the three of them and the rogue soul, their spell did not do what they needed it to do. The Mirror's soul kept drawing power from the people of Calimekka, and it kept getting stronger.

"Why isn't it working?" Kait shouted.

"We don't have enough power," Dùghall said. "Throughout all of time there have not been as many Falcons as there are citizens in Calimekka at this moment. We can never be as strong as it is."

"We don't need to be," Alarista said. "We're trying to pull it from something and force it into nothing—that requires brute force. If we channeled it into a ring, though, that would only take a little leverage."

Dùghall said, "But if it goes into a ring, we still have the same problem we have right now."

"We can destroy the ring physically," Alarista said.

"We don't have to." Kait focused on her body, standing with Dùghall's and Alarista's, the three of them holding hands around the Mirror of Souls, and she said, "We have a ring that will break the instant we step away from each other."

She felt Dùghall's horror. "You're saying we should use our bodies as the ring. No. It is so powerful it could take one of us over. With a flesh body, it would be more formidable than it is encased in the Mirror of Souls."

"We have to do something," Kait said.

A feeling of tremendous peace emanated from Alarista. "We have to do this. This—*this* is the thing that I must do and must succeed at. Dùghall, Kait, we have no more time. Repeat the spell with me, but offer our bodies as the ring."

The hooks the Mirror's soul dug into them dragged harder, pulling them away from flesh and life and toward death . . . or oblivion. It was a huge and burning light, a gruesome bloodred monster that filled the void of the Veil, grown so immense that they could no longer tell if it continued to expand. In the world of the flesh, people died to feed that obscenity. More would continue to die unless the Falcons succeeded in their task.

They chanted the spell of removal again, but, following Alarista's lead, changed the lines of destination.

". . . But give it safe house and shelter
Within the unbroken circle of our three bodies—
Unbroken that it may guard
This soul's immortality, and
Protect the essence of life and mind. . . ."

The flow of energy changed. The fierce grip that the Mirror's soul had on them relaxed for just an instant; then, with a horrifying rush, the red wash of its fire poured toward them, enveloped them, consumed them. Kait felt the souls of uncounted hundreds of Falcons brace themselves against the assault, and then she felt only the howling darkness of alien fury within her veins, within her muscles, within her skull. She fought to keep from drowning in the assault—thrown from the void of the Veil into the madness within her own body, she could only hang on to her identity and hope the others fared better against the monster that tried to consume them.

She was the weakest link—she was the Falcon least experienced in magic, least experienced in the safe control of energy, least capable of fending off the attacker that fought to strip her soul from her flesh. She could feel Dùghall and Alarista fighting beside her, trying to help her, but the Mirror's soul was merciless, and like an ocean pouring through a single hole in the bottom of the sea, it was unstoppable.

She lost ground and panicked, despaired of ever seeing another day. Dùghall fought to hold on to her; Alarista fought to hold on to her; but she felt the triumph of the

Mirror's soul and its glee and its certainty, and hope abandoned her.

"She's a mere child, and weak. Look at me. I have more to offer," Alarista said, and the Mirror's soul froze for half a heartbeat, and Kait could feel it evaluating her dull light, her slow responses and poorly shaped defenses, and then studying the brilliant purity of the light that poured through Alarista. It saw something that called to it—some hidden weakness that it could exploit, for a spasm rippled through Kait, through Dùghall, through Alarista, and suddenly Alarista was under attack.

But unlike Kait, Alarista wasn't fighting. Kait could still see Alarista's brilliance and feel the unfathomable power of her soul, but that soul was merely watching—Alarista let the Mirror's soul dig into her flesh and rip her soul's anchors one by one from the body that was rightfully hers. Dùghall and Kait fought the monster that consumed her, but without Alarista's help, they were losing the battle quickly.

Dùghall shouted, "Alarista! Hold on! Fight it!"

Her voice spoke into their minds. *Let me go. I have now completed my final task.*

And then her soul was gone and the *thathbund* shattered. Kait no longer had the strength and the wisdom of a thousand Falcons; she barely had the strength of one. Thrown back into the single limited reality of her own flesh, she toppled to the floor, weak and sick, her hands slipping free of Dùghall's and Alarista's.

Dùghall dropped to his knees as well, his hands splaying on the ground as he kept his face from smashing into the floor—and scattering a pile of glittering metal dust to the four corners of the room. Nothing else remained of the Mirror of Souls—but the soul of the Mirror was another thing entirely.

"I am flesh!" the monster in Alarista's body shrieked. "This is *my* flesh! I shall be a god!" Kait stared at Alarista's body dancing around the room. She saw the old bones leaping, the old muscles bunching and releasing. The old eyes turned to her, filled with a new and terrifying malevolence. "I shall . . . be a god, and you . . . shall be my first fodder." The monster began to laugh.

The laughter turned to coughing.

Alarista's lips turned blue and her skin blanched gray and waxy. The monster doubled over, wheezing, scrabbling at its chest with fingers turned to claws. Its knees gave way, and it toppled to the floor like a rag doll, limbs bouncing and flopping. It gasped, mouth opening and closing, trying to suck in air, spitting up frothy, bloody foam with every choking cough.

"No!" it managed to croak, but that was its last word. It glared at them and the red glow of its magic illuminated it—but Alarista's body was too near death. It ran out of time before it could successfully repair all the ruined organs, all the damaged flesh. Its eyes burned red, but red dulling to embers in a dying fire; its fragile chest heaved like a broken bellows; it clawed at the floor, and twitched. And then, with a final, gurgling gasp, the light went out of its eyes and it died.

Kait, on hands and knees, wept for the death of her friend Alarista, for her own loss.

"She saved us, Kait. She saved all of us," Dùghall said. "The Mirror of Souls would have won without her. And now she's with Hasmal." The look in his eyes grew thoughtful, and he whispered, "And that was the reason . . ."

Kait saw sudden guilt on his face as he glanced at her, then looked away.

"What?" she asked him.

"Had you and Ry and I formed the *thathbund,* we would have failed. Only Alarista could have done what she did."

"I know," Kait said, wondering what that guilty look

meant. "But she isn't with us. I've lost another friend."
She remembered Alarista as the red-haired beauty who
had met Hasmal on the road out of Calimekka—as the
slender woman who leaped into his arms and embraced
him with a joy so pure it illuminated them both; she remembered the woman who sat in her Gyru wagon with Ry
and Hasmal and Kait, struggling to find an answer to the
threat of the Dragons. She remembered the woman who
had given her youth to Dùghall for nothing more than the
chance to save her love from torture and death. And now
this same woman had given up her body and her life to
save the people of Calimekka, to beat the Mirror's soul, to
save Kait. "The world is diminished by her death."

A soft voice—bodiless and bloodless—reached out of
the darkness and touched Kait's ears. "We come to claim
our due."

She jumped and turned all around, and saw Dùghall
blanch. "The spirits of the Galweigh dead," he whispered.

Alarista's corpse began to glow from the inside, red as
a light shone through a ruby, terrible to see. It grew
brighter, and her flesh grew translucent, so that Kait could
see, briefly, the outline of her bones beneath her skin, the
shapes of her organs, the courses through which her blood
had once run. The light grew brighter yet, and she could
feel magic against her skin, in her gut, inside her skull—
magic that had been there in low levels since the day she'd
come home, but that now was strong and dangerous and
watchful. Alarista's body grew transparent as Strithian
glass, the light grew hurtful to Kait's eyes—and then both
body and light vanished. But the feeling of magic remained, patient and alert and somehow hungry.

She turned to Dùghall and saw tears on his cheeks.
"Every victory cuts us deeper and leaves us bleeding," he
said. "This is a bitter day. She is gone . . . but she is the
last to die. Uncounted Calimekkans have fallen in the battle we just fought—they should own our souls." He got to

his feet with difficulty and turned to the door. "The old Iberans were right to ban magic from their borders—to destroy every wizard they found. For all the good Falcon magic could do, the magic of Wolves and Dragons does as much evil. Better there was no magic. Better all wizards were dead."

He plodded from the room, head down and shoulders slumped, leaving Kait to stare at the place where he had been, wondering how much truth his words held.

Chapter 31

The bells of Calimekka tolled death—unending peals of grief and loss. Bodies piled in the streets, the living in little weeping groups beside them, mourning the loss of a father or mother, a child, a friend. Here, a woman knelt beside the bodies of her husband and her three young children, who lay unmarked where they had fallen, looking as though they could leap back to life at any instant. She contemplated their still forms with tear-blurred eyes, clutched the dagger in her hands a little tighter, and with a despairing cry rammed it between her ribs and into her heart. There, a child wandered through the streets, crying out for someone, anyone, to come and wake his mama. In the topmost apartment on the corner, a young father clutched the body of his infant son and screamed imprecations at the gods. Scenes repeated a thousand times, and a thousand more—few families within the boundaries of Calimekka came unscathed through the sudden silent flash of magical backlash—*rewhah*—that normal men and women would mistake for the onslaught of plague; some families were wiped entirely from the earth.

Life continued in Calimekka—but only in a grim and spectral mockery of itself. The carts rattled through the streets, but they no longer carried fruits and vegetables from the outlying farms or wondrous wares brought from across the seas; they carried only corpses. Men still worked, but they worked at building pyres, at burning the remains of all they had once loved and held dear. Women clutched not babies in their arms, but the ropes of the bells that tolled the souls of those dead babies through the Veil. They did not know that the soul of the Mirror of Souls, unchecked, would have devoured all of them—that the fact that any lived in Calimekka was a great victory. They could not see the victory in the streams and rivers and seas of the dead that rolled to the flames. They could see only inexplicable pain—inexplicable loss.

They could not see, either, the first wave of a new sea that rolled toward them. They could not see the misshapen bodies of the Scarred clutching their weapons like promises, clutching their dreams of humanity to their twisted breasts. They could not see the lovely young man and the delicate young woman who rode great fanged monsters down the slope of a mountain and across the southernmost border of Ibera, leading a horde of wild-eyed believers on a holy mission. They could not know that in the hearts and minds of the monsters who approached, *they* were the demons who had stolen a birthright, the monsters who stood between twisted flesh and the perfection of yearned-for human form.

They could not know.

But the Mirror of Souls was dead, and the last barrier was gone, and the army of the damned approached.

Chapter 32

Crispin stood on the balcony of his old room in Sabir House, staring up at Galweigh House. The red beacon was gone, the feeling that washed through him was that of magic shattered and destroyed. He had to assume that they had succeeded—that Dùghall, whose memories were imprinted in his mind, and whose soul he knew nearly as well as his own, had succeeded in destroying the Mirror of Souls with the help of his Falcons. He stared up at the alabaster House on the peak and wished a slow and painful death on Dùghall—the Mirror of Souls still called to his imagination with promises of immortality, of power beyond imagining. He would have made a good god.

But if he could not be a god, still he could be a father, and better than that, a father revenged. Where Dùghall was, there Ry would be, too—with his bitch Kait—and there, too, Crispin would find his daughter, Ulwe. Or if he did not find her there, he would find those who knew where she was, and what had become of her. He could make them tell him. And he could hurt them for whatever they had dared to do to her. He could. He would.

Sabir House had suffered losses. Ry's mother was found dead, clutching the throat of the demon she called Valard—

she'd ripped it out in her death throes. Much of the diplomats' branch would be lying in the pyre before the night fell, the paraglese included. Most of the trade branch lay dead, too.

But most of the Wolves survived. They'd felt the first stirrings of magic pouring from Galweigh House and they had shielded themselves. Now Anwyn and Andrew waited in Crispin's room, eager. They were about to hunt again, and they were impatient for blood.

"Everyone will have seen the beacon from Galweigh House," Anwyn said when Crispin turned away from the balcony. "We can tell the people of Calimekka that the last of the Galweighs practiced magic against them—against the whole of the city; we can tell them this sudden plague was a murder committed by Galweighs. We can offer revenge to those who survive, in exchange for their assistance. Galweigh House could stand against siege if it held an army, but it doesn't. We can throw people over the walls, drop them in by airible, send them up the cliffs, and we can overrun the place with sheer numbers."

Crispin shook his head. "That would work, but I want the people inside the House taken alive. All of them." He was thinking of his daughter, of her chances of surviving an all-out assault on the House. He didn't like her odds. "I don't think we'll be able to get Ry and Dùghall and whoever else they have in there out with their hides intact if we stir up the masses."

Andrew for once didn't giggle or titter or say something inane. He studied Crispin through narrowed eyes and said, "And just why do you care if they all get out with their skins intact? At this point, I'd think dead sooner would be as good as dead later—they've hurt us, and the longer they survive, the more they'll hurt us."

Crispin thought again that he was going to have to kill Andrew, and soon. He had more going on between his ears than he let show, and the fact that he'd managed to hide the truth of that from Crispin for so long made Crispin nervous. "Dùghall has access to forms of magic I want," he said coldly. "Ry . . . I have plans for that bitchson. As for the rest, each of them knows something. It might be something useful, it might not. But they eluded us for this long, they managed to destroy the Mirror of Souls, they overthrew the Dragons. I'm assuming we'll find what they know useful. I want them to live until we've had a chance to get to it."

Anwyn paced the room, his hooves making a sharp, clipping sound on the tile floor. "Like Andrew, I have my doubts about the wisdom of this. They've been disastrous to us up to now. I think we're better off if they're dead, no matter what knowledge they take with them."

Crispin couldn't believe this. Anwyn—his own brother—siding with Andrew?

He stared into his brother's eyes, hoping to see that Anwyn was playing a game with their cousin, but the eyes that looked back into his were dead serious. Anwyn, who had always deferred to Crispin's will, looked to have developed a sudden streak of independence, and at the worst possible time.

Crispin said, "No. I'm telling you, we'll go after them ourselves—the three of us and a few handpicked soldiers."

Anwyn's smile was that of the shark—his razor teeth gleamed in the harsh light of midday, and his eyes flashed. "And I'm telling you, we won't go in after them alone. While you've been busy with all your little projects, Andrew and I have had a lot of time to think and talk. And plan. We aren't going to get ourselves conveniently killed to leave your path to power clear. We aren't going on any suicide missions now that the paraglesiat of the Family is open; we aren't going to take on wizards or gods singlehandedly for you. We'll stay well to the back of the line and let the commoners die for us."

"We'll talk to the parnissas in the Prethin Quarter

today," Andrew said, and smiled. "They've kept their control over their people through the riots by acting like they were on their side. We've been getting good information from them all along, and we've financed some loyalty in the Prethin Quarter in spite of all the anti-Family activity elsewhere. We'll be able to start our army in that quarter— the rage will spread fast enough as word gets out." He giggled then, and twisted the lone braid on his shaved skull with fingers that moved like the legs of a nervous spider. "But we should let them burn the bodies first. Maybe I could go help them. I could find a nice one for me. Lots of pretty little girls out there just waiting for me, I should think."

Crispin was aware of Andrew's bright, clever eyes on him, aware that beneath the facade of madness those eyes were evaluating his reaction, testing him, deciding . . . something.

How much of it was an act? Andrew did like little girls, and he didn't care whether they were alive or dead—but every time he and Crispin disagreed, Andrew seemed less and less the perverse jester and more and more the conniving rival. In that instant, Crispin decided that Andrew would die by his hand. He would arrange it as soon as he could.

First, though, he had to get Ulwe away from her captors. She was probably trapped inside Galweigh House, held hostage. He hadn't gotten Ry's or Dùghall's demands yet, but no doubt those demands would be coming—very soon, since the Mirror had betrayed their hiding place. With his brother and his cousin bent on raising the countryside against Galweigh House, he would have to act.

An airible strike, he thought. With a brilliant pilot, a few handpicked soldiers, and an onboard landing crew that could slide down the ropes and drag the thing to its anchors, he could have her out of there and perhaps kill off most of his surviving enemies before his brother and his cousin could even realize he was gone.

Galweigh House had been haunted the last time he'd passed through its walls, but the haunting must have subsided if people were living there. He'd give the place a few new ghosts.

Chapter 33

Alcie stood atop the wall, staring down at the river of smoke that filled the valley. "The stink of smoke and the sound of the bells is going to drive me mad," she said. "And how is it that everyone within these walls lived when so many died?"

"You were shielded." Kait had explained it all to her before, but Alcie couldn't seem to understand it. "Be grateful you don't have my hearing. Their wailing carries up to me. It's far worse than the bells." They were keening in the streets below, mourning their dead. They had been for two days. The sound seemed to burrow under her skin, into her skull, behind her eyes—and it bound her to it with her guilt. She had brought the Mirror of Souls to Calimekka. She had poisoned the well, however inadvertently. All of these dead were her doing, dead by her hand. Their ashes rose up to her, ghosts coming to call on their murderer, and fell like gray snow on the cliff's shelves, on the ground outside the House, on the leaves and fronds of the jungle. But not on the House itself. Dùghall's spell remained in force—the Galweigh spirits consumed even the ashes of the dead as their due.

Below the wall, Ulwe crouched on the road that led

down into the city, her eyes shut, her fingers splayed against the dirt, her body tight as a coiled spring. She was as gray as the ash, her lips white with strain, her face a carved mask of pain. When finally she rose and waved to them that she was finished, she did so like an old woman.

Kait and Alcie went down to meet her.

"He comes," the girl said. "He's found a pilot who will bring him here in a flying machine, and soldiers who are to kill all of you, and men who have learned to land the machine with no crew here to help them." She staggered a little, and Kait caught her.

Alcie asked, "Are you ill?"

"The roads . . . they weep," the girl said softly. "Every mourner carries grief to the pyres. The road remembers every death—and I had to go through all of them to get to my father."

Kait hugged the girl. "I'm sorry. I'm sorry you had to feel that."

Ulwe hugged her tightly. "He's going to be here tonight—my father. And then you will have to kill him, won't you?"

Kait dropped to one knee so she was looking up into the girl's face. "Ulwe, I cannot promise that I won't kill him. He murdered my friend. He intends to kill all of us. If I have to kill him to protect my family, I will." She took Ulwe's hand. "But I promise you that if I can stop him without killing him, I will spare his life."

"You don't have to promise."

"But I do. I don't know how things could work out between you and your father, but I'll do everything I can to see that you get the chance to find out."

Ulwe nodded sharply, then turned away and ran back to the House. Alcie cleared her throat. Kait rose and looked at her sister.

"You're going to promise not to kill a murderous Sabir monster—one that even your Ry dreaded."

"I have enough blood on my hands already. I won't seek his death. But I didn't promise not to kill him. I promised that I would try to defeat him without killing him. There's a difference."

"The difference might be your life, and ours. If you go into a fight concentrating on how you can beat your enemy without killing him, and his only thought is on how to destroy you, he'll have the advantage."

"You want me to tell the child, 'Yes, I'm going to kill your father'?"

"I don't care what you tell her. Lie to her if you have to. She thinks you'll try to spare his life—that's sufficient. When he arrives, kill him and tell her you had no choice."

Kait laughed bitterly. "If you're so hot for blood, you could always kill him, Alcie. Run him through with a sword—feel his hot blood splatter against your wrists and taste it when it splashes on your lips. Smell the stink of his bowels and his bladder as they let go. See the life go out of his eyes, and know that yours is the hand that took that life—"

She was staring at her sister. When Alcie flinched, she stopped.

"Don't you like the idea of that, Alcie?"

Alcie looked away from her. "He needs to die."

"He probably does. But I wonder at your willingness to call for his execution if you aren't willing to be the executioner."

Alcie still wouldn't look at her. "I'm a mother. I'm not a killer."

Kait moved around to stand in Alcie's line of sight, and when Alcie tried to look away, reached up and caught her face with both hands. "I *am* a killer, Alcie. As a Karnee, I hunt down my own food and kill it with teeth and claws. I killed men who tried to kill me. In trying to save my Family, I brought about the deaths of half the people in the greatest city in the world."

"You don't know if it's half."

Kait held her annoyance in check. "No. I don't. The sky is black with the ashes of the people who died because of me, but I didn't go down in the streets and count the corpses. Alcie—listen to me. In order to live with myself—in order to live inside my skin and my head—I have to know that I won't kill a little girl's father—a *friend's* father—without at least looking for a way to let him live."

"He's evil."

"He loves his daughter."

"You don't know that."

Kait could still touch Crispin's memories—if she allowed herself to enter that place in her mind, she knew what he knew, and felt what he felt. Amid the horror and the evil and the foulness of his thoughts, a single chamber lay, filled with light and hope, with belief in something good. That one room he had marked with his daughter's name. That one part of his life he had kept apart and separate, had cherished and left unsullied. It was a ghost that haunted the halls of who he was, crying out for who he could have been, and its very presence chilled her and confounded her and made her wonder what would happen when the door opened and his actual daughter entered the room he'd kept for her. Would the goodness spill out, or would the evil flood in? How strong could a tiny fragment of love be against a sea of hate? "Yes. I do," she said, and did not elaborate.

"You'll do what you want," Alcie said bitterly. "And we'll probably all die for it. But when we die, we'll have no one to pray at our pyres, and no one to mourn our deaths."

She walked back to the tower that would take her to the top of the wall. Kait watched her for a moment, then headed to the House. She and Dùghall and Ian would need to plan their defense, and they hadn't much time.

Chapter 34

There were no better streets in Heymar than the mud river of Bayview Street: no lightly traveled back ways cobbled over, no boarded walks, no pleasant surprises where the filth gave way suddenly to firm roadbed or to mown grass. The whole of the town seemed to have been designed as a pig wallow, with no thought that people might wish to walk above the mire or even that they could.

Ry and Yanth and Jaim had waded their way through the filth from one end of the harbor to the other, studying ships. Most of those anchored in the deep bay were recognizable tramp ships, travelers from any harbor that would give them cargo to any harbor that would buy it. They carried settlers, too—immigrants from the crowding in Ibera's central region, from the poor eroding land of her North Coast, and from the unending appetites and expenses of Calimekka, civilization's jewel. Slavers lay in harbor, too; they brought new workers for the landowners in the New Territories, but many of the less desirable slaves would be sent to work in the lands opening up in Galweigia, New Kaspera, and the Sabirene Isthmus, harvesting timber from the forests and mining metals and gems from the earth. Only one ship was a diplomatic envoy—it flew the Masschanka Family flag and the banners of Brelst, seat of the greatest concentration of Masschanka power. Most of the vessels at anchor looked barely adequate to survive the mild temper of the Dalvian Sea; few would have any hope of making the harrowing crossing of the Bregian that the *Peregrine* had accomplished.

But near the west end of the harbor, they found a fine ship of Sabir make, a three-masted beauty freshly painted in viridian and deepest azure, the most costly of pigments, with bright brass fittings, sails that looked to Ry's practiced eye very like heavy silk, and fresh gilding on the figurehead—which was of a peregrine falcon. The decorative painting of the masts and cabins and rails spoke of time spent in Varhees among the Ko Patas, renowned for their woodworking prowess, but Sabirene ships traditionally eschewed paint, preferring the beauty of natural wood grains brought out by hand rubbing. It was a ship of contradictions; it bore no name glyphs and flew no flag, though it flaunted the wealth of kings. And the crew, dressed though they were in silks and velvets, were of mixed human and Scarred origin; they did not wear their finery as did those who were born to wealth, but instead as those who had come into it suddenly and with little preparation—as if, on receiving their first great sums, they had bought everything bright and expensive they could find without thought for style or taste.

No iridescent snow-haired beauties stood on the deck, but Ry had no doubt the ship was the *Peregrine,* or that the woman he had seen would prove to belong to the *Peregrine*'s crew.

Yanth was shaking his head. "Looks like a whore in her working paint," he said.

"Ian said the mutineers sailed with a hold full of first-quality Ancients' artifacts. I'd say they got good money for their treachery."

Jaim pointed down the road, away from the ship, and

said, "We seem to be drawing some attention. I suggest we pretend we just found what we were looking for elsewhere and move along."

Ry didn't spare the *Peregrine* another glance; he knew where it was and who was onboard. He walked with his two comrades back toward the town, toward their inn and their locked room and the bath they had been promised, which was to feature water both clean and warmed.

A woman approached them. In the style of Heymar, which was to say no style at all, she wore rubber boots that rose above her knees, and heavy homespun breeches, and a shapeless hooded shawl that draped around her shoulders, covering hair, clothing, and any weapons she might carry. It was testament to her beauty that on her the ugly clothing bore an air of proud daring. She smiled and said, "You are guests at the Long Comfort, are you not?" Her accent spoke of elegant dining rooms, of sweet music played softly, of exquisite silk dresses and measured dancing, and fine food served on silver platters and eaten with golden knives. She smelled of jasmine and musk.

"We are," Ry said, keeping wariness from his voice, bowing slightly, smiling politely.

"Then you are invited to sit at table with Captain Y'tallin of the *K'hbeth Rhu'ute*." The foreign words she said carefully. She was no native speaker of her captain's language.

"I know no Captain Y'tallin, nor any ship named *K'hbeth Rhu'ute*," Ry said, "and though I am honored by your captain's generosity, I cannot imagine why he has chosen to so honor me."

In her eyes, amusement flashed, quickly hidden by the formula of manners. "I am the captain's first concubine, and as such am not privy to the reasons for your invitation. I only tell you that a litter will be at your disposal outside the door of the Long Comfort at the first ringing of Dard, should you decide to accept the invitation. And I give you this, the captain's gift." She slipped a little carved wooden box into his hand; it had been wrapped in puzzle-wire and ribbon in the fashion made popular by the Five Families, and would take some time to open.

He accepted it and bowed again to the woman. "I will give your captain's invitation my fullest consideration," he said.

"Then I shall hope to see you tonight." She flashed a brilliant smile at him and for just an instant her shawl fell open, revealing an expanse of creamy skin and tight, high breasts barely covered by the sheerest of diaphanous silk blouses, between which nestled a fine gold neckchain stamped with the Masschanka crest. "I shall hope to see *much* more of you," she murmured, softly enough that only he could hear.

The shawl flicked back into place and the woman turned and squelched away, ruining with her noisy exit the aura of mystery and excitement she'd managed to create in the few short moments she'd been with him.

Ry laughed softly.

"She was a pleasant piece of work," Yanth observed. "Most beddable."

Jaim snorted. "She struck *me* as a woman who would make her own grandmother first guest at a cannibal feast for the right price."

Yanth was still watching her slogging back toward the harbor. "Wouldn't any concubine? I simply observed that she would make a delectable morsel if served between the sheets, preferably raw."

Jaim shook his head at Yanth and turned to Ry. "So, do we accept this dinner invitation?"

Ry was studying the box in his hand. "I haven't decided yet. Let's go back to the inn and see what sort of present the captain has seen fit to send."

The puzzle-wire, beautifully but fiendishly wound, gave up its secrets slowly. Before he even got to the box, he unwrapped three other gifts. First a lustrous pearl, oddly bluish in cast, of ordinary size. Then a bit of translucent white stone, carved into the shape of a tiny, beautifully detailed fruit tree by someone with extraordinary patience and too much free time. Finally, a silver coin unlike any he had ever seen. It was no bigger than the tip of his little finger and, like the stone tree, was exquisitely detailed. On the front, a woman staring forward, her heavy-lidded eyes, full lips, and oval face somehow both seductive and regal; on the obverse, a winged man, nude and powerfully built, holding a long-bow and some sort of flask. Both sides of the coin had writing around the perimeter, but it was almost too small to see, and even had it been clearly readable, Ry could find nothing familiar in the shape of the script.

He and Yanth and Jaim looked at the three tiny treasures, then at each other.

Ry shrugged. "I don't know what to make of them. Either of you care to make a suggestion?"

"Not yet," Jaim said.

Yanth was more daring. "The captain wishes to tell you that he is a midget. Or that he has a very small amount of money and would like to own an orchard by the sea. Or . . . or . . ." He grinned. "I guess I have no idea."

The box had no visible seam; it was a puzzle-box, beautifully made of a dozen kinds of wood, inlaid with geometric designs in ivory and tiny flower-starred vines of greenwood and shell. The vines circled out from a different inlaid flower on each of the six sides and wove through the ivory trellises. The box itself could have been the gift, but it rattled and whatever was inside was much heavier than wood.

Ry tried different strategies to open it—tapping the corners, trying to slide panels, and finally pressing the central flowers. When he did that, he discovered that each flower would depress slightly, but pressing one would cause the others to pop back up.

"I'll get a brick," Yanth said. "We can smash it open."

Ry arched an eyebrow at his friend. "No. That's all right. I'll get this."

He worked a bit longer, but without success. Jaim, who had been looking over his shoulder while he worked, finally said, "I think I see the pattern."

"I'm damned if I do."

"Try pressing the flowers by season of bloom."

Ry stared up at his friend. "The season of *bloom*? How in all the hells would I know that?"

"The central motifs are all common flowers in Calimekkan gardens."

"And you know how much time I've spent gardening."

Jaim held out a hand. "May I?"

Ry gave him the box without a word.

"Silkflower. Early spring," Jaim said, pressing one center. He turned the cube. "Nightmarch—late spring. Then sweet devil's heart—first of the rainy season, for about two weeks. Climiptera, also called Janisary rose—blooms right after sweet devil's heart, through the rest of the rainy season. Then cattle bole—right as the dry season starts." His finger rested over the last flower. The other five remained depressed this time. "The last is chilly slippers, which blooms at first dawn during the coolest and driest part of the year." He handed the puzzle-box back to Ry. "Your gift. You should open it."

Ry sighed. "One of these days you must tell me how you knew that." He pressed the final flower, and the box fell apart in his hand. In the center of the little panels lay a heavy gold ring, thick and massive, set with a flawless cabochon sapphire the size of a wren egg. The gold was heavily carved in fanciful forms—twisting vines again, like those of the box, with monkeys and deer and parrots peeking out from behind.

"Good gods," Yanth said. "That ring would buy passage around the world. Why would the captain give it to you?"

Ry shook his head and closed his eyes. An elusive scent tickled his memory. He lifted the box to his face and sniffed. Different woods, glues and resins, the fingertips of the person who had last touched the contents of the box— different than the hands that had held the outside. He opened his mouth slightly and breathed the scent through his parted lips, tasting it; then through his nose again.

Faint. Terribly faint, and masked by the wood, by the resins. But there.

He licked the spot on the wood where the scent was strongest, hoping to taste something that would make that enigmatic scent clearer.

Frustrated, he opened his eyes, found his friends studying him with patient curiosity. They knew his eccentricities, after all.

"Anything?" Yanth asked.

"Nothing clear. There's something familiar about the scent, but it's so faint I can't quite make the connection."

"Familiar. You think it's trouble?"

"Well, that's always the best assumption. It would help if we could figure out what the gift meant. The pearl and the single tree and the coin and the ring . . . hells, even the box, perhaps—I have the feeling that they're supposed to mean something, only I'm too dull-witted to figure out what." He looked at Jaim. "You saw the pattern in the flowers. Do you see any pattern here?"

Jaim sighed. "Well . . . perhaps. Pearls have always represented layers. Chip off the outer layer of a pearl and another pearl, equally perfect but smaller, lies just beneath. And beneath that another, and another, until you reach the center. The fact that it's blue . . ." He shrugged, palms outspread. "I don't know. Many people attribute significance to different gems and their colors, but I've never paid much attention to that. I have no idea what a blue pearl might signify."

Ry glanced at Yanth, who snorted. "Don't look to me.

When I buy a gemstone, I don't get it to convey some silly message. I buy it because I like the way it looks on me—or on the girl I give it to."

Ry looked back to Jaim. "The carved fruit tree . . . I'd guess that to stand for the Sabir crest if we're assuming the giver of gifts actually knows something about you."

"There are two trees on the Sabir crest, one which feeds good fruit to the friends of the Sabirs, and one which feeds poisoned fruit to their enemies. Which is this?"

"Assume poison until proven otherwise," Yanth said.

Jaim nodded agreement. "The coin . . . I can't even begin to guess the meaning of that. Perhaps one of the images on it is significant; perhaps the importance lies in the place where it was minted, or the time." He sighed. "The box and the ring leave me equally confused. They seem to belong together, but they don't seem to hold any meaning in and of themselves, except perhaps that the person inviting you to dinner has the wealth to give them."

"Perhaps that's it." Ry stood, the rest of the contents of the box and the pieces of the box itself lying on the thin mattress of his cot. "But now I'm not sure what to do."

"We go, I think," Yanth said. "And we take our weapons."

"Oh, I knew I would be going. My question was whether I should take the two of you with me—where all of us could be trapped—or leave you behind to come after me if something goes wrong, knowing that if I do, you might not be able to reach me. I'm not even certain that the two of you were invited."

"Which is all the more reason to take us with you when you go. If their goal is to get you there alone, you can't give them that."

Ry paced. "I'm not sure what I'll do."

Outside the door, someone knocked. Ry opened the door and found Shrubber's wife, Kelje, standing there. "Your bath is ready," she said. "You'll have to hurry, though—the water is hot enough now, but it won't stay that way for long." She smiled shyly. "There's a curtain up for you, and one warmer pot for each of you when you call."

"I'll go," he said—first dip in clean water was the prerogative of rank. "Stay here until I get back."

He took a change of clothes with him, stripped in the kitchen, then realized he wasn't alone. He heard female whispers coming from the pantry. He didn't look over. Instead, he stretched high, faking a yawn as he did, and twisted from side to side with his hands locked behind his back as if getting at a persistent crick in his spine. He was rewarded by admiring little *oohs*, and recognized the voices. The chambermaid and the evening tavern girl.

He dropped his dirty clothes in a pile by the stove, for he had agreed beforehand that Kelje would have the girl clean them for him, and stepped behind the curtain strung across one corner of the kitchen. The tub was generous enough in size, and Ry was pleased to see that it had been cleaned. He tested the water—a bit too hot, but he'd never minded that. He slipped into the bath, and grinned as he heard the chambermaid and the tavern girl whispering in the pantry beside the kitchen.

"He has very fine shoulders, doesn't he?"

"Good legs."

"And all his teeth—I saw them when he smiled. They're very white."

He washed himself slowly, enjoying hearing his good qualities enumerated.

"He looks so strong. And I wonder where he got that scar."

He took the pitcher that sat beside the tub, dipped it in the water, and poured the water over his head—and then lathered his hair with the soap Kelje had provided, and poured water over himself again, so he missed quite a bit of their conversation. When his ears cleared, he heard one of the girls say, "When he calls for his warming pot, I'll carry it to him."

"You're taking your clothes off?"

"I thought maybe he'd like some company in his bath."

Ry froze. He didn't mind being admired, but he most definitely did *not* want company in his bath—and he knew if the girl came, offered her naked charms, and he turned her down, she'd either accuse him of buggering little boys and leave nasty things in his bed or his food, or else she'd screech and yell rape and he'd have to find someplace else to stay. Assuming, of course, that the locals didn't hang him first—and that would be a big and risky assumption.

Forget the warming pot. He was clean enough, he decided.

He got out of the water, drying himself off with the coarse towel Kelje had provided, and threw his breeches on without thought to his appearance. He didn't bother with shoes or socks or underwear or shirt, and when he'd given the laces a cursory tug and tie, he hurried out of the kitchen and up to the room, only catching the barest hint of the whispered disappointment behind him.

Jaim looked up from studying the mechanism of the puzzle-box, his face a portrait of startlement. "That was a very fast bath, Ry. The water must have been ice."

"The water was perfect. I simply didn't fancy the company."

"The . . . company?"

"Apparently I paid too much for the baths. They seem to come with a girl."

Yanth's face lit up. "Oh, do tell."

Ry explained the two girls hiding in the pantry.

"And you didn't stay?"

"Which of them could compare to Kait?"

Yanth looked prim and said. "Well, we wouldn't know that, would we?"

Jaim, uncharacteristically, was smiling. "I rather liked

the look of the chambermaid," he said. "Nice little thing, good curves, wide hips."

Yanth said, "I'd take both of them, myself."

Ry said, "I'll let the two of you figure out who'll go first, then. Just don't leave your fight in the water—we've no idea what we'll be facing tonight. And mind the bells—I don't want us rushed to leave."

"We're all going, then?" Jaim asked.

"Yes, I think we are. We'll have a better chance of handling whatever they throw at us if we go together."

He pulled off his breeches and dressed again, this time doing it carefully. He wasn't wearing fine clothes—that would be too out of character for the person he was pretending to be—but he was wearing clothes that were clean and not too badly worn. Leather breeches and a soft linen shirt in pale green, dark green leather vest, green wide-brimmed felt hat with copper trinkets around the band.

Once dressed, he sat down with the gifts the concubine had given him, and tried to figure out what message they were supposed to send. He had a long time to think. When Jaim and Ry finally came back, more than a station had passed. They both looked well scrubbed, well sated, and very pleased with themselves.

And he knew nothing more than he had when the concubine presented him with the gifts and the invitation.

Chapter 35

Crispin and his men filled the airible's benches. Their weapons clanked and rattled at their sides; their packs formed mounds on the floor. They sat in silence as the steady thudding of the engines drew them ever closer to Galweigh House.

Crispin stared at the city that slipped below him. Only the faintest of lights shone all the way up through the haze of smoke from the burning dead. What a price to pay for the destruction of the Mirror of Souls—half the city dead, including most of his own Family, and for what? The knowledge wasn't gone. He could—he *would*—build another Mirror as soon as he had his daughter back. He would be an immortal. He would walk across the face of Matrin as a god for the rest of eternity.

But Ry and his bitch and her uncle owed him now for more than stealing away his daughter. The second Ulwe was safe, they were going to pay.

"How much farther, Aouel?" he shouted.

The pilot turned and said, "You can see it through my window."

The smoke that clogged the valleys didn't touch Galweigh House. It crouched atop its mountain as if astride an

island beset by curling white seas, touched by moonlight—
a cold and forbidding ruin. No lights burned within the
House, but Crispin knew his enemies hid in there. The Mirror had died there, the magic had exploded from there, and
his prey waited there. Huddled in the darkness, scared little
rabbits with the wolf digging down into their den.

He licked his lips. He could taste their deaths in his future; he could taste their blood on his tongue. He alone carried no weapon, for he would be his own weapon. First
Ulwe to safety . . . and then he would embrace the Karnee
monster; he would let his blood boil and his skin Shift. He
would give himself over to the ecstasy and the madness of
destruction. For Ulwe and for himself, he would extract full
measure from the deaths of those who had wronged him.

The pilot said, "Get the men on their ropes. They'll have
one chance to do this, and if they don't do it right, they'll
be smashed against the wall or dropped over the cliff."

Crispin nodded. The soldiers, picked by the pilot for
their night skills and specially trained for dangerous missions such as this, slipped out of their seats, through the
modified hatchway, and out into the night, to the anchor
ropes that coiled on the gondola catwalk. Each wore heavy
leather gloves, leather pants, sturdy leather jacket, and
heavy boots. At Aouel's signal, they each hooked an arm
around the rope and jumped off the catwalk, the rope un-
coiling as it dropped.

Aouel dared a quick, hard grin at Crispin's retreating
back. He'd worked for months toward this night and toward
this possibility. He had feigned loyalty, had kept his head
down, and worked like a donkey for Crispin . . . and had
made sure that the wrong men had suffered unfortunate accidents during drills, and that the right men had come
through intact. A good pilot could do that.

Now the future hinged on numbers, and on surprise.
Crispin had the numbers. But perhaps . . . perhaps . . .
Aouel still had the surprise.

* * *

Kait, Dùghall, and Ian watched from the main ground-floor doorway. Kait had heard the airible coming even before it rose from the sea of smoke like a diver reaching for air, but when she actually saw it, her mouth went dry and her heart began to pound. The three of them were ready—as ready as any three people could be against an army of unknown size with unknown capabilities.

Crispin had shielded his soldiers against magic, so even had Dùghall been inclined to attempt their defense with spells, he could not. He said he felt certain the dead of Galweigh House would still defend the living—but their strength came from the sacrifice of flesh, and the only flesh that had fed them in a long time had been Alarista's. The dead would be weak. Dùghall didn't think they could do more than slow down the approach of Crispin's army. They might not even successfully do that.

The airible had been moving steadily toward them, its engines thrumming steadily. When it came over the landing field, the pilot abruptly cut out the engines on one side, slewing around so that the airible was still moving toward them, but backward; he started the engines again, then stopped them all as it reached a point of equilibrium and hung in the air. In that brief moment, the air below the airible erupted with men dangling from strings, like dozens of baby spiders bursting from their mother's belly.

Kait almost couldn't breathe. "I've only seen one pilot stop an airible that way," she said. "He tried to teach me to do it, but it's very, very difficult. And he was one of few who would dare fly at night."

Ian and Dùghall looked at her expectantly.

"Aouel," she said. "My friend."

"That sturdy young Rophetian fellow who flew us out of Halles . . . and who burst me and the rest of the Sabir captives out of our prison the morning after we were all taken prisoner . . . yes. Yes. I remember him well," Dùghall said.

"I took him to task for teaching you to fly an airible, I believe. I don't imagine he remembers me too fondly." He looked sidelong at her. "The question is, how fondly does he remember you?"

"I would trust him with my life."

"Even now? Even when he's bringing the people who intend to kill you right into your hideaway?"

"With my life," she repeated.

"Well," he said thoughtfully, "that's good, I suppose. If we can get to him, perhaps he'll lift us out of here. Because I fear that's the only way we'll survive this encounter. I count forty men on those ropes, and that airible will hold more than twice that many. I think Crispin Sabir intends to see us dead tonight, no matter what the cost."

From behind the barred doorway, they watched the men gracefully drop down their ropes to the ground and run for the winches. In a matter of merest instants, they'd threaded ropes through winches and reeled them in, bringing the airible to the ground and anchoring it tightly.

"Sweetly done," Ian said. He unsheathed his sword. "The men who brought that ship to ground are as fine as any I've ever seen. It will be no shame to die at their hands."

Dùghall said, "Cold comfort. When my bones were old, they knew death as a friend who would come soon enough to gather them up and soothe their pains away. Now that they are once again young, I am as jealous of life as a man of his new mistress."

"Then grab your mistress by the soft bits and hold on tight," Kait said. "Because here they come."

Crispin dropped to the ground in the midst of the soldiers' formation. He would approach the House in human form—he wanted his daughter to see him as a man, not a beast. He wanted her to love him, to see him coming to her rescue and know all that he had done and all that he had

risked for her. He would become Karnee for the slaughter
. . . but Ulwe would not see that. He would shield her from
the darker side of his nature. She would be his gem, protected and cherished, and eventually she would become a
god with him.

His daughter, flesh of his flesh.

He strode across the ragged green of the landing field toward the dark House, his officers at his side, the men spread
out around them in all directions.

The pilot, as he had been instructed, waited on the
ground beside the airible—reassurance for Crispin that the
man would not panic while aboard the airible and strand the
Sabir forces in hostile terrain should things become risky,
but close enough to leap inside and get the great airship off
the ground in a hurry if the need arose. Two of his personal
guard stood with the pilot, an added guarantee of his continued loyalty.

Aouel took his place by the airible's ramp and waited.
Crispin's man Guibeall stood to his left, and to his right the
Manarkan woman Ilari—both bore their loyalty to Crispin
like tattoos of honor. He could no more reason with either of
them than with the rising of the sun. And though he liked
both of them personally, admiring their honor and their
courage, they fought on the wrong side of the war. They
were the enemy.

Two of the regular soldiers stayed back with them, one
flanking Ilari, one flanking Guibeall.

"Thought it was just to be the two of us on him," Ilari
said to the man beside her.

The soldier who answered was named Hixcelie—she
was another of the Manarkan fighting women, but attached
to the Sabir family forces on general duty. She said, "Parat
Sabir told us at the last instant we were to double the guard.
He said he smelled something out on the perimeter—not
that *smelling* something makes any sense to me. But he said

we were to face the four quadrants and keep ready, and under no circumstances let anything get through to the pilot."

Crispin's personal bodyguards exchanged meaningful glances. Guibeall frowned. "Smelled something, he said?"

Tschulscoter, the other added guard, said, "That's what he said. You have any idea what it might mean?"

"It means we face out and keep our eyes open," Ilari said. "When he smells trouble, there's trouble."

The four of them turned to face outward, surrounding him. Aouel smiled.

When the troops had crossed half the field, one of the soldiers cried out and fell to the ground. In an instant, the rest were on their bellies, and one of his guards had shoved Aouel facedown into the tall grass. He grunted, but his smile grew broader. He could hear more cries in the distance; beside him he heard rustling, the two thuds, and two soft moans.

He kept his face to the ground and listened for the signal. All seemed to be going according to his plan, but he could not know until the last moment whether he and his allies would succeed or fail. They had the advantage of numbers and of surprise, but that gave them no guarantee. Crispin's men were battle-hardened veterans, well treated by him and deeply loyal.

He heard blades crossing, and the screams of men injured and perhaps dying, and he prayed, Let them be not ours. Better that none should die, but if some must die, let them be not ours.

The fighting stopped. No more metal on metal, no more grunts, no more curses and shouts. Even the cries of the wounded quieted, though they did not die out completely.

And then he heard the call. "*Ebadloo tuoaneat?*" The words were the first line of a Rophetian sea chant; literally translated, they meant, "Husbands-of-the-sea, have-you-embraced-in-an-act-of-conjugal-procreation?" In that instance, however, their second and relevant meaning was that the conspirators had overpowered the assault force, and Crispin was taken prisoner.

On either side of him, Aouel heard a relieved sigh. Tschulscoter called out, "*Ooma, ama, ooma, oora,*" which were the words of the song's second line, and just nonsense syllables to keep the beat. They meant, as previously agreed upon by the conspirators, that Crispin's men guarding Aouel were no longer a threat.

Out of the tall grass the secret Galweigh loyalists arose, their Sabir captives bound and gagged at their feet, and Crispin Sabir held in iron bonds with a collar around his neck. Crispin glared and swore and struggled, his eyes full of murder. He saw Aouel walking toward him and snarled, "Yours will be the first head I hang on the pike. You accepted my coin. You broke the Rophetian oath of neutrality."

"I did not," Aouel said quietly. "I accepted your coin because I was told I would be killed if I did not. Rophetian code states that our oath is binding only when we are free to give it—if, held prisoner, we are forced to swear or die, Tonn permits us to save our own lives. I can make my case before the Captains' Council as a prisoner of war—I will not be punished or even sanctioned for my actions."

"You'll never see Captains' Council. You'll die with my teeth in your throat."

"Perhaps." Aouel studied him with an even look and said, "But you are bound and I am free. Yours is the throat you should be worrying about." He shrugged and turned to those who had helped him put together the coup. "Any sign from the House?"

"Not yet."

He nodded and stripped off his dagger and belt, then his shirt and boots. When he stood in his breeches alone, he said, "In a moment, I'll either be back or dead. If I die, kill the prisoner, then leave by the front gate."

Then he walked toward Galweigh House's great main door, his heart pounding in his chest. It was easy enough to say the words, "I'll either be back or dead," but harder to make himself walk forward knowing that they were true, and that a crossbow quarrel might sprout from his chest in the next instant.

He held his hands up, palm forward. He was stripped of his weapons, stripped of everything but a pair of broadcloth pants and a gold Tonn medallion that hung around his neck.

As a pilot in a position of trust, he had known most of the old Galweigh codes and signals. He remembered them—but they were old. If Galweigh House had new codes, and new guards, he could only hope that someone among them might remember the old ones. Or that someone might recognize him and believe what he had to say.

Kait, crouched at one of the crossbow slits beside Dùghall and Ian, listened to the fighting in the landing field die down.

"Betrayal from inside the ranks," Dùghall said, and managed a thin chuckle. "Even if we're unlucky and the enemy wins, we won't have as many to fight."

"We'll know one way or the other soon enough."

Ian stood and raised his crossbow, and Kait heard him carefully slowing his breathing. She looked through her narrow access across the ragged field, and saw what he was watching—a man, stripped to nothing but pants, his empty hands held high in the air, walking toward them.

Her eyes were better than Ian's—her Karnee vision picked up details his purely human eyes could not. By the weak light of the stars, she could see his Rophetian braids, the amulet to Tonn around his neck, the puckered flesh of the old scar that ran the length of the left side of his chest.

She said, "Lower your weapon, Ian. I know him."

"That you know a man does not mean that he is your friend," Dùghall said. "Vincalis—"

Kait cut him off. "Vincalis didn't know Aouel. I do. If he approaches, he does so as a friend."

"Aouel?" Dùghall pursed his lips. "I would be inclined to trust him, at least to a parley. Do you see any behind him who have their weapons aimed at him, not at us?"

"No," Kait said.

"I can't see anyone out there at all," Ian muttered. "Except the one who walks toward us—and him I can barely make out."

Kait watched him lower his crossbow. "I don't envy you your eyesight." She kept her own pointed at the ground and said, "So do we let him in, or go out to meet him?"

"I think we let him stand with his belly to a crossbow and talk through the slit," Ian said.

Dùghall said, "I agree with Ian. Let's hear what he has to say before we make any compromises. I could get Ulwe, I suppose. She could read his intentions as he came toward us, and perhaps those of the soldiers in the field."

Kait nodded. "Get her."

Ulwe, Alcie, and Alcie's two children hid in the first siege room, behind a secret panel in the wall just behind the great entry. The room had probably been intended originally as a place where the owner could position a platoon of his soldiers when he didn't trust his visitors, but the Galweighs, always secure in their own power, had never needed to use it in that manner. It had been, for them, the first of many secret rooms filled with food, water, armaments, and other necessary supplies—and the first of many rooms the conquering Sabirs had stripped bare.

Dùghall left, and returned a moment later, the little girl following him closely. Without saying a word, she crouched and closed her eyes, and her body went rigid with the effort of her concentration.

"He hopes you will recall the old codes," she said softly, "because he has no way of knowing the new ones. He planned this . . . trick. He overcame my father. They have *him* bound in the tall grass, surrounded by soldiers. He's very angry." She sounded so sad, speaking of her father held prisoner by the men he'd thought would help him win her back. "Your friend will bring you no harm," she said to Kait. "He still loves you—the things he does for your Family, he does in memory of you."

"In memory?"

"He believes you to be dead."

"He loves you, too?" Ian said, a hint of bitterness in his voice.

"He was never my lover," Kait said quietly. "He was always only a friend. The Karnee curse—"

"—guarantees you an unending supply of men who will throw themselves on the blades of swords and march into the teeth of death for you, apparently." Ian partially raised the crossbow toward Aouel, then lowered it and sighed. "I'm sorry, Kait."

"I understand. I'm sorry, too." Ian had not attempted to renew their romantic relationship once Ry left. He had never alluded to that time at all before that moment, and Kait had hoped that he had gotten over her. Apparently he had not.

"I want to see my father," Ulwe said. "When you open the door for your friend, let me go out to talk to him."

"That isn't safe," Dùghall said.

The little girl looked up at him. "I'm not your ward and not your responsibility. I came with you because I chose to. Now I choose to go speak to my father."

"I would recommend doing that later, when we have things more settled," Dùghall said, but Kait turned to face him and rested a hand on his shoulder. "Let her go talk to him. Now. Life is too uncertain for promises of later." She turned back to the crossbow slit.

Dùghall sighed.

Aouel came up the steps and stopped at the top one. "I come to tell you that your enemies have fallen into our hands, and that we who have captured them offer ourselves into your service," he said. "I offer as token of my good faith my own life, and the codes—"

Kait had moved at his first word to unbar the door. Now she finished unbarring it. She opened it and stepped into his view, and for an instant she could see hope warring in his eyes with disbelief. Then his face creased in a broad smile, and he said, "Ah, Kait. Ah, Kait. You're alive. I'll owe Tonn two more lifetimes at least for that."

Kait was aware of Ulwe slipping past her and hurrying down the stairs, but she only laughed and gave Aouel a warm hug. "Old friend, I owe him at least a lifetime now, too. I'll be reborn a Rophetian for sure, for I swore to him if he just got me out of that airible in one piece, I would dedicate a full life to him. And I thought about you often, and prayed that you were safe. If he answered that prayer, too, I am deeply in his debt."

She pulled away, and Dùghall said, "We can use the help, Aouel. How many troops have you brought us? And how many prisoners?"

Aouel didn't answer the question. Instead, he studied Dùghall. "I almost think I know you." He frowned, and Kait could hear the puzzlement in his voice. "Certainly you remind me of someone, and you know me—but I swear, Parat, I remember faces, and I have never seen yours."

"He's Uncle Dùghall," Kait said. She couldn't figure out how to explain her uncle's sudden youth in any brief manner, and finally decided on vagueness. "He's been through a lot since you saw him last."

Aouel arched an eyebrow and smiled at the understatement. "As have we all. And you . . ." He turned to Ian.

Kait again provided introductions. "Ian Draclas, captain of the *Peregrine*." She turned to Ian, "Aouel fa Asloodke den Kalemeke Toar," she said, giving his full Rophetian name. *Aouel, son of Asloodke, born of Calimekka, Full Captain.* "First captain of the Galweigh airible fleet."

The men did not exchange the bows customary of landsmen—they simply nodded, one captain to another. Acknowledgment that in their own worlds, they were both kings, and thus spared the posturing of lesser men.

Aouel turned to Dùghall. "I can see now who you are. I would love to hear someday how these last hellish years have been so kind to you." He looked like he wanted to say more in that vein, but he held his silence for an instant, then added, "Sixty of the men I count as ours. They hold eighteen prisoners. Three of those are lieutenants, one is a master sergeant, and one is Crispin Sabir." The corner of his mouth quirked into a tiny smile as he said that. "He shall not make a happy prisoner."

"No," Dùghall said. "He won't." He shook his head in amazement. "I would not have thought sixty Galweigh loyalists existed in all of Calimekka."

Aouel said, "I'm not sure sixty did. Some of these abandoned the Goft Family when it joined forces with the Sabirs. Some came home from the Territories and found everything changed. We've been gathering this counterforce for some time, waiting for an opportunity to rejoin the Galweighs, and uncertain if any true Galweighs still existed. Two days ago, one of the lieutenants let slip that we would be dropping by night into Galweigh House . . . and suddenly the loyal Sabir troops began having accidents while they trained, or becoming sick at their meals, or getting into trouble in their off-duty time."

"And now we have both a defensive force and a few bargaining chips," Kait said.

Dùghall said, "Does Crispin know how many of us held this place?" He shook his head and answered his own question. "If he had known that, he would not have needed such a force."

"He didn't know who or what you had in here. He thought to prepare for the worst that he might face."

Dùghall nodded. "Let's bring them in, then. The dungeon cells are clean enough, and if your men will post guards—"

"I'll handle it. We planned for this as much as for everything else. One moment." He stepped out onto the portico and whistled. The circle with prisoners in the center transformed itself into a thick-walled line with soldiers to either side of each prisoner, and soldiers at both front and back.

Kait watched the formation begin moving forward. "Lot of women in there," she observed.

"A lot of people dead in the city—and food is scarce and money worth next to nothing. Keeping a fighting force becomes harder by the day. Those who stay are those who have nowhere else to go, and no one else who might need them now that times are so hard."

"I don't like bringing them in here," Ian said quietly. "What if, among those you have judged loyalists, there are traitors? What if, when they come through the doors, the sides switch again and we find that we have opened the House and put ourselves in the hands of our enemies?"

"I vouch my life on those who have joined me," Aouel said.

"Ulwe said they were on our side, too," Kait reminded him.

Still, watching that line of soldiers and prisoners marching toward her, she felt a faint cold chill on the back of her neck, and sensed a rogue twisting in the ropes of fate. Crispin Sabir, she thought, would not go quietly into prison—and Crispin Sabir had the means to make a great deal of noise.

Ulwe stood outside the ring of soldiers. "Father," she said quietly, "I have come."

She looked at the man, the beautiful creature, who was her father. His lean features and light eyes had marked her own face—she could never doubt that he was her father. Looking at him, she could see no external mark of the cruelty and the evil that she had felt inside. How easy it would be to love him. How easy to trust him. If only she could not see what he was, she could be his daughter joyfully.

Briefly she cursed the Seven Monkey People for teaching her to walk the road and hear its stories. Blind and deaf to the truths it told, she could have run into his embrace and said, *Papa, I have waited so long.* On her long trip across the sea, that was the way she had envisioned this meeting. She had never thought to see her father bound in shackles, and certainly had never thought that she would be relieved to see him so.

"Ulwe," he said quietly. "My beautiful daughter. I did not realize you had grown so big." She saw his eyes fill with unshed tears, saw him swallow and look away. "You look very much like your mother. She . . . was beautiful, too."

"I had hope we would meet . . . better than this," she said, trying hard to find something to say that was both true and kind.

He looked back at her and his smile was self-mocking. "I seem to have overplanned for the occasion." His eyes flicked around the ring of soldiers, then down to his hands bound in metal bracelets, and he sighed.

The soldiers were watching the two of them. Ulwe stayed well back of their line, sensing their wariness even of her—of the uncertainty she introduced. They feared that she would somehow incite her father to rage; that she would try to cause a diversion that would allow him to escape; that she would suddenly draw a weapon and charge the nearest man in a futile attempt to rescue him herself. So she stood very still and kept her hands where everyone could see them, and did not look at anyone but her father.

"I'm sorry I didn't reach you in time," he said. "I'm sorry I was not in the harbor waiting for your ship when it arrived. I'm sorry that you were taken hostage, that you have had to suffer for my sake. It was for that reason that I sent you away."

"I know," she said. "I . . ." She had so many things she could not tell him. So many things she dared not even hint at. She could not let him know that she had not been taken hostage—that she had come willingly to the Galweighs because she wished to avoid him. She looked at the ground and said, "I have been well treated. I am well treated still. And they have promised me that they will not hurt you."

Crispin laughed at that—bright, merry, genuine laughter. "How kind of them to tell you so. Dear Ulwe, perhaps they care enough about you that they did not want to fill you with dread. Or grief." The laughter was gone from his face, replaced by pain and regret. "They will kill me. They must, or I will find a way to kill them."

"They believe you will fetch them a good ransom."

"They believe wrong. None at Sabir House would pay for my life. Not now. Not the way things have changed. My own brother, I suspect, will dance before the gods on the day my death is announced to him." He smiled slyly, and she caught the first sign of the other Crispin—the one who was not her father, but was instead the murderer, the torturer, the lover of power and pain. "Still, I should like to see them try. The negotiations would be . . . hilarious."

"I won't let them kill you."

"Ulwe, *chepeete,* don't let them kill *you.*"

One of the other prisoners said, "Parat, is she truly your daughter?"

"Silence, Sergeant," a guard said.

Her father looked at the sergeant. The man wore a different uniform than those of most of the rest of the soldiers. He and four of the other prisoners wore solid black, not black and green and gold. Something about the severity of those black uniforms, something about the looks in the eyes of the men and the one woman who wore them, sent a warning alarm through Ulwe's gut. She wished she dared rest her fingertips on the ground to hear what it had to tell her—she wanted to know why those soldiers looked different; she wanted to know why their eyes alone of all the prisoners held no fear. Crispin told the man, "She is my true daughter, my chosen heir."

One of the guards turned to Ulwe and, not unkindly, said, "Go back to the House now, child. This is no safe place for you."

Ulwe nodded, though she didn't want to leave. She had other things she wanted to say to her father. But Kait would let her speak to him again, she thought. Kait had promised that they would not kill him unless they had to—and he was sitting peacefully, letting these guards do what they wanted with him, offering them no threat. "I'll come to talk to you," she told him. "I promise."

Her father shook his head. "Never pass up the opportunity to say good-bye, daughter. Something I learned when I was younger than you—we have no promise that we will meet again. Do what they want you to do—escape if you can. No matter what they've told you about me, no matter how many lies you've heard, remember that I came for you as soon as I could." His voice grew softer. "And know that I love you."

She bit her lip. She wanted to cry, and indeed several tears escaped from her rapidly blinking eyes and rolled down her cheeks. She was the reason he was a prisoner. His chains were her fault. And she believed him when he declared his love for her—he didn't know her, but he had made a place in his heart for the person he thought she was, and he truly loved that person.

"I'm sorry this happened, Papa," she said. "I pray we have long years yet to come to know each other."

She turned away, and began to walk toward the House.

"Tell me good-bye, Ulwe. If you don't, there may come a time in your life when you regret that."

She turned back, feeling a lump in her throat, and said, "Good-bye, Papa."

"Good-bye, Ulwe."

She turned away and began to trudge toward the House, fighting to breathe around the sudden lump in her throat, hating her weakness and her childishness.

The man who had gone to Dùghall and Kait and Ian to declare peace stepped out onto the great stone landing and whistled.

Behind her, the guards began shouting commands and threats.

"Up on your feet, you!"

"Stand still or I'll run you through!"

"We're marching to the House, and the one of you who steps out of line or trips or coughs or so much as looks at me wrong dies for the privilege."

She walked faster—she did not wish to be in the way of the moving column. She did not want to be the cause of any man faltering or tripping; she did not wish to be the agent, however accidentally, of any death. She heard the first tramping of feet, the cries of the wounded being carried forward, the rattling of light shackles, and she bolted up the steps and into Galweigh House, thinking only of being out of the way.

But as the soldiers moved their prisoners up the stairway and into the House, something happened within the column. Someone shouted, and Ulwe heard cries of pain, the clank of chains, and thuds. Beneath her feet, the cool white stone reverberated with nearby pain, and cried out with fear and anguish and sudden death.

She saw the black-dressed soldiers fighting, shackled and weaponless though they were—they were using the chains that bound them as their armor and arms. One fell, a sword through her chest, and her red blood pooled on the white stone like a rose on snow, but locked in her dead embrace was a man in green and black, his neck twisted at an impossible angle and a chain around his throat and his eyes staring unblinking into the realm beyond the world. Two of the warriors stood back to back, swinging their chains in blindingly fast arcs, kicking with their feet at any who dared approach. Their chains caught the blades stabbed in at them, and for a moment Ulwe thought they would succeed, but the guards saw that they were the greatest threat and charged them in a mass.

And they fell, crying out in pain, and bleeding, and their cries turned to bubbling gasps, and they, too, died.

The air in Galweigh House grew chill. It seemed to swallow the sounds of fighting. It blew out the torch lit in the moments following the defeat of the Sabirs by the Galweigh loyalists, and threw the grand entry hall into darkness. Then, in the lightless, airless horror it made of the hall, faint lights appeared—bloodred lights that seemed at first to be candles lit within the bodies of the fallen, and then became fires that blazed inside their cores, and at last changed into suns that devoured flesh and bone and hair and blood and left only neat piles of cloth to mark the spots where warriors had given up their lives.

"Ahh," something whispered in her ear, and she would have screamed, but it passed by her, and she froze, fearing that if she made a sound or moved a muscle, it would turn and devour her as it had devoured the corpses.

"Ahh." A soft whisper, but that whisper was no sound of her world; instead, it echoed of the charnel house, of the funeral pyre, of the burial mound and the cold dark crypt.

Slowly, slowly, so slowly she could barely feel herself move, Ulwe slid into a crouch. She splayed her fingertips against the polished stone, and shut her eyes tightly, and sought the roadvoice.

And heard the hungry thoughts of uncounted dead who rose against the living, who sought those they called enemies, and grappled with them, and lifted them into the air. They longed for the flesh of their living enemies and for their blood, but magic constrained them—they could do no harm; they could neither maim nor kill, but only remove.

She had only an instant to decide, and only an instant to act. She leaped to her feet and raced back to her father. "I love you," he had said, and above all else she had felt the truth of those words. "Papa!" she shouted, and threw herself into his manacled arms, though the spirits of the dead had surrounded him. She clung tightly to him, and he to her, as the chill fingers of ghosts tried to pry them apart—and when the dead things left off and lifted both of them into the air, they held each other tighter.

Whispering, hissing, seeking for ways to break the oath that bound them, the spirits of Galweigh House stole away with their captives—out of the House, across the long swards of green, over the wall, onto the road that lay beyond Galweigh House and out of reach of the boundaries of Dùghall's spell. There they deposited them, and then they retreated.

Ulwe opened her eyes.

She and her father lay on the floor of the jungle. The earth beneath her spread hand quivered with coming death. And the protective wall of Galweigh House lay to the west of them; it's great gate, which would have kept them safe, now closed against them.

Chapter 36

The litters arrived for Ry and Jaim and Yanth promptly at the tolling of Dard—three fine open-sided seats with extendable mud ramps, each borne by six sturdy locals, which answered the question of who was expected for dinner. Ry had seen the litters in the streets before, and knew them to be for hire, but in his guise as a poor commoner, he thought he would be best to walk in the mud. Now he got into the litter with gratitude; how pleasant to ride instead of slogging, to be above the mud and the mire instead of right in it.

He and his two lieutenants rode to the bay, where a fine longboat nestled against one of the little docks, brightly painted in blue and red, with the top strakes and the high, arching stemposts carved with fanciful beasts and gilt. All the men waiting to row them to their dinner date were human, but the reptilian smell of the Keshi Scarred was strong on the wood and on the oars. Ry wondered if the fact that they were greeted by only humans was simple chance, or an attempt to hide the presence of the Keshi. He and Yanth and Jaim rode in silence, seated on the central thwart with eight rowers behind them and eight in front, two to each oar.

As he had expected, they rowed out to the ship he had identified earlier as the *Peregrine*. He reminded himself not to slip and use that name under any circumstances. He and Yanth and Jaim had discussed their options and decided that they would best serve their own interests by feigning ignorance of the true identity of the ship, at least until they could find out why the captain had sought them out.

A slender, dark-haired human woman greeted them as they clambered up the allus ladder and onto the deck. She bowed deeply in the fashion of the Wilhenes, and said, "*Salanota*. I am Katanapalita, your servant for this evening." Her accent was thick, markedly Wilhene. "If you have for needs, you have only for asking—I will do all I can."

Ry watched her carefully. She added no innuendo to that the way the captain's concubine had earlier. He bowed in return and answered her in the primary Wilhene dialect, Tagata. "Our needs will be light, and our gratitude plentiful."

Her face lit up and she answered him in her native tongue. "You speak Tagata? It's been so long since I heard it."

Jaim bowed and spoke in turn, also in the Wilhene dialect. "My friends and I once spent some time touring your fair city. We were there when the cherries were in bloom and every street was pink with their blossoms. It was quite lovely." His Tagata was, if anything, better than Ry's.

She smiled broadly. "There is no place more beautiful, I think; now that I have seen so much of the world, I am sure of it." Her smile became wistful. "I had a little house near the Temple of Winter Passing—I could hear the waterfall through my back window and watch the priestesses as they tended the sacred gardens."

Ry did not ask why she did not go back—people who made their lives on the sea often did so because something in their past had driven them from the land. Few wished to be reminded of what they had left behind. Instead he said, "I hope you have such joy again if that is your wish."

Her smile held gratitude. "Let me take you to the captain's dining room. She awaits you now."

The three men glanced at each other, surprised. She?

Katanapalita's back was to them, though; she did not see their reaction. She led them across the bleached stone-polished deck and down a gangway. Ry noted little places on the ship where the wood bore scars of previous fittings, where something new clearly adjoined something much older. The ship had been refitted recently—the work had been done by skilled shipwrights, but he saw a few places where corners had been cut, and most of the changes he could identify were cosmetic in nature.

Katanapalita led them to doors carved with fanciful beasts and heavily embellished with gilding, and stopped. "You must leave your boots outside," she said. Ry noted a rack built into the wall, scuffed from much recent use—this rule hadn't been created just for the three of them. He nodded, pulled off his boots, and slid them into one of the slots. Jaim and Yanth, after a barely perceptible hesitation, followed his lead. When they stood in their stockinged feet, she ushered them into a captain's dining chamber unlike anything Ry had ever seen. The table, built into the floor and with the traditional rim around the edge to keep plates from sliding off in high seas, had nonetheless been made to look like something that would have been at home in any of the great Houses of Calimekka. The wood, hand-rubbed to a beautiful sheen, was inlaid with as much detail and delicacy as the puzzle-box he'd received earlier that day—tiny patterns of leaves and flowers formed a border around the scene of a village nestled in the mountains. Every leaf of every tree was complete with veins and edges; each tiny person on the inlaid streets wore a different expression and a detailed outfit, and carried out a different task. Their flowing white hair had been worked in ivory, their iridescent skin in rare, black mother-of-pearl; they were not representations of humans, but were Scarred of the sort that Ry had seen sitting at the table with the Keshi earlier that day.

The tabletop had been the masterwork of a genius—Ry wondered how the captain could bear to set her plate on top of it.

Nor was the table the only thing in the room to catch the eye. Panels of pale gold raw silk and panels of deep carved black velvet alternated along the walls and a deep, plush rug of amazing softness and intricate design covered the floor, its black mazes, gold background, and red accents perfectly harmonizing with the silk and velvet wall coverings. The ceiling boasted a central light fixture that was clearly of solid gold, with the light itself of Ancients' make—a coldlamp that would prevent any use of open flame in this tiny mirror of palatial splendor. The pale cypress ceiling glowed with hand waxing and made the room seem both larger and more subdued. Ivory silk reclining couches in the Strithian style flanked the walls, the perfect final touch.

Opulence. Decadence. Power. The room spoke of all of them—and even, Ry thought, of good taste, something he hadn't noted in the rest of the ship's decoration.

"Please be seated," Katanapalita said, still speaking in Tagata. Ry noted that she had removed her shoes, too, and had replaced them with little satin slippers. She handed a pair of soft black doeskin slippers to each man and bowed her retreat. "I shall tell the captain that you have arrived. And while you await her, if there is anything I could bring you, please don't hesitate to ask."

"We await your captain's pleasure," Ry said, and took a seat on one of the couches.

Katanapalita left them with another bow, closing the door behind her.

"She didn't ask us to leave our swords outside," Jaim said.

Yanth snorted. "Or to bond them."

"She seemed quite charming."

"A bit old for my tastes." Yanth shrugged. "But nice enough, and certainly taken with you—you and that Wilhene jabber of yours."

Jaim gave Yanth an exasperated look. "Must every woman you see first pass through the filter of whether or not you want to bed her before you can decide on her other qualities?"

"What other qualities does a woman need to have?" Yanth ran his finger along the tabletop and raised an eyebrow. "It's the first thing you think, too, Jaim—you've simply spent so many years hiding the fact from yourself that you don't notice it anymore."

"And now you know what I think."

"I know what any man thinks." He waved a thumb in Ry's direction. "He'll tell you. Pretending you're some fine, civilized exception to the rule doesn't make you better. It just makes you silly. Isn't that so, Ry?"

Ry was looking around the room, only half-listening to this latest incarnation of their oldest argument. With senses sharpened to the aching point by his increasing nearness to Shift, he smelled fresh air and felt its movement over his skin even after the door was closed, but sitting where he was, he could see no place where it might originate. He suspected, too, that the three of them were being watched; he felt the little burr of tension that raised the hair on the back of his neck and on his arms, though he could hear nothing that would help him locate any watchers.

He rose and walked to the table, saying, "I suppose it's the first thing that most men think. I can't say all." He didn't look directly at either of his friends, but he could see them plainly from the corners of his eyes. They had taken positions on two of the other couches; Yanth struck a casual pose, leaning back against the couch's headrest-arm, with one slippered foot on the couch and the other trailing on the floor. He appeared to be completely relaxed, but his right hand rested near the hilt of his sword, and Ry had seen him leap from that pose to full fight before. Jaim, on his couch, sat with both feet on the ground, back stiff, hands on lap. He looked the part of a yokel out of his element, and that was as much a pose as Yanth's posturing.

"But isn't it the first thing you think?"

"Of course."

"There. You see?"

Ry ran his hands over the tabletop and said, "This is beautiful workmanship," all the while following the scent of that fresh air.

Yes. The back wall, the central carved velvet panel. He didn't look at it directly, but he'd bet his life that no wooden wall lay behind that panel—that it was, if not a passageway through which fighters could move with ease, at least a niche into which a single spy could drop from the deck above.

He smelled nothing that would tell him a spy already hid there, and he heard nothing out of place. But his senses, refined though they were, were not perfect. And the crawling skin on the back of his neck suggested that he and his men *were* being watched.

From the known hallway, a chorus of tiny bells jingling, and the light tread of several pairs of feet.

The door opened, and all three men stood and turned to face it.

Katanapalita came first, bowing again in greeting. She stepped to the side and said, "I present Captain Rrru-eeth Y'tallin, Princess of the Jerrpu of Tarrajanta-Kevalta, and her first concubine, Greten Kasta-woehr."

Ry returned her bow and said, "I am Ry dem Arin, and these are my friends and colleagues, Jaim dem Naore, and Yanth dem Fanthard."

The captain, dressed gorgeously in fitted red silk tunic and breeches and soft black calf-high suede-soled boots, was the iridescent-skinned creature they had seen in the inn eating with the humans and the Keshi Scarred. She smiled and said, "Sonderrans by name, with Calimekkan accents and the faces and bearings of those Family-born. What unusual birds you are who have flown into my nest. Greten brought you my gifts, I trust?"

Greten bowed and looked directly into Ry's eyes, her expression one of both challenge and seduction. The bells sewn to the hem of her nearly transparent silk dress jingled softly.

Ry looked from captain to concubine and back, and without a word held out his right hand—the ring adorned his index finger.

Rrru-eeth smiled more broadly this time, revealing small, pointed, perfectly white teeth. "And the other gifts?"

"Those as well, though I could not begin to guess their meaning." He held out his left hand and displayed the pearl, the tree, the coin, and the little box. "My gratitude—they are exquisite—and they were presented exquisitely." He bowed slightly in the Calimekkan fashion and gave both Rrru-eeth and her concubine Greten a warm smile.

He had a hard time reading Rrru-eeth's face—its configuration was nearly human, but her expressions were something other. He had an easier time reading her scent. She was excited, aroused, even . . . triumphant. He wondered who she thought he was; he wondered what she hoped to get from him. And he wondered how he could deliver her to the people she had betrayed.

Chapter 37

Rrru-eeth and Greten led them through every form of small talk as the dinner progressed; they discussed travel, trade, the weather, the odious condition of Heymar, and adventures they had experienced on the sea—though these last Ry suspected were carefully edited by each teller to reveal nothing of importance. By the time dessert arrived, Ry had noted that everyone who entered the room was a woman, and human, and that none of the women bore any sort of weapon. Each server wore a dress similar to the one worn by Greten, though without the bells—they could as easily have hidden a weapon on themselves when they were naked and fresh from the bath.

He and Jaim and Yanth found it easy to be charming and entertaining; but all of them remained cautious. They did no more than sip their wine, though both the captain and Greten drank freely. They always made sure their swords hung unencumbered at their sides, the hilts loose in their scabbards and easy to reach. They ate a food only after the captain or Greten had taken bites of it and swallowed them.

With the dessert behind them, the captain sighed. "You are fighters, ever wary, while we are women born to the arts of pleasure and love. Will you not relax just a bit and let us entertain you?"

Jaim, sipping cordial, inhaled it and choked, and emerald-green droplets sprayed from his nose. Yanth turned a startled laugh into a cough.

Ry, however, showed the women—and the guards he suspected of watching from behind the secret panel—nothing but a faint smile. He said, "Captain Rrru-eeth, I find your offer both generous and tempting, but we are strangers to you, and you to us. We have no idea why you've invited us to dine with you, nor what you hope will come from this meeting. Please . . . tell me why you have given me such fine gifts, why you have welcomed me as if I were a prince, why you have sought the three of us out to be your guests for this evening."

Rrru-eeth rose and walked to the back of the room, to stop in front of the panel that Ry suspected held the watcher he couldn't hear or smell. She stood with her back to the table, so that he could see the way her braid hung down her back nearly to her knees before looping back up to tuck in a coil into her belt. From the back, the narrowness of her shoulders, the almost stemlike quality of her waist, and the rounded flare of her hips were evident. "You would find it so hard to believe that I saw you sitting at that table and wanted you?"

"I remember how I looked and how I smelled sitting at that table, and I would have to say that if you saw me then and found me desirable, I would have to question your taste." He gestured at the room. "And from the appearance of this place, I would not dare to question that."

She turned and laughed. "What a very pretty way to call me a liar." Her pointed little teeth gleamed in the soft light. "And perhaps in a way I am, though not in the manner you might think." She settled on one of the white couches and sighed. "Ah, my lovely fellow, my story is such a sad one. I loved a man once—the previous captain of this ship, in fact. And he loved me. We sailed together for long years, and in those long years I never knew a moment of sorrow. We found a city of the Ancients on the far shores of Novtierra together, and gathered unimaginable treasures, and when our holds were full to brimming, we sailed back toward Ibera, hoping to sell our riches. From them we hoped to acquire the wealth to buy an island we both loved, far from the world that would never have accepted our love. Ian had promised me he would give up the sea. But fate was . . . cruel. We sailed into a Wizards' Circle, and the magic within it first becalmed us, then devoured many of those aboard the ship. He died trying to save the life of one not worthy to scrub the decks he walked on."

A tiny tear crept from the corner of her eye and slipped down her jewellike cheek, and the quaver in her voice sounded heartfelt. Ry was almost impressed. "I'm sorry," he said, managing to sound both sympathetic and genuine.

She smiled bravely, and her upper lip quivered the tiniest bit. Even the scent she gave off suggested absolute sincerity. Had he not known the truth, he would never have suspected her of lying.

"When I saw you sitting in the Long Comfort, I thought at first that I had seen a ghost. Then, that perhaps my eyes had deceived me, and I had not seen him devoured by the wizard-water. I tried to tell myself that he had, instead, been swept overboard and had somehow managed to survive, and had even more miraculously found his way across the vast expanse of the Bregian Ocean and into my waiting arms." She looked down at her hands lying still and small in her lap, and she shook her head sadly. "And then I realized that you only look very like him, and I had to hurry away from there before I started to weep in front of my officers." Her tiny smile when she glanced up at him offered to share a confidence with him. "That sort of thing is very bad for shipboard discipline."

"It would be," Ry agreed.

"So. I asked around about you—just a bit. You've been quiet about your reasons for being in this appalling mud hole. Very circumspect."

He nodded but said nothing, and after a moment of uncomfortable silence, she smiled again. "And you're now going to be circumspect with me." Her head tipped to one side, birdlike, and her enormous black eyes blinked.

They both waited. He felt her nearing her actual objective, and he could not on his life imagine what she wanted of him and his men.

Again she smiled, and again spoke into the silence. "Since you will not tell me your troubles, I will leave them for later. You may someday wish to confide in me." She shrugged. "You have clearly fallen upon hard times. You are no more Sonderran than I am. You are purely Calimekkan; you are, unless I miss my guess terribly, estranged from your Family, with no one in the world save these your two friends; and you are short of money and uncertain about the direction you should next take with your life."

Ry laughed and said, "You could not be more correct, Parata. You are an exquisite judge of the truth."

Rrru-eeth lay her head back on the curving arm of the couch and watched him through heavy-lidded eyes. "If I'm lucky, I will prove an equally good judge of character."

Ry waited.

"I miss my lover and my friend. I know you aren't him. But nothing I can do can bring him back, and you remind me of him so much that when I see you I almost can't breathe. I want you to be my concubine."

Ry thanked every god whose name he could recall in that instant for years of diplomatic training and years of practice in hiding what he was from the world; had he not had it, he would have burst out laughing. Or maybe he

would have strangled her. Instead, he simply nodded. "A
. . . *fascinating* offer, Parata."

Her smile was intended to be seductive. "Isn't it?" she
asked. "Of course I will keep Greten—she and I do so
enjoy each other's company. And no doubt you would
enjoy both of us. Together. You will want for nothing."
Her smile grew more suggestive. "Nothing."

To Ry's left, Yanth had grown so still he seemed not to
breathe. But beneath the table his right foot, crossed over
his left knee, bounced up and down so fast it was nothing
but a blur in the corner of Ry's eye. To Ry's right, Jaim
moved bits of crust across his dessert plate, staring downward as if he thought to read his future in those crumbs the
way seers read the patterns of the leaves left in a glass of
tea.

And Ry sat weighing all the meanings in her offer, and
considering what he could say that would get him what he
wanted. A trap lay in the room, in the puzzle she presented him, in her words and her actions—he could sense
it in the sudden weight of the air in his lungs and the
heaviness of the food that lay in his knotted gut and the
way her eyes and Greten's watched him while trying hard
to appear not to. He needed to thread his way through the
trap without springing it, and he could not see what it was
or even where it lay.

At last he decided that all he could do was be the man
he truly was. "I'm a freeman. And a fighter," Ry said quietly. "As are my friends. We were not born to spend our
days being bathed and perfumed and powdered, nor our
nights primping and dancing and posturing for the enter-
tainment of owners. I don't think I could turn myself into
a stud for pay. I won't pretend we aren't in trouble—we
are. And I won't pretend that an offer of a secure bed and
secure pay doesn't fall pleasantly on the ears. But not that
way. My men and I could offer you our services as bodyguards," he said. "We could protect you and your friends

and servants." He looked at her and shrugged slightly. "But, Captain, I cannot sell myself to you as your toy. I couldn't guarantee that the, ah, toy would even work under such circumstances."

She closed her eyes and sighed, but her smile grew broader. The feeling in the air lightened, and he sensed that somehow, that answer was the right one.

"You do sound so like him." She sat up then, and the seductress fell away from her and left in her place a woman used to getting what she wanted. "He could never have been a woman's plaything, either." She rubbed her hands together briskly and said, "Please bring me the gifts that I sent to you."

He removed the items from his pouch, and slipped the ring from his finger, and carried them to her. "You wish to have them back?" he asked, placing them in her hand.

She waved off the suggestion with a dismissive flick of her wrist. "I would not give a gift only to demand it back if I didn't get my way. But let me tell you about these," she said. "The little tree—it was something Ian had done for him when we were in the islands of the Devil's Trail. He said the tree was his Family's crest. He claimed to be of Sabir birth, but his name was Ian Draclas, and though he owned this ship, which is of Sabir make, he never flew the Sabir flag."

Ry said, "If he were one of the *uvestos,* that would not be so hard to understand."

"Uvestos?"

"In the highest Families, children born illegitimately who are acknowledged by their Family parent but not by that parent's legitimate mate still have certain Family rights. They cannot use the Family name, nor can they hold position within the Family or inherit title or land. But they can claim Family kinship, inherit and receive Family properties, and pass on these rights to their own children. These people and their sons and daughters are *uvestos.*"

"Ian never called himself such to me, but the story he told me would make him one of these." She looked at Ry. "So that was him. *Uvesto.* Unlike him, you are truly Sabir, are you not?"

"Not anymore."

She frowned a little. "You have the look, the bones, the carriage. And the crest on the hilt of your sword. You had it covered earlier today, but I see it clearly now. Forgive me for noticing, but I do recognize that. And if you ever were a Sabir, you still are. Blood is blood."

"Not Calimekkan blood," Ry said. "Any citizen can be declared never to have been born, and can be put under sentence of eternal banishment and worse. Not a happy fate." His smile to her as he said that felt strained. He had a hard time making light of the fate he had chosen. *Barzanne.*

"You have been disowned, then?"

"*Disowned* is such a simple word. I have been declared *barzanne,* which is not so simple, and not so kind."

"Then truly you have need of a patron. Second sons and first sons of lesser branches often do. And you have about you that lean and hungry look that I identify with the hunter, the hungry son, the one who desires more than what he can have. You have, unless I miss my guess, a great ambition for power and a great desire to get back all that you have lost."

Ry didn't care to tell her how far she had missed her guess. The only thing he wanted back was Kait. His Family—or what remained of it—could go hang itself. But Rrru-eeth would be much happier thinking that she was prescient, and would be much less difficult to deal with if she thought she understood him. So he said, "That I desire with all my heart."

"Well, I want things, too. I want more than this ship, more than money. I want my own House in Calimekka— a great House and a great Family that will be acknowledged the equal of any of the Five. I want to be recognized and accepted, I want to be invited to parties, I want to be envied by human women and lusted after by human men."

"You aren't human," Ry said, pointing out the obvious and hoping that he wouldn't enrage his hostess.

"No. I'm not. And Ibera has no place in it for the non-human but the Punishment Square or the gallows. Am I correct?"

"Yes."

"And still I want these things. I have accomplished so much in my life. I have risen from slave to freedwoman, and from freedwoman to ship's captain, and I will rise further yet. I am still young. Before I grow old, I will be a parata in Calimekka, and a paraglesa, and the head of a powerful Family." She looked past him, and he got the feeling that she was looking far beyond the walls of the room, far beyond Heymar's harbor. Her voice grew soft, and carried in it an undercurrent of rage. "I will own slaves and land and wealth beyond counting, and men will approach me on their knees."

She fell silent, and Greten and all three men found other places to look.

Her sharp laugh brought their attention back to her. "Well—I do have my plans." She touched the other items she had given Ry. "And you have a place in them. A place of honor." She touched the tree again. "You have the bloodlines to understand honor—and apparently you have some personal integrity, too."

Next she laid a finger on the tiny coin that she had given him. "This is a coin from my people and my land—I'm from up around the Wizards' Circle you call Lake Jirin. My own clan is no more, though there are others of my kind who still inhabit the region. This I have kept with me since I was a small child. For years, it was the only thing I owned, and if my master had known of it, he would have taken it, too." She smiled coldly, and he found himself wondering what had happened to her master. Kait had mentioned Rrru-eeth's grim past, and had said she'd had to kill the man who owned her to save a number of children—but Ry got the feeling that when she finally did kill him, she had taken her time with it, and had gone not for quickness and mercy, but for slow and exacting revenge. "This coin," she said in a voice edged with ice, "was the price of my sister's life. And it will buy a thousand lives like the one of the man who killed her before it is spent up."

She picked up the blue pearl and studied it. "These are reputed to be magical. They are supposed to symbolize fidelity, but more than that, they are supposed to enforce it. If you swallow one whole, the story goes that you become incapable of betraying the one to whom you swear allegiance."

She touched the ring. "And this was Ian's. One of the few things that he held dear that I have in my possession. It is the ring of a Strithian king, and how he acquired it, he never told me. And now I will never know. But it is a symbol to me of many things. Of my eternal love for him. Of the power I desire. Of the transient nature of life, and the way power can pass from hand to hand." She stood and looked down at him. If Ry stood, her head would come no higher than the center of his breastbone, but he sat and let her maintain that aura of command she seemed to want.

Ry said, "An unusual little collection of objects. Why give them to me?"

"You won't sell yourself, though you will sell your services. A fine distinction, but one I accept. I want to purchase your knowledge. And your loyalty. And your ambition. I want you to teach me what I must know to deal with Families—teach me everything you know about their structure, how they gather power, how they hold it, how they deal with each other."

"I would do this, but to what purpose?" Ry asked. "You cannot be accepted into Calimekkan society no matter how flawlessly you learn to act like a Calimekkan parata. You aren't human."

"But Greten is. And Greten will be my . . . *irrarrix*." The word trilled off her tongue. "I don't know of such a word in your language, but among my people, the one who holds true power does so from a position of great secrecy. His name is never known. The *irrarrix* speaks for him, acts for him, stands before the people for him at all times. The arrangement protects both the true master and the servant, for killing the *irrarrix* when something is done that angers the people accomplishes nothing—the true master will simply replace him with another, and will carry on as before."

"You could call them puppets, I suppose," Ry said. "But you're right. I know of no such word in Iberish."

"You see how I can make this work, then?"

"If you stay hidden. But if you are hidden, how do you intend to enjoy the fruits of your power? The *irrarrix*"— he stumbled a bit over the word, for the double set of trilled *r*'s threw him—"seems to me to be the one who benefits most from the arrangement. Men may come on their knees and bow, but they will bow before Greten."

"In public," Rrru-eeth said. "In public. What they will do in private is something else entirely."

"I see."

"Do you?" Those delicate eyebrows rose and fell, and the little feathery wisps moved in the breeze. She studied him intently, and he could see no emotion on her face. "Perhaps you do," she said at last. "You have no reason to love those who banished you. Perhaps you can see your way to understand the need for revenge—the justice in having it."

He smiled slowly. "I understand justice. With all my heart, I understand that."

"Then you will join me? You will teach me? You will travel with me to Calimekka and help me make Greten a parata there?"

Ry glanced at Jaim and Yanth. "I follow you wherever you lead," Yanth said.

Jaim nodded. "You have my loyalty if you choose to sail with her."

"You have good men," Rrru-eeth said.

"I do."

"Then wear the ring I gave you," she said. "Carry the tree and the coin, as reminders of who you once were and who I once was, and as a promise of who we shall become. And . . ."—she held out the blue pearl and dropped it on the table before him—"swallow that and swear you will be loyal to me."

He picked up the pearl and held it between thumb and forefinger. What a waste of a perfectly good pearl, he thought. But he held it to his mouth, and as he put it on his tongue, he thought, What if the tales have some truth in them? He could not swear loyalty to Rrru-eeth; he intended to give her to Ian and see her hanged for her treachery.

"I cannot swear loyalty to you as a woman," he said, taking the pearl off of his tongue. "In that capacity, another woman already has my oath. And my love."

"I don't want your love, and I don't require your body. I already have a concubine, and while I might lust for you in my bed, I can satisfy myself in other ways."

"Then I will swear my loyalty to your office as captain," Ry said, "because that I can give freely, and honestly, and without reservation."

"As your captain, I will accept that oath."

He nodded, and swallowed the pearl. With it still smooth on the back of his throat, he said, "Gods attend me." He stared into Rrru-eeth's fathomless eyes. "I swear on my life my undying loyalty to the true and rightful captain of this ship; I am your sword, Captain, to carry out your justice, and I am the hand through which your vengeance will be meted out. I swear myself the protector of your passengers, your crew, your honor, and your name." He spoke his words to Rrru-eeth, but he held his half-brother's face in his mind, and demanded that the gods hear that he had spoken only the truth; he owed his honor and his life to the *true* captain of the *Peregrine,* and to its rightful passengers whom these mutineers had betrayed—Ian, and Kait, and dead Hasmal, and Ian's loyal men, now also dead.

Rrru-eeth watched his face, nodded stiffly, and said, "A sincere oath—surely the gods heard you. But you should not swear before the gods more than is asked of you. You owe no loyalty to my crew, nor to my passengers. You owe loyalty only to me, and need work for justice only for me. Greten and any passengers we may take on will just have to take care of themselves." She smiled, but the smile was strained.

The pearl lay warm in his gut, and he thought he could feel that warmth spreading out and flowing through his blood. It was connection where he would never have thought to seek connection—Ian, who remained with Kait, now owned a part of him as surely as did Kait.

Ian would laugh, he thought, if he could hear what I've just done. Sworn my undying loyalty to him and the memory of the men who served him—I, who once swore to see him dead by my own hand.

He turned away from his thoughts and back to the practicalities of the moment. "We need to go back to the inn and gather our things," Ry said.

Rrru-eeth stood, smoothing the folds of her tunic. The beaded and feathered braids at the outer corners of her eyes swung back and forth, mesmerizing. "You do. And we shall have to arrange places aboard the ship to accommodate the three of you. At the moment, none of the cab-

ins are empty, and I do not wish to have you sleeping in
the galley with the common sailors. You must have their
respect from the first. So go back to your inn tonight, and
you shall take your places among us on the morrow. Join
us late in the day. Come the next high tide, we will sail for
Calimekka."

Chapter 38

Crispin was still bound. The metal around his wrists chafed, and the collar around his neck that forced him to keep his hands up against his chest was as tight as ever. But now he lay beneath the arch of trees, in soft grass, and the thing that stank of death and whispered perversities and touched him hungrily in tender places was gone. The wall that surrounded Galweigh House lay before him, but he was no longer within its confines. He lay outside of it. His daughter crouched beside him, worrying at the manacles with small, delicate fingers. His triumph—he had Ulwe, he was free of the House and its inhabitants, he had somehow pulled victory out of the jaws of defeat.

He sat up, thinking that if he Shifted, the collar around his neck would get tighter but the bracelets around his wrists and ankles would grow loose enough that he could shake them free. The question was, would the collar get so tight that it would strangle him before he could complete the Shift and return to human form? He had no wish to die in such an ironic fashion. Neither did he wish for Ulwe to see him as a beast. Someday he knew she would have to, but not yet. Not yet.

"Parat," a voice nearby whispered, "you've escaped as well."

"So it would seem." He searched out the source of the voice, and discovered that it belonged to Ilari, one of his personal guards. "How did you get away?"

"I had nothing to do with it. Some horror grabbed me and dragged me out here, telling me all the while what it wished it could do to me, and poking at me in the most disgusting fashion." She was crawling around the trees toward him, watching the gate for any signs of pursuit. She glanced at Ulwe. "You got her away from them."

"After a fashion." He smiled at his daughter.

"Good. I rejoice for you. But . . ." Ilari nodded toward the House. "They'll be after us before long. I need to get that chain off of you before we have to run."

"You can do that?"

"I'm good with locks. And I have my hairpins—no one thought to take them from me."

He saw then that she no longer wore her chains.

"Who else got free?"

"I'm not sure. We seem to be scattered about. Of our number, I saw Guibeall die—he and Hixcelie killed each other. And Theth died, too."

Crispin and Ilari could take Ulwe and escape together if they had to—if more of his personal guard had gotten free, so much the better. He suspected those nightmares from inside the House had carried the rest of his surviving troops outside and dumped them; he should have other loyal fighters to guard his back. And that gave him a sudden, tremendous advantage. The last thing the Galweighs would expect was another attack immediately. He would have Aouel's throat in his teeth before the night ended—he had sworn to it. And he would eliminate the Galweighs who still survived—he would make them pay for stealing his child.

Ilari, crouched behind him, neatly sprung the locks on the bracelets and collar, and they fell away. Crispin rubbed his wrists and ankles and throat briefly, then said, "Let's gather up the others who escaped. We're going back in. This time, we'll truly have surprise on our side."

Ulwe rested a hand on his forearm and shook her head. "No, Papa. You dare not. Trouble comes, and you must be well away from here before it arrives."

Crispin looked down into that earnest young face—the face in which he saw both a mirror of himself and of the one woman he had mistakenly loved so long ago—and for a moment he hesitated. He could take Ulwe from this place without exacting revenge; after all, he had the most important part of what he'd come for. But he felt Dùghall's memories in the back of his mind, and Ry's as well. He felt their distaste for him, their lack of respect for who he was and what he had accomplished as both a wizard and a man, and he knew that if he crept away without making them pay for what they had done, they would gloat. And they would spread stories of his weakness around the city.

Crispin had too many enemies. Any of them would leap at the first sign that he had lost his edge; he dared not let those who had stolen from him, who had shamed him, live.

He gently lifted Ulwe's chin with his index finger and said, "We go back in, Ulwe. But you will be safe. I will see to it." Then he turned to Ilari and said, "Let's hunt now."

Ilari grinned, and Crispin liked the way her teeth gleamed in the darkness. "We'll get them, Parat."

He flashed his own grin. "We will indeed."

They'll come back," Dùghall said.

Kait said, "Surely not. They barely escaped—by all rights they should be our captives."

Dùghall nodded. "But they aren't. They escaped, and they have Ulwe . . . and now Crispin must think of his pride and his reputation. We stole his daughter. He will have to kill us for the crime, or die trying."

Kait started to ask him why he thought that, but she already knew. Crispin's memories twisted inside of her mind, too, and when she allowed herself to touch them, she felt the utter truth in Dùghall's words. "But we'll beat them. We can get Ulwe back."

Dùghall was shaking his head. "She chose. For whatever reason, she decided to be with him. We have to let her go." He stared out into the darkness and said, "I don't like the feel of this night. I don't like the way the air moves, or the way sounds carry. Something is wrong."

"Something beyond Crispin attacking us again?"

Dùghall turned to Aouel. "How much fuel is in the airible?"

"Not much. And the right rear engine was knocking by the time we landed."

Dùghall said, "You have the men to fix these things?"

"We should find most of what we need—the Sabirs never could clear all the fuel from the wells. The House fought them too hard."

"Go, then. We probably don't have much time."

"Why must we flee? Why can't we let the House itself fend them off?" Kait asked.

"Because," Dùghall said, "the voices of uncounted dead Falcons whisper to me that now is the time to make a strategic retreat. If enough enemies come against us, the living will outstrip the capacity of the dead to remove them. The House can hold off small forces nearly indefinitely if it has the corpses to feed the spell. And it can clear large forces eventually—again, if enough die to keep the ghosts fed. But if we are overrun, we could be lost. Flight is *always* a better option than pointless death."

Kait stared out the window. "But there are no large forces. There are only those we have already defeated—and they are fewer now than they were the first time."

"Sometimes, Kait, it pays to listen to instinct."

She looked over at him thoughtfully. She would have argued . . . but in her gut, too, she felt the sudden urge to be elsewhere. Karnee senses, perhaps, or just the scent of wrongness in the night air. Whatever it was, it decided her. "There are a few things I would take with me."

"Fetch them then, but be quick."

Anwyn, his deformities hidden by mask and cloak and special clothing, had led his half of the mob up the easier incline of the Avenue of Triumph. His cousin Andrew had brought the other half up the Path of Gods. Both mobs kept silent—a surprising feat in itself, for they were not composed of trained soldiers, but primarily of angry survivors seeking revenge for the deaths of loved ones.

From his vantage point at the top of the great road of the Ancients, he could see the flickering of torches moving steadily up the distant Path of Gods. His own line had already come to a halt, deployed more or less in lines around the base of the wall from the west side of Galweigh House to its north. Andrew's forces would surround the House from the east to the north. The south, being built over the Palmetto Cliff, was inaccessible.

He moved his ladder carriers to the front of his ragged lines and, when he was sure his people were in place and fairly sure they would hold, ran north behind their lines to meet up with Andrew, where the two of them planned to give the sign to attack.

But instead of Andrew running along the cleared space between the great white wall and the jungle, he found Crispin loping toward him, with a pretty young girl, a few of his personal guard, and a handful of Sabir troops in tow, wearing a fierce grin on his handsome face.

Anwyn smiled beneath his mask, and held up a gauntleted hand. "Hold!"

Crispin slowed, then stopped. His grin faltered. "Brother," he said, "your timing is perfect. We can catch all of them in there if we hurry."

"Brother?" Anwyn's voice sounded hollow beneath the metal armor. "Who are you to call me brother?" Behind him, the mob shifted. A soft whisper—the hiss of a bag full of snakes poised to strike—rose from them. Andrew and a few of his horde closed the gap between them, boxing in Crispin and his people from the other side.

Crispin's eyes narrowed, and he said, "Anwyn, what game are you playing?"

"I play no game. We came to find those responsible for the death of half of Calimekka. We find . . . you. You and the brat you kept secret from your own Family. You claim you had no part in the disaster?"

"Of *course* I had no part in the disaster. I'm here for the same reason you are."

"And yet, you did not come with us, and you did not come with Andrew. And no one traveled these roads ahead of us. We posted guards. We sent scouts. How can you claim that you were not already here, that you are not part of the evil that comes from this place?"

"We came here to rescue my daughter—the Galweighs had her. We arrived by airible," Crispin snarled. "You moron, you *know* how we got here."

Andrew's people had cut Crispin and his daughter off from Crispin's troops; now Andrew and three of his men moved to surround them. "When he's dead, I get the little girl," Andrew said. He giggled.

Anwyn was disgusted. He needed to kill Andrew soon. But not tonight. Tonight he still needed him. "You can have the girl," he said. "When all of this is finished."

Crispin, one hand on Ulwe's shoulder, backed slowly until he could back no farther. He stood against the wall of Galweigh House with Andrew and Anwyn and their mobs between him and his people. He was trapped. He had only Ulwe at his side, and she would be useless in a fight. Worse than useless, he thought. A liability. He stared down at her, thinking that he had used girls like her any number of times as sacrifices to fuel his magic—but as a sacrifice, she would stand as far above those girls as a paraglesa stood above a commoner; she was, after all, his own daughter. His own blood. With the power he could draw from her life, he could utterly destroy those who hid behind the walls of Galweigh House—Dùghall, Ry, Kait, and the rest. He would have his vengeance on them. Further, he thought he would be able to craft a quick removal spell that would allow him to escape from his brother and his cousin and their horde of rabble. He could, if he aimed the spell carefully, destroy both Anwyn and Andrew; a sacrifice as enormous as a daughter would confer tremendous power. He might save Ilari or the others of his guard. He could certainly save himself. He could certainly hope for the immortality he so desired. He would not be beaten.

Andrew licked his lips and grinned at Ulwe, and beneath the palm of his hand, Crispin felt her shudder. A quick death would be better for her than what Andrew would do to her. And if he did not take some action, he would certainly die, and she would just as certainly become Andrew's toy. Eventually, she would also die. It was that "eventually" that so chilled him.

She looked up at him, and in her face he saw himself, and a poignant image of a love lost in his distant past, when he was a better man. When he had been less hungry for power, less frightened of life, less twisted by the choices he had made.

His options, then. Ulwe's merciful death at his hand, or his death at the hands of a mob and her slow, terrible destruction by Andrew?

And then a third option presented itself. It came not from him, but from memories not his own that resided within him.

He could use Falcon magic, and with Falcon magic, he could save Ulwe.

He had never followed the Falcon path—he had always known of it, as scholars in any field know something of the errant fools who practice bizarre offshoots of their own sensible discipline. But as he touched the old man's memories inside his head, he could feel Falcon magic. He could draw from his own life-force, from his own will and blood and flesh and spirit, and with his sacrifice of himself, he could send his daughter to safety. He could not use Falcon magic as a weapon; any magic that caused harm required sacrifice and also rebounded on its sender. So with Falcon magic, he could not destroy his enemies. He could clearly feel the range of his power, too, and, assessed as Dùghall would have assessed it, he could see that he was weak. He had not spent a lifetime developing the strength of character and the deep reserves of integrity that the old wizard had—he had propped his magic on the lives of others, and had never paid his own price. As a result, he had no hope of saving himself and Ulwe with Falcon magic. He would be lucky to save her.

And if he did sacrifice himself, where would Ulwe find safety? In that moment, he regretted terribly the fact that he had spent his life making enemies. He had no dear friend, no beloved companion, no sympathetic colleague with whom he could entrust his daughter's life.

Andrew said, "I want her now," and tittered.

Crispin heard Anwyn's disgusted snort; then, however, his voice boomed from behind the metal mask. "Give the child to Andrew; if you do so quickly and without causing difficulties, perhaps we can work something out for you."

Crispin's mind raced. He had so little time, so much to do. Both spells were clear in his mind, both sets of words as obvious and simple as if they were written in front of him. And his choices, too, were clear. Sacrifice Ulwe and save everything he wanted—even, perhaps, his chance of someday finding immortality. Or sacrifice his just vengeance, his pride, his future, and his life, and save his daughter.

Or do nothing and lose this brief opportunity, and with it everything—revenge, future, and daughter.

"Papa, give me to the bad man," Ulwe whispered, looking up at him. "Then they will let you go." Her face was pale, her body trembled, and he could see tears welling in her eyes.

His hands tightened on her shoulders, and his throat tightened so that he had to fight to breathe. "Not that," he whispered back, and kissed her lightly on the top of the head. Her hair was soft and smelled of hay and sunlight and girl; her skin was warm; and with his face so close to her, his Karnee ears easily picked up the bird-quick racing of her beating heart.

His hand slipped to the dagger at his hip, and he drew it quickly, before he could let himself think about what he was doing or debate further the rightness of his action. He tightened his grip around Ulwe with his left forearm so that she could not run, and tilted his left palm upward; he slashed the dagger across his exposed flesh, and when his blood poured from the deep cut, he bellowed:

"My flesh, my blood, my soul,
Vodor Imrish!
Yours for her life,
For her freedom,
For her safety.
Take what you will,
But first give me what I will."

"Papa, no," Ulwe shrieked. "They'll kill you!" She tried to break free from his grip, but he caught her up in both hands, lifted her feet off the ground, and flung her into the air, focusing his will like an arrow toward the parapet of the

wall high above him. The only place where he could hope
she would be safe was among his enemies—with Dùghall
and Ry and Kait. His shame was complete . . . but his
daughter would live.

She shot toward the parapet like a doll tossed by a child,
and landed lightly at the back edge. The stunned faces of
the mob turned from her back to him; Andrew screamed
like a pig at slaughter; Anwyn swore and called his personal
guards to surround him.

Crispin caught a quick glimpse of Ulwe's face staring
down at him, and then he heard her screaming, "Kait! Kait!
Come help him! They're going to kill him."

He did not have time to watch what happened atop the
wall, though, because in the next instant, Andrew was upon
him, knife drawn, snarling like a madman. The Falcon
magic had left Crispin weak and drained; he managed to
block Andrew's first thrust, but felt the second slip past his
guard and tear across his ribs, leaving a line of white-hot
fire in its wake. He yelled, and felt the beast within waken
and snarl and demand that he give himself over to it.
Crispin could control the beast—he had mastered Shift long
ago—but this time he did not. He let himself Shift; he let
the trappings of humanity fall away from him like symp-
toms of a sickness, and he set the fanged, four-legged monster free.

He heard screaming, but only peripherally. He tore off
the sleeves of his tunic with his teeth, shrugged out of his
cloak, and with a quick shudder worked free of boots and
breeches. He grinned, his lips pulling back over fangs long
as a man's thumb, and laid his ears flat against his head, and
in a growl dragged through Shift-mangled vocal cords, he
said, "Come a little closer, Andrew."

The guards around them backed away. Andrew said,
"Kill him, you fools," but perhaps none of the guards had
cared for Andrew's leering after a little girl. None approached, and Crispin launched himself into the air, ani-

mate fury with dagger-sharp claws, and tore eight long slashes in Andrew's left shoulder and the left side of his face as he vaulted past.

He landed, spun gracefully as any big cat, and coiled himself for the next spring.

Andrew swore, and Crispin caught the thickening of Karnee scent in the air. He waited; Andrew began to Shift. Crispin attacked again when his cousin was caught in mid-Shift—a clumsy creature neither man nor beast. He gouged out one eye and left the monster's throat a bloody mess. But the Karnee curse did not let its creatures die so quickly. Though the eye had ripped free of the socket and so was beyond repair, the gaping wound at Andrew's throat drew together and the bleeding stopped as quickly as the wound along Crispin's ribs had healed.

Crispin and Andrew braced themselves and attacked again. Andrew was the stronger and heavier opponent; Crispin was faster and more agile. They lunged and feinted and left chunks of each other's flesh and puddles of their own blood in an expanding circle on the ground. Speed, caution, and the fury of just rage gave Crispin the edge, though, and Andrew's blood poured faster, and his accumulated wounds slowed him more, until finally Crispin toppled him, held his teeth against Andrew's throat, and said, "Beg my mercy."

"Mercy," Andrew screamed, the sound a dark and horrible travesty of human speech.

"Louder."

"MERCY!"

"LOUDER."

"MERCY!"

"You never showed it, you'll never get it." Crispin sank his teeth deeply into Andrew's throat and shook his head hard—and felt the satisfying snap of Andrew's spine; his cousin went limp, and while he was paralyzed, before the Karnee curse had a chance to repair damaged flesh and damaged nerves, Crispin gnawed through both of Andrew's jugular arteries and, with a paw badly suited for the task, jammed his dagger through Andrew's ribs and deeply into his heart.

His heart sang with the triumph of the moment. He lifted his head from the bleeding corpse and, with Andrew's gore dripping from his muzzle, stared around him.

The faces that stared back at him were hate-filled, crazed, wild.

They were human—true human—and he had revealed himself as more than a collaborator with wizards. He had revealed himself as a wizard and as a monster.

He looked to Anwyn, wondering if he might kill him before he was taken down, but Anwyn was hidden completely within his armor. Pity I didn't sacrifice Andrew, he thought—I'd have done more good with his death than he did with his entire life.

"Kill it!" the mob was screaming.

"Kill it!"

He tensed his muscles, crouched, and sprang for Anwyn's head. He felt the catches that held Anwyn's gold mask in place snap, but the mask, caught perhaps on his horns, did not fall free. It stayed in place, and Crispin didn't get another chance. Anwyn's guard attacked him with swords, and when he fled toward the rabble who ringed Galweigh House, they picked up their cudgels and pitchforks and spears and beat him back.

He felt the first blows land—terrible silent explosions that tore his muscles and shattered his bones and ripped the breath from his body. And then one thunderbolt landed at the base of his neck, and after a stunning instant of pain worse than anything he had ever experienced, warmth suffused his body. He felt better.

He felt . . . good.

Sight faded, replaced with comforting darkness, womb-like darkness. Sensation faded. He did not feel pain. Did not feel touch. Did not feel anything. He floated in comfort. Smell faded, the stinks of sweat and filth and fear and hatred erased along with the sweet scent of the night air and the distant, haunting whisper of jasmine that was the last scent he could recall. And finally sound faded. The soft throbbing of his slowing heartbeat, soothing as the lulling waves breaking on a beach, washed away the screams and the shouts, the thin, high voice of Ulwe shrieking, "Papa, no! No!," the whisper of the wind, the rattle of palm fronds. And at last, even that soothing, pulsing wash of sound was gone.

"Monsters and traitors," Anwyn shouted, his voice carrying over the cleared ground that surrounded the House. "Two are dead. The rest hide within those walls."

He pointed up to the parapet, to the little girl who still stared down at the crowd and at the bloody tatters that were all that remained of her father.

Crispin's brat. His heir. Anwyn wanted her dead.

Then a woman appeared atop the wall beside the girl and stood staring down at the place where the child pointed. She looked painfully familiar, and after an instant, Anwyn realized why. She was the woman Anwyn had watched fall to her death from the top of the Sabir tower—the woman whose body had disappeared without a trace. She was a Galweigh—and something more. Karnee. A keeper of enormous magic. A woman who had to die.

The Galweigh woman covered the child's eyes and pulled her away from the parapet. She, however, glanced down at him for just an instant before disappearing, and in that instant he read cool assessment, and the promise of his own doom.

He suppressed his shudder. She wouldn't live to keep that promise. He would see to that.

"The ladders," he shouted. "Get the rest of the monsters!"

Howling, the rabble he and Andrew had gathered charged back to their ladders and threw them up against the wall at a dozen points. The ladders weren't tall enough to reach the top of the wall, but they were tall enough to get the rope-masters with their grappling hooks into position.

Ropes sailed over the parapets, and some skittered back again, their hooks finding nothing to hold. But others found purchase. And half a dozen men climbed the undefended walls, and dropped to the other side, and dragged up the rope ladders that the rest of the mob would climb, and anchored them.

But they had no more than settled the ladders into place when invisible forces picked them up and dropped them back outside the walls, carefully and gently.

"Keep going," Anwyn screamed, and the mob poured up the walls.

They, too, were picked up as soon as they were inside the walls and put down outside and unharmed.

"Faster," Anwyn shouted.

The mob, finding that it was not hurt by its removal, gathered courage and fueled it with rage, and surged back again, over each of the entry points.

And finally the invisible forces faltered, and those humans who entered stayed.

Now the bereaved vengeance-seekers poured in faster. Over the walls. Into the inner sanctum and onto the grounds of Galweigh House. Anwyn Sabir followed them in and rallied them and aimed them at the House itself. But they hadn't been fast enough. The House's invisible guards had bought just enough time, for as the mob neared its objective, the few inhabitants of Galweigh House escaped. The mob watched as the first rays of morning light caught the envelope of the airible as it slipped silently out of reach, motors off, buffeted by the dawn breeze.

Anwyn screamed with rage, and swore, and tossed his head as an angry bull would.

And the mask that hid his monstrosity from the mob he led fell to the ground. The dim light of new dawn displayed his naked, horned, scaled, fanged face to the mob that had just been deprived of its prey.

He heard the indrawn breath. He saw the shock in the eyes. He looked around for an avenue of escape, but there was no such thing.

The mob, hungry for blood and deprived of their rightful targets, turned on him.

He fought well, at least for a while.

And then the House's ghostly guardians received the night's final gift.

Chapter 39

The last strands of darkness still clung to the Long Comfort when a dozen shadowed forms slipped through the alley door. The innkeeper Shrubber came upon them as he carried wood into the common room—always an early riser, he'd been preparing the hearthfire for the new day.

One of the men slit his throat before he could cry out, and when he had finished thrashing, shoved his body into the hearth, piling the wood before it to hide it from immediate discovery. No one else stumbled upon the invaders, and they made their way quietly up the stairs to the guest rooms, and unerringly to the room occupied by Ry, Yanth, and Jaim.

"Knives out," one of the men said. "When they're dead, strip the bodies and take everything of value in the room. It has to look like a robbery."

That was the only sound any of them made, but it was enough for Ry.

Always a light sleeper, now near Shift and sensitive to changes in sound and smell, he was on his feet and had his sword in hand before either Yanth or Jaim could wake. He kicked their beds and snarled, "Up, quick, or we're all dead," and lunged forward, hearing them scrambling for weapons behind him.

When the attackers burst through the door, expecting to find three sleeping men, the first found a ready blade and death; the next, a madman who fought in the narrow space like a fiend possessed.

And by the time the weight of the attackers had pushed Ry into the room, both Yanth and Jaim stood with him.

They fought without words, the only sounds the scuffle of boots and bare feet on the plank floors, the clangs of sword on dagger and sword on sword, the thuds of flesh, the cries of pain.

And then one of the attackers won through Jaim's guard, his blade spearing between ribs and into heart and lung and out again with a hiss, and Jaim screamed once and folded double and dropped to the floor while his killer ripped the blade from him and turned and snarled, "For Captain Draclas!"

"For Captain Draclas!" the other attackers yelled.

"Ian Draclas is my *brother*!" Ry bellowed. "Truce! Truce! We fight on the same side!"

Yanth shouted, "They've killed Jaim—no truce!"

But the attackers had backed off, and Ry caught Yanth's wrist in his hand. They stood sweating and panting in the small room, with Jaim and two attackers dead on the floor in pools of their own blood, strangers staring at each other with expressions of bewilderment on their faces.

Below, someone started screaming, and the attackers said, "Run! Out the back, before the guards are called."

Yanth pulled his wrist free with a snarl and said, "I want them dead."

Ry was swinging his pack over his shoulder and wiping the blood from his blade onto the mattress where he had so recently lain. "Run with them, or we'll be charged with these deaths. We have no friends here and no one to speak for us; we'll be hanged."

Yanth's face went hard and cold. "What of Jaim?"

Ry knelt and quickly felt for any sign of life in Jaim's

body. The pulse was gone, the eyes—half-open—stared sightless and unblinking, the flesh had bleached a bloodless, ghostly white. He clenched a fist and fought back tears. "His body will stay with these others. His spirit will forgive us, I hope."

Yanth swore, then grabbed his own pack and fled down the hall with Ry, following the attackers. Through blurry eyes, Ry saw faces peering at them through the cracks of almost-closed doors.

They pounded down the stairs three steps at a time, leaped from the middle step on the last course to thud into the hallways, found Kelje and the kitchen wench crouched over the body of Boscott Shrubber, which they appeared to have dragged out of the fireplace—and then Ry and Yanth were out the door and running through the mud that sucked at their bare feet and pulled at their breeches.

Ry regretted the loss of his boots, but not as much as he would have the loss of his freedom. He and Yanth overtook the slower Keshi Scarred first, then caught up with and overtook the running humans. All of them reached the *Peregrine*'s trollop-painted long-boat together, and jumped in, and cast it off. Ry and Yanth took oars with the others and began pulling toward the ship with all their strength.

As they rowed, one of the attackers picked up where Ry had left off. "You're Ian Draclas's brother?"

"Half-brother."

"Then why in the hells-all have you consigned your soul to Rrru-eeth?"

"I serve Ian's interests."

"You serve that traitorous bitch," the speaker said. "With my own ears, I heard you swear your loyalty to her. We all did."

"I swore my loyalty to the *true* captain of the *Peregrine*. The true captain is my brother."

"Who is dead because of her."

"He isn't dead. I rescued him from the Ancients' city in

Novtierra not long after Rrru-eeth abandoned him there. He's in Calimekka now, and I intend to get his ship back to him—with Rrru-eeth aboard it. He can decide what to do with her once she's in his hands."

"He *did* swear loyalty to the true captain," one of the other men said. "Those were his very words: 'I swear loyalty to the *true* captain.' I thought it was funny at the time, because I knew she wasn't really the captain, but I thought he thought she was."

One of the Keshi said, "And he knowed the ship was *Peregrine,* not that damned Jerrpu name bitch-captain give it." The lizard-eyes blinked at Ry slowly, and the lizard tongue flicked in and out, in and out, sampling the air. "He don't taste like he lying."

Ry thought of Jaim, dead without cause, and he wanted blood in payment for his death. But if he sought his payment from the blood of those who could become his allies, when he needed allies more than anything else, he would be twice a fool. The one who needed to pay for Jaim's death was Rrru-eeth. He wanted *her* blood—for what she'd done to Kait, and now in repayment for Jaim.

He leaned into his oar. Bitterly, he said, "If you were loyal to Ian, why did you let Rrru-eeth leave him and Kait and Hasmal and your own people behind? Why didn't you fight with the others?"

"Rrru-eeth caught us by surprise," the man who'd done most of the speaking said. "She sent those she knew were loyal to Ian into the city, supposedly to gather the last few treasures before Ian and Kait and that wizard came back with whatever they'd gone after. A few of her people went with them, and when Ian's men were well away from the ship, Rrru-eeth's ran back, thinking to take the longboats and simply abandon everyone who wouldn't support Rrru-eeth. But Ian's men weren't asleep on their feet. They ran back to the beach, fought for the longboats . . . and lost." He hung his head. "We'd never made much fuss about our loyalties, and I guess we bitched as much as any about having a skinshifter and a wizard aboard our ship, so she assumed we were hers. We slept through the mutiny—we'd been in the city all day, hauling and digging; we were tired. . . ."

The Keshi who'd spoken before said, "We woke to find we were to sea, with that bitch calling herself captain of the ship, and those of us what supported Captain Draclas outnumbered. So we kept quiet. We waited—we-all're good at waiting. We stayed with her to make sure she paid for what she done. Gods say they get revenge for men who don't—but we didn't want to trust to no gods. We want to see her hang with our own eyes."

"Then why isn't she dead already?"

"She careful," the Keshi said. "She trust nobody, and she got better ears and a better nose than anyone—she know when trouble coming long time before it reach her."

Ry swept his oar forward and dug it into the roughening surface of the water. "I'll see her dead. I swore to that for my own sake, and for Kait and Ian. I wanted to kill her myself for what she did, but she harmed Ian and Kait more than she did me. They deserve to declare her fate—Ian most of all, I suppose. When she sails back to Calimekka, I'll see to it she won't leave again."

"Then we're with you. You have some plan to see her dead?"

"I have."

"Then lead." The man at the oar beside his said, "I'll follow you—and they follow me. So I speak for all of us."

The others nodded.

Ry looked at Yanth.

"They killed Jaim," he said. "They tried to kill you and me."

"They're our allies," Ry told him.

"Then they're our allies." Yanth's face remained cold. "But they aren't our friends, and if someday once Rrru-eeth is dead I have the chance to sink my blade into the heart of *that* bastard"—he nodded toward the man whose blade had killed Jaim—"his blood will feed my sword before he knows to draw breath."

The man Yanth had pointed out shrugged. "Name your time and your place, and I'll be there. I did not kill your friend out of any malice; if I had known you planned to put an end to Rrru-eeth, I would never have fought you at all. And I apologize for my mistake. But if that isn't enough for you and you want to test your metal against mine, I won't argue."

"It's not enough," Yanth said. "When this first matter is settled, you and I will settle our own score."

Chapter 40

The *K'hbeth Rhu'ute*, once the *Peregrine*, sailed out of harbor amid a flurry of accusations, demands for crew extradition to shore, and threats against both ship and crew should it ever sail into Heymar's harbor again. Rrru-eeth Y'tallin stood by her people, declaring that she, as a ship's captain both registered and sworn, claimed sovereignty over them and the disposition of justice. She said she would try those accused of murder when they were at sea, and would see that they received the fates they deserved. In the meantime, she wanted the bodies of her three crewmen back so they could have proper burial at sea.

It was testament to her ferocity that Jaim's body and those of the other two dead arrived at the dock promptly and were rowed out by townsfolk. Rrru-eeth found out that the woman standing on the dock watching the bodies being brought out was Kelje Shrubber, wife of the man her people were charged with murdering. She bade the burly dockworkers who'd rowed the bodies out wait, and went into her stores and came back with two small leather bags. "See that she gets both of these," Rrru-eeth said. "They are compensation for the loss of her husband and helpmeet, and though I know they are no comfort at a time like this, still they will keep the tax collectors and the estate dividers from her door." She smiled broadly enough that both men could clearly see the points of her teeth and added, "I'll just stand here and watch you, to be sure she gets it all."

"What did you give her?" Ry asked.

"Gold," Rrru-eeth said. Her voice held neither anger nor compassion. "It covers a multitude of sins."

When the dockworkers had handed the bags to Kelje, Rrru-eeth turned away from the shore and gave the order to sail. Ry stayed by her side.

"I want to know what happened," she said. "Why did my men come after you, why did they kill that innkeeper, why did you fight with them, then run with them? In your bare feet, no less."

Ry watched the sailors clambering through the rigging, freeing the great silk sails to drop and catch the wind so that they snapped in the breeze and bellied out. He felt the thrum of life surge in the ship beneath him as it started to move. Ships were made things, inanimate constructions of wood and metal and cloth and bone—but when the wind stirred the sails to life, those same inanimate creations began to breathe. He did not wonder that people named them, spoke of them as male or female, revered them and loved them—they were, he thought, in some ways as worthy of love as people. Certainly—and he glanced at Rrru-eeth—*more* worthy of love than some.

"Your men . . . questioned our loyalties. The trouble between us was a misunderstanding, and a bad one. We fought for our lives, and I am lucky to stand here right now."

"I would say so—they outnumbered you four to one. I would think you would have had no hope of surviving."

"Had we continued to fight, Yanth and I would have died with Jaim. But we did not. We convinced them instead that we were not traitors. Then, sadly, those below us woke and found the innkeeper dead—and that is as much a tragedy as any of the rest of this, for he was a good man, and deserving of a better end—and we had to run."

"But why did *you* have to run? You were attacked—surely you would have been asked only to testify. But by running, you as much as attested to your guilt when you had none."

"Your crewmen would not have stayed to stand trial. Yanth and I would have been alone, with three dead men in our room and another downstairs in the hearth, with only each other to swear that we were attacked and that we had done nothing to deserve the attack, and had nothing to do with the death of Shrubber. Strangers without resources in a town that had lost a man it cared for . . . I didn't like our chances."

"Nor do I, when you describe them in that manner."

They stood on the deck together, watching the *K'hbeth Rhu'ute* make its way through the scattering of other ships that dotted the harbor, heading for open sea.

"I will have to try my own men," Rrru-eeth said. "And you and your man, as well." Her voice had no more emotion to it than it had when she gave the gold to the dockworkers to pay off Shrubber's death. "I am little concerned about the death of a landsman; there are more of those than the world needs, and one or two removed from the world by accident matter not a whit to me. But I *am* concerned about why my men should so greatly question your loyalty that they would leave this ship without my knowledge to try to kill you. I am equally concerned by the manner in which you went from enemies to allies."

"I explained—"

"You did. But a trial brings out truths that explanations often don't. You can explain before me once you've sworn to the gods. With your soul forfeit, you can tell the same tale and the matter will end there."

Ry nodded.

Rrru-eeth smiled a tiny, thoughtful smile. "Or perhaps a different story will come out—and then I'll have to get out the gallows and have a hanging or two. It's a bad thing for a captain to wonder too much at the activities of her crew, and not to know why they should behave as they have."

"You won't have cause to wonder," Ry said.

"No. I won't."

He knew then that any hope he might have had of keeping his purpose and his true loyalties secret until he reached Calimekka had died with the attack. He and Yanth and Ian's loyalists were going to have to take Rrru-eeth prisoner, try her, and hold her for sentencing by Ian when at last the *Peregrine* reached him.

He wondered how many of the crew had sailed with her to Novtierra, and how many of those remained loyal. Probably a lot, he thought. The wealth they'd gotten from the sale of the Ancients' artifacts would buy a fair amount of goodwill among the crewmen.

This business promised to turn into a bloody mess. He wondered if he would ever see Kait again anyplace but beyond the Veil.

Ry? Can you hear me?

Ry, resting in his new bunk after the midday meal, opened his eyes, feeling Kait's presence for the first time in a long time. He had almost dared to hope that she was truly nearby, but as he let himself reach out to her, he could feel the long leagues that separated them—leagues growing longer by the instant. Her shields were down, though, and he sensed that though she had been in terrible danger, she was safe for the moment.

I hear you.

Beloved, please forgive me. I was wrong to want to change you, and wrong to want you other than as you are.

I forgave you before I even left.

I love you.

He wished he could pull her into his arms right then—he had to satisfy himself with touching her in his thoughts. *I love you, too.*

Come to me. Please. Find me again. I don't want to be without you anymore.

What happened?

The pictures that flashed through his mind—of Crispin's attack, of the turning of the guards, of the mob led by Anwyn and Andrew, who had destroyed Crispin before turning to attack Kait and all those with her—chilled him. He could have lost her that night, and he would have felt the truth only at the moment of her death, when she lost her grip on her shields.

Now she was on an airible with Ian and Dùghall and Alcie and the rest, fleeing south.

I have news for you, too, he told her, and showed her the images of the ship he was on, and the woman who captained it.

Shall I tell Ian?

No. If I triumph, I'll bring the ship and the mutineers to you, and Ian will have his justice. If I fail, better he does not know what I had hoped to accomplish.

Don't fail. I need you.

He felt her worry, and as best he could he reassured her. *If I failed I would never see you again. So I cannot fail—it is my fate to die in your arms.*

And mine to die in yours. Promise me.

I promise, he said.

The strain of reaching each other across the spaces became too much then, and Kait began to fade away from him. For as long as they could, they held each other, but at last she vanished from his mind.

But now he could not lose.

I promise, he told her, though she could no longer hear him. I will find my way back to you. And I will never leave you again.

Chapter 41

The main body of the Army of the Thousand Peoples moved into the pass, covering the ground like a living carpet as far as the eye could see. They rolled forward in a wide column, mounted outriders to either side, regular cavalry inside of their lines, foot soldiers in solid phalanxes inside of *those* lines, and in the center, the noncombatants—mothers with children, the elderly, the wives and young sons and daughters of various officers—and the supplies, loaded on sleds and wagons and travoises.

From the top of the pass, Har, the youngest of Dùghall's sons who had followed his father when he came requesting volunteers to fight at his side against a threat that back then was still hypothetical, watched them coming.

"We haven't a fraction of the men they have," he said. "And if our weapons are better, it won't matter much because they have so many more of them."

"Go." His older brother Namid, who watched the pass with him, closed his eyes, and rubbed his temples. "Tell Ranan what comes. We'll need men at Long Fall and Third Point and Highbridge to work the rockfalls. A goodly supply of fire arrows. The bags of poison powder for the catapults. . . ." He stared down at the enemy, who covered the ground beyond the pass like blades of grass, or like grains of sand on a beach. "And for the gods' sake, tell him to hurry."

Har fled, feeling death on his heels. The enemy scouts would be into the pass soon, and they needed to believe no resistance awaited them. If they gave a report of all clear, the enemy would march into the pass unaware, and per-haps—*perhaps*—Dùghall's army could trap them and slaughter them without being wiped out in the process. Har knew the stories of small forces who had held off massive armies by benefit of terrain and intelligence and plan-ning—and he and his brothers and their men had planned, and prepared, and made use of every niche and cranny and drop the mountains offered.

But who could have imagined so many would come against them? The land was blackened with the enemy as far as the eye could see. How many arrows did they have? How many bags of poison powder? How many deadfalls, how many rocks?

He raced into camp, and men raised their heads to stare after him and eyes went flat and faces grew grim. Soldiers put aside their guitars and their wenches and their cook pots, and stood, and shook off all vestiges of play. In his eyes and his expression they saw a small reflection of what he had seen, and they knew.

Ranan caught him by the shoulders as he bolted toward Ranan's tent. "Tell me."

"They . . . come . . ." he gasped. "Thousands of thou-sands. In lines. Like . . . army ants. Namid said . . . fire ar-rows. And men at Highbridge and . . . Long Fall and Third Point. And the poison powder for the catapults. And hurry."

"Scouts?"

"Not yet."

Ranan nodded.

Another brother, Tupi—he from the island of Bitter Kettle and a mother who had begged him not to go—raced

into camp from the western side and charged up to Ranan.
"Men to Second Pass now," he panted. He stood for a mo-
ment with his hands on his knees, his head hanging down
while he tried to catch his breath. The watchpoint above
Second Pass was farther from camp than that above Main
Pass.

"How many?" Ranan asked.

"We thought at first a shadow moved across the distant
hills toward us, but there were no clouds. We could not believe what we saw."

"Scouts?"

"We could see them breaking off in the distance.
Mounted, some of them. And the enemy has fliers of some
sort."

"The Scarred would."

"We're well hidden. But we'll need all the reinforce-
ments we can get."

Ranan nodded. "Both passes, then."

Har watched his oldest brother's eyes, and shivered at
the bleakness in them. People were going to die this day,
and Ranan was the one who would command them to their
deaths. And one of those so commanded might be him.

"Get back to your post," Ranan said, looking at Har but
seeming not to see him. "Tell Namid he'll have full forces.
Don't touch the scouts unless you're in danger of being discovered, and if you have to kill them, try to do it dis-
creetly."

Har nodded.

"Run," Ranan said, and turned to Tupi.

Har ran back the way he had come, praying that he
would survive to see another sunrise.

The scouts came first—a dozen beastly riders astride
their deformed mounts galloping into the pass, a dozen more
batlike flying Scarred soaring overhead. The men who held
the foremost positions lay flat beneath their camouflage of

cloth painted to look like rocks, grateful then for Ranan's repetition of Halifran's Maxim: "What the enemy *might* do is irrelevant; plan against what he *can* do."

They had muttered, "Can our enemy see through solid stone? Can he fly?" when creating the shelters—and Ranan had shrugged and said, "Perhaps. We won't know until we find out who our enemy is."

And now they found out—they, who had thought the whole exercise a waste of time, and Dùghall and Ranan deluded, and the gold Ranan spent to have men trek into the mountains to haul rocks and paint canvas and build deadfalls money for nothing. Ranan looked increasingly brilliant as the scouts flitted overhead, blind to the traps that lay ahead of them, and soared back the way they had come.

When the scouts were gone, the full force of Ranan's troops moved into position. Still hidden beneath painted awnings, they loaded the sacks of poison powder into their catapults and tested the wind to make sure it carried down into the pass from them. They moved their fireboxes close to the fire pits where wood and tinder, neatly piled and dry, waited to fuel the fires from which they would light their arrows. They tested the blades with which they would cut the ropes that held back the great stone deadfalls. Then they crouched, barely breathing, watching the massed forces of the monsters beginning to move forward, and their guts clenched and twisted, and their hearts beat against their ribs, and their mouths went dry and tasted bitter with fear.

Har, still in the foremost position, offered fervent prayers to the island gods of home, and a quick, hopeful prayer to the Iberan gods who watched over the mountains and the cold, foreign land in which he huddled.

Then the first lines of the fighting forces arrived, and he and those who hid with him waited for the signal. He knew it would be long in coming—the pass needed to be full of the enemy before the defenders dared attack.

So the first hundreds of the Scarred monsters passed un-accosted beneath the waiting, huddled humans, dragging catapults and siege engines and weapons Har could not identify on great wooden-wheeled wagons behind them. The pass was broad enough that a dozen men could ride abreast—it easily accommodated the attackers and their weapons and their hideous war beasts. The enemy moved forward alertly, keeping scouts constantly in motion, but the troops of the Scarred showed no fear and no awareness of the trap into which they moved—they chattered among themselves, clusters of enormous gray shaggy beasts bel-lowing at each other as they marched, and little black-and-silver furred things chirping and squawking, almost like monkeys except for the clothes that they wore, and brown-furred monsters with faces like friendly bears who growled and trilled at each other, their ears flicking as they saun-tered toward disaster.

The first part of the pass filled, the troops below moving out of sight around the sharp curve the defenders named First Point. There seemed as many of them yet to come as there had been before—but now some of the noncombat-ants were moving into range, traveling in the center of the thinned-out column. Females with their babes in arms; chil-dren running among the wagons or riding atop them, play-ing games and shouting; the old and the infirm clustered together on the padded benches of special wagons. Watch-ing them, Har began to feel sick in a different way. He had feared his own death at the hands of the soldiers below—had feared their retaliatory strikes on their preemptive at-tacks should their scouts discover him and his comrades before they could strike.

Now, though, he realized that innocents traveled among his enemies, and that those innocents would die, and that he would have a part in killing them. Being from the Imum-barran Isles, he had never developed the hatred for the Scarred that Iberans had—the Scarred traded with his people often, and some made their homes in the outer isles. He saw the creatures below as people—and he wanted to cry. How could warriors bring their wives and children with them? How could they risk everything they held dear? What did they hope to gain?

"They want Ibera itself," Namid said, when he dared a whispered question. "They're leaving the Scarred lands of the Veral Territories, looking for a home well away from the poison of the Wizards' Circles." He sighed. "I guess attacking Ibera looks easier than attacking Strithia."

"Well . . . *Strithia* . . ." Har said, and fell silent, thinking that no one could be mad enough to try to invade the Strithians.

They stared down at the unending column that poured beneath them. The fighters kept their places to either side, the flying scouts soared past, usually still below Har's position high on the side of the mountain but sometimes above it, noncombatants traveled in the center with the weapons and supplies, and the whole force looked to Har like it would never end.

"At the speed they're going, they'll be to Third Point at any time."

Har said, "There aren't enough of them in the pass yet."

"As many as will fit. We can't help the fact that there are too many of them still outside it."

"Their fighters will come up over the sides at us."

Namid nodded. "When we drop our deadfall, we're going to have to run. The ones outside the pass will mark our position quick enough, and some of those flying scouts carry arms, too. We can't hope to have much effect on them."

"So we'll run to First Point."

"Have to. They have archers there. They'll be able to give us some cover."

Har nodded. "If I don't live, tell my mother I fought well, would you? And that I thought of her."

Namid held out a hand. "I'll swear on it. And you tell my mother the same thing, should I die."

"What about Father?"

"He'll know. He's always known what happened to all of us."

Har took Namid's hand and said, "You're right. So I'll swear to tell her." They clasped hands, then quickly turned back to the pass.

From Third Point, they heard the sounding of a horn—high and clear and mournful in the early morning air.

Neither of them hesitated, though Har fought tear-blurred vision as he worked. The brothers sawed through the thin ropes that bound the heavy ropes which held the deadfall boards in place. The boards fell away, tearing at the painted canvas that hid them from the enemy—and rocks and boulders, carefully piled behind those boards, burst free in a torrent and crashed down into the pass with an avalanche's roar. Har heard the same roar repeated farther up the pass.

The screams started, and the neatly ordered column scattered like ants stirred with a stick—the attackers ran madly, some fleeing out of the pass, some running deeper into trouble, some trampling their own and racing in circles in their desperate attempt to find safety. The rockfalls blocked the pass at Third Point and at Highbridge and at Long Fall, and at the mouth as well.

Once they had the enemy trapped—or as much of the enemy as they could hope to hold—the defenders launched the bags of poison powder from their catapults. The bags had been carefully designed to burst upon impact—the powder was light and billowed up in huge clouds when it struck. From within the white clouds, Har heard coughing. Then cries of agony, and screaming, and retching.

"Run now," Namid shouted, and burst from their hiding place. Har followed him, keeping his eyes on the narrow, treacherous path that led along the uneven ledge to First

Point. The enemy's flying scouts were nowhere to be seen, the first wave of the enemy's army, trapped in the pass, was dying, and Har began to hope that some of the gods might have heard his prayer and cared that he and his many brothers and the soldiers who fought with them might live to see another day.

He tried to keep himself from hearing the anguished cries that reached him from below. He tried to keep himself from picturing the horrors that lay down there—the bodies of men and women and children of the Thousand Peoples crushed beneath rocks, writhing from the poison, burning from the rain of flaming arrows. He was protecting his own people, and the evil he had done he did for them. For the men and women and children of the small villages in the mountains who went about their lives, blissfully unaware of the marching death that bore down on them.

He tried, but he was no callous killer. He was a boy, far away from his home and the people he had loved all his life, and he had been forced to kill because he believed he had no choice. He *still* believed he had no choice.

But he wanted to hide his face for shame that such slaughter should be the only solution to the danger his people faced.

He and Namid reached First Point and dove beneath the sheltering camouflaged awnings and watched the archers shooting down at anything in the powder-coated mess below that still moved.

"Time to retreat soon," one of the men said.

"We're winning," Namid said. "Why would we retreat now?"

"Because we're out of poison, almost out of arrows, and have no more deadfalls built. And *they're* already pulling down the first of the deadfalls. Didn't you see them?"

The one thing they had not been able to see from their position was the area directly below their ledge—which was the location of the first deadfall.

"No," Namid said. "We didn't see them."

"We aren't going to be able to hold this position for long. Ranan has already warned us to be ready to fall back to Third Point when the horn sounds again. We're to resupply from the caves there. Maybe we'll be able to clear a second wave before we're out of everything—but that second wave won't just march up the pass like this one did. We're going to have to fight like demons."

"And then what will we do?" Har asked.

The veteran's mouth twisted into a weary smile. "Then we run like hell and hope they've braced themselves back behind us."

Ranan, from his aerie atop Highbridge, watched both the main pass and the small secondary pass and felt a moment of triumph. The failed second wave of attackers faltered and the few survivors fled backward. He counted his own casualties, dead from aerial attack and enemy catapult fire and the one bag of poison powder that burst in midair and rained back on a friendly position, and guessed that of the near-thousand men he'd led in the morning, some seven hundred survived in fighting condition. Bodies of the enemy filled both passes, in places three and four and five deep; he could only guess at the number of enemy dead, but his guess numbered ten thousand. If he went by the numbers, this Battle of Two Passes would make him one of the great generals of history.

He would not take pride in his victory, however. Most of the enemy dead had fallen in the first wave, and a good half of those had been noncombatants. The bodies of mothers and babes, of children, of old men and old women, lay trampled with and tangled among those of the soldiers they'd followed. And it wasn't over. He had hoped that the enemy, twice slaughtered by a force it could not kill and could not intimidate, would turn back, and thus would not discover that he and his men had reached the end of their resources and would not be able to offer resistance to a third wave.

He had dared hope that even if he had not won such a substantial victory as a full retreat, this Army of the Thousand Peoples might halt for a while, reconsider its plan of attack, and in so doing give him and his people time to regroup and resupply.

The enemy, however, was setting up a third wave—a force that would launch itself into both passes under cover of the coming darkness. From what he could see from Highbridge, this third force was as large as the first two combined—and it would not include noncombatants.

Ten thousand armed fighters against seven hundred men who had nothing left but their personal arms—swords, daggers, cudgels, slings, and shields. Behind the forming third wave, enough of the Scarred remained to launch a fourth, and perhaps a fifth. He and his force had succeeded in slowing the enemy down—nothing more. The army of the Scarred would have to clear away rockfalls and bodies before it could move its war machines through the passes, but when its path was cleared, it would come on. Inexorably, it would come on.

Ranan turned to the young man beside him, the son of his favorite wife's best friend, and said, "Sound retreat."

Chapter 42

Danya, astride her giant lorrag, watched over the removal of the dead from the pass. They were bringing out some of the children of the Kargans: children she had once ferried across the Sokema River to pick berries; children who had taught her the subtleties of language and culture in her adopted home; children whom she had liked.

Their backs arched; their mouths stretched open in silent screams; their eyes bulged wide and frightened, the corneas no longer clear and shiny, but clouded, dull, coated with dirt and powder.

Children.

She stared at Luercas, standing near the mouth of the pass, who was directing a group of Trakkath soldiers in disposal of the bodies. He remained untouched by the deaths; but then, why could she have thought he might be moved? He'd led her to destroy her own child, then stolen his body. What could the deaths of other innocents mean to him?

He saw her looking at him, mounted his lorrag, and rode to her side. "Mother. Dear. If it's going to upset you so much, perhaps you ought to go hide with the rest of the helpless."

She said, "I'm not upset."

"I could feel your distress from clear over there." He nodded toward the growing pile of bodies. "You can't have a war without a few corpses."

She lifted her chin and looked at him coldly. "Why those corpses? Why mothers and babies? Why grandfathers? Why little boys and little girls?"

"If you want to ask those questions, then why anyone?" Luercas shrugged. "Why is the life of a little girl more worthy of tears than the life of a trained soldier? Why do you weep for the lost children but not for the lost men?"

Danya, the daughter of Galweighs, born and raised with Family duty as the core of her existence, had no doubts on that score. "Those whose duty it is to serve must be prepared to offer as much as their lives."

"But do they love life any less to go so unmourned, their sacrifices so unquestioned? Has the soldier in the flower of his manhood lost less or more than the ignorant child, or the all-but-unknowing babe?"

Danya glared at him. "Now that we have come this far, would you convince me to leave off this war? To retreat to the Veral wastes again?"

"Not at all." Luercas turned and studied the soldiers who were pulling out the last few bodies and adding them to the pyre. "I would only alert you to your own hypocrisy. You act as if ignorance and innocence add value to the worth of a life, and act as if you believe that those who have the most to gain have the least to lose. But the fact that those soldiers walked into that pass for you knowing that they might die does not make the price they paid less than the price paid by the children who died unaware of their danger. Rather, I would think they paid more, and hold them in higher esteem." He turned to study her face, and when he saw that she was giving his words serious consideration, he laughed. "I would value them if they were truly men, of course. These are just smart beasts—but those they kill on your word in the coming days will be as human as you."

He started to ride off, then turned back and grinned at her.

"As human as you once were, anyway."

She wanted to scream at him. She didn't—that would give him too much satisfaction. She contented herself with imagining him groveling at her feet, begging for his life with the rest of those she would make pay for their sins against her—those in her Family who had failed to ransom her, those in the Sabirs who had raped her, hurt her, twisted her with their magic, those among the Kargans who had turned their backs on her when she regained most of her human form, and the others since that time who had slighted her and looked sidelong at her as if questioning her right to call herself Ki Ika, the Summer Goddess. And now those soldiers who had poisoned the Kargan children who had cared about her, even when she was no longer Gath-alorra, the Master of the Lorrags.

She would call forth cries for mercy. Begging and pleading. Desperate offers of penitence. And then she would have the blood of those who had hurt her. The promise of vengeance against those who had destroyed her life was all that sustained her, all that kept her moving forward. But it was enough.

Chapter 43

The great airible *Morning Star* limped through the darkness on two engines, almost out of fuel, tugged by winds it grew less and less able to fight.

"We're going to have to land," Aouel said.

Kait looked down at the rough coastal terrain barely illuminated by moonlight. "Where are we?"

"Not yet to Costan Selvira. I would have been happier to land us there. We could have gotten fuel from the Galweigh Embassy, perhaps repaired the engines on the landing field, and then we could have gone wherever you wanted. If we land below, we're going to have to cut the airible free."

"Why?" Kait asked.

"To preserve the secrets of the engines."

Kait rested a hand on his shoulder. "The days of the Families are dead. My Family can no longer control the secrets of airible flight. *No* Family will be able to buy artisans and keep them in seclusion to rebuild from the Ancients' designs—the people who controlled that power are dead, and the mechanisms that kept the power in their hands are dead, too. If we cut the airible loose and let the sea claim it, we will have consigned the work that went into making it to oblivion—and there will be no more fine engines pouring from Galweigh workshops to replace those that we drown."

Aouel frowned at her. "Don't think that. The Galweighs still hold land in the Territories. They still hold Waypoint and Pappas and Hillreach. And in South Novtierra, Galweigia. You can't call the Families dead yet."

"Yes, I can. Money ran from Calimekka to the Territories, the daughter cities and the new colonies; trade goods came back. If our dependencies don't keep getting their ships full of gold and supplies, they will slip away from us like water spilling through open fingers. The true Family was in Calimekka. That's gone now."

"Then what shall we do with the airible?"

"Land it. Anchor it. Leave it. Most likely it will go to ruin before anyone can make use of it, but I'd rather someone figured out a way to fix the engines and perhaps even copy them than think that flight would be lost again—for a hundred years, or a thousand, or maybe forever."

Aouel said, "Who will know what to do with it? The fishermen who live along this shore? The farmers who work the ground inland?"

"If we leave it behind, there's a chance," Kait insisted. "Not much of one, I know. But any chance is better than none." Kait ran her fingers over the controls and sighed. "It took my Family fifty years to decipher the secrets in the Ancients' diagrams and tables, and to learn to create the machines they could use to build such engines. It took them the gold of a nation to build the airibles, test them, keep their designs secret—and only in the last ten years have we had any sort of reliable service in the air. I don't want all of that to be lost."

"I know." Aouel looked at the ground, and Kait saw sorrow in his eyes. "When I step out of this airible, I will probably never touch the sky again. But I, too, hope that someone will."

The men and women sworn to serve the Galweighs

moved out of the cabin and onto the outer gangplank, ready to slide down the ropes and find anchorage for the airible on the rough terrain below. Kait didn't envy them their task—they would drop, not onto a smooth and grassy field, but onto a rock-strewn stretch of land bordered on one side by cliffs and on the other side by forest, and they would have to make their landing in darkness. Behind the navigator's station Kait could hear Alcie soothing her children, promising them that everything would be fine, that they would be safe, and that she would protect them.

Kait wished for just a moment that she had someone who depended on her, someone for whom she had to be brave and calm and reassuring.

Aouel pulled the chain that blew the steam whistle, and the guards crouched, waiting for their second signal. He fought for response from his two remaining engines and slewed the airible around so that it fought against its own inertia with its engines, and even with the buffeting wind it hung still in the sky for a moment. As he came fully around, he pulled the chain again, and the guards leaped over the rail, sliding down the rope toward the ground. He'd taken them in as close to the trees as he dared, thinking that the trunks would make good anchors, but he couldn't get them in as close as he would have liked, for fear of dragging some of the guards into the trees and skewering them.

Kait held her breath, and Aouel said, "They'll get us down. We've done this maneuver more times than I can count in the last few months, practicing with every conceivable obstacle. They haven't come this far to die here, and neither have we."

She rested a hand on his shoulder and nodded. "Forgive me. It's been a long day following a difficult night."

"Things are going to get better now." Aouel smiled, though he didn't look away from the instruments and controls on his console. "I promise you that."

"I believe you," Kait said, and wished she weren't lying when she said it.

Dùghall had not thought an airible could make such a rough landing. The envelope snagged in some trees, the whole damnable contraption screeched like a pig in a slaughterhouse, and then without warning one end shot straight up while the other dropped down until the thing was standing on its nose.

His feet skidded out from under him and he slid against the first bulkhead behind the pilot's cabin, which suddenly became a floor. He grabbed Lonar as the boy went skidding past, aimed for the doorway into the front cabin; Ulwe, graceful as a cat, landed on the bulkhead without mishap. Alcie, though, with a tight grip on the suddenly wakened Rethen, found herself suspended in the air on the couch, which, fixed firmly to what had once been the floor, now served as a precarious ledge. She howled louder than the squalling infant, but only once. From below him, Dùghall heard Aouel roaring commands out the open hatch, and Kait swearing steadily.

The soft light of the glowlamps inside the airible prevented him from seeing anything that happened out in the darkness, but he could hear frantic screams, and thumps along the side of the cabin and passenger area.

"We've lost the aft gas chamber," Aouel was shouting. "Get out of the way so I can vent the forward hold!"

That didn't sound promising.

"How am I going to get down from here?" Alcie managed to ask Dùghall in an almost conversational tone; years of experience with hardship, a good Family upbringing, and the fact that she'd been terrifying her own children gave her the strength to sound brave even though she was suspended four times higher than his head on a perch that pitched forward crazily with every passing breeze, threatening to throw her and the baby to their deaths.

"Mama!" Lonar wailed, and clung to Ulwe, who patted his head and pulled him close to her.

Kait poked her head through the hole in the floor that had been the doorway to the cabin, and saw Alcie and the baby high above her, staring down.

"Hang on," she said. "The forward gas chamber tore when we hit the trees, but Aouel will have the ship leveled soon. Don't try to get down on your own."

Alcie clung to Rethen and nodded, and Kait disappeared back into the cabin.

The next sound they heard was the gush of water. "That will be the ballast," Dùghall said.

The back end of the ship started to come down, slowly enough that both Alcie and Dùghall could compensate and keep their positions steady.

Still the feeling of having nearly died didn't leave him when at last his feet touched solid ground again. He was grateful for every breath he took and for every bruise he bore. The narrow escape from the House, the rough flight and harrowing landing, all combined to make the fact that he was a long way from anywhere and uncertain about what his next move should be seem trivial—something easily overcome.

He walked through the darkness toward the beach, and suddenly realized he did not walk alone.

"I thought when I was hanging by that aft rope and the ship went tail up that I was dead for sure," a female voice said out of the darkness.

One of the guards, Dùghall realized, and chuckled. "You weren't alone. When the room tipped sideways I nearly pissed myself. I could see all of us being sucked out over the ocean and dropped into the water a thousand leagues from land."

"You hurt much?"

"Some bruises. You?"

"Twisted my right wrist all to hell. That's why I'm not unloading—can't carry anything for a bit."

They reached the rocky shore and stood watching the moonlight reflecting on the pounding waves.

"Have you ever seen anything so beautiful?" the woman asked him.

"No," he said, and meant it. "I cannot remember when last life tasted so sweet."

A hand slipped into his—calloused but small, warm and strong, vibrantly alive—and he rubbed his thumb along her palm and felt a thrill he hadn't felt in years. His now-young body suddenly tasted the hungers he had been denying; he turned to her and touched her cheek with his other hand, and felt her lips brush against his fingertips in a soft kiss.

"We're alive. Dance with me," she said with a soft laugh, and he found himself enchanted by the reflection of moonlight in her eyes. The two of them kicked off their boots at the edge of the beach and danced in the coarse, damp sand, arms draped around each other, whirling in circles that grew slower and tighter and closer, until at last they stood, breathing hard, bodies pressed tightly together, and realized the inevitability of that which must come next.

Not speaking, they sought out a flat rock well out of the reach of the spray. It still held the warmth of the day; when Dùghall touched its water-smoothed surface it almost seemed alive. He caught the woman around the waist and lifted her onto it, then climbed up after her. They knelt on the boulder facing each other and slowly began to touch, and then to kiss.

Alive! his body sang. Alive! Escaped! Free!

Her left hand fumbled with the ties of his breeches, and impatient, he undid them himself and pulled them off. How awkward undressing was—something he had forgotten in the last many years when sex, when it came at all, came in the careful confines of a bedroom, with clothes made to be removed.

With growing urgency, he and the young guard undressed each other, met, coupled, plunged and thrust in rhythm with the steady roar and hiss of the sea. Wild things, they lost themselves in the intensity of pleasure so great it became almost pain, and consumed themselves in their own reckless abandon. Lust, passion, and over all sheer grateful joy at finding themselves miraculously alive fueled their hunger, so that when they sprawled together, spent, they only lay that way for moments before hunger drove them to seek the comfort of each other's bodies again.

When at last they tired of their sport, they clung together laughing, and sat on the shore watching the first graying of the sky to the east. The guard pulled a flask from her hip bag and twisted the cap from it. She took a short drink and handed it to him. He followed her example, and felt the delightful fire of good Sonderran liqueur burning its way down the back of his throat and warming him with the friendliest of glows.

"Watch," she said. "The sun will come up right there. There's such magic in watching it rise."

They sat on the rock, both partially clothed, arms around each other, and the sky grew purple, then pink, then orange.

Then he saw it. For just an eyeblink, a ray of purest green shot above the horizon. It vanished before he could even motion toward it, swallowed by the brilliance of the sun that followed in its wake, but she'd seen it, too. He heard her gasp and whisper, "Fair fortune follows an emerald sun."

But that flash of green had sent his mind reeling back to the day he'd parted from Ranan—and the words of his eldest son's benediction. "Love a woman well before you take back your years," Ranan had said. "Fight once, drink once, dance once . . . and once, watch the waves on the shore with young eyes, and see the flash of green as the sun rises over the water's edge."

In that moment, that loving benediction seemed almost a

curse—in a single night he had touched all the points of true living his son had wished for him but one; he could almost think that the only thing which lay between him and imminent doom was the fight he had not yet had.

Chilled, he shivered and broke the spell that he and the guard had spun between them. She turned to him and smiled, but her smile was sad. "A good night," she said softly. "But now the day's work awaits. I should be getting back."

He nodded, and impulsively stole another kiss from her lips. "The best night I can remember in more years than I can count," he whispered. He squeezed her left hand gently and said, "Thank you. Perhaps . . ." And he thought, *Perhaps we could do this again,* but he stopped himself before he said it. This moment would never come again—bound to the ground, she became a guard again, while he became one of the Family she guarded; no road ran between those two points that could withstand regular travel and not destroy the terrain over which it ran. Within the single span of a night they had been equal—survivors on a rocky shore. But daylight brought the world with it.

She smiled sadly and kissed him back. "I'll cherish this night always. Always."

And he nodded and fell back on gallantry. "As shall I, beautiful one."

He did not ask her name. He would learn it in the coming days, and when he did he would hold it close to his heart, but he told himself he would not speak it aloud. They pulled on the rest of their clothes and walked together up the bank, gathering their boots that still lay above the high water mark. They shook out the little blue crabs that had lodged in them overnight, laughing softly as they did, and then they walked slowly back to the airible.

"I know he isn't here," Ian said, "but this won't wait. Where did he go?"

Kait knew exactly where Dùghall was, and knew as well how he had occupied himself during the hours of darkness. "He'll be back soon enough. What's wrong?"

"Ulwe asked me to take her to the road. What she's discovered bodes poorly for all of us. She's waiting by the road and she's afraid. She said she'll go back to what she's found once, but she doesn't want to have to do it twice."

Kait rose. "I'll go get him," she said, but that proved not necessary. Dùghall joined them at the campsite, a small smile still curving at the corners of his mouth. Kait hated to see it go—she saw a wistfulness in his eyes that made her feel sad for him. Still, Ulwe and her news, whatever it might be, should not be kept waiting.

Ian led the two of them to the road, and to the little girl who stood beside it.

"We've come," Dùghall said. "What have you found, child?"

"Trouble comes," she said, "on too many feet to count. The road screams with the pain of the dying, and with mourning for the dead. It brings me stories of suffering and fear and death, but not from sickness. From war."

"From which direction does war approach?" Dùghall asked. Kait saw that his lips had thinned; his face became a mask of calm, but she smelled his sudden fear.

"That way," Ulwe said, and pointed south and west.

Directly back to the mountains above Brelst, to the place where Dùghall's sons waited with the army.

"What else does the road tell you?" Dùghall asked, and his voice shook, though he tried to hide it. "Can you tell me who lives and who has died?"

Ulwe shook her head. "They are all strangers to me, and too far away. Single voices drown in all the noise." She paused, then said, "I can tell that many live and flee for their lives, that many others pursue. Nothing more, except that they run toward us."

Ian, Dùghall, and Kait exchanged glances. Kait said, "This is the attack you foresaw?"

"I think so," Dùghall said. "My heart says it is. And my gut. Let me spend some time with my *zanda*. When I've done that, I'll know for sure."

He left, and Kait crouched and hugged Ulwe tightly. "How are you feeling?"

"I want my father to have been someone better," Ulwe said. "I want him to be still alive, and to be someone I can love."

"I know. I'm sorry."

"I was looking for some sign of him when I found out about the war that comes to us," Ulwe said softly. "I wanted to find his ghost, to find that he still looked for me." Tears were running down her cheeks, and her voice caught when she spoke, but she kept on. "I wanted to know that he loved me. He *did* come for me."

Kait said, "You were the best thing he ever had a part in, Ulwe. And he did love you. I have his voice inside of me still; I can touch his memories. The place he made for you in his heart was truly good. You can hold on to that."

Chapter 44

Dùghall took his *zanda* back to the rock where he and the guard had spent the night. He spread out the black silk on the weathered surface, then settled himself cross-legged in front of it, silver coins in his left hand.

Everything we do in life, we do for a first time and a last time. We usually remember the first, but rarely suspect the latter. Vincalis's introduction to his Book of Agonies. Dùghall couldn't shake that line from his thoughts. The sun felt warm on his face, the rhythm of the surf and the scent of salt water soothed him, the soft cries of the shore birds that raced to the water's edge and then away as if terrified of wetting their feet seemed to him a detail of the moment that was both homely and poignant.

In his young body he was still an old man, with an old man's memories and an old man's fears. Young men could not conceive of doing something for the last time; old men thought of little else. Now the night that had left him behind loomed like a suspected last time.

In his hand, the coins lay heavy and still. He closed his eyes, summoned a calm he did not feel, and let the silver fall to the worn silk surface. And then he sat there a while longer, eyes closed against the morning sunlight, because he did not wish to see what the future held.

In the end, he looked.

Well, this was the unpleasant travel his earlier reading had foretold—the journey that he had to take if he hoped to triumph. And that unrecognized enemy that he'd discovered was on the way to meet him. Almost surely the Dragon at the head of the army that pursued his sons, he thought darkly.

The Duty quadrant told him that his payment would be due soon, and he found himself wondering what exactly the gods wanted from him, if he could not be seen to have done his duty *yet*.

Only the godless man can know true happiness, Vincalis had written in one of his darker moments, *for nothing can be asked of him that he must give to preserve his soul.* Later in the Book of Agonies he had reversed that, but Dùghall found some comfort in knowing that he'd thought it, anyway.

One part of the reading seemed to him to point directly to Kait and Ry—lovers parted by his doing as well as their own who, for the good of all, faced their own destruction . . . or not.

The most enigmatic part of the reading that lay before him was that every outcome lay in an either-or position. Either those he loved faced utter destruction, or else they didn't. Either the forces that had gathered against Matrin would destroy it, or they wouldn't. Either his health would continue strong and robust and his wealth would expand . . . or it wouldn't.

He'd never seen such a pointless cast of the coins, he thought. And then he started trying to puzzle out the meaning of the *Self* coin that lay, obverse and reversed, dead center on the *zanda* cloth, perfectly inside the circle where all the quadrants intersected.

The obverse of *self* was *selflessness*. And not the selflessness of conscious thought, of awareness, which the coin would have indicated if obverse but upright. No. Selflessness that came from the core, that came not from what he thought but from who he was. Unconscious openness, a thing the body knew so well it did not need to ask of the mind in order to choose its actions or follow its path.

That was the thing that lay at the heart of the reading, that touched the outcome of every quadrant equally—that was the thing that the gods would ask of him. Soul-deep selflessness.

And he didn't think he knew a more consciously selfish human being in the world than himself.

At some moment in the near future, he would be asked to make a choice. He would have to make it in a situation of great duress, and the choice he had to make was going to hurt. He was going to have to give up something he loved—the *zanda* suggested that strongly, though it did not point to any specific thing. If he chose one path he would be healthy and wealthy, Matrin would prosper, those he loved would survive. If he chose the other path, Matrin would fall to ruins, those he loved would be annihilated, he himself would lose his health and his wealth and probably his life.

Or, he thought grimly, those combinations could change. Nothing on the *zanda* said one outcome would be all good and the other all bad. It might be that he had to sacrifice his loved ones to save Matrin, or sacrifice his wealth or his health to save his loved ones, or sacrifice the Matrin that he had served his entire life to save the people in it. The sun-touched coins gleamed up at him from the black silk—silver possibilities touched by the sun, the eternal golden fire of the universe. And for that moment he sat at the center of those possibilities like a spider at the center of its web. The gods were telling him that they intended to throw the problems of the world in his lap, that they intended to say, *Here, you choose,* when the choice was one that even a god would dread making.

His fingers shook as he gathered up the coins, wrapped them carefully in the folded silk, stored them in their bag. He sat on the rock a while longer, thinking. Even refusing to choose would be a choice—and almost certainly the wrong one. He could run away from the enemies who approached. He could run away from his duty. The gods always left a door open for those who decided running was the best option. If he did, though, he had little doubt but that the worst of what he had seen on the *zanda* would come to pass.

At last he rose to a standing position and lifted his face to the sun. "I am still your sword, Vodor Imrish," he said. His voice was calm, firm, and sure. "Draw me at will, use me as you must."

Chapter 45

Five days into the voyage, the *K'hbeth Rhu'ute* sailed through the northern edge of the Thousand Dancers and into Goft's harbor. Ry, still mourning Jaim's death and still stinging from the funeral at sea, was not ready for what he had to do next, but this would be his single best opportunity.

He gave each of those who still bore loyalty to Ian a cautious signal; those who could do so without arousing suspicion would stay aboard the ship with him, while those who could not would meet with Yanth at the Coral Goddess. He and Yanth had gone over both prongs of their planned attack in the dark hours when everyone else slept, committing to memory the acts that they dared not commit to paper. If they could succeed and reach Ian and prove him alive, they would be heroes; if their plan failed, they and all those who followed them would be adjudged mutineers—they'd be hanged from the *K'hbeth Rhu'ute*'s mast and would not be afforded even the coarsest of burials at sea; their bodies would simply be dumped over the side like offal from the galley, food for fishes.

When most of the men had departed for their brief shore leave, Rrru-eeth called together all those who remained. She called her first mate, who was loyal to her, her chief concubine, also loyal, her purser, who hid his loyalty for Ian, and Ry.

Outside the room, two Keshi Scarred guards watched the door.

The five of them sat at the table with a sumptuous feast spread before them—fried plantains glazed with honey butter; mounds of sugared beans; lightly sweetened cocova molded into the shapes of fanciful fish; platters of steamed dolphin on black rice and kettled tuna and baked tubers stuffed with cheeses, meats, and grapes; fingerling pastries and sour pies and sweetcakes. And to drink, water clear as the air itself, filled from goblet bottom to goblet top with spheres of lemon-flavored ice—a treat of such great rarity and such enormous cost that Ry, scion of one of the two greatest Families in the world, had only had it three times before in his life.

"Eat and drink, my dear comrades, my beloved colleagues," Rrru-eeth said, spreading her delicate hands expansively over the repast.

"You feed us as you would feed kings," Ry said.

Rrru-eeth smiled. "We shall all be kings, my friend. Tomorrow we sail for Calimekka, and for the new life we shall win there." She rested one palm flat upon the table and held the other to her heart. "A toast to all of us—to Bemyar, who shall sail us to our new destination and command the crew who shall keep us there; and to Kithdrel, who shall guard and dispense the funds with which we shall buy our kingdom; and to Ry, who shall teach us the ways of kings and lead us to our paraglesiat; and to Greten, who shall be paraglesa in name, and to whom all knees shall bow; and lastly, to myself, who shall be paraglesa in fact, and to whom all hearts shall at last turn with worship and awe."

The other four placed their hands on the table and heart and said, "To us."

During the meal, they listened while Rrru-eeth talked—about her dreams of the future, about the grand roles each of them would play, and about the glories and honors each of them would receive when she was paraglesa of her own Family, living in a great House on a high hill in the greatest city in the world. Ry let her feed the dreams with her words, and when he judged the time to be right, he said, "A single thought, Captain, that I offer so you can protect yourself. Calimekka is a city of rumors and tales, where gossip is a minor deity honored most in the highest halls. There are in the city those who are called Finders, whose entire life revolves around discovering the secrets of the powerful and selling them to the highest bidder. If any of your crew could speak an honest word of ill about you, you would be best to leave him on these shores and replace him with someone who cannot malign you."

"You are suggesting that I have secrets?" Rrru-eeth asked.

"I know you have secrets. *Everyone* has secrets. I am suggesting that you alone know if any of them might be harmful—if someday one of your crew will be offered a thousand pieces of gold by a Finder to tell everything about you that might be worth money, and one of your crew will take the gold and tell."

Rrru-eeth frowned and looked from Bemyar to Kithdrel to Greten. Each of them shook his or her head fractionally, and Kithdrel said, "We are all officers, and share guilt for any decisions you might have made."

"But the regular crew does not," Rrru-eeth said.

"No." Greten was frowning into her iced water. "They do not."

"You know of something that could be used against you?"

"I do."

"How many know of it?"

"More than half the crew."

Ry gave a low whistle and said, "You cannot count on loyalty from so many."

"I cannot. So I must act." She closed her eyes and rubbed the bridge of her nose between two fingers.

"Goft has sailors aplenty to fill out an interim crew," Kithdrel said.

Bemyar nodded. "It's a good port; I'd have no trouble replacing most of our roster from here. Some of your current crew might resent being left here."

"Generous severance pay would prevent that," Kithdrel said.

"Not so generous that it would interfere with my plans."

"Of course not. That would be pointless."

Greten said, "Perhaps a message to the old crew that you have heard of sickness in the city of Calimekka, and you are going to continue on, but that you refuse to put them at risk."

"No," Ry said. "The simplest stories are the best—and where no story will adequately serve, none should be offered. Simply tell them that you release them, offer more than the money they were due, and take on your new crew. If they don't know why"—he shrugged—"well, that is your privilege as captain."

Bemyar nodded. "He's right. No explanation is best. I should go over the list with you of those we'll keep and those we'll release."

"Release all of them. Let there be no appearance of favoritism."

Greten's eyes went wide and she started to protest—then, without making the slightest sound, she closed her mouth and looked down at the table, her face gone pale and her lips pressed into a thin, hard line. Rrru-eeth didn't notice. Interesting, Ry thought. With whom among the soon-to-be-departed crew did she share a secret? And how much of a secret was it? Enough to make her a possible ally?

Ry liked Greten—and Yanth, who had found hiding places aboard the ship in which to meet with her every day since they'd sailed, adored her. Ry thought it would be happier for all of them if she were not hanged with her mistress—and if she helped the ship return to its rightful captain, she would be absolved of any previous guilt.

Something to think on, and something to tell Yanth.

As they finished eating, Rrru-eeth said to Bemyar, "Gather the remaining crew on deck, and tell them the whole ship is released on leave for a week. Go ashore with them, and begin quietly hiring on new crew. When we have enough people aboard to be sure we will not be overrun, we will announce that the old crew is permanently released." She turned to Kithdrel. "At that time you will give out final pay and severance bonuses. Any who dispute you are to receive the pay, but not the bonus. Make that clear at the outset."

She closed her eyes. "I think, however, that I will keep my Keshi guardsmen. They owe me their lives—I can trust them as much as I can trust each of you."

Maybe even more than that, Ry thought, and had to suppress the smile that tried to reach his lips. He and Ian's loyal crewmen that Kithdrel would sneak back on board, and the new crew that would do anything to avoid being tarred by the mutiny of an old crew, would have little trouble containing Rrru-eeth, the few loyalists she would retain, and two or three Keshi Scarred.

Bemyar and Greten had already proved unwitting allies. He hoped they would prove as useful in the next stage of his plan.

"I can find not a single sailor who will board a ship sailing for Calimekka," Bemyar said a day later. "The city has been devastated by plague, and all who have heard of it fear for their lives should they sail even within the harbor. They say ships lie at anchor there, some with corpses still rotting on the decks from the day that they fell. They speak of rats that pour like rivers through the streets, and of a river so clogged with corpses that the water will not flow, and of flies so thick in some places that when they take to the air they darken the sun."

Ry thought of the blast of magic he'd felt all the way in Heymar, the blast that told of the death of the Mirror of Souls. The Mirror had not died alone—he'd known that at some level, but had not thought through to the consequences that fact might bring. The sailors would be happy enough if they knew they were going to sail south along the coast; he would be able to get a full crew. But he couldn't tell the first mate the truth; Bemyar was loyal to Rrru-eeth.

Kithdrel, he thought, and smiled. "Bemyar, send Kithdrel to hire them. He knows to the tenth-piece what you can afford to pay crew. I'd bet anything he'll be able to find *some* who will willingly sail into the jaws of death itself for the right price."

Bemyar thought about that for a moment, then shrugged. He glanced at Kithdrel, who said, "I'll do what I can. I don't have *his* confidence, but I might find enough for a skeleton crew to get us into harbor—though we may have to work double stations, and I know I'll have to pay more than the going rate."

"It will be worth it." Ry smiled at Bemyar. "The captain wants to find her way into Calimekkan society. Moving in now, while society is in confusion, will give her an edge. If she can appear and offer stability when stability is the thing the people of Calimekka most need, she'll build a base of loyalty that nothing will later dislodge."

Bemyar rose from his bench and said, "I'll go talk to her. Perhaps you should come with me, Ry, to tell her what you've told me."

They sailed a day later, their scant new crew secretly augmented by Ian's loyalists, who of necessity stayed hidden in the holds. All of the new crew, once under way, were told Rrru-eeth was a mutineer who had stolen the ship from its rightful captain and abandoned him and some of his crew in

Novtierra. The old crew confirmed this, and added that the ship was to be returned to its true captain, who was to be restored to his rightful place—much was made of the gratitude he was sure to feel and the rewards he was sure to pay to those who helped him regain what was rightfully his.

So when they were off the southern point of Goft, in what could truly be called open sea, Ry gave the signal, and Ian's men caught Rrru-eeth, Bemyar, Greten, and Rrru-eeth's Keshi guards and brought them onto the main deck at swordpoint.

When they were assembled with the new crew gathered around them, Kithdrel stepped forward and held up a paper, and read from it. "You, Rrru-eeth Y'tallin, cabin girl of the *Peregrine* sailing under Captain Ian Draclas, are charged with capital mutiny, and with inciting mutiny, and with inciting the murder of crew and participating in the murder of crew by willful abandonment in a place hostile to human survival, and further, you are charged with the attempted murder of your rightful captain by the same means, and with impersonation of a deeded captain, and with capital theft of a deeded ship. How plead you to these charges?"

Rrru-eeth looked around her, at the strangers who stood on the deck facing her, and she smiled to Kithdrel. "Is that what you told them, Kith? That I was a mutineer? Do you, then, plan to become captain of the *K'hbeth Rhu'ute* by lying about me? You know as well as I do that I was first mate of this ship under Draclas, and that he and much of his crew were lost in battle with a Wizards' Circle off the coast of North Novtierra. You've seen to it that none remain who can vouch for the truth save these you hold with me . . . but you seem to have forgotten that you have left none aboard who can vouch for your lies, either."

"Call the witnesses," Kithdrel shouted.

Ian's loyal crew stepped out onto the deck from the holds below, and Rrru-eeth's face went hard. "Ah. So you've found a few who will lie with you in hopes of gain,

I see. Have you promised them riches, Kith? Have you promised them my portion of the wealth in the holds?" She turned to the new crew and said, "Beware, all of you. If you conspire with these traitors, you will be as guilty of mutiny as they are—and I'll see you hang for your crimes. The only one who could judge the truth of this matter is Captain Ian Draclas, and if he were still alive, he would be the first to tell you of my brave service as his first mate, and my valiant attempts to save his life."

Ry stepped out of the crowd and gave Rrru-eeth a mocking bow. "I'm so glad to hear you say that, Lady Captain, for we sail to meet up with Captain Draclas this very moment."

For an instant he saw raw fear flash across her smooth, dark face. Then that vanished, replaced again by arrogance. "If Kithdrel told you he knows where to find Captain Draclas, he lies. He had found someone who will pretend the part, and has convinced his *witnesses* to say the imposter is truly Draclas."

"I think not," Ry said. "I know my own brother."

"Lies," she shrieked. "Lies! Ian is dead! You all conspire against me." She turned to Greten. "Tell them! Tell them the truth!"

Greten said, "I was not with you when you sailed to Novtierra. I don't know the truth."

"Bemyar! You were with us. You know what we faced! Tell them."

Bemyar looked at Rrru-eeth and saw his neck in a noose, for he shook his head and backed away from her as much as the swords at his back would allow. "They speak the truth, Rrru-eeth. Whether the captain lives or not, I don't know. But I do know that you did everything they said you did."

Her eyes narrowed and she snarled, "You coward. Do you think if you turn on me now that will save your neck from the noose it so richly deserves? G'graal, G'gmorrig, tell these poor fools the truth, and save them from themselves."

The two Keshi Scarred gave each other long, measuring looks, and stared down at their feet in unison.

Rrru-eeth said, "Tell them! I command you!"

But neither Keshi said a word.

"I am the captain of this ship," Rrru-eeth howled, "the master of your destinies! I will see you all dead for your betrayal! Dead!"

"Confine her in the brig," Kithdrel said. He turned to Bemyar. "You can earn your way clear of capital mutiny charges if you help us now. Take over the helm of the ship and sail us toward Costan Selvira. We go there to meet up with Captain Draclas—Ry knows where he is."

Bemyar stared at his hands. "I'm a coward, Kith. I always have been. I'd join you just to save my own life."

Ry said, "If what you know to be right is also the thing that will save your life, there's no shame in taking the safe path. You do not brand yourself a coward by doing so."

"No. I branded myself a coward when I let myself listen to Rrru-eeth. I'll never rid myself of that mark." He hung his head. "But I'll serve you now. If I cannot repair the damage I did in the past, I can at least prevent myself from embracing new sins in the present."

Kithdrel said, "Then take the helm, First Mate. Ian Draclas will see that you have served him well." He turned to the concubine. "Greten, you were not a part of the mutiny, but you are loyal to Rrru-eeth. If you attempt to cause us trouble, we'll have to kill you. Do you wish to be confined to the brig with her? You will not face capital charges, but you will be set ashore when we take on Captain Draclas and his people."

"I don't know what I want," Greten said. "Confine me to my quarters if you choose—I swear on God Dark that I will not cause you trouble."

"I hear your oath and witness it," Kithdrel said. He looked at Ry.

"I, too, bear witness to your oath. Gods adjudge you if you break it."

"You need not confine yourself to your quarters. You may not, however, approach the brig. The rest of the ship is yours, as ever."

Greten nodded and left the deck.

And that left the two Keshi Scarred. "She owns the two of you," Kithdrel said. "Does she own your loyalty?"

Neither Keshi said a word.

"As acting captain of this ship," Bemyar said, "I have the power to grant them their freedom. Once she does not own them, they may speak as they choose, and decide their loyalties without incurring the death penalty for betraying an owner."

"Free them, then," Kithdrel said.

Bemyar said, "Before Tonn, god of the sea, I declare you freemen. Your only bonds are to your gods and your consciences from this day forward."

"I hear and witness your oath," Kithdrel said.

And Ry said, "I hear and witness."

"Gods adjudge you if you break it," Kithdrel added.

The Keshi looked at each other, and one, though Ry could not tell whether that one was G'graal or G'gmorrig, said, "I will take oath, then, as a freeman, that the charges Kithdrel brings are true." His voice was so deep and his accent so thick that Ry had a hard time making out his words.

The other Keshi said, "I take oath with my brother."

Kithdrel said, "Then you are free aboard the ship, save only that you may not approach the brig. If you do, you will die."

The Keshi nodded.

Kithdrel turned to the sailors. "The matter rests until we take on Captain Draclas. I hereby turn the ship over to Acting Captain Bemyar Ilori. Captain." He bowed. "Ry Sabir will tell you how to find the captain."

Ry said, "South. Toward Costan Selvira."

Bemyar pointed at one of Ian's men and said, "You, Wootan. You're acting first mate. Tell the men to set all sails and take us down the Inner Current, fast as you can."

"Yes, Cap'n." Wootan began shouting orders, and the sailors scattered to their places. The white sails dropped and filled, the ropes sang in the stiff breeze, the ship cleaved through the chop like a knife through boneless flesh.

I'm on my way, Kait, Ry thought. And I'm bringing help.

Chapter 46

Kait, carrying a pack full of the few things she'd managed to save from the House, trudged along the road with the rest of the refugees, headed for Costan Selvira. If she looked back, she could still make out the top curve of the airible's envelope behind the growing wall of trees. When they topped the short rise they were climbing and headed down into the next valley, she would lose that view for good.

She felt less torn about leaving the House this time. She had her sister and niece and nephew with her, as well as Dùghall, and Ry was sailing back to her. She could feel his presence in the back of her mind; he was using her as the compass by which he directed the ship that raced toward them.

They could have stayed on the beach where the airible had landed, but the road south from Calimekka was a dangerous one inhabited by bandits, and the airible would certainly draw those bandits to investigate. She and the rest of the grounded escapees didn't want to fight, and Kait knew Ry would be able to find her no matter where she was, so long as she left her shield down at least a little.

She hoped the bandits wouldn't destroy the airible when

they found it empty, on the theory that what they didn't understand would be worthless to anyone else. They'd make a nice profit off of the machinery if they managed to hang on to it; the Gyrus paid richly for anything mechanical that still worked, and two of the airible engines were still in working order. The other two could be salvaged for parts. The envelope, though badly damaged, was of high-quality waterproofed silk that would surely be useful for something; the bladders inside were made of specially treated airtight skins—also bound to be useful for something, though Kait couldn't imagine what at the moment. Even the furnishings and struts would have some value in the barter market, provided the bandits could find a buyer who would believe they truly happened across the abandoned vehicle and didn't murder Family to get it.

Or maybe that wouldn't matter in these new days—perhaps the murder of Family wouldn't raise so much as an eyebrow, much less send the countryside scurrying for cover in fear for their lives. Who, after all, was left to avenge a Family death?

Even in the midst of the soldiers sworn to defend her, she didn't feel truly safe. The pressures of Shift rose inside of her, and she knew before long she would have to break free from the group and run and hunt alone. The old order might be falling apart, the reverence for Family dying or even dead, but the tradition of killing anyone not fully human she felt sure would remain. She stared longingly at the forest as she trudged, hearing the animals that moved just out of sight, smelling prey, hungering for the hunt, and she yearned for the radiance of the Karnee world, and the unheeding simplicity—hunt and be hunted, kill or be killed. There was little of diplomacy in the jungles.

To keep her mind off her appetites, she ran to catch up with her uncle.

"You've been quiet," she said. He walked along the road between a pair of equally silent guards, head down, pack slung carelessly across his shoulders with no thought for its balance or his own comfort.

He seemed at first not to hear her, and she had almost decided to repeat herself, but a little louder, when he turned and looked at her with bleak eyes. She felt again the shock of seeing his hair black, his face unlined—but this time felt it so strongly because his eyes looked ancient and haunted.

"By Brethwan, Uncle, you look to have danced with the ghosts!"

He nodded, but said nothing.

"You said your auguring went well enough, and we have had no bad news from other sources. . . . Oh! I've been stupid. You're worrying about your sons."

He sighed. "I fear for all of us."

She gestured at the group that surrounded them. "Us?"

"The whole of the world, Kait. The whole of the world."

"Why? What have you seen that's so terrible?"

"A choice that I must make. A sacrifice that I must offer willingly."

"What sacrifice? And when?"

He managed a hollow laugh. "I don't know. Not where, not when, not what. I only know that the choice will be hellish, and that it will test me to the very core of who I am . . . and if I fail, we will lose . . . not just a war, but the world. I have cast the *zanda* a hundred times the past few days. I have summoned Speaker after Speaker until I have near bled myself dry asking for answers, and I know an answer exists. But I can't find it. I am blind to it, deaf, walled into a windowless, lightless room with only my knowledge of some pending doom." He glanced over at her and she saw the fear in his eyes. "And facing that knowledge, I don't know if I will ever sleep again."

Kait reached out to comfort him, to rest a hand on his shoulder, and as she did, she heard a voice in the back of her mind.

That which you so desperately seek, you already have.

She froze. The voice spoke to her from the dead. Or did it?

Hasmal, she thought, *I would know your voice anywhere. Where are you? Have you found a way to come back to us? What can you tell us?*

Hasmal didn't answer any of her questions. Instead, she heard again the single sentence she had heard before. *That which you so desperately seek, you already have.* It echoed inside her skull, slipping away from her like the vapors of a ghost; the more she reached after it, the more elusive it became.

That which you so desperately seek, you already have.

She closed her eyes and stood still in the middle of the road and sought the source of the voice, for she had learned from hard experience to fear voices that whispered into her mind. She chased after it, and came up against the place inside of her that she had shielded and shuttered and walled up—the place where she had buried Hasmal's memories, and Dùghall's, and Crispin's . . . and Dafril's.

Dafril's memories.

Yes.

She had blocked them away because she could not bear the touch of that evil inside of her. She could not bear to feel that any part of the monster who had been removed from the world at such great cost still lived in any way, and when she brushed against those memories, she could feel Dafril himself stirring inside of her.

But she *had* touched those memories, and in one cursory brush with them, she had learned something. Something about the evil that came, the evil that Dùghall feared. She *knew* something.

Or perhaps she didn't. But she knew where she could learn it.

Eyes tightly closed, she pulled down the shields that had kept Dafril's poison from spilling onto her. She touched those memories tentatively, hating the feel of the creature that twisted where she prodded. Surface images flashed behind her eyes, pictures of a tall and handsome man, tiny shards of conversations, the briefest bite of dread.

Dafril had feared someone. Dafril had lived in terror of someone. And she thought, Why would the most powerful wizard who had ever lived fear anyone?

She moved into his memories, embracing them, accepting them, following that fear.

Dùghall kept the soldiers back from Kait, who stood in the center of the road, eyes shut, body rigid, unresponsive to anything or anyone.

"Just wait," he said. "This is nothing of magic, nor is she ill."

"Then what's the matter with her?" Ian demanded.

"Wait," Dùghall said.

They stood that way for long moments; he probed the Falcon sea within himself, looking for some sign that the tide of Falconry had swallowed her, but she was not within reach of the Falcons. She stood unshielded, but no magic touched her. She was gone from her own mind, oblivious to her own body, and he thought that rationally he ought to be frightened. But he wasn't. She was doing something she had chosen—he was sure of it.

Suddenly her eyes flew open, and with a cry she crumpled to the ground. She landed on the dirt road facedown, arms barely managing to catch her. She vomited, and when she had emptied her stomach she continued to retch.

Ian shouted, "Help her, damn you!"

Dùghall felt helpless. "Kait! What do you need? What has happened?" He placed a hand on her back, and she shook it off. "Kait? Can you hear me?"

She shook her head weakly, wiped her mouth on the back of her forearm, and pushed herself upright so that she knelt in the road, head hanging down, eyes focused some-place very far away.

"I know," she said at last, and hers was the voice of a week-drowned corpse animated by some nightmare magic to speak from beyond the grave.

"You know?"

She looked into Dùghall's eyes then, and a hellish spasm gripped his gut and his bowels, and fear stabbed its knives up and down his spine and flayed his every nerve.

"I know," she said simply. "I know who comes, I know what he desires . . . and I know why, even if it costs us every life around us, he must never be permitted to reach Calimekka."

"Tell me."

"His name is Luercas. He was the only wizard Dafril dreaded—where Dafril and his colleagues created the Mirror of Souls, Luercas alone created the Soul-flower."

"Soul-flower?"

"The wizardly device that, when loosed within the great cities of the Hars Ticlarim, the civilization in which the Dragons ruled, slaughtered five and a half billion people and created the Wizards' Circles."

Dùghall felt the world begin to spin. No one had really known the genesis of the circles—only that they had been born at the end of the Wizards' War, and that they were places of great death and great evil. "Luercas . . . the circles . . ."

Kait nodded. "Five and a half billion souls, all trapped there still. Held within the Wizards' Circles by a carefully wrought spell, waiting against the day that they could become the final, refined fuel for the Dragons' immortality engine. Now they are to be fuel for Luercas alone." She pulled her flask from her hip, took a swig of the water in it, and rose shakily to her feet. "It is no accident that Calimekka was spared the destruction that swallowed most of their world's great cities. It was a minor city at the time, and within it the Dragons created for themselves a fallback location in case something went wrong in Oel Artis." She managed a weak smile. "All that was left of Oel Artis was the Wizards' Circle that almost destroyed us when we sailed through it on our way to retrieve the Mirror of Souls, so I suppose we can assume something went wrong. In any case, Calimekka did not fall to the Soul-flower; its towers remain intact."

"What towers?"

"All the lovely spires of the Ancients that grace the city."

"Oh. Those towers. What of them?"

"The towers themselves are devices made to stand against time. The proper spell will awaken them; a portion of that spell has already been used once, when the Mirror pulled the souls from innocents so that the Dragons could steal their bodies." Kait looked away again, and in her eyes, Dùghall saw afresh the horror of the vision she'd uncovered.

"We've destroyed the Mirror of Souls," he said. "We've destroyed the Dragons. Surely he can't replace everything the rest of the Dragons worked so hard to do—"

Kait held up a hand, and Dùghall almost knew what she was going to say before she spoke. "He doesn't need to. He alone carries the full knowledge of the Soul-flower within himself. The work the rest of the Dragons did, they did because they did not know and could not uncover the spell that would reawaken the Soul-flower. What they hoped to do by mechanical means, Luercas can do with a word."

"And that word?"

Kait shrugged. "Dafril didn't know, so I don't know. But if Luercas stands in the heart of Calimekka, he can speak the word and the towers will hear him, and all within the walls of the city will fall first to feed the towers' magic . . . and then five and a half billion trapped and tortured souls will die forever. And Luercas will become a god incarnate."

"And every other living thing on this planet will become his slave."

"Until time itself turns to dust. Yes."

"I see. And where shall we find Luercas, that we may stop him?"

Kait's voice grew soft. "He's on his way to us now, approaching from the Veral Territories at the head of an army of countless Scarred, wearing the body that he stole when Danya murdered the Reborn. Ulwe told us something approached from the south on countless feet—Luercas and his army *are* that something. If we still had the Mirror of Souls, we could use it against him and tear his soul from his flesh—we would do so at the cost of our own souls upon our deaths, but at least we would have something with which to fight him. He owns the flesh he wears by rights, however, so the spells we used to call the other Dragons from their stolen bodies won't touch him."

Dùghall laughed bitterly. "Don't go breaking things you can't fix."

Kait frowned. "What?"

"A bit of practical advice I got from a Speaker. When I demanded that she tell me something useful, she said, 'Don't go breaking things you can't fix.'"

"We *had* to destroy the Mirror of Souls."

He clicked his tongue and arched an eyebrow. "It certainly seemed the best path at the time. But you must admit having it would be useful now."

"Considering that we have no other weapons with which to fight this monster . . . yes."

Dùghall became aware of the fact that the two of them were standing in the center of a road. That Ian, the soldiers, Alcie, and Ulwe surrounded them, staring at them. That not a single listener seemed to dare to even breathe.

"Well," he said softly. "I still don't know what decision

I'll be called upon to make, but at least I know what will happen if I fail to make it correctly." He gave a grim smile to those who surrounded him and said, "A bit of pressure is good for the soul, I hear. Come. Let us get to Costan Selvira; maybe we'll find better news there."

Chapter 47

The Army of the Thousand Peoples swept out of the pass and down the good mountain road that led toward Ibera and civilization. The way lay clear ahead of Danya and Luercas and their throng—the first three villages they passed were ghosts, the houses abandoned with every belonging still inside.

The soldiers hunted for occupants and found none—deprived of a fight, they looted the homes and shops and took in stores of food to add to their supply wagons, and kegs of wine and beer, and tiny caches of silver, and even smaller caches of gold. They were satisfied enough with those things. But the quality of the household goods they found disappointed them—these were little different in quality from what they'd had at home, and the exotic shapes and patterns couldn't change the fact that the treasure everyone had been hoping to uncover eluded them.

So far the Green Lands, the Fields of Heaven, looked as bleak and rocky as any mountains, and the troops began to whisper to each other when they thought they were well away from their Ki Ika and their Iksahsha.

Danya told Luercas, "They've lost children and lovers, and they're beginning to lose faith."

"Nonsense. Their natural greed hasn't been slaked by tempting prizes. They'll perk up when we reach a good city. A hard fight, some rape and murder and a good haul—and the sight of rich green farmland and fine city houses—and they'll be ready for more."

"You're loathsome."

"Perhaps. But I'm right. We'll get to Calimekka, and we'll take the city easily. My prediction."

"I'll laugh at you when you prove wrong."

"Will you? But if I'm wrong, you won't get your revenge." He smiled, jabbed his heels into his lorrag's ribs, and rode away.

And the army moved on.

Glaswherry Hala fell in less than a station, and every human being still within its walls when the Scarred took it died at the hands of the invaders. Brelst stood no more than two stations, its wall crews at last succumbing to the aerial attacks of the Scarred flying forces, and to the tunnelers who breached the walls from beneath and permitted the waves of Scarred to pour into the heart of the city and kill from the inside out as well as from the outside in.

Humanity fled in a steady stream, pouring northward ahead of the implacable, unstoppable tide that rolled toward it. Villages and towns along the Great Sea Road offered no resistance; their populations—less fond of their belongings than their lives—raced toward the promised safety of the great city of Calimekka, whose greatest walls had been made by the Ancients, and whose soldiers were acknowledged the fiercest and most skilled in the world. If Calimekka could not stand against the horde, what place in all the world could?

Chapter 48

The refugees from Calimekka got the news from the first of the southern refugees a week after Glaswherry Hala fell—and the news was bad. A few tatters of the army that Dùghall had placed in the pass still survived, leading guerrilla attacks against the outer edges of the Scarred army, but the damage they could do was minimal and the effect they were having was minimal, too.

"When will they be here, then?" Dùghall had asked one man.

"Our army—what there is of it—in a day. The leading edge of the enemy forces only a few stations later than that. The full army of the damned—two days. Maybe three. I won't be here when they arrive. They don't take prisoners and they don't leave survivors."

Dùghall, seated in a small inn near the harbor, rested his head in his hands and closed his eyes.

"What's wrong with him?" the man asked Kait.

Kait did not go into detail. "His sons lead our army."

"Yes? Good men, them—but if they want to be living men, they better lead it to Calimekka and get inside the walls there. The only way we're going to live to see another day is if the Families take these monsters out."

Kait did not tell him that Calimekka had fallen from the inside or that if any remnants of the Families survived there, they would be powerless to stop the approaching enemy. He left, thinking that he headed toward safety, toward a place where someone else would look after him and his children and make sure that they survived.

"Dùghall," she said when he was gone, "to that bad news I can at last add a bit of good news."

"You've met up with Falcons who've answered my call?"

"No—not yet. But Ry just sailed into the harbor."

"Thank you, Vodor Imrish," Dùghall whispered. "For that at least we can be truly grateful."

Neither Kait nor Dùghall had told Ian what waited in the harbor for him. They had decided between themselves that since Ry had found the ship and won it back for his brother, he deserved the honor of returning it to its rightful captain. Ry wasn't sure whether he anticipated the moment when he would tell his brother what waited for him with dread or pleasure.

They met at the Copper-Walls Tavern, Kait bringing Ry from the dock, Dùghall leading Ian from the inn where they'd all stayed.

Ry saw the pain in his brother's eyes in the instant when he first saw Kait with Ry and noted their arms around each other; he hid it quickly and completely, but Ry knew Ian still loved her. His jumbled emotional response to that knowledge surprised him—he felt triumph and jealousy and fierce possessiveness and a sharp stab of guilt, all at once. More than that, however, he felt a deep, quiet current of love for his brother—something he would never have expected he could feel. They had been through so much together, and at every turn Ian had deferred to Ry. Now, finally, Ry could do something for Ian.

By way of greeting, Ry told Ian, "I brought something

back for you from my travels, brother." He did not use the formal, Family term for brother, *sibarru*, but the informal and affectionate *boshu*.

Ian looked surprised. "Considering the troubles you faced on the trip, I'm surprised you found time to think of me."

Ry shrugged, suddenly awkward at having to express this newfound affection for Ian. "You've become a real brother to me." He looked away, and said with a gruffness that attempted to mask embarrassment, and probably failed, "We must be going. Come—I'll give you what I found."

He would never forget the moment when they stepped onto the dock together and Ian's eyes focused on the refurbished *Peregrine* sitting at anchor in the bay and his mouth dropped open. Ian turned and stared at Ry, then looked back at his ship. "Where . . . ?" His face was pale as death, his eyes glittered, and for a moment Ry feared that Ian might topple to the dock in a dead faint. But he said, "You brought her to me?"

"Your ship. And Rrru-eeth. *She's* in the brig. The crew helped me win the *Peregrine* back for you—they're your people now. Captain."

Ian's lips pressed together in a thin line, and his eyes glittered with unshed tears. He rested a hand on his brother's upper arm and squeezed. "Thank you," he said softly.

Ry only nodded—the words he had thought he would say when he presented his brother with his ship fell away and left him mute.

The crew standing by the longboat for the final trip out to the ship were the survivors from the mutiny of the *Peregrine*. Each of them bowed deeply and formally when Ian entered the longboat, and the first mate, Bemyar, hugged him and whispered, "He paid more than you know to bring her back to you," into Ian's ear. Ry's Karnee hearing caught the words easily, but he gave no sign. "We tried to kill him and his friends, thinking they meant to aid *her* in getting her way in Calimekka—we did kill one of them. He forgave us and worked with us. For your sake."

Ian's face betrayed nothing, but his soft response—"Thank you for telling me. I didn't know"—betrayed an intensity Ry had only thought his brother possessed in relation to Kait.

Ian strode back to the longboat's tiller and displaced the man sitting there. When Dùghall, the last passenger to board, took a seat on the thwart, Ian put a hand to the tiller and said, "Take us home, men."

And the men said, "*Yes*, Captain," and dug in with a will.

In the instant he regained his ship, Ian changed. The bitterness he had carried since Ry rescued him from Novtierra fell away. His eyes looked clearer, his head lifted, and the faintest of smiles curved at the corners of his mouth.

Ry knew what they still faced—he knew that likely the only fate they would find in Calimekka would be death. But for the first time since Ry had known his half-brother, he saw Ian as an equal and understood both the power Ian held and the loyalty he had earned.

The trip had cost him his friend Jaim. He could not forget that, though he truly had forgiven the men who thought only to serve Ian. But Ry realized in that moment that it had won him a brother who was family, too, and not merely Family—and that was something he had never had.

Kait didn't know the boy who stood outside the door of the cabin she shared with Ry. He was one of the crew that Rrru-eeth had hired on to replace those killed or abandoned for dead in Novtierra. Thin, waifish, and poorly dressed, he didn't look like he had profited from the riches that had spilled over onto the mutineers. He stared up at her with wide, worried eyes.

"What do you want, boy?" she asked, but kindly.

"Your uncle sends an important message. He requests

you meet him in his cabin as soon as you can." He glanced over his shoulder, then back to her. "He's really your uncle, the *themmuburra* Dùghall?"

"My mother's older brother."

"Then you are a *themmuburra,* too," he whispered. He quickly kissed her hand and ducked his head to his knees in a low Imumbarran bow. Then, without looking back up at her, he turned and fled.

Ry had come up behind her. "And that was . . . ?" he asked.

"One of Uncle Dùghall's worshipers," Kait said softly. "They show up in the strangest places."

"He really is a god in the islands?"

"Fertility god." Kait went to the cabin wardrobe, and pulled out the only really decent outfit she had, and started putting it on. "Forty years ago, the birth rate in the islands had fallen far below the death rate. The men fathered no children, the women were barren. The Imumbarrans prayed that they be delivered from extinction—and then Uncle Dùghall was assigned to the islands as part of his diplomatic rotation. He . . . got along well with the natives. And he apparently produced a few miracles for the girls he got along well with. So young husbands sent their wives to him, and they became pregnant, too. And then more came, and they went home happy." She pulled her tunic over her head and tugged the beaded belt into place. "He was the answer to the islanders' prayers—which was the answer to Galweigh House's prayers. In exchange for his services, which he apparently enjoyed rendering, we received exclusive trade with the islands, and first pick of all the caberra they grew. Then, when the first of the daughters born to Dùghall reached the age of childbearing, the islanders discovered that she could be fertile with an Imumbarran. The other daughters were, too. Dùghall's miracle was complete. At that point they declared him a god." Kait shrugged. "He has hundreds of children. By now, perhaps thousands. Uncountable grandchildren. In another generation, most of the people in the islands will be related to him to some degree. And all of them seem to have inherited the Galweigh fertility."

"They breed like rabbits."

Kait sighed. "Yes. In a few more years they'll be everywhere."

Ry laughed. "Think how the islanders will react when Dùghall returns to them as a young man."

Kait laughed, too, but then she shook her head. "He doesn't have any reason to go back anymore. There is no Galweigh House in Calimekka for him to represent."

"He could go back to be with his family."

"I've never gotten the feeling that it worked that way . . . that there was much feeling of family involved in his . . . duties. He talks about his children, and I've met any number of my cousins when he brought them to the city for visits, but Dùghall was never really a father to them. Their mothers always had Imumbarran husbands, and their husbands raised the children as their own. My cousins called Dùghall 'father' while they were visiting with us, but I didn't learn until years later that the word they used when they spoke to him in Imumbarran was the formal one, *ebemurr*—or that the word children affectionately call their fathers in the Imumbarras is *peba*." She finished dressing and quickly brushed her hair. "I don't think anybody ever called him *peba*. And I think he's felt the lack of that his whole life."

"That's rather sad."

"It is. I have always suspected that he looked on me as a replacement for the children he fathered but didn't get to keep."

She and Ry tapped on Dùghall's door only a few moments later. He greeted them with a grim expression, ushered them into the cabin with some haste, and bade them be seated. He was pale, Kait noticed, his eyes were red-rimmed, and he smelled of grief and despair.

Kait looked past the lavish decorations of the room to Dùghall's *zanda,* spread out on the room's little table with its coins scattered in a pattern that meant nothing to her, and she felt her heart skip a beat.

"I apologize to you both for calling you away from your other activities," Dùghall said. He carried himself like a man who had been told he must die the next day. "You have had only a little time to be together, but what I have to tell the two of you must not wait any longer." When they took the two seats beside the table, he turned away from them to stare out the room's tiny porthole.

Kait watched him, hating his stillness and the cloud of doom that emanated from him.

"You finally got the answer to your auguring," she said.

"Yes."

"You know the choice that you will have to make when the moment comes."

"Yes."

Kait reached for Ry's hand under the table, and held it tightly.

Ry said, "Kait told me about the oracles you sought. About the confusing answer you received."

Dùghall turned and faced the two of them. "It is no longer confusing. It has become terribly clear."

"And . . . ?"

"And I am Vodor Imrish's sword. I have sworn my life to serve him, to serve the Falcons, to serve the good of the world. I am making that choice now."

Kait felt a soft burning on her instep, where she had been branded by the Falcons. In the back of her mind, like the tugging of the moon on the tide, she felt them pulling on her. She, too, was a Falcon—different, apart, but still sworn to serve. *Listen,* they were telling her. *Listen.*

Dùghall, still staring out the porthole, said, "Luercas approaches with allies so numerous they make the earth tremble when they move; with magic honed during a thousand years of waiting; with an appetite that will devour the world. Every *zanda* I have cast in these last few days has been clear about one thing—we cannot beat him in a straight fight. Even if we could get all of the Falcons banded together and hit him force against force, he would still annihilate us."

Kait nodded. "We suspected as much. Tell us what you *know*."

"That we will die," he said quietly. "But we will try to do it in such a way that the world will survive behind us."

Kait and Ry both grew very still at those words—so still that Kait was uncertain if either she or Ry still breathed. Or could. They both waited for Dùghall to qualify his statement, to give them some hope, to offer *anything* beyond that flat statement of their coming death. But he said nothing.

Finally Ry said, "You mean we *may* die, don't you? I mean, you cannot be certain of the outcome until we fight our fight—"

But Dùghall shook his head. "I am certain. I have entreated Vodor Imrish himself for a path that did not end in our certain death . . . and there is none. If our world is to live, the three of us will die together."

Kait gripped Ry's hand harder, and felt his fingers tighten around hers. She turned to him and said, "I'm sorry I cost us the last real time we could have had together." She moved around the table and dropped to her knees, resting her head against his chest. She could feel his heart pounding beneath her cheek; she could hear the smooth, sweet sound of the air moving in and out of his lungs. She could smell his pain, his grief, his longing for her. He held her; one hand to stroke her hair, one arm to pull her close.

"From the time we knew who Luercas was, we thought this might be our fate. The only thing that has changed is that now we know. Don't waste the little time we have left in this life blaming yourself, Kait. You were no more wrong than I was. I'm sorry I left."

Kait wiped at her cheeks, startled to find that they were wet; she had not realized she was crying. She felt almost as if she were outside of her body—as if already she were moving toward the Veil and the next life.

Ry rested a hand on her chin and gently turned her back to face him. "We will die together," he said. "And beyond the Veil, we will live together again. I did not find you at last and after such difficulty to let such a small thing as death separate us. You and I are forever."

She gripped his hands in hers. "Promise me," she said fiercely. "You said you would never leave me again."

"I promise. Not in life, not in death, not beyond eternity."

"Nor I, you."

Something was wrong with Dùghall. Kait could sense it, and when she turned away from Ry, she could see it. She could almost smell it. His cheeks were streaked with tears, his eyes would not meet hers, his hands gripped each other as if fighting for their lives. He was hiding something—something important.

"What are you not telling us?" she asked.

"The . . . sacrifice of our lives . . . it is only the beginning," Dùghall said. His voice shook.

Kait shook her head. "What more can the gods ask of us than our lives?"

"In order to have any chance to win against Luercas, we are going to have to draw him into the Veil and beat him there. Any Falcons who join us in Galweigh House will create the shield that will protect the rest of Calimekka. But we three will be unshielded. I am the only one strong enough to draw Luercas into the Veil against his will and hold him there, but I cannot both hold him and fight him at the same time. You and Ry share a bond that is beyond my understanding—you can communicate with each other without effort, without words, and without resorting to magic. Because of this, only the two of you may hope to draw him into the trap that I will build to capture him." Dùghall stared down at his feet and whispered, "But by the very nature of that trap, the two of you will only be able to pull him in if you go with him."

"Into the trap."

Dùghall nodded.

"And what will be in the trap?" Ry asked. "How are our souls to escape once they have entered?"

"They aren't." Dùghall sighed. "Inside the trap will be oblivion. Annihilation." He shook his head, and his hands twisted against each other, endlessly moving. "He would find his way free of any trap that had a way out—sooner or later, he would return to the world, and resume his destruction of it and the people in it. So his soul must die."

Kait said, "But destroying souls—that is what the Dragons do."

"Yes. And no. The Dragons use the souls of others to pay the price for their magic. We are Falcons, and will not follow that path."

Ry said, "You're saying that we will pay for our magic with our own souls."

"That is the Falcon way," Dùghall said.

Kait finally understood. "If we do as you ask, Ry and I will go into the trap with Luercas. And with Luercas, we will cease to exist. Forever."

Dùghall finally looked into her eyes. "If you do this thing, there will be no second chances for you, no meetings beyond the Veil, no rebirth." He sat on the edge of his bunk, his movements so loose-jointed and weak that it seemed more a collapse than any intentional movement. He gripped his knees and closed his eyes tightly. "This was the meaning of the terrible oracle that I cast. I cannot give my own soul to win this fight—if I could, I would. You and you alone can do this thing that will save our world. Two souls to save the millions born and yet to be born, and the billions trapped and held in pain and madness for a thousand years."

"And what of the fact that we are Karnee?" Ry snarled. "What of the fact that those we will give lives and souls and eternity to save would kill us and cheer our deaths if they knew what we were?"

Dùghall said, "If you yearn for revenge against all those who persecute the Karnee, you couldn't find a more permanent kind than to walk away from this thing I ask of you."

"I *yearn* for an eternity with my Kait," Ry said bitterly.

"I know. If you walk away, perhaps you could somehow have it. You might hope to escape Luercas. Certainly you would have each other longer than you will if you do what I must ask of you."

Kait looked into Ry's eyes and saw her own pain and despair and disbelief mirrored there. That they faced death—yes, she had already found a way to deal with that. But that they faced oblivion . . .

Ry's mind touched hers. That subtle bond, strengthened and refined by their time apart, filled her with his love, and with ironic acknowledgment; the bond they shared was the very thing that would, if they chose to fight Luercas, consign them to oblivion. No one else could do what they did. No one else could replace them. If they refused, there would be no brave replacements to step into their places and fight in their stead.

She touched his thoughts with pictures of all the things they would be giving up, not just for this one lifetime, but for eternity. Laughter and music, the sweet scent of the wind blowing across a sun-warmed meadow, the touch of warm rain on skin, the taste of a fresh-picked berry. They would never have children together; they would never grow old together; they would never fight again, nor would they ever again cherish the pleasure of making up. For them, all of those things would cease to exist. *They* would cease to exist. It was unthinkable—and yet it was the path they were being asked to take.

Dùghall had once quoted Vincalis to Kait, and the words came back to her in that moment: *Men forge swords of steel and fire; gods forge swords of flesh and blood and tragedy.*

Ry read that quote in her thoughts, and their reaction echoed back to each other. *We were chosen for this moment from the time of our birth. We were born to face this path and make this choice. Every struggle, every hurt we have ever faced, has made us stronger and pointed us toward this day.*

They pulled away from each other at last, and stood together facing Dùghall, and once again their hands sought each other out and clasped tightly.

Ry looked down at Kait. "I doubted the hell of the philosophers," he said. "I was wrong to doubt. There is a hell, and this is it—to know heaven, and to cast it away for yourself rather than see it destroyed for everyone."

Kait smiled at him, though her lips trembled and her tears slid along the corners of her mouth so that she tasted salt. "You will not cast heaven away alone. I will be with you—every moment that we have yet to breathe, I will breathe with you at my side."

"You will do this, then?"

Kait turned to face her uncle. "I am Galweigh," she said. "He is Sabir. We are born of *Family*. We know our duty to Family, to Calimekka, to Matrin. To the gods. At last I discover the meaning of the Galweigh motto: *Kaithaeras tavan.*"

"All before self," Ry said.

"Let not the gods say that I cowered at the moment of their greatest need." Her voice began to shake so hard that she couldn't say anything else. She pressed her face against Ry's shoulder and fought to stop the tears.

"We will do what we must do," Ry said to Dùghall.

Then, softly and just for her to hear, he added, "Nevertheless, we have some time yet together before we reach Calimekka. If all of eternity is to be denied us, we'd best not waste this flicker that remains."

She did not look at Dùghall again. Instead, she kept her face averted as she followed Ry back to the cabin they shared. "How do we make these few days last forever?" she asked him.

He smiled and shook his head and kissed her. "We cannot make time stand still," he whispered. "But we can make it run."

Ian stood at the door of the brig. Rrru-eeth, shackled to the wall, glared up at him. He took a deep breath—no one knew where he was at that moment, or if they knew, they did not suspect why he was there.

"Come to tell me it's time for my hanging?" she snarled.

"No." He looked at her. She was—she had always been—beautiful in her odd way. He had cared about her once, had trusted her with his life, had thought her a friend. And then she had betrayed him. But he was not her. "I've come to talk to you of our friendship."

She snorted. "We aren't friends."

"We were once."

"Once. We could have been more—once. I loved you."

"I cared about you."

"But you didn't love me. I thought it was because I was Scarred—I could live with that. I was Scarred, and you were not, and that was the wall that stood between us."

"It wasn't that."

Rrru-eeth turned her face to the wall. "Of course it wasn't. Because then she came along, and she was Scarred, and you loved her anyway. So it wasn't that I was Scarred. It was just . . . that you didn't love me."

"But we were friends," he reminded her. "We were good friends."

She stared straight into his eyes with a fury that chilled him. "Not so good as you might have thought."

He stared at his boots and sought the right words. "I'll let you go, Rrru-eeth. I don't want to hang you. I cannot pardon you—mutiny cannot be pardoned. But I can let you escape . . . I can help you escape. We'll be sailing through the western edge of the Little Summer Chain soon. There are a dozen or so islands there—they're livable, they get some ship trade from time to time. You could hide there until you could find passage elsewhere."

"I don't want your help. I don't want anything from you."

"If you stay aboard the ship, Rrru-eeth, I have to hang you. Shipboard discipline will not permit me any other alternative."

"Then hang me. Have my blood on your hands and my soul on your conscience. And know that my ghost will haunt you through this life and every one that follows, cursing every step you take." She spat at him, but missed.

He stepped back, shaking his head. "For the next three stations, if you change your mind, call the guard. He'll know how to get me if you request it. If you don't . . ." He turned away. "Then you will die, but your death will be on your own hands, because it is the path that you have chosen."

Chapter 49

In Costan Selvira, the last city that stood between the Army of the Thousand Peoples and Calimekka, the main gates clanged shut and the inhabitants, warned by Ranan of the oncoming horde, swarmed behind the walls, stacking explosives and torchbombs and poison powder for the catapults; twisting cloth into wicks for glass pineapple projectiles; restringing bows and refletching arrows; sharpening swords and pikes. Those few who remained outside the walls cleared the trenches and buried the rows of spikes in them, and spread out caltrops and pressure-mines to slow the advancing lines. No children would be able to play outside the walls of the city for a long time after the battle, Ranan thought—if, indeed, any children returned to Costan Selvira.

They were being sent away, along with their mothers and those too old or weak or sick to fight—three ships would sail out to one of the tiny barrier isles just off the coast to wait for word of the battle. If the news was bad, or if there was no news, the captains of those three ships would assume the worst and sail north to Calimekka, or if the rumors of plague proved true, to someplace beyond.

Ranan stood atop the wall, staring down the slope of the

hill on which the town sat, studying the preparations his men and the Costan Selvirans were making. He also watched the road that ran south. If the Scarred followed their previous pattern of attack, the enemy scouts would approach from the sides, well away from the road, but the main army would march along it—it was in fairly good repair and unless a sudden rain turned the dirt portions to mud, it would withstand the sudden traffic with only a little damage.

He caught a flash of red at the edge of the clearing, and a man on horseback erupted from the jungle pursued by a pair of dozen-legged monsters that nonetheless ran upright like men.

A pair of the Scarred scouts. Ranan shuddered and pointed two of the crossbowmen at them, and a pair of archers as well. A storm of arrows and bolts arced across the sky, sprouting in the oncoming enemy. The pursuers toppled and the human scout galloped on.

Ranan hurried from the top of the wall to the gate to meet him. Within moments, the scout arrived. His horse trembled and frothed, its head hanging between its knees. The scout looked not much healthier. He bled from several wounds, and though none of them singly had been fatal, Ranan thought the man would be lucky indeed if the entire collection didn't kill him.

"The jungle stopped their side columns, except for their winged attackers. The whole of the rest of their force now comes by the main road. If you split your ground forces to defend against a three-way attack, they'll overwhelm your main force in an instant and all will be lost. Keep . . . keep only the archers from the side positions to hold off their fliers."

Ranan nodded. "What else?"

"Their catapults and siege engines and battering rams are to the fore. The fliers took off in clouds and approach just above the tops of the trees, carrying something . . . but I know not what."

"How long until they reach us?" Ranan asked.

"They are almost upon us now."

The army of the Scarred, then, would arrive with full daylight still to aid it—though from what Ranan knew of the Scarred, that would make little difference; there would be those among them who had no need of daylight. Watching them moving into the pass and sniping at them from ambushes, he had seen creatures with no eyes; creatures with ears or noses so huge and complexly developed that he felt certain their eyes were only of secondary importance to them, rather as his nose was to him; creatures who wore a luminous bluish haze around them that he could only wonder at. When it came to a full battle, he did not know what the enemy could do. He and his men had run a guerrilla campaign, attacking from the sides, wearing the enemy down as best they could, trying to get the people from the little towns that stood in the approaching army's way to flee to safer ground. This would be the first time they'd had enough men to dare a real stand.

He turned to his signal captain and said, "Signal the ships with the noncombatants to leave harbor now."

"They have not yet finished loading, sir."

"I know that. But if they don't go now, they won't get out at all."

"What of the ones who couldn't board?"

"Send them home. And pray we win the day."

The Army of the Thousand Peoples pushed forward at its fastest pace, its wings flanking the main column from the air, the main column pounding inexorably forward—three spears racing toward Costan Selvira.

Danya, atop her lorrag, took her place with Luercas at the head of the ground forces. Almost home, she thought. Resistance up to this point had been almost nonexistent.

The army that had caused them such losses going through the pass hadn't been able to press any truly devastating attacks since. They'd hit from the sides a few times, killing a dozen here and a hundred there, but they were poorly armed and vastly outnumbered—they couldn't penetrate into the core of the column to threaten supplies or damage the great siege weapons. They couldn't touch the flying wings. They could only harry and harass and stalk—and among the Scarred troops were those who were better harriers, better harassers, better stalkers. The enemy forces had lost many of their own in these last weeks.

Now they appeared to intend to make a stand.

Good. Danya was ready to finish it with them.

The leading edge of the column moved out of the heavy cover of the jungle and into a huge clearing. Costan Selvira lay before the attackers like a treasure box—unplundered, virginal, full of promise.

To the Scarred, who had faced the disappointment of discovering both Brelst and Glaswherry Hala abandoned and stripped of most of their riches, that lovely white-walled city that sat before them with its gates up and soldiers along its parapets and ramparts was a long-delayed gift of the gods. They began to cheer.

"Deploy the battering rams," Luercas shouted.

The great wheeled rams separated themselves from the main column and began to move forward. Their crews, protected from arrow fire by metal roofs affixed to the central part of the rams, tucked in close to the rams, put their heads down, and began to run toward the city's gates.

Danya paused. In Calimekka, she had people she hated. She had a reason to seek blood, destruction, and death. But here . . . ? These people in this city had done nothing to her. What business did she have with them, and how could she assuage her conscience at their spilled blood?

She set her jaw and squinted at the parapets of the city wall, making out the shapes of strangers who stared back in her direction. This was the road to Calimekka—if they did not take this city, kill these defenders, they would leave an armed enemy at their backs, and place themselves between the crushing jaws of a deadly vise. She raised an arm. "Deploy the ladder-men!"

Behind the rams ran the thickets of ladder-men, who would attempt to breach the walls by flinging their ladders up against them and climbing into the city before they could be shot down or toppled over. With each team of ladder-men ran twenty archers who would give any of the enemy who dared poke a head over the wall to give a ladder a shove something else to think about.

"Deploy the moles!"

The Scarred diggers nicknamed the moles trudged forward, little eyes shielded from the light of day by circles of polished obsidian strapped over them. They trotted behind the ladder-men with their attending archers, and when they reached a point just beyond comfortable arrow shot, went nose-down to the dirt and began to dig. They would tunnel into the city from beneath, weakening the walls, creating paths that fighters could run through, and sniffing out armories so that they could be cleaned out from the inside, giving the Scarred more weapons and the defending humans fewer.

Danya raised a gold and red flag and waved it high. That was the signal for the two flying wings to circle the city and clear any defensive positions from behind. The wings carried bags of poison dust that the Scarred had swept up from the pass and stored—simple justice, Danya thought, to kill the enemy with their own weapons.

She squinted, and saw the wings soaring out in two thin lines toward sailing ships that were racing away from the harbor. She could barely make out the dark shapes of the fliers, but she knew whoever hid aboard those ships would die within minutes.

I hope they suffer, she thought. I hope they cry out for mercy. I hope they hurt the way I have hurt.

Their suffering wouldn't be enough. It couldn't be enough, not ever, because no matter how much her enemies suffered, their pain would not take away her pain. But at least she knew that now, now, she did not suffer alone.

Smoke curled up from the remains of Costan Selvira, and fires from a hundred little battles lit the darkness like the eyes of hellish hunters. Ranan, bleeding and battered, gave word to Har, who had stayed at his side throughout the last stations of the fight. "Flee. Take word to Father in Calimekka that we have lost the day." His brother would run to Galweigh House if he could get out of Costan Selvira alive. He would let Dùghall know that now nothing stood between Calimekka and the Scarred.

Har nodded. Ranan slipped a ring from his finger onto the boy's hand and said, "Give this to him to give to my mother, and tell him we did everything we could. Now run."

Har fled down the stairs of the central tower from which Ranan had directed the last frantic stages of the fight, down into the darkness of the long tunnel that lay beneath the tower, silently as he could through the darkness, not even lighting his way with a candle for fear that he might betray his presence. He felt his way along the damp stone walls, wet and slick with moss; he hurried with fingers dragging the wall to keep himself from getting lost. He trotted, but he dared not run. Blind, he heard a thousand sounds that might have been Scarred monsters taking up pursuit; that might have been the breathing of some hideous talon-handed monster poised in the path before him, waiting to snatch his eyes out or bite open his skull; that might have been beasts hanging from the ceiling waiting for him to pass beneath so that they could drop on top of him and suck the life-juices from his flesh.

He had seen such horrors from his place beside Ranan in the high tower. He had watched the monsters come, and he had watched humans fall to them and die in ways he could not have imagined in his worst nightmares. The monsters knew no mercy; they did not take prisoners, they did not spare any living thing.

The children who had been sent away from the city were all dead, and with them their mothers and the sick and the elderly—vengeance, he thought, for those moments in the pass. Some of their children. Some of ours. This evil thing we all do to each other.

His terror nearly paralyzed him—only the thought that the monsters were more likely to appear behind him than in front of him kept him moving at all.

To Calimekka, he thought. To Calimekka, to Dùghall, with my news.

To Calimekka. I'll be safe in Calimekka, if only I can reach it.

To Calimekka.

He would never be certain how much time he spent beneath the earth, or how far he ran before the tunnel finally sloped upward and disgorged him into the heart of a jungle. He wept, though, when fresh air brushed his wet cheeks and when he looked up and saw stars overhead, winking at him from breaks in the jungle canopy.

He would never be able to enter such a closed space again, nor would he ever be able to stomach the slick feel of moss beneath his palm. And ever after, the sound of dripping water and of wind blowing through stone passages would send him racing for lighted places, for the warmth of a hearthfire and the presence of other people.

He ran through the jungle, heading north, north, north, to the promised safety of Calimekka.

The whole of Costan Selvira belonged to her. Danya rode through the streets atop her lorrag, staring at the human dead who lay in piles, and she waved her Scarred hand at their corpses and laughed. "You would have killed me," she shouted. "I could never have been one of yours, could I? But I'm alive and you're dead! Dead!"

The dead watched her with unblinking eyes, with faces stretched by horror or grief or pain, and she found herself growing less happy the farther she rode into the heart of the city. She came upon a nest of girls—certainly sisters—dressed alike, their hair cut in the same silly fashion, who lay in the street in a neat line. Eight of them, the youngest no more than two or three, the oldest in her late teens. All dead, all on display, wearing their Family colors, their Family lace.

They could have been Galweighs—they could have been Danya and her three sisters. Dark hair, dark eyes, small stature—she could have seen their likeness in her own mirror. Their young faces accused her silently, and she glared at them. "This is what I came for," she told herself as she rode forward. "I came to see my enemies brought low. I came to see those who abandoned me spread at my feet, to see them crushed. This is the first taste of my reward. This is my first moment of triumph."

The dead cared not about triumph. Their faces accused, and Danya felt the weight of dead stares at her back, and heard in their silence the simple truth: *We did nothing to cause you harm, either by action or inaction.*

Slowly her elation died.

Costan Selvira is not my city, she told herself. So I cannot expect to feel the joy I deserve as I ride through these streets. But neither must I take blame for the dead here, because we must go through here to get to Calimekka, and we cannot leave living enemies at our backs.

I'll have my joy in Calimekka, when my Family kneels before me and begs for their lives, and when the Sabirs crawl on their bellies to me, their entrails dragging in the dirt beneath them, and beg me to end their suffering.

And when I watch Crispin Sabir and Anwyn Sabir and Andrew Sabir die slowly from a thousand tiny cuts—when I hurt them myself and hear their screams and when I take their lives from them as they took my life from me, *then* I'll know satisfaction. Then I will be happy.

She turned her face from the grotesqueries of Costan Selvira's dead and sought out the living; she wanted to see Luercas. She wanted to picture him on his knees beside Crispin Sabir, the father of his flesh. She wanted to watch him and imagine the two of them begging for their lives together.

I will see that, she promised herself. Soon now, I will have the satisfaction of fulfilling my own dreams.

Chapter 50

Dùghall bent over the table in the little cabin, with the ship rocking steadily beneath him. He fought to keep his pen moving over the parchment, but the form of the spell he had to cast to trap Luercas eluded him. He sought its image in his mind—he had hoped to make it look like something that it was not, something that would seem to offer Luercas shelter or even sustenance as he fought, but what he created was a soul-devouring void, and his mind could not move past that fact to embrace frills and pointless artistry that would not fool Luercas anyway. He was no idiot to be tricked by appearances. He was a master wizard, the greatest wizard of his age, and far more powerful and talented than Dùghall would ever be.

In the back of his mind, Dùghall felt the movement of the living Falcons. Summoned, those who could were responding to the call for help that he'd sent out, traveling across Ibera to Calimekka and moving through the city and up the Path of Gods to Galweigh House. They would wait in the jungle outside the walls—those who survived the trip, anyway—to serve their part in the final battle between Falcons and Dragon. Some of them, Dùghall thought, might survive to see another day.

But that didn't help him in his task. This single most important spell he had ever conceived had to be perfect—cast right the first time, made without weakness or escape. He would only have one chance to create it, and the souls of Matrin would live or die on his success or failure. One chance.

He closed his eyes and rubbed his left temple with fingers stiff from being clenched into a fist.

He opened his eyes, sanded the ink, put aside that sheet of parchment, and pulled out another. The trap was only the first part of Dùghall's final spell. The Veil was not void. It had its own inhabitants and its own resources.

The shape of the battle that was to come formed itself in his mind, and he began to write furiously, laying out the spells he would cast, and as he wrote, he prayed:

I commend my soul to you, Vodor Imrish,
That you remember me in my hour of need.
I commend my soul to you, Vodor Imrish,
That you use me in your hour of need.
I commend my soul to you, Vodor Imrish,
That in my last moments, I will not shame you.
Make me the instrument of your will.
Make me the sword in your hand.
And once before I die, Vodor Imrish,
Let me understand the love
For which Solander died twice.
Only once, please let me feel this gift
For which I sacrifice myself.

Chapter 51

The long bay in Calimekka lay almost deserted. A few abandoned ships rocked at anchor, the skeletons of their crews scattered across the decks and fat gulls picking at the leavings. But the *Peregrine* alone sailed into the harbor, and when she dropped anchor near the Galweigh docks, no long-boats full of traders greeted her. She lay in silence, with her full crew on deck staring at the deserted wharf.

"My crew and I will travel with you," Ian told Kait and Dùghall and Ry. "I'll make sure that you and Alcie and her children and Ulwe arrive safely in Galweigh House. When the fighting is over, I'll return to the *Peregrine*—assuming that I survive, of course—and I'll resume my trading. If you wish to have me trade on behalf of Galweigh House, I'll fly your banners." He shrugged.

"What of Rrru-eeth?" Kait asked.

"You must be present for her hanging. In the final sentencing, you must speak against her, since you are one of those she wronged."

Kait and Ry glanced at each other, and Kait said, "We have no time for that now."

"Then after the battle."

"After . . . assumes much."

"Perhaps it does." Ian stared out at the mouth of the long bay and at the curve of the ocean that beckoned beyond it. "You should not have to risk yourselves in the city after this fight you seek with Luercas. Still, Rrru-eeth must be hanged. I find no joy in it—I will never forget that once she was my friend. But mutineers cannot be pardoned, for Captain's Law becomes a fragile thing if it can even once be broken with impunity." He sighed. "I'd rather leave her in the brig until her final moments, but I'll have her shackled and bring her with us. She can be hanged from the walls of Galweigh House as easily as from my mast."

"And if I die and cannot speak against her?"

"Many remain who can and will."

Kait felt the faint stirring of intuition, almost of prescience, and she said, "Bring all who can speak against her. Every one."

"I can't. Many of those she wronged are Scarred. Within Calimekka's walls they will be sentenced to immediate death."

"No. The city lies half-empty, with whole streets abandoned, the harbor full of nothing but ghosts. Your Scarred will pass safely to Galweigh House. Bring them—they must have their speech and their justice, too. We will hide them if we can, and let them walk under the Galweigh banner if we must, but I feel that they must be present to state their charges."

"Very well," Ian said. He frowned and rested fingertips on her forearm. "Tell me honestly, Kait, do you think we will survive what comes?"

"Honestly . . ." She looked down at his hand on her arm and said, "I think you might. Your crew might. Ry and I . . . will not. We know this."

"I thought as much. I can take you away. Across the sea in the Novtierras, there are lands so vast and rich that you could wander in them for a lifetime and never tire of the wonders you find. We could go there, all of us. Luercas would never find you." His fingers tightened in a gentle squeeze, and he said, "It's not too late. Not for any of you."

Kait looked up at him and then over at Ry. "It was too late the moment we were born. We are who we are, Dùghall and Ry and I—we were born for this moment. We could choose not to accept our fate, but we would do so knowing that we condemned uncounted innocents to death and worse. Three lives for a world—that's not such a bad bargain."

"If one of those lives is yours, it is."

Kait smiled up at him, and he saw bittersweet acknowledgment of what they had once shared. "Remember me," she said.

"I will."

Chapter 52

Carriages had been easy enough to come by; horses harder; drivers who would travel the road to Galweigh House were not to be had at any price. So those among Ian's crew who had some experience with horses and carriages drove them through the nearly empty streets of the city, past endless rows of houses with their shutters drawn shut, past scattered tribes of gaunt and filthy children who watched them from the shadows, past young men grown old in months, young women bent with loss and pain, past silent watching.

From the south, the storm of the Scarred approached, and those within the carriages felt its pressure spurring them onward.

Kait was first out of the carriages when they reached the top of the Path of Gods and came to a halt outside Galweigh House's gate. She ran to the carriage in which Alcie and her children and Ulwe had ridden together. When Alcie stepped to the ground, Kait hugged her. She hugged her nephew and Ulwe, and kissed the top of her niece's head.

"I have to believe you'll survive this," Alcie said. "We didn't find each other just to lose each other now."

Kait said, "Don't waste your time in false hopes. Just

promise me that each time you see the sun rise or feel the rain on your face, you'll think of me."

"It isn't fair," Alcie said, and Kait raised an eyebrow. Alcie managed a brittle laugh. "I know what the Family said: *The search for fairness is nothing but the meddling of men in the affairs of gods.* But it still isn't fair. You're my sister and my friend. I love you."

"I love you, too, Alcie. That's part of why I have to do this."

Alcie closed her eyes and knotted the hand that didn't hold the baby into a small, tight fist. "If I don't see you again in this world, I'll see you in the next."

"Yes," Kait said, knowing that she was lying, but knowing, too, that Alcie would refuse to accept the truth. "Until we meet again, be well."

Alcie cleared her throat, and Kait waited. "I was wrong about Ry," she said softly. "Sabir or not, he's a good man, and the two of you deserve each other, and all the happiness you find in this life or any other. Should you come through this . . ."—she held up a hand to ward off Kait's remarks—"and I know you don't think you will, but should you . . . you'll have my blessing."

Kait fought back tears. "Thank you. I'm glad you told me that now."

She next dropped to one knee and hugged Ulwe, looking up into that serious young face. "Your path is clouded, Kait," Ulwe said. "I cannot find the thread of it that leads beyond the House."

Kait hugged her tighter. "Look for your own path, Ulwe. The world can be wonderful—find the beauty in it and the joy, and never let them go."

Ulwe said, "I have something for you."

Kait stroked the child's cheek with her thumb. "I won't have much use for gifts where I'm going."

"This isn't a gift. It's . . . a message. A man came to me

in a dream, and said I was to tell you: *I wait for you within the Veil, Kait. I never left you.*"

Kait felt a shiver slip down her spine. "Who told you that?"

"I don't know. I couldn't see a face. I saw only light . . . but I felt . . . love."

"Oh." Kait barely breathed.

"You know who it was."

"I . . . perhaps. I will look. Perhaps I will find . . . him."

"He was good," Ulwe said. "He was very kind."

"Yes." She stood. "I have to go now. But . . . thank you."

She turned to face her future—the little of it that remained. The walls of Galweigh House stood before her, and the gate lay open. The House was empty once again.

Of course, Kait thought. The Galweigh ghosts would have claimed the bodies of the fallen, and once strong again, would have removed the rabble who had come to kill those the House sheltered. Dùghall's spell still held them. It would hold them a little longer—as long as he lived. Then the ghosts would subside to their graves, or to the Veil beyond, and the House would fall prey to whomever chose to claim it.

Now, however, for just a while longer, it was hers.

A stray scent from the edge of the jungle caught her attention. When she lifted her head and sniffed the breeze, she realized the jungle hid many men and women. She began to move toward them, not loosening her sword in its scabbard. Their scents, their movements, and the distantly felt tug of their thoughts named them friend.

First one stepped forward from the shadows, then a handful, and a dozen, and a dozen more. They were male and female, old and young, ugly and beautiful; all of them studied her with eyes old from having seen too much of the evil that the tribes of humankind inflicted upon each other. All had come to stand against this last and worst evil, to fight and if necessary to die in the service of life. In their eyes, Kait saw a hundred shades of fear—the same horror she felt, the same dread she would face down and fight through when her time came.

She knew them, though she had never met any of them before. She found them within the Falcon tide that washed through her—found the shapes of their faces and the shapes of their thoughts, and knew that they were good allies—that though they were afraid, they would not run. And she could see in their eyes that they knew her—knew who she was and what she was. They knew what she went into the House to face. The doom that marked her touched them, and they reached out hands to her as she passed them, and offered wordless thanks for her sacrifice. In that moment she was one of them more truly than she had ever been part of anyone or anything, save only Ry and the Reborn. In that moment, the awful secrets of her birth and life were forgiven and put behind, and she was theirs, wholly and without reservation, as they were hers.

Then she was beyond them, stepping through the gate into Galweigh House, and her eyes saw everything fresh and new, as if for the moment she had Shifted and become Karnee a final time.

I will never walk through that gate again, she thought. I will never step on this ground, never smell the sweetness of this air, never hear the wind through these palm leaves. These are my last sights, my last sounds, last touches, last scents, last tastes.

She drank it all in, and it wasn't enough. It could never be enough, because it was the last of everything, and she was not ready to say good-bye.

Ry came behind her and rested his hand on the small of her back. "It's hard to believe how beautiful everything is, isn't it?"

She nodded, not speaking.

"I wish we could be Karnee together one last time. I

would have loved to have hunted these hills with you, to have run the cliffs with you."

"I know. But we . . . had good lives. We flew together in many ways."

"I would have loved you forever if forever had been ours."

They stopped at the bottom of the stairs that led up into the broad front doors of Galweigh House, and kissed slowly. "And I, you," Kait told him quietly. "I wish forever *had* been ours. I like to think we would have spent it well."

Dùghall came up behind them and stopped. They looked into each other's eyes, and then, with sad smiles, moved apart. "It's time, isn't it?" Kait asked her uncle.

"I'm sorry. It is. The Army of the Thousand Peoples approaches the city. My son Har was waiting here for me—he tells me that he alone of our army survives. Costan Selvira fell the day after we left it and the Scarred raced here. We have little time."

"The Falcons are casting their shield over those who survive in Calimekka?" Ry asked.

"They have begun. They waited only for us to arrive before they started their work. When Luercas tries to draw on the souls of Calimekkans to fuel his magic, he will find only his own troops. That may slow him, at least a bit. It should weaken him."

Kait said, "It won't change our outcome, will it?"

"No," Dùghall said. "That we already know. Either the three of us win together and die together, or Luercas wins and all the world dies separately."

"Well . . . I suppose we should get started," Kait said.

She took Ry's hand in hers and together they ascended the stairway.

Chapter 53

The Falcons ringed the outside of the wall around Galweigh House—nearly a hundred of them, all sitting cross-legged with their backs against the smooth, translucent stone-of-Ancients, their eyes closed, their bodies so still they seemed not to breathe. They had said they would cast a shield over the people of Calimekka to protect them from the coming battle. Ian couldn't feel anything, but he assumed they cast the same sort of shield Kait had cast over those within the longboat that time they had escaped through the Thousand Dancers with the Mirror of Souls. He found their silent sitting unnerving—he would have felt better if magic looked more like doing something useful and less like taking a nap. Or being a corpse.

Ian set his own men in a loose guard at the head of each of the two roads that led down to the city. Like them and the Falcons and even Alcie and the children, he stayed outside the walls of Galweigh House—Dùghall had asked that none but the three who went in to fight Luercas enter through those gates until after the battle.

Inside the House, he knew Kait and Ry and Dùghall prepared for war. It being a magical battle they would fight, they were probably sitting, he thought. Sitting with their eyes closed, looking like they were napping.

He hated magic. He couldn't get his mind around it; he couldn't get past all the strangeness of it to the place where it became a fight between two people. *I wish I could fight the bastard with swords,* he thought. *I wish I could call him out like any other man and cross blades with him and run him through. Or have him run me through and that be the end of it.*

That was the way men should fight—with their hands and bodies and minds. The one who was faster or smarter or stronger won, and the loser died, and the issue was settled forever. It didn't crop up again a thousand years later when the bastard stole somebody else's body and came back from the dead to fight again.

Ian paced the semicircle around the back of the House, from east cliff edge to west cliff edge and back, stopping in the center each time to look at Rrru-eeth, who sat, shackled at throat and wrists and ankles and waist, with her chains bolted into a huge whitegum tree right at the edge of the clearing. Four men guarded her—all four were those who would speak against her in her final sentencing. Only one of the four was human. The other three were Keshi Scarred.

"You know I love you," Rrru-eeth shouted at him as he passed her yet again. "I was jealous of *her*. I wanted you to love me, not her. You can't hang me for jealousy."

He looked at her and said nothing. Mutiny wasn't jealousy, and she knew it, but she sought to win his pity and the pity of the others she'd wronged. She wanted to twist things, to reshape the past so that it became favorable to her. He thought of the young girl who had risked her life to save the lives of all those slave children, and he wondered how that girl had become a woman who could abandon her comrades to die in a hostile land and who could betray the man who had given her sanctuary and a new life and her freedom—a man she claimed to love.

"No good deed goes unpunished," he whispered to himself, but that was too cynical and too bitter. The children she had saved and that he had transported to safety had gone on to live free lives. Some of them he'd watched grow up in the Thousand Dancers. Some had moved on. None of them had grown rich yet, but none of them had ended up the sex toys of perverse and brutal old men, either, to be thrown away when they were broken.

I got the good from my risk, he thought. If it wasn't all good, well, nothing is.

It was like Kait. He'd loved her, fought beside her, wanted more than anything to make a life with her, and then she had turned away from him and found someone else. It didn't change a minute of what they had shared. Now Kait said she would fight and die in a battle in which he could not even lift sword to help her, and he was left feeling useless and wasted; he would gladly have fought in her place. He would gladly have died if she might live. But he could not do what she had to do, and so he paced from road to road, looking for threats that didn't materialize and enemies that didn't come.

What he and Kait had shared together had been good, but it was gone forever. He tried to accept that, tried to come to some accommodation with the reality of his world.

He wouldn't have changed the past, he finally realized. He would have simply made it last longer.

Chapter 54

The wings of the Army of the Thousand Peoples over-flew Calimekka and returned to Luercas and Danya to report.

"The city seems almost empty," the captain of the Gold-Fire wing reported. He shifted his leathery wings awkwardly and ducked his head into his left side to arrange an errant fold of skin. When he lifted his head, he continued. "Gray rags hang over most of the doors to houses and shops, and most shops are closed. The wharves are deserted, the harbor empty of all but dead ships, and great smoking piles of bones lay in every square and empty lot."

Luercas frowned. "I wonder why the city would be empty. That doesn't make sense—everyone from the towns and villages to the south has been running toward Calimekka ahead of us. The city ought to be bursting at the seams. There ought to be mobs camped outside the walls."

Danya said, "Gray rags, you said?"

The captain nodded.

"That's your answer, then." She turned to face Luercas and said, "Plague is loose in Calimekka. The gray rags are the signal that someone within a house is dead or dying of it. Gray rags will hang on all the gates, warning all those who come that if they enter, they will die. The people who fled ahead of us to this city will have kept on running— most likely they will have scattered west to Crati or Man- ale or Halles, or gone on north to Radan." She stared at him and started to laugh. "All your planning, all your care, all your grand designs, and you've brought us at last to a pest- hole, a plague-hell, a disease-ridden cesspool." She stood and began to laugh at him. "You who would be king—can you be king of corpses? Can you chain the souls of the dead to your will?"

Luercas smiled slowly and his eyes narrowed. "So funny you should ask me that—it is, in fact, something I have long planned. But you, bitch-mother—tell me, how will you exact vengeance on the dead?"

Danya frowned. "Surely the plague did not reach the great Houses. The Families have stores and walls—at the first word of disease, they would have closed their gates and waited out the sickness as they have always done. Those who owe me their lives will be waiting in comfort in the midst of their riches when I go to claim them."

"Will they?"

"Of course."

"Why don't you seek them out? Why don't you see for yourself?" He smiled at her, smug and secretive. His eyes said, *I know something you don't know,* and she wanted in that moment to drive her dagger through his heart and watch him writhe and die on her blade. But she had not the power to kill him. She knew that.

She felt sure that the Galweighs and the Sabirs would be intact behind their walls, waiting out the devastation that was claiming the rest of Calimekka. She determined that she would prove this to Luercas. Raised a Galweigh Wolf, trained to the darkest of known magics and, hardened by bitter experience, she felt the slick, seductive channels of Wolf magic coursing through muscle and blood and bone like black fire. She welcomed that flow into her mind, and out of it she spun around herself a globe of white light, and into that light she sent her vision. She cast globe and vision away from herself, toward the city, toward the Houses of the great Families. She went first to the citadel of the Sabirs, and saw the gate on it closed. But gray silk bunting hung across the smooth white stone-of-Ancients on either side of the gate, and as she guided her vision-light inward, she found funeral pyres in which blackened fragments of bone lay like sticks of shining coal. She found servants scuttling through vast, empty halls and hiding in store-rooms. She found the body of an old Wolf-woman, Scarred beyond any remembrance of humanity, bloated and rotting, left lying on the floor where it had fallen, fingers still clutching the ripped throat of a dead man. She found a blank-eyed man lying on a bed staring at nothingness, alive and whole but lost in the darkness of his own mind, and elsewhere a starving child locked in an empty store-room, too far gone even to cry or claw at the door any-more.

But she did not find Crispin, and she did not find Anwyn, and she did not find Andrew. She cued her magic to them—to her memory of the shapes of their bodies and the form of their souls—and she sent her vision-light quest-ing beyond Sabir House. She found nothing. She grabbed one of the Scarred who stood beside her throne and dug her two talons into his throat, and as his blood gushed across her hand and onto the floor, she drew power from his life and sent the vision-light farther. But still she found nothing. The Unholy Trinity were dead.

She searched next through her own House, and there found strangers ringing the wall, and behind that wall . . . emptiness. In a central room she found her cousin Kait, her uncle Dùghall, and a stranger kneeling around a silver bowl in the center of the floor, but in all that vast House they were the only living things.

Goft, she thought. The Family has fled to Goft. She sent

her vision farther. But the gates of Cherian House had been ripped from the walls and traders and vagabonds had set up a market within the walls, and tramps and thieves and whores camped inside the House itself.

Gone. They were gone. Her Family, the Sabir Family, all those who had wronged her and abandoned her. Gone not just from their Houses but from the face of Matrin. They were dead. All dead.

She had sworn her life to see them grovel at her feet, to hear from their own mouths their pleas and their contrition; she had killed her own child in sacrifice to her oath, and now here she was, outside the gates of the very city where they should have been, her army around her, her time for vengeance at hand—and her enemies were all dead and gone.

She shattered the vision-light with a scream, rose from her throne, kicked the corpse of the creature she had sacrificed away from her, and turned on Luercas.

"You knew," she raged.

He smiled at her and said nothing.

"You knew they were all dead! You knew!"

"Of course I knew. If you had paid more attention to what was going on in Calimekka, you would have known, too."

"If you knew of the plague, why did you come here?"

"There was no plague. The breaking of the Mirror of Souls killed a few people—that's all. No one within the city is sick. No one is dying of some dread contagious disease."

"A few people! The city is nearly empty."

"The citizens thought it was a plague," Luercas said, and shrugged. "Stupid people. Those who could, fled. Those who remain are too poor or too weak to run away, or they have simply ceased to care whether they live or die. That suits me well enough."

"We were to get the riches of the city," one of the

Scarred said. "We were to become lords of the greatest city on Matrin."

"And so you shall," Luercas said. "That you'll have little resistance before you claim what is yours is no great tragedy. The city itself is the prize—the people who inhabited it were merely obstacles."

"And what of me?" Danya screamed. "What of my vengeance?"

"What can I say? You made a bad bargain. Those who live only for revenge usually do. They never get the satisfaction they imagine; that you didn't, either, is no surprise to me."

She attacked him then, two claw-tipped fingers slashing for his throat, and the guards who stood at either side of Luercas's throne grabbed her and pinned her between them. She howled her rage, and Luercas laughed. "That took a bit longer than I'd anticipated, but it was as delightful as I'd hoped it would be. How charming to see you exhibit some spine at last. Themmias, bring the chains."

One of the Dethu Scarred ran from the tent and returned a moment later with heavy chains and manacles. The guards put them on Danya and chained her to Luercas's throne, though some of them looked askance at Luercas as they carried out his orders. Luercas said, "I think you've had your weapons long enough." He touched her with his index finger, and her right hand, Scarred by the two talons, began to melt. The white heat of fire raged through her hand; no matter what she did to try to shield herself from his magic, he simply shifted his spell's approach and kept burning her. The pain drove her to her knees—she screamed and begged; she shamed herself and her Family . . . but no, she had no Family. She had nothing.

He did not stop until her right hand ended in a stump at the wrist.

"Enough for now," he said, and patted her on the head. "You may sit at my feet like the good little lapdog that you are, and later perhaps I'll think of some amusing tricks to teach you. I think humiliation is good for the soul, don't you?"

She could only whimper. The pain where her hand had once been was still so great it nearly blinded her.

"And now," she heard him say, "if I am not mistaken, the time has come for my enemies to challenge me directly. I feel their magic building—they should be summoning me at any time."

"Why do you not go into the city and take the fight to them?"

"I have a single task I must take care of when we enter the city—a little thing, the matter of a moment. When I've finished it, I will lead you through the streets as the conquerors of Calimekka, and we shall all be declared kings and lords. But if I do not destroy them first, they might strike at me as I am about my business, and hit me in the single moment when I will be . . . vulnerable. I choose, rather, to meet them in a time and place of my choosing, and at a moment of strength." His voice grew soft and solicitous. "After all, I don't want anything to stand between you, my people, and your well-earned triumph."

Chapter 55

Dùghall stood across from Kait and Ry. "You'll cross into the Veil, and immediately after you arrive, you'll see a dark sphere surrounded by lights. This is the void that I've created to destroy Luercas. Under no circumstances allow yourself to fall or be pushed into it unless you can pull Luercas in with you. If you cross over in Shifted form, you may have an edge against him—he will not be expecting predators like the Karnee to meet him."

"What difference will it make? We have no true bodies within the Veil—only seeming bodies as insubstantial as light," Kait said.

Dùghall said, "Your mind acts upon what it knows. If you cross in human form, you will take human senses with you. If you cross in Karnee form, you will take Karnee speed and Karnee talents."

"And Karnee temper," Ry said.

Kait nodded. "In Karnee form, I am easily enraged, always hungry for blood and flesh, wild and barely able to control my own impulses."

Dùghall knelt across from them and leaned forward, his eyes focused intently on their faces. "I know. This is part of why I believe the two of you were chosen by the gods for this task. Luercas will have fought against many things, but he will never have challenged a pair of Karnee—your kind did not exist in the world when last he lived as a man. You will control all the magic you ever did as humans; you will be able to communicate in thought as only the two of you can, without any touch or taint of magic . . . and you will think as Karnee think—as wild things hungry for the hunt and free from fear. *This* I believe is the key that will give us the battle if anything can."

"And yet you have doubts."

"You are overmatched. The three of us together are overmatched. Even if we give everything we have—even if we lose everything we have—we will almost certainly fail. And yet we must fight."

Kait held the faces of those she loved before her in her mind. Her sister Alcie and Alcie's two lovely children; Ulwe, who was so young and frightened and brave in the face of loss and disappointment; Ian, who would have done anything for her. These were the people she could save. And there was Ry, whom she loved more than breath, and Dùghall, who had become friend and father figure and inspiration to her. These two she could not save; they would fight with her and die with her. Around them lay a world, her world, which she loved from blade of grass to ray of sunlight to grain of sand, and the people who were to her faceless and nameless—they, too, would benefit from what she did, but in the end she would not fight for them, and she would not die for them. She would die for Alcie, for Ulwe, for Lonar, for Rethen, for Ian, for Ry, for Dùghall. For the memory of Hasmal, who had died a hero that she might live. For the memory of Solander, who had given his life twice for love of all of life.

She turned to face Ry and rested a hand on his thigh. "I'm ready," she said.

"Not yet." He pulled her into his arms and kissed her passionately, and she responded with everything in her. She fought to silence the voice in the back of her head that screamed, *Last kiss*—she held herself in the moment, focused only on his touch and scent and taste, and for that single moment joy filled her and overflowed—her mind touched Ry's and they became one as fully as if they were joined flesh to flesh.

When at last they moved apart, he said, "Now we're ready."

Dùghall took one of Kait's hands in his left, one of Ry's in his right. "I am proud to have known both of you. I love you both as my own children. Good fortune find you, and courage and strength." He squeezed their hands, then leaned forward and gave each of them a kiss on the cheek. "Now let us do what we must do." He released their hands, took a deep breath, and the anxious, sad man he had been fell away. Dùghall seemed to grow taller. His chin lifted, his shoulders went back, and a fierce, determined smile crossed his face. "Shift first," he said. "Then move into the Veil. Wait by the void you will find there. I will issue the challenge to Luercas—he will respond. He knows that until we are defeated he cannot move forward with his plans."

Kait shivered and stared into Ry's eyes. Then she found the wildness inside of her, the Karnee hunger, and her blood began to bubble and her muscles grew hot and slippery beneath her skin. She stood and quickly stripped off her clothes. Beside her Ry did the same. Within moments, they were furred, four-legged hunters in a world where colors were brighter, scents were sharper, tastes were richer—and now Kait yearned for the hunt, for the chase, for the kill. Now death was a stranger to her, and though the human Kait within still cried out at the knowledge of the loss she faced, Kait the beast longed only to be set free against the monster that was her prey.

Within the blood-bowl, light shimmered, and she crouched onto all fours, her belly pressed against the cool stone floor, and closed her eyes tightly, and Kait the human stilled the mind of Kait the beast and brought both of them together in this single final task they faced, and Kait the forbidden stepped out of her Scarred flesh and into the incomprehensible vastness of the Veil.

Ry, formed as she was in the spirit-flesh of a four-legged hunter, joined her. They stood in the midst of the terrifying infinity of the Veil. Before them lay a circle of utter darkness, a cold and evil twisting in the fabric of the universe, ringed about with tiny sparkling lights that marked its boundaries; it was the void Dùghall had created; their killer; their grave; their end. It was, too, the gate to the salvation of their world and those they loved. Kait howled out against the darkness, a cry that shivered through the Veil and touched eternity. Ry's voice echoed with hers, telling her in wordless wild song that they were together, that they would be together as long as they had life and breath and soul.

Then, as one, they fell silent, and awaited the coming of the one with whom they would go down into eternal oblivion.

"Now he comes," Luercas said, and at his feet Danya rattled her chains and snarled.

"Death to you. Death and pain, shame and humiliation."

Luercas gave her a hurt look. "I would never have wished such a thing for you. You were supposed to be my ally. My companion. I tried to give you what you said you wanted," he said. "I'm truly sorry I had no way to keep your enemies alive long enough for you to kill them yourself. You're being unreasonable in demanding that I should have."

"I sacrificed my child, my soul, my honor because of you!" she screamed.

"Everything you did, you did of your own free will, by your own hand and your own choice, and for your own reasons. You did nothing for me. You did it for yourself." He smiled down at her and shrugged. "That's all anybody ever does."

The gloom of the tent brightened, and a swirl of light appeared at the foot of Luercas's throne, and the Scarred stepped back as one. The ghostly form of a man appeared, tall as the tallest warrior, fierce as any lorrag, with a cloak of night that whipped about him in a wind that did not reach those who watched. He smiled coldly at Luercas, and more than one among the Scarred shivered. His smile was Death, the gleam in his eye was Death, and when he spoke, his voice was the icy voice risen from the lone forgotten grave. "Within the Veil our champions await. Come, fight, defeat them or die; you will not sit upon the world's throne until the Falcons have fallen."

Luercas did not tremble at the apparition before him. He only smiled, waved a hand in negligent dismissal, and said, "Go. Play your little games, you and your champions. I'll be along in a moment—I'll give you enough time to commend your souls to your gods, for when I come they'll be my meal." He snapped his fingers and the messenger dissolved into smoke, and in the breathless silence of the tent, the messenger's startled cry, cut off, hung in mockery of the brave front he'd presented and the fierce threats he'd made.

"They are so small and so weak," Luercas said to the Scarred who waited on him. "They would war with gods, but they are only flesh and blood." He settled himself comfortably into his throne and with the practice of centuries, prepared himself to tread the trackless Veil. "Await me here," he said. "Guard against intrusion. I will rejoin you shortly, and when I return, we shall ride forth to claim our world."

He spun the silver thread that led from the realm of flesh to the realm of the spirit, and followed it into the cold and the dark of infinite night.

Kait, hanging in the formless darkness of the Veil, remembered Ulwe's message—that one had said, *I wait for you within the Veil. I never left you.*

Perhaps I will find him here, she thought, and wondered where she might have to search—but she did not need to search. In the instant she thought of Solander, her mind was filled again with that all-encompassing love, with the touch of the soul that had first given her hope that she might be loved as she was—that she might be truly worthy of love.

Little sister, the radiance whispered into her mind, *I came only to tell you what I have learned—perhaps you will find a way to use it.*

Tell me, she said.

I was wrong, Solander told her. *I thought that I had to hang on, that I had to defeat the Dragons a second time because without me, they would not have been defeated the first time.*

But we needed you, Kait said.

No. I thought you did, so I held on and I staved off the natural order of life and death and fought to experience rebirth unchanged by that which lies beyond the Veil. I could not accept that heroes are born anew in each age that needs them; I could not accept that my fight was over or that the world could go on without me. In my own way, I was as wrong as the Dragons. Yours was never my world, nor was your time ever my time. This is your moment, Kait. Your time upon the stage, to fight and triumph or fall in defeat. And no matter what happens, when it is over your time will pass and you will have to let go. Then the world and its fate will belong to others.

The love touched her again, embraced her, comforted her. *In that moment, love . . . and let go. Know that evil is always weak, for it is born of cowardice. Courage is eternal, for it is born of love. And love never dies.*

Then Solander was gone, and again she faced the darkness.

Light moved in the distance—radiance that billowed forth from nothingness and swirled into the shape of a man. Now Luercas came. He was beautiful, Kait thought—as beautiful as any god. He shimmered with strength and life—nude, perfectly formed, and gently smiling, he walked toward them with his long golden hair blowing in the wind of the Veil and a trail of starlight scattering behind his every step.

On his left breast, two dark scars marred his flesh—two puckered triangles that drove like poison into his heart. Kait saw those scars and coldness gripped her; she knew without knowing how she knew that they were the genesis of Luercas, and their poison was as much a part of him as he was a part of them.

Move away from me, Ry said, speaking directly into her thoughts. *Keep your distance.*

She slipped to Ry's left and moved forward in a slow and easy lope, ears cocked forward, nose sifting the air for any hint that scent might bring, mouth partly open to keep her dagger-sharp teeth ready.

"Oh, come, now," Luercas said with a laugh in his voice. "I made a dramatic exit in front of my troops, but my intention is that we work out our differences and go our separate ways. You can't expect us to actually fight. You couldn't win against me, and I have no wish to destroy those who could be valuable to me someday . . . and who are, in any case, quite lovely. I am no barbarian to destroy that which is beautiful simply because it is not mine."

Kait and Ry said nothing. They kept circling, looking for an opening.

Luercas sighed. "Quite a nasty trap you people have built for me there," he said. "Impressive use of magic. The fellow who actually created it didn't have the courage to come in here with you, I see, but the two of you seem to have enough courage for everyone—if not enough sense."

He glanced over his shoulder at Dùghall's void, and in that instant Kait saw an opening and leaped into it quickly, slashing Luercas's thigh with unsheathed claws and darting out of reach before he could react. He snarled and made a gesture with one hand, and Kait realized he meant to summon forth power.

And she felt her second victory when a startled look appeared on his face and magic failed to flow into him at his summoning. Luercas glanced from Kait to Ry and said, "Nicely done. I commend you. It doesn't matter that you have shielded the souls of the Calimekkans, however. My Scarred have souls, too. If necessary, they will serve me in death instead of in life." He started to make the gesture again, and as he did, Ry leaped for his hand and his teeth ripped through Luercas's wrist, and in the same moment, Kait, knowing what Ry was going to do, feinted behind Luercas and her teeth flashed in and ripped into the back of his leg behind his knee and she darted out again.

They were out of easy range as quickly as that. But this time Luercas summoned magic that responded to him— his wounds healed as quickly as they had been made, and the faint shield that had surrounded him from the instant of his appearance grew bright and hard.

"Stop before I have to do something you'll regret," he said quietly. "Listen to me for a moment. We three can reach an accommodation. Your world will be better for the gifts I bring to it. Matrin swarms now with murderers, rapists, slavers, and thieves; with diseases and poverty and addictions to a thousand poisons and abuses of a thousand vices. It doesn't need to. There's a better way."

"The Dragon way?" Kait snarled, fighting her Karnee form to speak. "We've already seen that way. The Dragons would have built a lovely world, but they wanted to use the souls of the innocent to do it, as if human souls were appetizers before a banquet, to be devoured by the dozens or hundreds and then forgotten."

"Dafril and his colleagues were wasteful and greedy."

"And you're not?" Kait asked. She and Ry kept circling Luercas, watching for another opening, but he'd become much more careful.

"That's correct. I'm not. I am a man with simple wants and simple needs. I have eminently sensible goals." He sighed. "I want to live forever; what sensible man does not? I differ only from most men in that I have found a way to have what I want. I want to make sure I spend eternity in comfort and happiness, and in pleasant and agreeable surroundings, free from want and suffering and ugliness. Again, my desires are such that I share them with every living human being. I differ from everyone else only in that I have been intelligent enough and determined enough to overcome the considerable obstacles that separate me from my dreams. I can live forever only if I am a god—I can guarantee eternal comfort and happiness to myself and everyone else only if I control the world in which I live."

He spread his hands in a placating gesture. "In wanting pleasant surroundings and beauty, I must create a world that will offer these things to everyone equally. Don't you see? Ugliness is offensive whether one faces it daily or is simply forced to know that it exists in the shadows at a distance. I will not wantonly waste lives or souls—the best gamekeeper is the one who remembers that if he kills all his deer today, he shall starve on the morrow. I do, however, accept the maxim that no one can eat venison who does not kill a deer."

Move in a little, Ry said into her thoughts. *Edge him toward the void.*

They moved, and Luercas laughed and was suddenly behind them, farther from the trap than he had been before. "I'm not going to step into your trap," he said gently. "Please stop trying to maneuver me into it. Listen to sense. Not all souls are deserving of immortality. Not all lives are equal. Can you truly tell me that a peddler in the flesh of young children is as worthy of eternity as the two of you? Or what of his customer, who buys the children, uses them as sexual playthings for a time, and then throws them away, ruined and scarred and broken for the rest of their lives—if they even survive? How has the woman who poisons her husband and her children in order to gain control of the family estate and become parata of it all earned eternity? Tell me—what of the man who slaughters strangers for the pleasure of watching them die; what of the raper of the helpless; what of the thief who in the name of his god or his Family or his city steals the poor into oblivion, and calls his thievery taxation, and claims it as his rightful due?"

Ry growled, "What of the petty demagogue who lays claim to souls not his own to buy himself eternity?"

Luercas smiled indulgently. "Better worlds are not built without cost. I will bring peace and safety to the streets; I will bring food to the tables of the poor, security to the aged in their time of great need, education and civilization and employment to those who now are ignorant and struggling. No disease will ravage any city under my care, no child will suffer abuse or die of hunger."

"And all you want in exchange," Kait said, circling and circling, "is our free will. Our bodies. Our souls."

"The bodies of the irreparably damaged. The souls of the evil. Any good gamekeeper culls out the sick and the foul—it improves the herd." Luercas shrugged. "And free will—"

"Free will," Kait interrupted, "is the thing that makes us not a herd to be kept and culled and *improved*. Free will gives us the drive to improve ourselves. Or not, if we so choose."

Ry slipped closer, teeth bared in a feral grin, claws out. "All men are evil sometimes. It is the immortality of the soul and the mortality of the flesh that gives each the opportunity to be reborn—to learn and grow and improve. The very thing you would strip away is the thing we most need."

"What? An endless cycle of pissing, shitting, helpless infancy followed by stupid, weak childhood and pigheaded adolescence; then a few brief years of glorious adulthood followed by senility, senescence, and decay—and a final ignominious return to shitting, pissing helplessness in the form of a second, aged infancy? And then dying. Ah, dying. Hideous, humbling days or weeks or months or years that rip every vestige of self-respect from a man and leave him gasping like a fish tossed on a bank for just a bit of air he can breathe? That leave him begging his gods for an end to the pain, groveling for the simplest of mercies, for the end of everything he once held dear so that those he loved will no longer see him writhing in his cowardice and his shame? And then death itself, which should be the end of it all—but it *isn't*. Because then we must come back and do it again. And again. And again. Learning every time. Becoming *better* every time—or so the gods would mislead us to believe."

They moved closer to Luercas and he lashed out at them with magic—not enough to damage them; just enough to fling them away from him as if they were toys.

He snarled, "*That* is the fate you would demand for all of us equally. Well, I applaud your idealism and your fine and shiny belief that all souls, given time, will become worthy of life, but I don't share your optimism. The evil stay evil; the good wear down from the weight of bitter lives one piled upon another and *become* evil. I see a better way to spend eternity. My way helps many, hurts only those deserving of hurt, and removes me from a cycle of existence that I find pointless, humiliating, and disgusting."

"And the billions who are trapped in the Wizards' Circles?" Kait asked.

She saw surprise cross his face, but then he shrugged. "They're lost, ruined a thousand years ago, damaged now beyond repair. Their madness grows deeper and more terrible with every passing day, and the magical poison they spew out into the world grows worse. For them—and for the survival of Matrin—oblivion will be a mercy. I do a service, really. To them. To all who live or ever will live in Matrin again."

"You delude yourself if you think there is anything but evil in your plan," Kait said.

"You may believe what you wish. I am a good man, though, and I will prove it to you. You may walk away from this battle unscathed, right now, if you will only swear on your souls that neither you nor your Falcons will attempt to hinder me again. Your only other option is to die, which you don't want and I don't want. You cannot win. Surely you can see that; you haven't the talent or the strength to stand against me."

Kait felt him probing at her mind as he turned, as they circled; he was digging for her thoughts. She shielded herself as best she could, and so did Ry, but Luercas was right: He was stronger than both of them together, and he tore through their meager shields and into the secrets they had tried to keep as easily as a child would tear through ribbon and paper to get to the treat beneath. She felt him pawing through her thoughts and through Ry's.

He did not gloat at what he found, though. Instead he

grew still, and stared at the two of them with an expression of sudden uncertainty that bordered on fear.

"You *planned* to die," he whispered. "You planned to go into the void with me—you accept eternal oblivion for yourselves as the price for my death. Your uncle has abandoned you to me, and yet, knowing that you cannot win, you still intend to fight. What manner of madness has gripped you? Have your lives no value to you?"

He gestured again, and his body became brighter and began to expand. "How can a god bargain with those who embrace oblivion? I cannot offer you heaven; I cannot threaten you with hell. I can only destroy you regretfully, then use the energy I draw from your destruction to create something good."

Kait kept circling, keeping Luercas between her and the void, keeping Ry always in position where one of the two of them might have a chance to lunge in again if Luercas became distracted or dropped his guard.

Dùghall *should* have been there, she thought. He had said he would be with them—if he were there, he could have provided a third distraction, and perhaps she or Ry might have gotten a clean shot at Luercas's throat, could have dragged him into the void.

What had happened to him? Had he faltered at the last moment? Had his fear grown to be too much for him?

In her mind, she felt Ry's comforting touch. *If it is to be just us, then it will be just us. Hunt, love; hunt with me as we would have hunted in the hills together. We have only this moment. Let us make it count.*

Between them and the void, Luercas shook his head. "Your choice, then. I offered reason, you picked annihilation." He made a single, simple gesture, and power began to pour into him as if it were water from a broken dam. He began to expand and to brighten, filling with cold white light, stretching upward and outward.

They weren't going to be able to destroy him, Kait realized. They simply didn't have a prayer.

Nonetheless, she leaped at him, and in the same instant, Ry leaped, too.

Chapter 56

Dùghall, his spells awaiting only the trigger of a single event, crouched inside his chalk-drawn circle, staring at the still Karnee-Scarred forms of his niece Kait and her soulmate, Ry. They lay in each other's embrace, lovely creatures even in their altered flesh. He would miss them, he thought—and then he thought, no, he probably wouldn't. He probably wouldn't miss *anything*.

He peered within the Veil through the tiny connection hidden within the decoy he'd built—his pretty little sphere of void, surrounded by lights, marked DANGER, DO NOT ENTER—and dangerous though it truly was, completely useless for the purpose he'd claimed for it.

It was quite useful, though, as a way to watch without being seen or suspected.

He'd told Kait and Ry the truth when he told them that they would have to fight Luercas within the Veil. He'd lied to them, though, about everything else. He had no choice. Had they known the truth, they might have accidentally betrayed it to Luercas—that innocent betrayal would cost them not just their lives, not just their own eternity, but a world.

Dùghall stared at their unmoving bodies for a long moment, and he shivered. No matter what reassurances he had given them, he had known all along that neither Kait nor Ry, nor even the two of them together, had any hope of defeating Luercas.

He did fear they might fall prey to Luercas's carefully worded, reasonable-sounding arguments. He heard the Dragon offer them life within his safe new world and Dùghall snarled at the arrogance of the bastard. Luercas offered Kait and Ry the same bargain a herdsman would offer wild beasts: *Come to me and I will protect you from the hunters, care for your old and your young, give your lives purpose, shelter you, feed you, improve you and your lot. And all I ask is that you work with me.*

And what he did not say was what the herdsman never said: *I will rip your young from your side because I covet the taste of their tender flesh and in any case I would rather have your milk for myself than let you feed them with it; I will care for your old by destroying them because the old will only slow me down, eat expensive food, and give me nothing I desire in return. I will shelter you in a cage of my making and kill any who try to escape. I will feed you the cheapest and foulest swill I can obtain, because while your continued existence serves my purpose, your happiness is meaningless to me. I will improve you to my preferences and needs, not yours, culling out the intelligent and the curious and the adventuresome in favor of the docile and the stupid and the slow, because docility and acceptance make my work easier. Your burden will be anything I wish it to be, and nothing you do will ever be enough to earn you my gratitude or your own freedom; when the day comes that you have borne me your last offspring or given me your last drop of milk, I will slaughter you for your bones and your skin and your teeth, because those who can no longer serve me in life must serve me in death.*

And the bargain you make with me will be binding on your children and your children's children through all of time. You will pay for your illusion of safety with everything you have and with everything you ever could have hoped for, as will your heirs. And in the end, only I will gain anything from this bargain we make, for security is only an illusion, and safety is a prison. Only those who risk losing can ever hope to win.

If either Kait or Ry believed Luercas's lie, the battle would be over before it could even begin—but neither of them faltered for a single instant.

Dùghall nodded grimly; his time to act would come soon, then, for when Luercas discovered he could not enslave Ry and Kait, he would be forced to kill them. No herdsman dared tolerate rogues.

Dùghall crouched in the circle with his hands pressed together, biting his lip. He was afraid, as deeply and wholly terrified as he had ever been. He alone had a chance of defeating Luercas. He alone controlled a power strong enough to pose any challenge to the ancient Dragon. If he was given an opening. *If* he was fast enough and brave enough to take it.

He held the last word of the last spell on his tongue, kept the magic he had gathered together and formed with a focused concentration that left him sweating and trembling— and fought against the fear that consumed him. His body shook and his soul cried out for reprieve. He had never been so alone.

On the other side, Dùghall felt his enemy begin to rip the souls from his own followers to give himself power to shatter Kait and Ry. He felt Kait and Ry bunch their muscles, bound into the air in a twin leap that they knew even as they took it was futile, and doomed.

Time slipped through his fingers like quicksilver; the harder he tried to hang on to it, the more it ran away. *Give me the strength to do what I must do,* he said to any gods that might be listening. He embraced the energy that connected him through his created void to the hopeless drama that unfolded within the Veil, and distanced himself from the horror that scrabbled in the back of his mind, shrieking with the certain knowledge of things worse than physical death.

He found the darkness of the Veil, and within it, the pale lights that were Kait and Ry, and the bright, hard light that was Luercas. The three of them closed in a single awful collision, focused completely on each other. In that single instant, Luercas dropped the shields he had maintained around himself so that he could release the power he had stolen in one hard, fast, devastating thunderbolt that would obliterate Ry's and Kait's souls.

In that one instant, after Luercas's shield dropped but before the magic flew, Dùghall erupted through the link he had created, screaming the final word of his final spell, swarming at and into and *through* Luercas so that the essences of their two souls occupied the same space. Their energies melded and the fire of their blended lives blazed like an exploding star. *Get away from us,* he screamed at Kait and Ry, and felt Kait protest and felt Ry catch her and pull her far from them and their battle. His spells swirled around himself and Luercas; one wrapped them within a mirrorlike ball that kept reflecting every cast spell back at them—instantaneous and brutally effective *rewhah,* which blocked them from doing any damage except to each other . . . while simultaneously and equally damaging themselves.

The second prepared spell raced off into the darkness of the Veil, screaming like a banshee, blazing like a meteor, and vanishing into silence as quickly as it had appeared.

The spell which Luercas had released, intending to destroy Kait and Ry, slammed instead into him and Dùghall, its energy ricocheting within the mirrored ball that confined them. Pain tore through them both, a blinding, deafening, nauseating hot white agony that melted their souls, twisting them and binding them together so that they became one soul—but one soul with two minds.

"Release me or die," Luercas howled. "I have the strength of a thousand men . . . and a thousand women . . . and several thousand children. You and your Falcons are not and can never be my equal."

"I know what I can do," Dùghall said. "And what I can't."

"I'll tell you what you cannot do. You cannot win, you jackass. You'll expend yourself in fighting me and gain nothing for your loss. You should have stayed hidden in your house on the hill. I might have left you there—I might have let your little nest of wizards and freaks survive."

"I cannot win," Dùghall acknowledged. "But I can fight."

"You can die eternally. And when I'm done with you, the rest of them will die, too, and die forever."

Dùghall felt a shift in the darkness that surrounded them. He rested for just an instant, then struggled to drag Luercas toward the void he had created.

"You think to take me with you into oblivion?" Luercas began to laugh. He resisted Dùghall's struggles easily, simply drawing more power into himself to counter Dùghall's efforts. The mirror that surrounded them both did not keep him from drawing out the souls of those who served him—it simply prevented him from loosing their power on anyone save himself. "You noble fool."

"I am the gods' sword," Dùghall said, feeling an indescribable weight streaking toward them, knowing that the end came quickly now. "I was forged out of need, for this day, against this moment. The gods unsheathed me and aimed me for your heart, and in this moment I strike."

Luercas in that moment heard the first soft noises that rapidly became banshee screaming, and saw the first flicker of light that became with horrifying speed the return of

Dùghall's meteor-spell, tearing through the Veil straight toward the two of them.

In the instant after, he became aware of that which moved silently behind it.

"No," he whispered, and in that moment, Dùghall felt his enemy's fear.

Luercas tried to disengage from Dùghall, but they were completely enmeshed. "Release me," he said. "Quickly. One of those which hunt between the worlds approaches."

"I know," Dùghall said. "I summoned it."

"*No!*" Luercas struggled harder. "Those which hunt between the worlds devour souls. It will . . . it will eat us. We'll cease to be forever."

"I know."

"It isn't like the damned Mirror of Souls, you whoreson! Nor like a gate—we can make ourselves a Mirror or a gate if we hurry, and even if we're trapped inside for a thousand years, we'll eventually find a way out. This—*this* will be the end of us. Both of us!"

Now Dùghall's voice was sad. "I know." He resisted Luercas's increasingly frantic attempts to break the mirror-ball and cast a spell that would create an escape for the two of them; he buffered the mirror-ball with every drop of strength he had and every drop of magic the collective souls of the Falcons could feed him. And he held them steady, in the path of the approaching hunter. The energy that fed into the two of them burned ever brighter, drawing the mindless devourer to them all the more certainly.

"I know I'll cease to exist. But the tools of the gods are often broken in service—and I will serve. You've cared nothing for the uncounted souls you've devoured. And with your destruction, your evil will stop."

Luercas suddenly stopped struggling. He began snapping the ties that bound him to all his captive souls. "If we go dark, it won't notice us," he said. "It's drawn to our energy. Just send that spell of yours past us and let us release our strength and hide in darkness. It isn't too late. We can save ourselves." The light the two of them cast began to dim as he broke away from soul after captured soul.

"It was too late when you decided that you would pay for immortality in the world of the flesh with the souls of others. In that instant, the gods themselves cast lots against you. And I was chosen to be the vehicle of your destruction."

"At the price of your own immortality? Let me go, Dùghall. Let us both go—make the bastards who chose you to die come after me themselves. You have my word—I'll never touch you or yours again. My word—sworn on my soul."

"No. I accept my fate."

"Why?" Luercas screamed. The nightmare was almost upon them. "Why would you accept oblivion?"

Dùghall was quiet, watching the immense, dark shape gliding toward them.

"Why?"

"Because I love them," Dùghall said, realizing in that moment that it was true. "I love all of them. It was Solander's final gift to me, that I would know what it meant to truly love—to love every living thing with all my soul."

"What gods could claim to love you and send you to oblivion?"

"No gods could make me do this. I was their chosen sword, but I alone strike the blow that will end you. That is the Falcon way—at the final moment, we can offer only ourselves, and only if we give ourselves freely."

They were a small, dim sun by that time. In the merest fraction of a heartbeat that had passed since Luercas first sensed the presence of the soul-eater and began trying to hide, he had broken free from all the souls with which he had fed his body.

Alone, without the strength he had stolen from others, Luercas was weak, Dùghall realized. Weak enough that

Dùghall might hope to trap him within a soul-mirror and so save himself—but Luercas had spoken truly when he'd said that, given time, he would find a way to escape.

The decision of the gods was final—had to be final. Luercas had committed the only crime for which there could be no forgiveness. And the only way Dùghall could be certain that the justice of the gods was meted out was to stay with Luercas and hold him until the soul-eater devoured them both.

So he held fast while the coldness and utter lightlessness of the hunter between the worlds descended on him, maw gaping.

He thought of life—of sunlight and the warmth of summer evenings in the Imumbarran Isles. In his last remaining instants, he remembered the sounds of laughter in the streets, the touch of lips against his cheek, the way his first daughter's hand had felt when, newborn, she gripped his finger and looked into his eyes. Their souls had known each other always, he realized. Their time together had been a gift. He remembered Galweigh House, and the struggles of the Falcons to bring love to the city of Calimekka. He thought of Kait and Ry, and saw for just an instant the battles that still lay ahead of them—a lifetime of struggling, endless chances for defeat, a single path that might, if they were strong and faithful, lead them to triumph. But through the struggles they would have each other . . . and when it was all over, they would have forever.

He had given them that chance. The chance to struggle, the chance to live. The chance, at last, to rejoin the gods.

"Let me go!" Luercas screamed. "Let me *go*!"

Dùghall blended himself more completely with Luercas and held fast. "Vodor Imrish," he prayed, "I offer myself freely that others may live. I know there is no other way to do this . . . but I'm afraid. I love life. I don't want to die to all of eternity. If some part of me can survive, please . . ."

He stopped short of asking for a reprieve. What he did,

he did for Kait, for Ry, for Solander and Vincalis, for Hasmal and Alarista, for his many sons and daughters and their many sons and daughters, for his friends, for the Falcons, for strangers he would never meet whose souls were nonetheless good and deserving of life. What he did, he did for life.

What he did, he did for love.

I truly love them all, he thought, and was filled with wonder, for in that instant, he was no longer alone.

He filled with love, growing brighter and warmer, expanding, stretching out, filling the universe. Luercas shrank inside of him, recoiling from that all-accepting love. I love even Luercas, Dùghall realized. He cannot continue to do his evil, but I love him nonetheless.

You are my brother in truth, a voice whispered in his thoughts. *And you will not go alone into the darkness.*

In that last instant before the soul-eater reached Dùghall and Luercas, Solander linked his soul with theirs. Their combined brilliance became a fire that erased the darkness of the Veil—their love poured into the emptiness of the void, filling it for an instant with perfect music, with perfect hope.

Then oblivion swallowed them.

Chapter 57

From their vantage point well away from Dùghall's void and the struggling souls of Dùghall and Luercas, Kait could see a darker form growing in the darkness of the void. Immense, unspeakable, it was a cancer in the flesh of eternity.

She knew what it was without having ever seen such a thing before—her soul knew, and cried out in terror, and she tried to flee back along the silvery line that connected her still to her flesh self.

But Ry, trembling himself, held her tightly to his side and said, "Wait. We may yet be needed here."

She fought to find her courage. She thought of Dùghall, of how he had come to save her and Ry from Luercas when she'd been so sure all was lost, of what he was doing at that moment to end the horrors of Luercas's reign. She grew calm, she centered herself, and she said, "I'm strong now. I'll wait."

For an instant, the radiant sphere that was Luercas and Dùghall grew dim, and Kait feared that Luercas had beaten Dùghall, and that the dimness came from the destruction of Dùghall's soul. Then, suddenly, the sphere grew brighter and brighter, until it blazed more brilliantly than any sun.

From far away, she felt its warmth, its light, and its love. At the touch of that love, she rejoiced.

"Dùghall's won! He's won!" She danced through the infinite Veil, rejoicing in the wonder of the miracle that left her and Ry and Dùghall alive when they had known they would die. "Feel that—there is nothing of Luercas in that."

Ry said, "There is, Kait. He's still there. But he's weak, and Dùghall is powerful. And feel . . . that isn't just Dùghall and Luercas anymore. Listen, too . . . you can hear them if you're still. Solander is with them."

She could hear them. Dùghall and Solander—and deep within, hidden, cowering, hate-filled, and afraid, Luercas—still pleading for his life. How, she wondered, could anyone so weak and pathetic have done so much harm? Surrounded by the immense loving light cast by Dùghall and Solander, Luercas seemed like nothing. Their light filled everything.

Except for the hunter that bore down on them. They were immense—but it was bigger, and it expanded as it reached them, flowing over the brilliance of their love of life, of their joy in existence, and it blotted them out, wiping them from the universe as if they had never been.

"No!" Kait screamed. "No! It can't end this way."

But it did. The unspeakable maw of the hunter between the worlds shuttered closed, and where there had been light and warmth and hope and joy, there was only the cold and empty void of the infinite, oblivious Veil, and the expanding bloated horror of the hunter.

"No," Kait wept.

Beside her, Ry froze—stunned, still, devastated. "I've felt that love twice in my life," he whispered. "And twice it's been ripped away from me, and twice, destroyed. What is immortality," he screamed to the heavens, "if it ends like this? If love dies and evil remains, what use is anything?"

The hunter between the worlds continued to expand, its outlines changing as it grew. A thin sound cut through the silence of the Veil, a single, low, shivering rumble.

"Run!" Ry shouted, but this time Kait held fast.

"Something's changing," she said, and gripped him so tightly their souls blended at the edges. "Something is happening within the soul-eater."

The lines of blacker nothingness that marked the soul-eater's body were beginning to ripple and waver. The rumbling grew louder—still that same low note, now felt more than heard, a shifting and tearing of the very stuff of the universe. The note expanded, and Kait felt the vibrations of it grab her and shake her and fling her across the void as if she were a gnat in a hurricane; she and Ry clung together, all thought of escape lost as the unbearable ripping, tearing, screaming wall of erupting sound smashed them flat and rolled over them, as tiny cracks of light formed in the unthinkable nothingness of the hunter's hide, and those cracks ripped into blazing gashes, and the gashes exploded, and uncountable shimmering streaming beautiful fountains of multicolored light burst from nothingness into the Veil, pouring music over the roar of their creation.

And above that note, a sudden ripple of awe and joy, and a voice she knew, a voice she loved, a voice that was born of Dùghall and Solander, born of love and compassion and self-sacrifice and hope and faith that there were things worth living for and things worth dying for, said, *In the end, love is everything, and nothing is ever lost. Love reshapes evil, it births new life, it creates the universe. Love . . . survives.*

At the sound of that voice, Kait recalled words Dùghall had once said to her:

"I would give my life, my soul, my eternity, to feel that kind of love. . . ."

In that moment, in spite of the pain of her loss, she understood and she rejoiced for him—and for all of them.

Chapter 58

Danya had been torn soul from flesh and fed into darkness; in hellish noise and hellish pain, she'd felt herself poured toward oblivion. Yet at the last instant, the god of vengeance granted her a reprieve. Luercas cut her loose and she burst into her own flesh self again, and power poured into her that had never been there before. She caught the shape of what was happening; Luercas, caught in a trap within the Veil, was against all odds losing his battle, and had decided his only hope of survival was to divest himself of all the power he'd stolen from the lives and souls of his victims.

Which meant that, against all odds, she could still win her own battle.

She opened her eyes and saw the Scarred around her fallen to the floor. Some breathed, some did not, but none had recovered as quickly as she had—they were none of them wizards, and the sharp pains of this sudden encounter with magic would leave them stunned and senseless for a short time.

"Brethwan smiles on me indeed," she murmured, and used the gifted magic Luercas had fed into her body to rip a sword from the sheath of the nearest fallen guard and send it flying straight at Luercas—into the puckered scars on his chest where once her talons had buried themselves, through his heart, out his back, and into the hard wood of the throne behind him.

It wedged there and blood spurted from his chest—and as his flesh self died, she stripped the power from his magic-altered body and fed it into her own wounded flesh. She rebuilt her hand, and still he did not die, so she made herself stronger, taller, and faster. She fed on his death, and when his body twitched its last and no more red froth bubbled from the corner of his lips, she wrapped her hands around the collar that bound her to the corpse's throne and ripped it in two. The metal screamed protest and her heart filled with furious joy. And her mind embraced a single compelling thought. Galweighs waited within Galweigh House—two of them, who had not suffered as she had, who had not been shamed, humiliated, or tortured, who had not felt their flesh twisted into a hideous travesty of itself. Two remained—Dùghall, beloved uncle and ambassador of the Family, and Kait, favored daughter.

She could not, perhaps, have her vengeance against the Sabirs, nor against those of the Galweighs who had harmed her directly. But she could still have her satisfaction.

And she would.

The Scarred at her feet began to stir. As they sat up, shuddering and frightened, she moved away to one side of Luercas's corpse and said, "I, Ki Ika, have destroyed the false Iksahsha and have pulled your souls back from oblivion. Ride with me now, and we will claim this city and this world which are your birthright . . . and mine."

Shaken, uncertain, but obedient, the Scarred followed her outside the grand tent, and brought her lorrag to her as she commanded, and gathered her weapons, and saddled her beast—and when she pointed to the finest company of cavalry in the Thousand Peoples' army and indicated that they and they alone should follow her, the company she commanded wheeled to a man and galloped after her through the gray-draped gates of Calimekka and into the ghostly, silent streets, toward the heart of the city and the great House that had once been and would again be her home.

Ian saw the trouble coming long before it reached him—the company of Scarred astride their monstrous six-legged beasts charged up the Avenue of Triumph at a pace that would have killed horses, led by a dark-haired woman astride a toothy, gaunt-faced nightmare that had never been intended as a beast of burden. He deployed his men as best he could—pikes to the fore, archers behind. He was outnumbered but he held the high ground and the enemy approached only by one road, a bit of shortsightedness that left him grateful if confused. The enemy commander could have forced him to split his meager forces and arms and could have pinned him between pincers had she chosen to approach using both the Avenue of Triumph and the Path of Gods.

But perhaps attack was not the whole of her plan.

The sailors pressed into duty as soldiers sweated as they watched the approach of the Scarred company. They held fast, but Ian thought he saw weakness in them—some of them would break ranks and flee at the first exchange of blows. He frowned and held his breath and waited.

Ringed around the wall, the Falcons held their unmoving vigil.

I wish I could force them away from whatever they're doing to help me guard the road, he thought. But he did not bother them. They had their duty, no matter how pointless it looked to him, and he had his.

The enemy company came to a halt just beyond the line where Ian's archers could have started doing damage with their arrows, and the human woman astride her nightmare-beast raised a hand. "My name is Danya Galweigh," she called out. "I have come to carry out my sworn duty. If you stand aside and allow me to pass into my home unmolested, my troops will let you live. If you attempt to stand against me, they will slaughter you like sheep and I will rip your souls from your dying flesh and destroy them to feed my magic. And *then* I will go into my home and carry out my duty."

Behind her, the Scarred troops cheered.

Ian saw his own lines waver in the center, but he'd judged his outside men well enough, and nobody broke ranks to flee. Yet.

He walked forward, measuring his distance as carefully as she had done. The Scarred carried bows of an odd configuration, stocky but relatively short, with short arrows. He could not be certain they would not be able to hit him where he stood, but he thought his odds fairly good. "Danya Galweigh—the woman who murdered her own son?"

"I sacrificed to the gods an infant conceived from rape," she said coldly, "in exchange for a promise of vengeance against Sabirs and Galweighs. The Sabirs are dead. But I will have vengeance against the Galweighs now."

"How?" Ian asked. "The Galweighs are as dead as the Sabirs."

"Two are not," Danya said. "Dùghall Draclas and Kait Galweigh. Their deaths will serve."

Behind Ian, someone moved. "I'm not dead, Danya," Alcie shouted, her voice clear and firm. Ian's heart sank. He would have had Alcie keep silent—instead, she had managed to mark herself as a special target for the enemy if fighting started. "Surely you remember me."

"Spoiled, pampered bitch," Danya called. "I remember you. So kind of you to stand up. I'll be sure to kill you as I pass." She looked beyond Alcie and saw the little boy holding his baby sister, and her mouth twisted into a cruel smile. "And your son and baby, too. I've grown to hate children."

Ian sighed and muttered, "Get out of the way, Alcie." He shouted, "You've overlooked the best part of your target, Danya. Not all the Sabirs are dead. *I'm* Sabir. And I'll be happy to let you try to kill me—*if* . . ."

"If?"

"If you accept my challenge to fight in single combat. If I win, your troops become mine; if you win, my troops become yours." He guessed that she stood half a head taller than him and had a correspondingly longer reach. He had no idea how good she would be with a sword, but he knew that Kait was devastating, and that Families made sure their people could defend themselves if necessary. She wouldn't be an easy mark.

She laughed, and he saw a flicker of light flash between her fingertips and realized that he had misstepped. Her brag about tearing the souls from the dying to feed her magic had not been mere bluster; she was a wizard—one of the Galweigh Wolves.

"I accept your challenge," she said, and jumped lightly from the back of her mount. She gave a command and her archers lowered their bows and unnocked their arrows.

Ah, hells, he thought. All I wanted was a straight fight that I might hope to win. All I wanted was a way to help Kait.

"You heard our bargain," he shouted to his own troops, and Scarred and human alike, they lowered their weapons. "If I win, we claim her men; if I lose, you obey her. Either way, when this is over, you and they stand as allies." He pointed to the Scarred company.

Danya strode toward him, sword unsheathed and faintly glowing, and he drew his own weapon.

"Where?" she asked when they met at the point in the road that lay equally distant from both forces.

"Here is as good as anywhere."

She shrugged. She was beautiful, he realized—she looked like a much taller, much more powerful version of

Kait, but her face did not have in it any of the kindness or the softness that he had seen and been touched by in Kait's. Cruelty was no stranger to her. She said, "If you concede defeat now and beg my forgiveness for the sins of your Family, perhaps I will have a little leniency on you. Perhaps I won't make you eat your intestines before I slaughter you. Maybe I'll only consign your soul to hell for a thousand years instead of tearing it into uncountable shreds and devouring the shreds."

"Yes. And maybe you'll shit gold, too," Ian said. "Let us be what we're about."

She smiled. "As you wish." She raised her sword, and its glimmer blazed into a blinding green flame, and she leaped for him. His own blade came up in honed reflex and parried her cut, and he dove out of the way, keeping his feet, but she was fast—faster than she had any right to be, and stronger than even the luckiest combination of muscle and bone and nerve and sinew could explain. Magic fed her, magic fueled her, and magic gave her an edge he couldn't compete with. She was going to kill him. The best he could hope for was that he could buy Kait and Ry and Dùghall enough time to do what they needed to do.

She moved in again, blade flashing, and this time as he parried, her blade's edge caught the tip of his and sliced it off. He felt a jolt run through his hilt into the bones of his fingers and all the way through both his arms to his shoulders.

"Concede," she said through gritted teeth, and her lips skinned back in a brutal smile.

"Why don't you?"

She slashed at him in sudden fury, and the flame of her blade grew brighter—and then, suddenly, impossibly, it flickered out. Her eyes widened in surprise, and she shouted words in a tongue he did not know and pointed at his troops. Nothing happened—her sword remained merely a sword, and while her face bore a look of frustrated rage, he charged in at her, blade held up and brought down in a two-handed cut that would have cloven her in half had she not leaped out of his way at the last instant. As it was, he scored her shoulder and drew first blood.

She was a good swordsman even without the magic, though. She danced out of his reach and brought her weapon up and stepped in at him again, and he parried her blow with difficulty.

She shouted the alien words again, this time pointing at her own people. Again whatever she had hoped would happen failed to occur, for she screamed in rage and pointed the index finger of her left hand at the men and women who sat around the wall of Galweigh House.

He realized two things in that instant. The first was that she had hoped to draw magic from the lives of those around her to fuel her spell, in the manner of the Wolves; the second was that the shield that the Falcons had cast to protect the people of Calimekka from Luercas was also protecting them from Danya. Whatever magic she'd had access to, she had used up, and as long as the Falcons held their shield, she would have no more. In that instant he had the fight he'd wanted all along—a fight of flesh and blood, mind and body, and nothing more.

He laughed and attacked, and saw his enemy, with her greater reach and greater strength and greater speed, flinch beneath his onslaught.

"Concede," he shouted as he cornered her against the wall of the Avenue of Triumph. "Concede and live."

She snarled at him and screamed, "The gods will give me my vengeance!" She swung at him but misjudged her stroke; he caught her hilt guard on the broken tip of his blade and ripped her sword from her hand. It flashed into the air, spinning, catching the sunlight as it arced away from the great arch of the avenue, out into empty air, and down in lazy circles to the ground far below.

"Concede," he said in a softer voice, but one both commanding and sure.

Danya pointed to her troops and screamed, "Attack them! Save me!" But her troops stood on the bridge, still as stones, hands well away from their weapons.

Perhaps they had true honor, Ian thought. Or perhaps they simply hadn't cared for the fact that when she couldn't draw her magic from his people, she tried to draw it from them. Either way, he had her.

"Concede," he said a third time.

In her eyes he saw fear and rage and a sudden cold determination. "I concede only to death," she snarled, and flung herself backward over the wall of the avenue. She fell silently—she did not in her last moments cry out for the mercy of the gods, nor did she howl in fear. Instead, she brought her arms to a point in front of her, as a pearl diver would when leaping from a cliff into the sea, and raced to the rocky slab below her as if it were a friend that she expected to open up and embrace her.

It didn't.

She hit the rock at the bottom of the cliff so hard Ian could hear the sound of it from where he stood. He stared for a long moment at the smashed form that lay on the flat rock; at the bright star of blood that circled the pale shape; at the faint pennant of black that was some of her hair blowing in a breeze.

Behind him, he heard a commotion. He turned warily, and was stunned to see Kait and Ry walking toward him, with his men parting to let them pass, and behind them the Falcons standing and embracing each other silently, tears running down their cheeks.

"You live," he said quietly.

"We live."

"Dùghall?"

Pain flitted across her face, touched with strange wonder. "No. He . . . did not live. And yet . . ."

"Does that mean we've lost?"

Kait shook her head slowly, and slowly a disbelieving smile found its way to her face. "We've won," she said. "By all the gods who ever loved us, Ian . . . we've won."

Chapter 59

Those whom Rrru-eeth had wronged stood and spoke against her one by one, human and Scarred together, with the Scarred company from the Army of the Thousand Peoples looking on with silent attention. And when the last had spoken, Ian stood and said, "The sentence for mutiny is hanging, and all here agree this woman has committed mutiny. If any remain who would say otherwise, let him stand now and speak, or forever hold his peace."

None stood.

Rrru-eeth shouted, "I am guilty only of love. He betrayed me!"

Two of the Keshi Scarred prepared to place the rope around her neck, but Ian raised a hand. "Under Captain's Law, I would demand fulfillment of the sentence of death; for without law applied equally to all, we are nothing." The Keshi began to move forward again, but again Ian stayed them with a gesture. "But a further tenet of Captain's Law is that the captain is master of his ship as if it were his kingdom. Here, on solid land, I have no authority. I cannot command the death of Rrru-eeth, even though she has been found guilty."

Kait, standing beside him, started. She knew how he had

dreaded Rrru-eeth's trial, and how he had fought the fact that he would have to hang her. He did not want her to die—even after all she had done to him and to all of them, he held the friendship they had once shared too dear.

The Keshi stared, and Ry said, "Then what are you going to do to her? She's a mutineer. A traitor. A murderer. You cannot consider setting her free."

"I can remand her over to your custody," Ian said, his voice carrying to the farthest ranks of the Army of the Thousand Peoples. "As Family, and within your domain, you have jurisdiction."

But now Kait raised her hand. "She committed her betrayal on the sea. As the last yanar, the last speaker for the Galweigh Family, I cannot judge her actions here on land. If none is found who has true jurisdiction over her, I declare that she will be freed by virtue of mistrial."

Among the ranks of the Army of the Thousand Peoples, murmurs began and spread, voices growing quickly louder and sharper. Suddenly three archers leaped to their feet and loosed arrows in Rrru-eeth's direction. All three sprouted from her chest. She gasped, then toppled. Ian cried out and dropped to one knee, and put a hand on her shoulder. Kait saw the tears that ran from his cheeks, and saw him turn his face to the wall.

One of the archers, a lean, silver-carapaced creature, stepped forward and stared levelly at Ian and Kait and the others who had stood before the crowd. Through the translator who had been passing the proceedings on to him, he said, "We claim jurisdiction, for she is Scarred, and we are Scarred. She lived among humans and was accepted by humans. Treated as human. Befriended by humans. And she shamed herself, and shamed all of us who are not human. Thus has she been judged by her own kind—by the damned and the forsaken. For even the damned and the forsaken have their honor, and we will not have one such as she besmirch ours. This is our gift to you . . . our promise that if you will have us, we will live as humans within human lands, under human law. And those among us who will not live honorably . . . will die."

Kait turned to the observers—human, Keshi Scarred, and Scarred of the Thousand Peoples, and first in Iberan and then in Trade Tongue, she said, "We face a new world today—in Calimekka, the Scarred who have conquered will claim a place within the city, but the humans who have struggled and fought for their city will also claim a place. If the old hatreds rule, then each shall devour the other and none will prosper. If the old hatreds rule, all of us will lose the one thing we fought for—Calimekka itself."

She took a deep breath. "The Army of the Thousand Peoples is now Calimekka's army—Danya offered it with her battle and sealed the bargain with her death. You"—she pointed to the Scarred company—"are now a part of us. As the last yanar of the Galweigh Family, I declare you human, that you may live freely and without fear or persecution within Ibera's borders and Calimekka's walls—I revoke the judgments of the parnissery and create a new law: Any creature who can state that he is human, by word, thought, gesture, or deed, shall be declared human. I declare this law by blood." She drew her dagger and cut across her palm so that blood welled up, and held her hand in the air so that all could see the blood that ran down her arm. "Let gods and men attend."

She turned to the Keshi and said, "Give her decent burial. I will not have anyone gloat at the spectacle of death. Not now." She knelt beside Ian and touched his shoulder lightly. "They did what had to be done, Ian. Can you forgive them?"

He lifted his head and nodded slowly. "She would have been poison had she lived. But I could not remember the girl who had risked her own life to save all those children, and sentence her to death."

"Neither could I." Kait closed her eyes. "But she would have been poison."

He rose. "Her death is a blessing."

"If you can see that, I have a favor to ask of you. Can you ride with the Army of the Thousand Peoples to their main camp? Tell them what has been decided. Bring them in. Lead them to homes where they can live. There are enough places within Calimekka's walls for all of them."

Ry said, "Those who wait outside the gates have killed humans."

"And those within the gates have killed the Scarred, and reveled in their deaths. This is no easy thing they'll do—building a city in which all of the Thousand and One Peoples can find a home. But Ian has given us a chance to win this . . . to win all of it."

Ian looked at her and smiled. "I always hoped I would see the day when the people who served aboard my ship could be people in the city of my birth. I'll tell them."

He took a horse and a few of his men, and the company of Scarred rode with them, down the Avenue of Triumph. Toward the new world Kait barely dared to imagine.

"The Calimekkans will try to kill you for this," Ry said in her ear. "They'll never know or never believe what we've done to save them—they won't be able to imagine what the world would have been if we'd failed. They'll know only that you were the one who told the Scarred they could stay, and they'll do everything they can to destroy you."

"Probably. But Galweigh House is strong. We have Falcons here now. We have Ulwe, with her ear always listening to the voice of the roads. We have each other. And we have love, Ry, and how can something as small as hatred hope to stand against something as powerful as love?"

"You want to stay in Calimekka, then?"

"How can we not? Billions of souls lay trapped within the Wizards' Circles—they must be released. Ibera is no more stable or secure than it ever was, and Calimekka is now weaker. We have much to offer . . . you, me . . . the Falcons. A new world awaits in the city below—and perhaps for the first time, if we stay and fight for what we need, it will be a world that has room for the two of us in it."

About the Author

Holly Lisle, born in 1960, has been writing fantasy and SF novels full-time since November 30, 1992. Prior to that, she worked as an advertising representative, a commercial artist, a guitar teacher, a restaurant singer, and for ten years as a registered nurse specializing in emergency and intensive care. Originally from Salem, Ohio, she has also lived in Alaska, Costa Rica, Guatemala, North Carolina, Georgia, and Florida. She and Matt are raising three children and several cats.

She maintains a large readers' and writers' Web site at www.hollylisle.com/ and offers a free biweekly writers' newsletter, readers' mailing list, active readers' and writers' communities, games and contests, sneak peeks at new work, and much, much more.

Holly's e-mail address is holly@hollylisle.com. She reads every letter and e-mail, though she cannot promise to answer all of them.

A thousand years before the events of THE SECRET TEXTS, the Dragons rule an empire that spans oceans and more than 3000 years of history. In this world of wondrous magic, fueled by cruelty and evil, a young man named Wraith, who can neither use nor be used by magic, befriends Solander, the son of one of the most powerful Dragons in the empire, and together they discover the source of the power that feeds their world.

Driven by a thirst for justice, and their vision of a better world and a better way, they attempt to right the wrongs they find. Two young men, a mission of mercy—and the fury of the greatest empire and the mightiest wizards in the world of Matrin arrayed against them.

The conflict that follows will reshape their world forever.

VINCALIS THE AGITATOR
(0-446-67899-6)
by Holly Lisle

Coming in early 2002
FROM WARNER ASPECT

VISIT WARNER ASPECT ONLINE!

THE WARNER ASPECT HOMEPAGE

You'll find us at: www.twbookmark.com then by clicking on Science Fiction and Fantasy.

NEW AND UPCOMING TITLES

Each month we feature our new titles and reader favorites.

AUTHOR INFO

Author bios, bibliographies and links to personal websites.

CONTESTS AND OTHER FUN STUFF

Advance galley giveaways, autographed copies, and more.

THE ASPECT BUZZ

What's new, hot and upcoming from Warner Aspect: awards news, bestsellers, movie tie-in information . . .